Mastering the Art of Deception

Marlowe Edison

Mastering the Art of Deception

This is a work of fiction. Names, characters, places, and events are either the product of the author's imagination or used fictitiously. Any resemblance to actual persons, living or dead, events, or locales is entirely coincidental.

Publisher: Edison Publishing

ISBN (ebook – Amazon Kindle): 978-1-7638026-0-5

ISBN (paperback – Amazon KDP): 978-1-7638026-1-2

ISBN (paperback – IngramSpark): 978-1-7638026-2-9

For permissions and inquiries, please contact:

Edison Publishing

Sydney, NSW, Australia

Cover design by Kari Brownlie

First Edition: September 2025

Advance Reader Copy

This advance reader copy is provided for review purposes and may differ slightly from the final published edition. Please verify any quotations against the published book.

For Delaney,

My steadfast listener, my sounding board, and my greatest cheerleader. Thank you for indulging my endless ramblings, for your patience, and for always believing in me. This story is as much yours as it is mine.

Author's Note

Dear Reader,

This story takes place in a fictional city of my own creation. While some aspects may feel reminiscent of London, the setting is deliberately distinct, with a climate that's noticeably milder and details that don't adhere to real-world geography. The city, its landmarks, and the surrounding countryside exist solely to serve the needs of the story. The conservatory, too, is entirely fictional.

As you read, I invite you to immerse yourself in this world without searching for real-life parallels. It is a place shaped by its characters, their ambitions, and the intrigue that unfolds within its streets.

Enjoy the journey!

Marlowe Edison

Chapter One

The phone slipped from Antony's fingers and hit the floor with a heavy clunk, cutting off the dispatch officer's voice as thunder growled through the walls. He sank to his heels, breath catching, eyes fixed on Sara Miles's body sprawled across the bed. Strands of bronze hair tangled with the blood on her arms, thighs, and breasts. A penknife lay discarded on the bedside table.

But it was the purple bruising around her neck that told the story of her final moments.

A tremor crept up Antony's fingers as he untied her hands and folded them gently over her chest. He steadied his breath, stroked her tear-streaked cheek—a futile gesture in the face of death. For one terrible moment, he almost sank to the floor. Gave in. Let it crack him wide open.

Instead—

He stood.

Fists clenched, he stumbled down the corridor, shoving the scene from his mind.

On the kitchen counter, an open bottle of Macallan beckoned.

He grabbed it, took a long swig, and stared through the back door. Another swig. Then—

He squared his shoulders and stepped into the study.

The glow of Sara's computer cut through the dark, guiding him to the desk. He squinted at the blinking cursor, still pulsing as if waiting for her return. He read the scandalous opening paragraph, set the bottle down, and leaned in.

The tremors eased as his fingers found the keys.

Clack. Clack. The sound rose above the wind stirring through the open doors. With a final tap, her words vanished.

He turned away—then stopped.

A gleam of polished wood.

He pivoted. Eyes locked on the box on the shelf above her desk.

A chill slid down his spine.

African blackwood. Carved from a single piece. Mother-of-pearl inlay. Seamless. Keyless.

Now stained with Sara's blood.

The third piece of Rebrisi's masterpiece—*The Three Elements*—sitting there like some kitschy thrift-store find.

His jaw tightened. He crossed the floor. Paused—just for a moment. Then reached. Hands steady. Jaw set—

Bang.

He froze, his breath loud in his ears. Wind howled through the doors. Beneath it: voices—low, clipped, professional. A car door slammed. A radio crackled.

A knock. Followed by boots on pavement.

"POLICE. OPEN UP."

His throat tightened.

The evening—already catastrophic—was about to get worse.

The box—forgotten. Sara's body—cooling in the next room.

He rolled his eyes. Of course—discovered . . . with blood on his hands.

There was only one thing left to do.

He lifted the bottle—

And drank.

* * *

"You're here about a disturbance?" Antony asked, eyeing the two officers across the threshold.

Detective Katrine Ratcliffe stepped forward.

Five foot seven, platinum-blond, and radiating restless energy, she moved with a predator's grace—cool, composed, and taut with threat. She carried the presence of someone used to commanding the room.

Her partner, Detective Kyle Saunders, loomed a half step behind. Broader, with linebacker shoulders and a flattened nose, he looked more like her muscle than her equal.

Antony exhaled slowly, hiding his bloodstained cuff beneath his palm as he stepped aside. Ratcliffe was already scanning the space with practiced eyes. Saunders followed, his bulk filling the doorway.

A dark blur shot through the entrance, claws skittering on hardwood.

"Shit!" Saunders flinched. "What the hell was that?"

A hiss answered as the Maine Coon crabwalked toward the kitchen, tail puffed out like a feather duster.

"Tib!" Antony dropped to his knees, his cool façade slipping. The cat halted, sniffed, and returned, pressing against his leg. A loud purr filled the foyer.

Ratcliffe's eyes flicked between Antony and the animal, one brow raised. "Friendly, isn't he?"

"Depends on who you ask," Antony muttered. "He bites."

"So do I."

Ratcliffe's gaze snapped to the back of the house. "Right, then. What's this all about? Dispatch said it was a domestic dispute."

Antony scooped the Maine Coon into his arms and led them into the front room. Ratcliffe planted herself in front of the fireplace, arms crossed—the picture of quiet judgment.

At the bay window, Saunders scanned the street beyond.

Antony's voice darkened. "Not exactly." His chest constricted, stomach churning. He lowered himself onto the silk sofa, the cat curling into his lap. "There's been a murder."

Ratcliffe's brow lifted. "A murder? So, we've got a body, then?"

Antony nodded, stroking the cat's fur with unsteady hands. "Before you ask, it wasn't me. I tried to resuscitate her."

She stiffened, shooting Saunders a look. He vanished into the corridor.

Minutes later, he returned, speaking into the mic clipped to his jacket. In his gloved hand: a Stanley knife and a roll of duct tape in an evidence bag.

"Affirmative, sir," he said. "I'll relay this to Ratcliffe now."

Thunder rolled overhead as he released the transmit button. "Scene's secure. Victim's in the back bedroom. CSI's already on the way."

Another rumble shook the room. "We've logged multiple calls to this address tonight." He paused, his gaze fixing on Antony.

Antony's hands stilled.

Ratcliffe gave a grim nod. "I'll say it—looks like the work of the Bayside Ripper."

* * *

Over the next hour, Sara Miles's swanky bungalow transformed into the epicenter of a full-blown crime scene investigation. Police cordoned off the front and rear of the property, the driveway, and the garden, weaving a giant spiderweb of yellow tape. Inside, forensic techs in coveralls and nitrile gloves combed the bedroom, the living room, and the kitchen.

They spent the first thirty minutes photographing the body from every conceivable angle. Then came the bagging and tagging. Antony groaned as—despite his protests—the bottle of Macallan vanished into an evidence bag. With a resigned sigh, he returned to his perch by the window, settling Tib into his lap as more news crews gathered on the lawn.

Vans with swiveling satellite dishes jammed the street. Cameramen jockeyed for position, their broadcast lenses trained on anything that moved, while predatory reporters whispered into mics held just centimeters from their glossy lips. Antony pressed his forehead to the cool glass, fingers sinking into the ruff at Tib's neck. The cat's low purr deepened.

Outside, Ratcliffe and Saunders stood on the veranda, their voices drifting in through the open doorway.

"You've been keeping tabs?" Saunders folded his arms, casting Ratcliffe a long, judgmental look.

She shrugged. "Gut feeling." A beat. No longer than a breath. "On paper, she's renting in Bayside, but no one's seen her. Then she shows up tonight. With Landvik."

Thunder rolled in the distance.

"He's up to something—I can feel it."

Saunders sighed. "So bring him in."

Footsteps creaked behind Antony. He turned as an officer approached, carrying a pet carrier.

"What the hell?"

The officer gave a weary shrug. "I've been instructed to take the cat down to forensics."

"Why?"

"Detective Ratcliffe says he bites. If he bit our perp, there might be DNA."

Antony's brows lifted. "You're kidding."

She shook her head. Tib growled low in his throat as she stepped closer, the door of the cage clinking open.

Antony's grip tightened on the cat. "He won't go in that."

"It's a workplace health and safety issue, sir."

"Then do it here."

"It has to be at the lab," she said, her mouth set into a firm line.

He arched a brow. "Why bother? Seems like a long shot."

Her voice softened, though her patience was wearing thin. "Because any small detail might lead us to the Bayside Ripper."

Antony huffed. "Well, I suppose you'll take anything you can get. What is it now—four murders? Five? I'm losing count." He turned back to the window and the circus on the lawn. Grief threatened to crack his tightly held façade.

"Your cooperation would be much appreciated," she said, frustration creeping in. "It won't take long. Just a DNA swab. I'll return the cat personally."

Tib growled again.

The officer sighed. "Fine. Have it your way. Keep the cat. But that means we'll need both of you to come down to the station."

Chapter Two

Annouie Bach stepped off the last train to Haynes Park, her boots thudding softly on the platform. She moved with loose-limbed precision, scanning her surroundings, unfazed by the unseasonable warmth. A bronze statue loomed—some forgotten general astride a rearing horse—but she barely glanced at it. Something was off. She could feel it.

The river path lay ahead. Warehouses lined the edge, their shadows spilling into the night. She felt him before she saw him: the man tailing her, keeping his distance. Easy enough to lose him in the warren of streets south of here—but as she already knew who he was and what he wanted, she didn't.

She ascended the ramp into the wooded park. Beneath a flickering streetlamp, she checked the time. Just on two. Her tail lingered in the dark, watching.

Through the deserted play area, then out onto River Street. She didn't break stride. Halfway down, the old mill rose—four stories of crumbling brick swallowing the sidewalk in shadow. Faded print on a plaque: THE OLD PAPER WORKS, CIRCA 1876. A gust tugged at an official-looking notice taped to the door.

She ripped it down. FINAL DEMAND glared in red ink—a sharp reminder she was behind on the protection payments. As she crumpled the notice, a flicker of flame lit the street. Her tail stepped into view, cigarette glowing.

Mentor. Handler.

The reason her dad was in prison.

"John Chrysler Anderson," she muttered.

Tall. Dark hair curling against his scalp. A broad nose hinting at African ancestry.

He flicked ash to the pavement.

"You're off the Denny Maxwell case," he said, mellow baritone cutting through the air.

"What?" Her voice cracked. "Why?"

He pulled a tablet from his coat. "Got something else for you. More urgent. And it pays better. You can say no, of course—but you won't."

Her eyes narrowed. "If this is another shitty honey trap—"

"Not a honey trap. Surveillance. But you'll need to get close." He passed her the tablet.

Newspaper headline. Transcript. A headshot.

Antony Meyer-Edwards. Disgraced concert pianist. Devil-may-care glint in his eyes.

She stared for a long beat—then shoved the tablet back. "Go fuck yourself."

Anderson leaned in. "What if I told you he has Rebrisi's *Second Element*?"

Her breath caught. "The missing manuscript?"

For a moment, her eyes lit up with curiosity. There were whispers on the dark web: the first piece, a painting, hanging in the Fonteyn Gallery. If the second was in play—

She snapped her defenses back up. "Still won't touch it."

He smiled. "Not even for two hundred grand?"

Her heart kicked. "Two hundred thousand to get close to him?"

Tempting. *Too* tempting.

"What's the catch?"

"No catch. You're a world-class musician. You've got the look. The attitude. All you have to do is audition."

"I was expelled from the Conservatory."

"All taken care of."

She blinked. "How?"

He shrugged. "Everything has a price in this world."

He handed her the tablet again. "So. You want back in?"

She did. But Antony Meyer-Edwards? Arrogant. Infuriating. Magnetic.

The man was trouble in an Armani suit.

"Study your mark," Anderson said. "Know him better than yourself. I can't interfere with the selection process. It's all up to you."

"Anything else I should know?"

"You're up against hopefuls who've had months to prep. Bring your A-game."

He flicked his cigarette to the pavement and buttoned his Louis Vuitton jacket.

She hesitated. Two hundred thousand. Reinstatement. It was almost too good.

"I'll take it."

A flash of teeth. "Knew you would." His gaze roved over her face, settling on her lips. "I'll be at the Dorset."

She exhaled slowly. "One more thing—I want half up front." A calculated risk—but who else could he get?

Anderson blinked. "You want what?"

"One hundred thousand now. Or find someone else."

His jaw flexed. "That may be difficult to arrange."

"Then we don't have a deal."

He sighed. "Fine."

"And the phone call you promised. I want that too."

A flicker of irritation crossed his face. "Anything else?"

"That's it."

She watched him disappear into the dark, then put her shoulder to the door.

The factory yawned open—ruined floor, stacked beams, broken bricks. Moonlight spilled through clerestory windows. Beneath them—a battered broom and a wheelbarrow. She moved through the space, climbing the new metal stairs to the foreman's office.

The French doors hung open. She crossed to them.

The river surged below, muscular and dark, moonlight catching on the current like spilled milk. The air was briny, laced with a pungent note of rotting fish. For a moment, she lingered—a tiny concession, barely a heartbeat, to remember who she had been before Security and Risk.

Before Anderson.

Not the spy. Not the thief. Just Annouie.

A moment. Then—

She turned away.

In the bathroom, a claw-foot tub gleamed, its antique showerhead a lucky thrift-store find. The boiler beside it, salvaged from the curb, wheezed softly.

She twisted the ancient tap. Water hissed from the bronze showerhead. Stripping, she studied herself in the mirror: a purple bruise on her hip. Jagged scratches across her back. Reminders that sometimes even her skill wasn't enough.

She stepped into the tub, the hot water stinging. Then soothing. She scrubbed until the last traces of the night's mission—and Denny Maxwell—swirled down the drain.

Gone.

But not forgotten.

She shut off the water and stepped from the tub, pipes singing as she knelt beside her bag. Inside: Denny's files. Decrypting them would be tough. Linking them to the numbered accounts? Tougher. But without them, there was no proof her dad hadn't known about the art, the auction site, or the embezzled millions.

She had to crack them. There was no Plan B.

She reached for her corset. Removed the drive.

And the business card.

The elegant typeface glistened in the poor light.

Timothy Gibson
Artist

What it didn't say: forger, criminal, the architect behind her dad's imprisonment.

Below: a number and the Fonteyn Gallery address.

She had the accountant.

It was time to go after Gibson.

She flicked the card onto her desk and began to dress—already running through her next moves.

* * *

Three wooden barstools stood before the marble-topped kitchen island—paid for with five percent skimmed from the Milan job. The matte navy cupboards mounted on the cement-rendered wall? Ten percent from a surveillance gig. The freestanding oven, all old-world charm and a gas stovetop? Covered entirely by her six grueling months undercover as a paralegal.

Annouie stepped onto the factory floor, eyes narrowing as she scanned her surroundings.

Dust coated the unfinished floorboards. A pair of carved wooden columns framed the divide between the kitchen and dining room. Between them, flanked by a half-rendered wall, stood a gleaming oak table—the room's centerpiece.

A nine-foot grand piano sat on a riser in the far corner, the golden letters visible even at a distance—*La Belle Dame.*

A scuff drew her attention. Then a rattle.

The front door burst open.

Andre Landvik—former MIT tech prodigy—strode in, right on

schedule, his Jimmy Choo high-tops whispering across the concrete floor. A leather messenger bag thumped against his chest; a paper bag swung from his hand.

"Coffee," he called, his dark Eurasian eyes glinting as he set two large paper cups on the kitchen counter.

Annouie turned from the piano, eyes closing as the aroma hit her. Medium roast. Arabica blend. With chai.

Andre slid onto a stool and nudged her cup toward her. "What did the dean say?"

She sat opposite, lifting the cup to her lips. "Never got to speak to him," she lied, taking a sip. "He canceled at the last minute."

We won't be overturning your expulsion at this time.

Andre's mouth flattened. Without a word, he pushed his coffee aside, slung his bag onto the counter, and withdrew *Version One Point One*—his sleek laptop prototype.

"Say the word and I'll expunge the record for you," he said, flipping open the lid. The screen flared to life as his fingers hovered over the keyboard.

"No need. Anderson took care of it," she said, watching him over the rim of her cup.

"He did what?" Andre's fingers flew over the keys, hacking the conservatory firewall in seconds. "If Anderson did that—" He sucked in a breath. "Your record's gone. Not even a blip." He turned to her, eyes sharp. "What's he up to?"

"We have a new assignment."

"And?"

"The mark is Antony Meyer-Edwards."

Andre's brow lifted. "The musician?"

She nodded. "I'm auditioning for him at eleven. Catch is—if he doesn't choose me, the deal's off."

The clacking resumed, sharper now. "He'll choose you."

Annouie offered a tired smile. Her gaze drifted to the clock above the stove. Almost three. She smothered a yawn. "How's our crooked accountant?"

Andre flicked his pastel-pink hair from his eyes. "Denny's pissed, as you'd expect. Not thrilled about sitting tight at the safe house. But once I explained his role—and the immunity deal—he came around."

"He agreed to link the accounts?"

Andre nodded.

"And the files? Can you decrypt them?"

He pounded the keyboard. "Depends on the algorithms. Won't know until I take a crack at it." He held out a hand. "Stick."

Annouie pulled the drive from her vest and slid it across the marble.

Andre plugged it in and waited for the directories to load. With a few deft clicks, he selected all the encrypted files and dragged them into an app labeled Decryptomagic.

"This'll take a few hours to run," he said, watching her over the screen. He gave a sharp exhale. "You don't have to do this. I can handle it. You could lie low until it's over."

She shook her head.

"What if you get caught?" His eyes shone. "You heard what happened to that operative in California. They still haven't found the rest of his body."

Lightning cracked over the river. Rain began to pepper the pavement beyond the windows.

She shrugged. "I'm not getting caught. Because unlike Enrico Sanchez—I don't get sloppy."

* * *

A few minutes after five, Annouie's phone buzzed.

Anderson:

> A phone's been smuggled into Isidore. I hope you appreciate the lengths I've gone to for you.

She let out a dry, bitter laugh, the sound bouncing off the walls.

Sitting cross-legged on her bed, she glanced toward the open French doors, where the river's low rumble mingled with the rush of a cool morning breeze.

Lengths?

The wrought-iron bed creaked as she shifted. She dialed, hit speaker, and held her breath, counting each ring as it echoed through the room.

Isidore picked up on the fifth.

"Oh God!" she whispered, her throat tightening.

"Breathe," he said, his voice crackling through the line.

She closed her eyes, letting the familiar warmth of his mellow tenor wash over her.

"I—" She exhaled. "Isidore—"

"Call me Dad."

A beat.

"Dad." The word slipped out on a breath, vanishing into the chill air. "I found the accountant."

The words hung there, suspended.

Finally, he broke the silence—his voice low, strained. "My lawyers came today. They're confident. Think they can mount a good defense. I'll be out before you know it."

She leaned forward, gripped the phone tighter. "That's what they said last time. I have a plan—"

"Annouie." His voice cut in, sharper now. "Stay out of this. Some very bad people engineered those accounts. They'll do anything—and I mean anything—to protect their interests."

Her jaw clenched. "So will I."

A rasp of breath slid down the line. "Let it go. For all our sakes." A pause. Then, softer: "I'm fine. That's all you need to know. Trust me on that."

Another beat. Then a hurried whisper—

"I'm sorry—I've gotta go, sweetheart."

She opened her mouth—

But the line was already dead.

Chapter Three

The police cruiser rolled up to a red light. Saunders swiveled to glance at Tib. "You really think this furball's gonna help us catch the Bayside Ripper?"

Antony scratched behind the cat's ears. Tib snuffled once, curled up in his lap, and began to purr.

Police chatter crackled from the radio, underscoring the lull. The light turned green, and the V-6 surged forward.

Ratcliffe flicked the turn signal, guiding the cruiser down a narrow side street.

"If the cat nipped our perp, forensics might pull DNA," she said.

Antony tightened his hold as the gray bulk of the precinct loomed ahead.

"How long is this going to take?"

No one answered.

The cruiser bounced over the curb-cut, passed through the security gate, and slid into a space at the back of the lot.

The moment it stopped, Saunders and Ratcliffe stepped out without a word.

Antony grabbed the door handle. Nothing. He yanked harder.

Saunders leaned in and popped the lock.

"You locked the damn doors?" Antony muttered, climbing out with Tib in his arms.

"Standard procedure," Saunders said with a shrug.

"Thought I wasn't a suspect."

"Everyone's a suspect."

He gave Antony a light prod toward the building.

They climbed the stairs. Saunders swiped his access card, and the rear door buzzed open. Harsh fluorescent light spilled into the narrow corridor as they stepped inside.

Ratcliffe pushed through a metal door, leading them into the station's busy reception area.

She pointed. "Take a seat. We'll be right back." The door clanged shut behind her.

Antony scanned the room. Behind the plexiglass counter, an officer helped a drunken woman file a report. Phones rang. Emails pinged. Voices buzzed in every direction.

He sank onto the nearest metal bench, nose wrinkling as the sour reek of vomit wafted his way. A man two seats over muttered to himself, swaying.

Antony shifted away, murmuring to the cat in his arms.

A door creaked open. Ratcliffe reappeared—this time with a pet carrier.

Her eyes locked on him. "Mr. Edwards," she said crisply. "Give me the cat."

Tib squirmed, claws digging into Antony's sleeve.

She stepped closer. "Can't have animals in here. Hand it over, and then we can talk about what happened tonight."

She set the carrier on the floor and reached. Tib hissed.

Antony stood, grip tightening. "Tib stays with me."

Her scoff was sharp. "Not procedure. It can't come into the interview room."

"He's a *he,* not an *it.* And I'm keeping him with me."

Ratcliffe turned toward the glass. "Detective Saunders? A little help here."

Moments later, Saunders emerged. "Would you mind stepping into the hallway, sir?"

Antony exhaled and followed, Tib clutched to his chest.

The door clicked shut behind them. Saunders turned, brow furrowed. "I feel like I've seen you before."

Antony shrugged. "Yes. At the house."

Saunders squinted. "Never been booked?"

Antony's pulse ticked higher. "Never."

A small lie.

They locked eyes for several long seconds.

Saunders's jaw clenched. "We can do this the easy way or—"

He lunged.

Tib exploded from Antony's arms—an eruption of claws, teeth, and fur.

* * *

Antony winced, his face throbbing as he pressed the ice pack to his swollen eye. Tib was gone—locked somewhere in the precinct. He sank into the seat as the interview room door swung open.

Ratcliffe strode in and dropped a stack of folders onto the desk with a dull thud.

"Apologies for that," she said. "Things got out of hand. Detective Saunders will be along shortly, as soon as the medic finishes with him."

Antony raised a brow. "He's hurt?"

Her lips twitched. "He'll live. Mr. Edwards, correct?"

"Meyer-Edwards," he corrected.

"Right. Meyer-Edwards. Apologies for the wait—it's been a busy night. Would you like something to drink?"

"Bourbon, neat."

Her smile was quick, razor-sharp. "Just tea or coffee, I'm afraid."

"Fine. Coffee. Black. Lots of sugar."

She stepped into the corridor, issued instructions to someone unseen, then returned—posture straight, boots clicking. Everything about her—crisp white shirt, tailored navy jacket—broadcast calm control.

"Food?" she asked.

Antony grimaced. "God, no."

She didn't press, sliding into the plastic seat opposite. A moment later, a uniformed officer arrived with a mug, a teapot, and a plate of sandwiches. Ratcliffe nudged the mug toward him and claimed a sandwich for herself.

"Should take the edge off," she said, biting into it as she flipped open the top folder. *Statement of Mona Rees* was scrawled across the top.

"Before we begin, this interview is being recorded. For the record, please state your full name, age, and address."

He rattled off the information while she leafed through more pages, then—

She pulled a pen from behind her ear, opened her notebook, and fixed him with her predatory ice-blue gaze.

"You told my colleague you'd spoken to the deceased earlier tonight."

He nodded.

"You argued?"

"We disagreed."

"About?"

"An article she was writing."

Her brow lifted. "So you went to confront her about it?"

"To talk."

"And when you arrived, she was already dead?"

"Yes."

"What time was that?"

"About eleven-thirty."

"Anyone who can verify that?"

"No."

She flipped to the next page and slid a typewritten report across the table. Antony squinted, scanning the redacted lines.

Incident Report 1

At 5:22 a.m. on February 12, I was dispatched to 56 Turnbull Avenue. Mrs. Gilda Forrest reported finding the body of her neighbor, Rita Holmes.

Holmes returned home around 8:00 p.m. with a man believed to be Mr. Peter Darby of Lomanville. Reddish-brown hair. Over six feet. Lean. Notably handsome.

They entered the house. Three hours of quiet. Music started around 11.

Mrs. Forrest went to bed. Woke again at 2:00 a.m. to loud music. Knocked. No answer. Saw Holmes through the sidelight: naked, bound, gagged. Hair hacked off. Multiple stab wounds.

Called emergency services. Confirmed deceased upon entry.

Antony pushed the report away. "What's this got to do with me?"

"I was hoping you could tell me," Ratcliffe said, pen poised.

He frowned. "I'm not sure what you're driving at."

"Ring any bells?"

"No bells ringing."

She made a note. *Denies knowledge of previous victims.*

"What about Sara Miles?"

"What about her?"

"You were overheard arguing. In your dressing room. Want to explain?"

His irritation flared. "It was over the phone. And 'arguing' is generous. It was a discussion."

"Did you take a prohibited substance this evening?"

He blinked. "Excuse me?"

"Did you do drugs before the concert?"

"I have a prescription. For anxiety."

She arched a brow. "Why did you go to Belmont Beach?"

"To talk about the article. As I said."

"Did you threaten her?"

He met Ratcliffe's gaze. "Only with legal action."

"Care to elaborate?"

He sighed. "No. Not unless you're planning to arrest me. Am I under arrest?"

Her smile thinned. "Were you and Ms. Miles ever romantically involved?"

"Briefly."

"She ended it?"

"Yes."

"Because she found something out about you?"

He tilted his head. "Such as?"

"Shady past? Drug habit? Moonlighting as a serial killer?"

"Jesus."

"Well?"

"Am I under arrest?"

Her tone cooled. "Did she have a reason to fear you?"

He snapped, "Answer the damn question. Am I under arrest?"

Ratcliffe leaned back. "We can detain without charge if needed to secure evidence."

"So, no," he said, already rising. "Not under arrest."

"Sit down, Mr. Meyer-Edwards."

"Either arrest me, or I walk."

She slid a photograph across the table.

A blonde woman, her hair hacked off like Sara's.

"The Bayside Ripper's first victim," Ratcliffe said.

Another photo followed. Deeper wounds. Bloodier.

"This was his second. Those injuries? Done with a penknife."

Antony stared at the photo. "Like Sara's?"

"These women were murdered in Bayside. Until tonight, we thought our perp favored the Lower North."

She slipped the photos back into the folder.

"Where were you on August 12th?"

He shrugged. "No idea. Not Bayside."

"September 15th?"

"Probably in a bar. Still *not* Bayside. Are we done now?"

The door swung open. Saunders entered, ice pack pressed to his cheek.

"Chief wants us in briefing."

Antony stood. "Guess that means I'm free to go."

"Afraid not." Saunders shook his head. "Knew I'd seen you somewhere. Warrant was on my desk."

"What?"

Saunders straightened. "Mr. Meyer-Edwards, you're under arrest for disorderly conduct and public disturbance."

Antony froze. "You're joking."

"Nope." Saunders shrugged. "Acting on a complaint."

"Whose?"

"Thibault Messier. On behalf of the Friends of the Town Hall."

Antony scoffed. "That old fraud!" He dropped back into the chair with a bitter laugh. "Fine. Do I at least get a phone call?"

"Sure," Saunders said. "Right after we book you."

Chapter Four

Early morning briefings were the worst. The sky outside was still black—dawn a good hour away. Katrine Ratcliffe dropped into a hard seat at the back of the precinct briefing room and rubbed her eyes, struggling to stay alert as she flipped open her notebook.

The room buzzed with tension, bloated at the edges with too many bodies crammed together. Despite the hour, everyone had shown up. They'd come for updates—hoping last night's homicide had cracked something open. Katrine wasn't holding her breath. She knew better.

At the lectern, Detective Chief Inspector Greg Dunbier—a six-foot-four ex-rugby forward—fiddled with the microphone.

His face was etched with exhaustion. He had nothing. And everyone in this room was about to learn just how deep the impasse ran.

Her phone buzzed inside her jacket. She slid it onto her knee, angling the screen away from prying eyes.

ENCRYPTED MESSAGE – SHIRUKU

> SHIRUKU: `Sending you a file.`

Her new source. Her pulse quickened, hope pressing in like a knife.

Dunbier moved to the whiteboard, grabbed the electronic pen, and started scribbling. The network was lagging, his words trailing behind his hand. His nostrils flared in annoyance.

"Give me the good old days when pens were actually pens," he muttered, trying to reattach the stylus to the underside of the screen. It dropped to the carpet with a dull thud.

Katrine's phone pinged. Shiruku's file had landed.

She tapped it open, her focus on the attachment as Dunbier turned to the room.

"So. As most of you know, the Bayside Ripper has claimed another victim."

Silence thickened the air. Katrine's knee bounced. The killings were meticulously staged—obsessive, ritualistic—but Shiruku's intel suggested something more: an intricate agenda. Not just a predator's gratification, but a calculated motive.

Dunbier's voice droned on about stalker profiles and repetitive behaviours. Katrine scrolled, her attention locked on the file.

"We know how. That's about it," he said, gesturing at the spiderweb of notes on the board. Two lines glowed yellow. "Good detective work starts here." He jabbed at them. "How are the victims connected? And—what does our killer want?"

The murmurs began. Furrowed brows. Confused frowns. Saunders looked like he was moments from punching the wall, his jaw working overtime.

Katrine's mouth curled into her first smile of the day—Saunders always looked like he wanted to punch something.

She tuned out Dunbier, his voice fading into the background as she continued to scroll.

Her breath stilled.

> SHIRUKU: The first three victims are connected to the antiquities industry (see Annexure 1). The first victim was an art recovery agent investigating Timothy Gibson at the time of her death (see Annexure 2).

> SHIRUKU: Sara Miles—primarily a gossip columnist—was rumored to have met Gibson at a black-market auction in Paris last month.

Katrine's stomach hollowed out as the pieces began to slot into place.

> SHIRUKU: Gibson isn't our perp, though. And the Ripper's not trying to frame him. He wants us to think it's a stalker—hence the rituals.

Her head snapped up.

Shit.

Stolen Art. The murders were about stolen art.

Her fingers flew across the screen.

> RATCLIFFE: We have to meet.

> SHIRUKU: Not if you want me to keep feeding you intel.

The room was beginning to stir.

> RATCLIFFE: What if I can promise immunity?

> SHIRUKU: You can't.

She began to type—

The chat window closed without warning.

Katrine surged to her feet. "Son of a bitch!"

Every head turned.

At the front of the room, Dunbier crooked a finger. "That reminds me—Ratcliffe. My office. Now."

* * *

Annouie paused, fingers hovering.

`> SHIRUKU: You can't.`

She took a slow breath—the detective was getting too close. VPN tunneling, encrypted comms—it all helped obscure her identity—but Katrine had a knack for unearthing things—things better left buried. Just the week before, a surveillance camera at the Albert Street safe house had caught her rifling through Annouie's mailbox.

Posing as a black hat hacker was growing more perilous by the day.

She tapped the keyboard, exhaling quietly as the chat window vanished from her screen.

Perilous or not, the job remained. Shaking off the tension, she refocused, fingers tapping quickly over the keys. In the Oria2 window, lines of data scrolled upward—rapid, efficient, unstoppable.

She leaned back, eyes flicking to Timothy Gibson's business card, propped against her monitor. The gold-embossed lettering caught the light. His name seemed to crop up everywhere lately.

The AI's response pinged onto the screen.

> ORIA2: `Cross-correlation complete. Anomalies flagged. Common denominator: Timothy Gibson.`

A thin smile touched her lips. Timothy Gibson. Again.

Andre's AI assistant was as sharp as a scalpel—precise, logical, ruthlessly efficient. Oria2 had already linked a cascade of dark web activity back to Gibson. But he wasn't the killer. Innocent or not, he was knee-deep in something the killer wanted:

Rebrisi's *Three Elements*.

Annouie rose and stretched, joints cracking as she moved to the windows. Outside, the clouds shifted, and light spilled across the water—heralding the break of day.

For a moment, everything faded: the murders, the accountant, Antony Meyer-Edwards.

She stepped onto the balcony, filling her lungs with the crisp, briny air. Below, a riverboat drifted lazily downstream.

Eventually, she turned from the view and eyed the bed. Crossing the room, she slipped beneath the covers and looked up at the rafters, mind already drifting.

Would a well-placed palm strike to Dr. Messier's nose get her disqualified from the audition?

A tempting thought. One she couldn't entertain—at least, not if she wanted that two hundred grand.

Still, she couldn't deny the satisfaction the thought brought.

Minutes later, she was asleep, a faint smile lingering on her lips.

* * *

Katrine followed the Chief Inspector into his office, eased the door shut, and dropped into the nearest seat.

"Why aren't we investigating Timothy Gibson? He's connected to all three victims."

Dunbier leaned in, sighing heavily. "He's not our perp. And the higher-ups say that means hands off." His tone was clipped.

She sat back, folding her arms. "Higher-ups? Let me guess—Gibson senior?"

His mouth flattened into a line. "Yeah. And he's sent a clear message: get results, or he'll launch an inquiry into why we're failing."

"Politicians," Katrine muttered.

Dunbier nodded. "Which brings me to why I called you in here . . ." His gaze swept over her clothes, the deep shadows under her eyes, the washed-out pallor of her skin. "Have you looked in a mirror lately?"

She waved him off. "I know I look like hell. But I've got something—a new source. A black hat. Goes by Shiruku. He's got access to some top-tier tech."

Dunbier held up a hand. "Stop. I know where this is going. And you can tell me all about it this afternoon—*after* you've slept. You're officially off the clock."

"What?" Her voice sharpened. "You can't be serious. At least let me show you what I've got. Gibson's breathing down our necks—we need a new angle."

Dunbier waved dismissively, settling into his chair. "Sure. Pass the details to Saunders. He's running point."

Already typing, Katrine said, "I'll send you everything Shiruku shared. All I'm asking is that you look at it—now. Then direct me however you want."

An alert chimed on Dunbier's screen. He sighed and dragged his keyboard closer.

"Alright. A quick look—seeing as you asked so nicely."

As he scrolled, Katrine rattled off key points. His scrolling slowed. His brows lifted.

"Shiruku put all this together?"

She nodded. "He can also track the victims' movements from the past two years. See if anything flags."

Dunbier's eyes narrowed. "Here's how it works. Go home. Sleep—minimum eight hours. I'll send this down to Tech. They'll track this hacker. Cyber can bring him in."

Katrine's spine snapped straight. "I've spent hours gaining his trust. If you come down on him like a hammer—"

Dunbier cut her off. "Black hats don't get free passes, Ratcliffe. Those are my terms. Take them or leave them."

* * *

Early-morning light was already filtering through the frosted glass windows along the east wall of the building. Katrine stalked through the noisy bullpen toward her workstation beneath the red brick sill.

Without the black hat, her options were limited. She could go home, sit in front of her computer, and trawl law enforcement databases. Most perps were identified through solid research anyway.

But playing by the rules was getting her colleagues nowhere. That left one option.

Katrine Ratcliffe didn't like hackers. As a rule, they were self-interested bastards—like Andre Landvik—always looking to beat the system, no matter the collateral damage.

But Shiruku wasn't Landvik.

Katrine slid into her seat and logged on. The familiar cacophony of office banter, whirring printers, and dinging elevator doors swelled around her—oddly reassuring, considering what she was about to do. Her inbox overflowed with demands, but she ignored them, eyes fixed on the encrypted VPN channel blinking in the corner of her screen.

Shiruku was still offline.

Her fingers hovered, then typed a single line:

```
> RATCLIFFE: Watch your six.
```

"Heading home?" Saunders's voice cut through the din.

Katrine locked her screen and turned, masking concern with bland resignation.

"Yeah." She grabbed her jacket and phone, slipping the latter into her back pocket.

"You've been pulling a lot of double shifts," he noted, watching her closely.

She shrugged. "We all have."

She slung her tote over her shoulder and moved toward the foyer.

He quick-timed to keep pace, falling in beside her near the shiny bank of elevators.

Katrine counted to four, then exhaled. Now or never.

The words came faster than she meant.

"The murders are connected to stolen art—works moving through a black-market auction run by Timothy Gibson." She jabbed the call button. "See what else you can dig up on him while I'm getting my regulation eight hours. Dunbier won't green-light us bringing him in until we have something solid."

Saunders blinked. "How did you—"

The elevator dinged. The doors parted.

Katrine stepped inside and fixed him with a stare. "Just look into it," she said, and the doors slid shut.

The car rumbled down five floors as she replayed Shiruku's findings. The hacker had tools most law-abiding officers could only dream of—breaching secure networks, tearing through classified data like it was there for the taking.

It was wrong.

It was illegal.

And it might be the only way to trace anonymous dark web addresses to someone real.

Katrine sighed. Black hats were the scum of the earth. But Shiruku wasn't like other black hats. Even through their faceless, encrypted chats, he'd shown a surprising core of decency.

And now the cowboys in Cyber were gearing up to take him down.

If only they put that kind of effort into nailing Landvik.

She ground her teeth, leaning against the elevator wall. *Landvik.* She was almost certain he was leading Annouie down another dark path.

The elevator slowed. Katrine pushed off the back wall as the doors parted. She clicked her fob; her sedan chirped from the corner. Her boots echoed across the concrete as she strode toward it.

Annouie was fearless—but blind to Landvik's true nature. Somehow, Katrine had to make her see the threat without blowing classified intel.

But she couldn't do that if she was sleeping.

Eight hours, be damned. Six would do.

Sliding into the driver's seat, she connected her phone to Bluetooth and hit dial.

She gunned the engine, V-6 growling.

If Annouie wouldn't cut ties, Katrine would put Landvik under surveillance—he was already flagged.

And when he went off script—as he inevitably would—she'd be ready.

To read him his rights.

Again.

And this time—

Make it stick.

Chapter Five

Annouie Bach rolled onto her back as a relentless ringing shattered the surface of her oblivion, dragging her from sleep. Groaning, she flailed an arm toward the makeshift bedside table. Her hand missed, sending the phone clattering to the wooden floor, where it continued its clamor undeterred.

She sighed and leaned over the edge of the creaking bed to retrieve the Samsung Flip. The caller ID flashed across the screen.

KATRINE RATCLIFFE.

She froze, then dropped back onto the sheets, leaving it to ring. She was in no mood to defend her relationship with Andre Landvik. Her eyes traced the darkness above—the rafters disappearing into the gloom.

No ceiling. Just shadow. Like the vaulted interior of a cathedral. Even the pigeons were watching—unblinking.

The mill was her sanctuary. A place to push herself through punishing drills. A place where she could forget the lies.

Forget she was lying to her best friend.

The phone fell silent, leaving only the low rumble of the river churning beyond the property's edge. Annouie sat up, rubbing her arms against the chill seeping in through the windows.

Left open again. Rookie move.

She sighed. Who was she fooling? She was a wreck. The mill was falling apart. The furniture was secondhand and worse than shabby. She owed everything—including the roof over her head—to the man who betrayed her father.

Clothing lay strewn across the floor. She stared at it.

She was a wreck on a deadline.

She rose, stretching, and padded toward the bathroom, thumbing the power button on the TV remote as she passed.

The morning's headlines echoed off the bare walls. She turned the tap, listening as the cantankerous hot water system hissed and whined.

"Police remain close-lipped about the identity of the latest victim," the anchor said. "If anyone has any information regarding this man—"

A composite sketch flashed onto the screen—so generic it could have been anyone.

"—please contact authorities at the number below."

Annouie caught her reflection in the mirror. Long, tangled blonde waves. Hollow eyes. Her body radiated exhaustion.

Going to bed at six.

Waking at seven.

She lifted her arms and winced at the deep ache in her shoulders. Then she stepped into the shower. A jet of water hit her face, hard and fast.

Last night's wildness—the dancing, the drinking, Katrine catching her with Andre, then the new mission—it was already fading. She braced her hands against the cold tile, letting the water ground her as the weight of the impending audition settled over her.

It hit like a fist.

No walking out in a fit of pique this time.

She'd apologise to Thibault Messier. Swallow his smirk. Endure whatever smugness he threw her way.

Because—

She had two hundred thousand reasons to play nice.

And her dad's freedom depended on it.

* * *

Gull cries drifted through the open bedroom windows, mingling with the faint hum of a waking city as Annouie stepped out of the shower. She wandered to the glass and lingered, gaze sweeping the river path below.

Lone joggers moved in steady rhythm, earbuds in. Others strolled, coffees in hand, recycled brown cups tipping as they scrolled their phones. Students in hoodies and backpacks darted past, hurrying toward the station, their footsteps almost audible from the mill's first floor.

The ambient babble rose—carefree, detached. Human. For a moment, everything felt so . . . normal.

Annouie pulled on a hoodie and headed downstairs, wondering if Katrine had finally given up.

At the fridge, she crouched and rummaged through the crisper. As she straightened, the glint of metal caught her eye—the Japanese Chef's knife, forged from high-carbon shirogami steel, its black-smithed edge honed to perfection, the grip textured for better control.

She reached for it, letting the polished blade catch the light as she began slicing—quick, clean, precise.

Her phone pinged.

She set the knife aside, grabbed the device, and swiped.

Hitting the gym in ten. You coming?

Annouie groaned. She still hadn't decided what to say to Katrine

—or more precisely—what lies might convince her to drop Andre Landvik for good.

But whatever she said, she already knew—it wouldn't be enough.

* * *

It took most people twelve minutes to jog to the gym. Annouie did it in nine.

She burst through the entrance, her bag slipping from her shoulder. Hands on her knees, she forced air through burning lungs. Too fast. Too reckless. But she refused to slow down.

A shadow fell across her.

Katrine Ratcliffe loomed, peering down with the predatory stare of a hawk.

"Andre Landvik. Spill. And don't feed me that crap about him being your childhood bestie. We both know that's a lie."

The burn in Annouie's lungs faded. She straightened, drawing a slow breath.

"We took the same classes at uni." The lie slipped out easily.

Katrine narrowed her eyes.

"No way you got into MIT."

Annouie suppressed a smirk—Katrine truly believed her Shiruku alter ego had graduated with honors.

She rolled her shoulders. "That's a hurtful thing to say."

Katrine jabbed a finger toward her. "And just because he got off on a technicality doesn't mean he isn't a criminal."

Annouie tilted her head. "Is this really about Andre?" She grabbed her discarded bag from the floor.

Katrine hesitated, glancing toward the mats where the rest of the class was warming up. "What else would it be about?"

"You tell me." Annouie shrugged off her hoodie with practiced indifference. Her hands, though, were taut. She stuffed the garment into her bag, dumped it in the corner, and strode to the mats, her snug-fitting shorts and black T-shirt drawing a few lingering glances from the men.

Katrine sighed and followed her. She dropped into a deep lunge.

"Fine. It's about the flat in Bayside." She bounced back, reset, and lunged again.

Annouie mirrored her. "What about it?"

Katrine held the position, counted to four, then straightened and began a side-to-side stretch. "I know you're not staying there."

Annouie turned to face her. "So what if I'm not?"

Katrine kept stretching, her voice quieter. "I was hoping—praying—you'd take your safety seriously for once." She hesitated. "If you were living in that nice, secure, really expensive apartment, I wouldn't be so worried. But you're not. You're lying about where you're staying, and that's a red flag. Especially with that freak still on the loose—"

"You mean Andre?"

Katrine snapped to attention. "Do you even watch the news? I was talking about the Bayside Ripper. Unless you're trying to tell me Landvik's moonlighting as a serial killer, too."

Annouie shrugged. "Right. The Ripper. Good thing I'm not living in Bayside—"

"Make jokes," Katrine said, "but he's out there."

"And I'm taking self-defense classes." Annouie's arms flailed.

Katrine snorted. "You don't know the first thing about self-defense."

"That's not true."

Not even close. Annouie was trained in close-quarters combat, fluent in five languages, passable in three more, and proficient in infiltration and network intrusion. She could hack most firewalls and assume multiple covers. Playing the clueless undergrad was just another mask.

She knew exactly how to keep herself safe.

A sharp grunt cut through the air as the instructor strode onto the mats. He planted his hands on his hips and scanned the room.

"All right. Listen up. You're all here to learn how to defend yourselves—except for Detective Ratcliffe, who's here to make you all look bad." He swept the room, then locked eyes on Annouie.

"Bach. Word is you've been tapping out too much. So, new rule. Anyone who taps out in the first two minutes drops and gives me twenty."

Chapter Six

The holding cell was damp and cold. Antony huddled at the far end of the bench, a thin, scratchy blanket draped over his shoulders. Sleep had eluded him completely. He sat wide-eyed, the chill gnawing through to his bones.

In the corner, the toilet dripped incessantly.

Plink. Plink. Plink.

The sound echoed off the cinder-block cell, erratic and maddening.

Antony stifled a groan. There was no escaping the truth: he was going to miss his first lecture. And when that happened, Messier would pounce—likely demand his resignation.

He drew in a shaky breath. His hands trembled. The craving ate away at his resolve, clawing its way into his thoughts.

A uniformed officer appeared at the bars, tapping them with practiced indifference. "Meyer-Edwards. Time to go."

Antony lifted his head, squinting against the flickering fluorescent light. The bruises around his left eye throbbed with each heartbeat. "Go where?"

The officer shrugged as he unlocked the door. "Booking and processing. After that, you're being released."

* * *

The booking office was a grim continuation of the rest of the building: a narrow corridor, more metal benches, and storage cages behind the counter where confiscated belongings were held.

Antony fixed his gaze on the blank gray wall as the charging officer guided his trembling hands onto the fingerprint scanner. The tremor had worsened, the craving eating away at his focus.

"Hold still," the officer said as his fifth finger spasmed again.

"Sorry," Antony muttered, willing it to stillness.

"We're almost done. Just need to process this, issue the complaint, and then you're free to go." She gestured toward the row of metal seats. "Why don't you wait over there?"

He nodded, shuffled to the bench, and collapsed onto the hard, unyielding surface. Leaning his head against the painted bricks, he closed his eyes.

Today was supposed to mark his triumphant return as Head of Performance Studies—a day he should have been at his best. Instead, he had a mottled bruise on his cheek, reeked like a urinal, and his bloodshot eyes scraped against his lids like sandpaper.

A fine start.

"Edwards." The officer's voice cut through his thoughts. Antony dragged himself upright, knees stiff, and wove his way back to the counter.

"Complaint and summons." She slid a stack of papers toward him.

He gave a tight nod, staring down at the documents.

"And this—" she added a pamphlet, "—has information about the lower court and how to access legal aid."

Antony added it to the growing pile and returned to the bench, the weight of the morning settling over him like a storm cloud.

Then he heard it.

Tib's angry hiss echoed through the booking office, presaging the arrival of the cat carrier. Tib scratched and fretted at the door—a furious bundle of fur and frustration. Antony gave a low laugh and stepped up to the counter.

"Your cat, sir," the officer said, not hiding his irritation.

"You've got a lockup for cats now?"

The officer's pen tapped against the desk. "Of course not. It spent the night with the vet—who wasn't pleased. Wanted to send it back. Insisted we put it in a cell on the basis that it was agitating the other animals."

Antony signed the form, his laugh hollow as he took the cage. Tib glared at him through the bars, tail lashing like an accusation.

The officer pushed a few more items across the counter. "Your phone, wallet, a packet of cigarettes, house keys, and a stick of gum."

"Gum's not mine."

The officer frowned at the page and nudged the stick aside. "Sign here and here."

"How much longer is this going to take?" Antony asked as he scrawled his name. He pocketed his belongings and lifted the cat carrier.

"You're free to go whenever you're ready."

* * *

As Antony maneuvered the cat carrier through the station's revolving front door, his phone began to ring in his hip pocket. He paused on the top step, set the cage down, and shielded his face from the sun as he fumbled for the device.

The screen lit up: twenty missed calls.

He frowned and swiped to answer. "Hello?"

"Oh, thank God!" a woman gushed. "I've been calling all morning! I thought I'd never get through—Mr. Hogan insisted I handle this before lunch."

Antony wiped a hand across his brow. "Handle what, exactly?"

Across the road, a bus hissed to a stop beside the shelter, releasing a stream of commuters onto the pavement.

"My name is Shari Vanamali. I'm a partner at Hogan and Ryan, and I've been assigned your case."

Antony sidestepped into the shade of the building and leaned against the warm brick. In the garden beyond, a pair of honeyeaters darted from flower to flower, utterly indifferent to his unraveling morning.

"My case?"

"Mr. Hogan called me in first thing. Said to make you my top priority."

He checked his watch—eight-thirty. "This is a joke."

"I assure you, it's not."

"Oh, I get it. You're one of those firms that chase ambulances."

There was a faint gasp on the other end, distorted by the phone's tiny speaker. "Mr. Meyer-Edwards, we're one of the top firms in the city. I've been instructed to ensure you receive the best representation money can buy."

Antony laughed, sharp and bitter. "Now I *know* it's a joke, because I won't be paying you."

A beat of silence, then Shari dropped her voice to a conspiratorial whisper. "I'm not supposed to say, but that's all been taken care of."

His stomach clenched. "'Taken care of?'" His tone hardened. "Please tell me this has nothing to do with my uncle Luigi."

The rustle of papers filtered through the line. "I can't disclose details, but your benefactor is connected to the conservatory. Could you hold a moment?"

Antony rubbed his temples, exhaustion pressing down like a weight. A benefactor? Dread coiled in his gut. Only one person would go to such lengths. He stared up into the sky—too bright, too deep, almost nauseating.

Tib yowled as Antony picked up the carrier. He descended the ramp quickly, brushing past a bearded man in tattered track pants who muttered a curse.

The hold music cut out abruptly.

"Mr. Meyer-Edwards?" Shari's voice brightened. "You didn't hear it from me, but I can confirm it was the dean who contacted Mr. Hogan this morning. He wants the matter handled discreetly. I'm optimistic we can make the charges disappear—but I'll need your full cooperation."

Antony froze. "The dean?" The name hit like a lightning bolt, confirming his suspicion.

"Like I said—cooperation is key. I'll send the paperwork to your address as soon as we hang up."

He opened his mouth, but the line went dead.

Sliding the phone back into his pocket, he broke into a run, heading for the bus shelter where a double-decker was just pulling in.

The doors had already begun to close as he reached them. He jammed his foot between the panels, forcing them open, squeezed through, and swiped his card as the vehicle jolted forward.

He collapsed into the nearest seat, the carrier perched precariously on his knees. Tib yowled again, claws scraping in a desperate frenzy, drawing stares from passengers on the lower deck.

Antony flashed a radiant smile. "Don't ask. It's been one of *those* mornings."

As the murmuring subsided, he leaned back, still gripping the cage. A wave of exhaustion rolled over him.

His smile lingered as he eased the cat cage onto the seat beside him and finally surrendered to sleep.

Chapter Seven

Katrine Ratcliffe was waiting, leaning against the change-room wall.

Annouie emerged from the showers, dropped her bag, and began towel-drying her hair. Katrine sat on a nearby bench, cracked the seal on her water bottle and took a long sip.

"You didn't try to fight back," she said quietly.

Annouie tossed the towel aside, opened a locker and pulled out tailored pants and a fitted blouse. She turned to the mirror, twisted her damp hair into a knot and clipped it into place. She bent and shoved her towel and gym clothes into her bag.

"Got an interview?" Katrine asked.

"Audition." Annouie zipped the bag.

"Look, about last night—"

Like a dog with a bone.

Annouie slung the bag over her shoulder and headed for the exit.

Katrine sprang to her feet, hurrying after her. "Just tell me you're not being sucked back into that world again."

Annouie kept her gaze forward. Katrine Ratcliffe wasn't a dog with a bone. She was a *bloodhound.*

She lengthened her stride.

"Landvik's dangerous," Katrine said, matching her pace.

"He's a nerd with an unfinished PhD. Dangerous? Please."

The Colombia mission had been a disaster from the outset. If Andre hadn't broken protocol—

"I know things about him that would shock the hell out of you," Katrine said.

He had overseen the entire exfil—ground crew to medics. Without him—

She'd be on a slab in a Bogotá morgue.

"He's the one person I trust most in the world."

Katrine grabbed her arm. "Listen to me. He's a black hat—"

Annouie shook her off. "I don't have time for this. I've got thirty minutes to get to the old school, pull myself together, and audition for Thibault Messier."

She shoved through the entrance and strode for the nearest bus shelter.

Katrine ran after her. "You're auditioning for Messier? You didn't tell me—"

"Because you only ever talk about Andre," Annouie said, joining the nearest queue.

"I don't want to argue with you."

"So don't."

The line inched forward.

"Fine," Katrine said quietly. She stepped closer, exhaled slowly. "Why don't we start over?" She paused. "Breakfast. Jamisen's. Tomorrow."

Annouie glanced at her. "And not a word—"

"Scout's honour."

No way the detective was giving up that easily.

The bus pulled in, brakes hissing.

No way in hell.

Annouie exhaled, gave a tight nod. "Sure."

Katrine brightened. "Seven sharp?"

"Make it eight," Annouie said and climbed aboard.

"Hey! No swipe, no ride," the driver barked.

Annouie backed up, tapped her card and gave the scowling man a shrug. He shoved a lever forward. The doors sealed shut behind her.

The bus lurched into motion as she navigated the narrow aisle, stepping carefully around a man slumped near the stairwell. At first glance, he looked like a vagrant—battered face, stained clothes.

But his shoes told a different story.

Valentinos.

She stepped over his outstretched leg just as the bus jolted. She stumbled, catching herself on a handhold. Then the smell hit—sharp and pungent. But beneath it—something familiar.

Caron Poivre.

His shirt was expensive. His suit—dark blue *Savile Row*. His tie—Hermès silk.

The man stirred but didn't wake. Beneath the grime and stubble, his face was striking—handsome in a way that hinted at danger. A man carved by conflict.

Her stomach tightened.

Antony Meyer-Edwards.

What was he doing here? Looking like he'd lost a fight with the world—and sleeping it off on public transport?

She inched closer, fingers reaching for the inside pocket of his jacket. The bulge of a wallet was obvious.

A hiss broke the silence.

She flinched. A pair of glowing blue irises glared from behind the bars of the pet carrier beside him. The cat swished its tail, its gaze sharp with disdain.

Annouie laughed under her breath. "I suppose you're the bodyguard?"

Meyer-Edwards stirred, stretched sinuously like a man in his own bed, and mumbled incoherently.

Annouie headed to the upper deck. Sliding into a window seat, she popped two painkillers and leaned back, forcing thoughts of the rich vagabond to the edge of her mind.

A crumpled newspaper lay abandoned on the seat beside her. She smoothed it over her knee.

The headline screamed: BAYSIDE RIPPER CLAIMS ANOTHER VICTIM.

She sighed.

The Ripper again? Just what she needed.

Another damn complication.

* * *

The 529 University bus was just turning onto Harborside Road as Andre struggled out of what had been, for once, a pleasant dream—birds, the slap of sailcloth, an outboard. At least, it had been until an irritating buzz cut through the haze of sleep.

Outside, the 529 bus groaned and wheezed up the hill.

He cracked a lid. The quiet murmur of the harbor slid through the master bedroom's open balcony doors.

Beside him, Paul snuffled and rolled away, dragging the sheets with him.

It took Andre a moment to pinpoint the source of the vibration. His phone. He reached for the black case.

> Went to the gym with Detective Ratcliffe. Spent most of it talking about you. Did you know you're dangerous? Speaking of which, Anderson wants us to attend a lecture at nine at the Old School. That's where we'll get eyes on our latest mark.

It was just after eight-thirty.

"Shit."

Andre pushed himself upright, flicking spiky pink hair out of his face.

"What's the matter?" Paul grumbled, his voice muffled by the pillow.

Always chasing a deadline. Living life on an edge.

"Running late," Andre said, swinging his legs over the side of the bed. He hurried to the walk-in closet and grabbed a pair of lemon-colored pants and a slim-fit shirt.

Paul peeked out from beneath the covers. "Call in sick and come back to bed."

Andre laughed, the sound rumbling through the room as he squeezed into the tight-fitting pants. "Wish I could." He found the Jimmy Choo high-tops under the bed and shoved his feet into them. "Gotta hand in that report."

Paul groaned, rolling to face him. "The one you spent all night on?"

"Yeah. That one."

Paul snuggled back into the pillow. "Sucks to be you."

Andre grabbed the leather messenger bag hanging on the back of the door, then leaned to press a quick kiss to Paul's lips.

"See you tonight. Then we'll go for that drink. No assignments. Promise."

Paul struggled upright, now fully awake. "About tonight—you have to be on time."

"Six-thirty, right?"

Paul shook his head. "No. I told you already. Six. If you're late, I can't let you in."

Andre was already halfway out the door. "Don't worry. I'll be there."

He had to be. Paul was already showing signs of frustration with his unorthodox work hours.

The Porsche Carrera sat beneath the swaying elms lining the driveway. Andre slid into the driver's seat and gunned the engine. He slammed the gearshift into reverse and the car shot out into the middle of the street. He hit the brakes, shifted again, and the car flew down the hill, tires squealing as he swerved around the 529 that was just turning into the bottom of the street.

He tapped the rims of his specs, activating the data feed as the Carrera sped through an orange light, its engine growling. "Oria, send Annouie the following text: *Sorry. Slept in. Meet you out front in ten.*"

Chapter Eight

The double-decker turned onto University Road, and Annouie slipped down the internal staircase, merging with the crowd waiting to disembark.

The bus hissed to a halt alongside the curb. The doors snapped open, and students spilled out, streaming toward the campus.

Meyer-Edwards remained slumped in his seat, dead to the world. If Anderson's intel was right, he had twenty minutes to make it to the Old School. Annouie edged closer, her gaze flicking to the cat carrier. She prodded him gently.

His eyes blinked open—pine-green, glassy. He muttered something incoherent, straightened with a groggy shake of his head, and staggered toward the exit, cage in hand. Annouie followed, stepping into the heat.

Outside the Davies Building, students sprawled across the lawn in loose clusters. Annouie hung back as Meyer-Edwards worked his way through the crowd.

"Isn't that him?" a boy with a cello case murmured to his friend.

They turned to stare, expressions flickering with awe, as Meyer-Edwards stumbled toward the curb.

"Heard he did time in one of those Eastern European prisons," the boy whispered.

His friend shrugged. "Maybe. Heard he's got one of those mob tattoos. Could just be a myth."

Meyer-Edwards shot them a dark look. His eyes skimmed over Annouie—just a beat—before he turned and zig-zagged through the crosswalk, vanishing into the grounds.

"Total mafia vibe," the boy added under his breath.

Annouie resisted the urge to follow. Instead, she waited for the lights to change and crossed, slipping through the university gates and into the Davies Building.

Andre was waiting near the food court, his neon-pink hair impossible to miss.

"You look like death warmed up," he said, strutting toward her, arms wide. He swept her into a crushing hug as students flowed around them like water around a rock in a fast-moving stream. "You're not sleeping again?"

She wriggled free. "I need caffeine before we hit Meyer-Edwards's nine o'clock lecture."

Andre's lashes fluttered. "It's nine now."

Her eyes glinted. "I know. But I'm pretty sure he's going to be late."

"Oh?" He tilted his head. "Do tell."

She shrugged, stifling a yawn. "Just a hunch. But you're right—we should hurry."

* * *

"He's not here, Mr. Deluca."

The voice drifted through the open doorway of 112 Thomas Street as Antony stepped lightly over the low gate. The garden path crunched beneath his shoes—uneven and half-swallowed by weeds. The steps squeaked. The veranda moaned. He set the cat cage on the wicker rocking chair beneath the sagging bay window.

Inside, a door slammed. A heavy tread thundered down the staircase. Stewie Hewson—Luigi's man for the grubby, day-to-day jobs—hit the foyer like a battering ram. Big, loud, unmistakable. Antony slid into the shadows, jaw tightening.

No way he was making it to his lecture now.

Stewie loomed in the doorway, framed by the gloom. A phone rested in one meaty hand, casting an up-light across this face.

Antony stilled, ears pricked.

"Gave the place a good going-over. No sign of Vallone."

Antony suppressed a curse. Jack was in trouble again.

Stewie paused, listening. He nodded—once. Twice. Then again and again, like a puppet. His expression dulled. "Yes, sir. Got it. The fixer will take it from here."

Antony grabbed the cage, vaulted the veranda railing, and landed silently in the side alley. He crouched low as Stewie emerged and trudged to a black sedan beneath the elm.

The engine roared to life. The car peeled off downhill, tires shrieking at the turn.

Silence settled over the neighborhood.

Antony exhaled, hefted the cage, and slipped down the long side access.

The back garden was another world—neat hedges, shaded tiles, wisteria-draped pergola. He ducked beneath it, set the cage on a table, and crouched in front of the wire grille.

"Well, Tib," he muttered. "Luigi's out of his cage. Time to start locking the doors."

* * *

Tib had barely settled in the garden when a courier in a fluorescent-yellow jacket strode up the front path of 112 Thomas Street. He rapped on the door, pivoting on the thick sole of his work boot as he scanned the tree-lined street.

The neighborhood had that polished urban-chic air—except for 112, a glaring outlier with its peeling paint and sagging veranda.

He tapped the large envelope against his thigh, stifling a yawn.

Footsteps approached—cautious, deliberate. The door creaked open, revealing a tall man with dark, tousled hair. The courier clocked him instantly: chiseled jaw, artfully messy haircut, and a faint disinterested look—like he had better places to be.

The man muttered something under his breath, scrawled his signature on the digital pad, and flipped the envelope over with a frown. "Wasn't expecting anything," he said, tossing it onto a cluttered antique console.

The courier caught a glimpse of the interior—worn wood floors, oversized furniture, the faded charm of something once-loved, now mostly ignored.

He retrieved his pad, gave a nod, and turned back to the street.

Nice neighborhood—if you overlooked the house at 112. Funny how a place could stand out for all the wrong reasons.

* * *

Antony Meyer-Edwards shut the door and snatched the envelope. The Accademia's address was stamped on the back. Why would Alberto Aguirre—former Peruvian master and now estranged mentor—be sending him mail after all this time?

He ripped it open. Inside, a second envelope spilled out—photos, letters, and a large unbound musical manuscript. His pulse quickened as he flipped through the pages of the coverless book.

Rebrisi's "lost" *Second Element.*

Aguirre's dead man's switch had been triggered.

His breath caught. First the box at Sara's place. Now this.

A scuff echoed down the hallway.

Antony froze, fingers tightening on the manuscript. A shadow loomed at the rear doorway.

Then a man stepped into the kitchen, and the tension broke like silk under a blade.

Short. Stocky. Ruggedly handsome. A grin that promised trouble.

Professor Giacomo Vallone.

Antiquities expert. Ex-con. Half-brother.

"Jack. Why are you here?" Antony asked, though he already had a good idea.

Jack's grin widened. "Can't I drop in on my little brother?"

Antony shoved the manuscript beneath the mound of unopened letters on the console.

Jack's eyes tracked the movement. A furrow creased his brow.

Antony gestured toward the front room. Jack lingered a beat, then followed him in.

The place was a war zone. Books, papers, dirty glasses, and empty wine bottles littered every surface. A Chesterfield sofa sulked beneath a mountain of crumpled pages. Tall bookcases flanked the entrance, their contents spilling onto the antique rug. In the corner, a grandfather clock ticked steadily, its pendulum slicing the air with methodical precision.

At the center of it all, the grand piano lay buried beneath bills, final demands, and a disconnection notice stamped in aggressive red ink.

Antony moved to the drinks trolley and poured himself a Scotch. "This is a social visit?" He shot Jack a disbelieving look. "No. You're in trouble. Just cut the crap and tell me what you want."

Jack smirked. "I heard a rumor—you've got the manuscript."

"Not this Rebrisi shit again!" Antony downed the drink. The burn did little to soothe the tension in his shoulders.

Jack's smirk vanished. "Is it true?"

Antony sighed. "Look, I don't have time for this. I spent the night in jail. I'm late for work. And I need a goddamn shower."

Jack's lips thinned—his only tell. "I know where the box is. And I'm going after the *Venus* tonight. Forget work. This is the only thing that matters."

Antony stilled.

Jack was close.

Too close.

He exhaled slowly. "Why should it matter to me?"

Jack's eyes swept the room again. "Antoine's desperate to collect all three pieces. And he's not the only one." His gaze settled on Antony. "I need this."

Antony's voice flattened. "Let him chase his red diamond."

Jack stepped closer. "No one gives a shit about the diamond. It's what's *now* in the box that matters."

"What's in the box?

Jack's lips curled. "That's the question, isn't it?" He paused. "What I do know? Antoine offered me Deluca Industries for it. That means whatever's in there is worth more than his entire empire."

Antony shrugged. "Still not my problem."

Jack's voice cut sharper. "Luigi Deluca's been sniffing around."

That landed.

Antony's jaw clenched. Luigi. Antoine's son. Heir to the empire.

Out of jail and already circling.

He turned away, the tension coiling through his spine. "It doesn't interest me."

He rounded the trolley and headed for the door. "Now, if you'll excuse me—"

Jack followed him into the foyer and slapped a ticket onto the console. "Rose Chambers Room. Fourth floor. Fonteyn Gallery. Tonight."

Antony eyed it. "What's that?"

Jack's grin returned. "Preview ticket."

"I told you—I'm not interested."

Jack backed into the hall, still grinning. "You'll be there," he called, voice edged with certainty. "Seven o'clock. Don't be late. And bring that manuscript."

Then he was gone—his footsteps fading, the grandfather clock ticking in his wake.

Antony exhaled and glanced at the envelope half-buried in the stack of neglected mail.

No way he was handing over the manuscript.

Not to Jack.

Not to Antoine.

And definitely not to Luigi Deluca.

Chapter Nine

A gust of wind blasted a flurry of brown leaves across the pavement as Annouie and Andre sprinted toward the Old School. They took the wooden steps two at a time—the boards groaning underfoot—and burst into the foyer.

Annouie skidded to a halt, catching her breath. She smoothed her blouse, ran a hand through her hair, and stepped into the room at the far end.

The long nave-like space was nearly full. The low hum of conversation bounced off the high ceiling.

Wading through the crowd, Annouie made her way to the last two seats in the back corner. As she sat, the murmur around her swelled. Snippets drifted in:

". . . Bayside Ripper . . ."

". . . an anonymous tip-off . . ."

". . . Meyer-Edwards seen leaving the police station this morning . . ."

Her brow creased. That explained his earlier appearance.

Andre leaned in, voice dropping to a conspiratorial growl.

"Alright. Listen up. This is the plan for tonight." He tapped the screen of his phone and angled it toward her. "This is the Rebrisi *Venus*."

Annouie studied the image. Rebrisi's *First Element* was breathtaking—a young woman poised atop a water-slicked rock, feet planted, sun blazing down as the sea churned behind her.

"Oria predicts Timothy Gibson will try to auction it off on the dark web within the week. Her best guess is it's being stored on the fourth floor—Rose Chambers Room. Your job is to get in and verify its authenticity. Gibson's known for near-perfect forgeries. Odds are it's fake. But we won't know until Oria analyzes it."

"Piece of cake."

Andre's tone sharpened. "Don't underestimate Gibson. Security doubled last week. Eight guards total—two on the fourth floor. Stay on your toes."

She flashed him a grin. "I'm always on my toes."

The murmur in the hall rose again as a tall, commanding woman entered through a side door—Judith Pasolini: political pitbull in pumps, acting dean of studies and the conservatory's unofficial enforcer. Flanking her was Dr. Thibault Messier, professor of Advanced Harmony and Counterpoint . . . and a low-life worm.

Annouie's stomach twisted as Messier's sharp gaze swept the crowd and locked on her. He stiffened, leaned into Judith and tugged urgently at her sleeve.

His voice rose—agitated, scornful. "I told you this would happen . . . unreliable . . . shouldn't be here . . ."

Judith waved him off, then stepped onto the platform at the front of the auditorium. She took her place behind the lectern, flanked by the Old School Steinway and a gleaming fortepiano. Gripping the podium, her knuckles whitened as if bracing for the worst.

"I must apologize," she began, voice tight. She hesitated, glancing toward the rear doors. "It would seem—"

A scuff echoed through the hall. All heads turned.

A beat. A whine. Clicking. Then—

A man strode through the doorway, his steps purposeful, his expression a blend of irritation and charm. He raked long fingers through carefully tousled hair, the bruise on his cheek expertly concealed beneath layers of makeup.

He smiled—disarming, electric—as he moved down the central aisle. Every stride drew eyes.

"Ah, Judith. Apologies for my lateness. As always, traffic was abysmal."

Judith's frown softened. "Better late than never," she said, casting Messier a satisfied glance. "As promised, Mr. Antony Meyer-Edwards will speak today on the finer points of nineteenth-century performance practice."

Annouie nudged Andre. "That's him. Our mark."

Andre muttered under his breath. "You sure this isn't a honey trap?"

Meyer-Edwards ascended the stage with effortless grace. Tall. Arresting. He had the wiry strength of a greyhound and the magnetism of a fallen rockstar. Rumors of a torrid affair with former student Sophie Muxlow still lingered.

He radiated danger. The women in the front row were practically swooning.

Despite appearances, Anderson was right—winning him over would take more than just Annouie's good looks.

"Anderson promised it's not," she whispered.

Andre snorted. "And when did you start believing that man's lies?"

At the lectern, Meyer-Edwards flashed a crooked grin. "As many of you know, I specialize in nineteenth-century music." His voice was layered with warmth. "We talk endlessly about period instruments versus modern and the relative strength of the upper partials." He made air quotes, adopting a theatrical tone. "You know what I mean when I say "upper partials", don't you?"

He glanced at the palm cards Judith had handed him, sighed, and tossed them into the air.

Judith gasped. The front row tittered.

Meyer-Edwards gripped the lectern and leaned forward. "You've heard it all before—the usual claptrap about the upper partials, the clarity of modern instruments, et cetera, et cetera." His tone turned sly. "But no one explains the physics behind it. Let me enlighten you."

He stepped away from the stand and moved to the Steinway.

Lowering himself onto the bench, he closed his eyes as if listening to something far off. The room fell silent.

Then he began.

Rhapsody. Brahms. B section.

His fingers glided over the keys, each note deliberate yet effortless, his command over the sound absolute, filling the hall with the Steinway's bright, bell-like tones.

When he stopped, the room held its breath.

Annouie swallowed.

He was every bit what his legend promised: a master of performance.

And if she wasn't careful, he might become her honey trap.

* * *

"He's an asshole," Andre muttered, slinging his messenger bag across his chest as they rose from their seats.

"But brilliant," Annouie countered, lifting her cold coffee to her lips.

Andre shot her a look. "Sure. One-part genius, nine parts dick. Little does he know, I could ruin his life with one line of code."

She snorted. "I hear he's doing a pretty good job of that on his own."

Andre nudged her forward. "Speaking of the Armani-wearing prick—"

The floor creaked. Meyer-Edwards appeared in front of them, clipboard in hand.

"Sorry to interrupt," he said, eyes on Annouie. "The conservatory requires feedback for all lectures now. Apparently, I have to ask random attendees what they thought. So . . ." He flipped open the clipboard, pen poised. "Comments?"

Caught off guard, Annouie stammered, "Er—yes. Very helpful."

Meyer-Edwards tilted his head, lips pursed. "In what way?"

Her mind scrambled. "That bit about 'it's not rocket science'."

The corner of his mouth lifted. "Yes. I thought it had a nice ring to it. What else?"

"Your playing was superb."

"Yes, yes." He sighed, as though praise were a tedious inevitability. "But are there any other adjectives you'd like to use? More specific ones. About the *lecture*."

Andre grabbed her arm, trying to steer her away. "Let's go. We've got prep to do for tonight."

"One more question," Meyer-Edwards said, voice cutting through the noise. "The conservatory is running master classes in nineteenth-century performance practice next term. Would you be interested?"

Annouie shrugged off Andre's grip and turned to Meyer-Edwards, head tilted. "I didn't think you taught regular classes."

His smile returned, sharper now. "There's nothing *regular* about what I do." He scribbled a final note, snapped the clipboard shut, and tucked it under his arm. "Well. A pleasure."

With a pivot, he strode toward the exit, the click of his Valentino heels echoing against the floorboards.

He was nearly at the doors when a loud, deliberate throat-clearing stopped him mid-stride.

"A word, Mr. Meyer-Edwards."

Judith was already closing in.

He turned stiffly. "Yes. Of course. But it'll have to be quick—I'm on a tight schedule."

"A *private* word," Judith said, gesturing toward a quieter corner. She didn't wait for a reply.

Annouie feigned interest in her phone as they passed. She tucked her hair behind her ear, popped in a noise-suppressing earpiece. and leaned closer.

"Whatever plans you have can wait," Judith said. "We're convening in an hour. But the board needs to speak to you first. Some concerns were raised this morning."

He scoffed. "Let me guess—raised by Messier."

Judith's gaze swept the room. "We're meeting in ten minutes. Studio One."

"Fine. We'll have our cozy little chat. Messier can make a prat of himself. Then I'll rush off to my three o'clock because—you know—lawyers."

He turned to go.

Judith's voice stopped him cold. "Aren't you forgetting about the auditions?"

He paused. "Auditions?"

"To select a student," she said, voice weighted.

His expression soured. "Do I really need to be there? I stipulated —no students. That was the agreement."

"Everyone takes students. It's part of the role."

"I'm not everyone."

"Which is why concessions have already been made," she replied.

But he was already gone, the doors swinging shut behind him.

Annouie turned to leave, but Judith stepped in front of her, a stack of papers in hand.

"Ms. Bach."

Annouie forced a smile. "Dr. Pasolini."

"You got my message about rescheduling your interview?" She smoothed a strand of gray hair into place.

"Interview?" Annouie blinked. "You mean the audition."

Judith's brow furrowed. "No. *Interview*. It's part of the reinstatement process. It's been moved forward."

Annouie's throat tightened. "What about the audition?"

"What audition?"

"I heard Meyer-Edwards is taking students again."

"It's *Mister* Meyer-Edwards," Judith corrected, her tone sharp. "And that audition is by invitation only. Your name isn't on the list."

Annouie flushed. "But Dr. Pasolini—"

Judith's tone softened. Slightly. "There are other fine teachers. Focus on proving your commitment to the panel. Dr. Messier remains unconvinced about your return."

"I need to be on that list."

Judith's lips thinned. "Dr. Messier compiled it. He's insisted on strict adherence to the process."

Annouie's voice rose. "But I was told—"

"Mr. Meyer-Edwards wouldn't be my first choice for you." Judith looked almost apologetic.

"But I *need* to audition for him."

Judith rubbed her temples, her resolve hardening again. "It's out of my hands. You're not on it. That's all there is to it."

Before Annouie could press further, Judith turned and walked toward the foyer.

Andre peeled away from the wall, face grim. "This won't work if you're not allowed to audition."

Annouie exhaled sharply. No list meant no two hundred thousand. She had to get on it. "Can't you work your magic? Put my name on it?"

He shook his head. "I wish I could. But didn't you notice?"

He nodded toward the door.

"It's handwritten."

* * *

Studio One was exactly as Antony remembered it—mirrors lining the front wall, ballet barres along the sides. Three tables stood in an arc before the glass, the two outer ones angled inward. A single chair sat at the focal point, solemn and alone.

A class in the late 1800s had dubbed it the *Arc of Inquisition.* The name had stuck.

Antony took his seat at the third desk. Messier—the balding little viper—was already at the second, his thin lips pressed into a self-satisfied line. At the first table sat Judith, commander-in-chief, fingers steepled in a posture of forced authority.

"We have a situation," she began. "The charges against you have raised some red flags with the dean. He's asking questions."

Antony rolled his eyes. "It's a misunderstanding. The drugs are medicinal. It'll all come out in the wash."

Judith's expression suggested otherwise. "Be that as it may, it's causing problems. This could bring the conservatory some very bad press."

Antony leaned forward, tone sharpening. "What are you suggesting?"

Messier's mouth twitched toward a smirk. "Suspension, at the very least. Possibly termination."

Antony shot him a look of open disgust.

Judith raised a hand. "Fortunately, there's a way to make this disappear. But it will require cooperation—from *both* of you."

She turned on Messier. "As I understand it, the complaint was instigated by you, Thibault."

Messier stiffened. "Where did you hear that?"

"From our lawyers," she said flatly. "We can't let this drag on for months while the matter bounces between legal teams."

Messier's smirk sharpened—full of glee. "Then Meyer-Edwards must resign."

Judith exhaled through her nose. "That's not an option. The press would crucify us. The simpler path is for you to withdraw your statement so the charges can be dropped quietly."

Messier recoiled, appalled. "I won't."

"Not even for a seat on the board?"

He froze. "A seat?"

Antony spun in his chair. "You're joking. The drugs are prescribed. He knew that when he filed the complaint. And now you're offering him a board position?"

Messier's grin returned, self-righteous. "Where's the certificate, then? Show me." He slapped the table with his palm.

Antony's jaw flexed. "I don't carry it around."

The table shuddered as Messier struck it again. "Because you don't have one."

"Gentlemen," Judith snapped. She dragged a hand through her hair, then turned to Messier. "The dean is offering you a board seat. What's your answer?"

Messier leaned back, blinking. "Yes. Of course. But I still want proof."

Judith looked to Antony. "Well?"

Antony grimaced. "I'll bring it tomorrow."

Judith nodded. "Good enough?"

Messier sniffed but didn't argue.

"I'll take that as a 'yes'," she said.

Antony adjusted his tie and shoved back from the table. "If that's all, let's hear the candidates so I can get the hell out of here."

Judith shook her head. "Not quite. There's also the matter of the mandatory drug and alcohol testing clause in your contract."

"What about it?"

"You're going to rehab."

His hands flew to his hair. "Now see here—"

"It was our best option," she said. "That, or resignation. And I assume you're not resigning. Our lawyers have already arranged everything. Shari Vanamali will be in touch."

He stared at her. "Unbelievable."

"Take it up with the dean."

His voice dropped to an icy whisper. "And what if I do resign?"

Judith adjusted her glasses. "Don't be so dramatic. You have a habit. Deal with it."

Her tone shifted, darker now.

"There's one more thing. The dean was very clear. You will draw a hard line in the sand with students. No fraternizing. *None.*"

Antony's jaw clenched.

He knew what was coming.

"Because none of us can afford another Sophie Muxlow incident."

Chapter Ten

Carillon bells shimmered through the stiff midsummer air as Annouie stepped beneath the East Wing archway and mounted the staircase. The air smelled of beeswax and lavender. From the floor above, faint murmurs drifted down.

The sound grew louder as she climbed. At the top, she stopped. A wide corridor stretched left, ending in two massive wooden doors. Fabric-covered seats lined both walls—every one of them occupied by audition hopefuls in jeans and T-shirts.

She padded forward, stopping beside a blonde girl with glossy pink lips and a name tag that read "Soraya".

"Is everyone here to audition?" she asked, scanning her competition.

Soraya sniffed and leaned back, raking Annouie with a slow, appraising look. "Isn't that why you're here?"

Annouie shrugged, her face carefully neutral.

Soraya huffed. "Well, if you're not sure, maybe you should leave."

The heavy doors swung open. A lined, gray-faced professor ambled into the foyer. His expression brightened as he spotted her.

"Ms. Bach," he called, beckoning. "We're ready for you."

Groans rippled through the corridor as the other students slumped in their seats.

"She only just got here," someone muttered.

Annouie hurried after the professor, heart hammering.

"Professor Wayne," she said, catching up. "About the audition . . . any chance you could put me on the list?"

He gave her a bemused look but said nothing as he ushered her into Studio One.

"Studio" was apt. The room was vast, filled with natural light and dominated by a gleaming Steinway grand beneath the overheads—not quite as imposing as the one at the Old Paper Mill, but still a masterpiece.

"You already know Dr. Pasolini," Wayne said, dragging her attention back to the panel.

Judith, seated far left, didn't bother to rise. She nodded once, already returning to the stack of documents before her.

Wayne introduced the others, pausing when he reached Thibault Messier.

Sixty-six. Bald. Irritable. He crouched in his seat, glowering. With dark irises and heavy brows, he resembled a bedraggled crow, watching vigilantly for weakness.

Wayne's tone warmed slightly as he turned to the last man. "And finally, our new Head of Performance, Antony Meyer-Edwards."

Annouie's gaze snapped to him before she could stop it. Wherever he went, whatever he did, Meyer-Edwards was magnetic. Tousled hair. Pine-green eyes. An aura of effortless control. He stretched, lacing his fingers behind his head, as if already bored by his own authority.

Judith gestured to the lone chair. "If you would."

Annouie lowered herself into the seat, aware of every eye on her. She straightened her spine, lifted her chin, and folded her hands in her lap.

"We'll be with you in a moment," Judith said, turning to Messier.

Their whispering carried across the otherwise silent room. Annouie cleared her throat.

"Is there a problem?"

Judith straightened, her tone sterner now. "Dr. Messier has brought a serious concern to my attention. There is the matter of an audition—"

"And rules are rules," Messier cut in, fingers laced, voice smug.

Annouie's gaze flickered to the Steinway. "The special audition?"

Meyer-Edwards leaned forward, a rebellious lock falling into his eyes. Amusement glinted there.

Judith shook her head. "Expulsion, no matter the circumstances, is serious. Even if overturned, it can't be ignored. Thibault informs me that, per conservatory regulations, returning students must audition again—on an equal footing with other applicants."

Annouie's pulse ticked faster.

"This means, despite any prior assurances, your place is not guaranteed," Judith continued. "You must demonstrate your competency. It is a late-stage condition agreed upon by all parties. Your sponsor may have misunderstood the terms."

Annouie lifted a brow. "Sponsor?"

"John Chrysler Anderson," Judith said, her tone clipped. "From IB International."

Annouie's lips twitched. Another item for the "Reasons to Screw with Anderson" list.

Judith neatened her papers. "We could, of course, defer your application until next semester. Auditions begin the second week of November. I'm sure Mr. Anderson would understand if we advised him that Ms. Bach has chosen to delay her return." She glanced at Messier, who nodded.

Annouie tilted her head, eyes drifting toward the Steinway. It was a fine instrument—she knew it well.

Judith gestured to the door. "Now if you wouldn't mind? The clock is ticking, and we need to hear the special placement applicants." She turned to Messier.

Annouie cracked her knuckles. "I can audition now."

The room stilled. Judith blinked, clearly caught off guard.

"You do understand you'll need to present quite a—" Her gaze swept the panel. "Substantial program."

Messier leaned forward, sneering. "A work of note by at least four composers, each from a different period. Given your lack of preparation, it may be best to wait."

Annouie shrugged, her tone cool. "I'm sure I can cobble something together."

"We don't want cobbling," Messier snapped.

"What would you like to hear?" Her eyes glinted. "The Bach aria? Some Liszt? A Chopin nocturne? Or better still, the Prokofiev? I remember you were quite partial to the third movement."

"The *Barcarolle,*" Messier said, tone mocking.

Annouie stood, her chair scraping loudly. She dropped her bag on the seat and strode to the piano. Circling it once, she ran her fingers along the polished surface, then sat, leaning over the keys.

Then, without warning, she struck the opening notes of Prokofiev's *Precipitato.*

The Steinway responded just as she remembered—bright tone, perfect balance. The polyphonic textures unfurled like silk.

And the stunned silence from the panel as she landed the final chord?

The most beautiful sound she'd heard in weeks.

She let it hang. Then, without glancing at them, she leaned forward again and began the opening of Chopin's *Barcarolle.*

Out of the corner of her eye, she saw Meyer-Edwards.

No longer slouched. The amusement gone.

He sat upright, eyes gleaming. Flushed. Surprised.

Hungry-looking.

As her fingers danced over the keys, a smile pressed against her lips.

* * *

As the Studio One doors shut firmly behind her, Annouie found herself in a foyer full of stunned faces.

"Guess the audition is over," one boy snapped, breaking the silence as he grabbed his bag and stormed off toward the staircase.

Others followed in a rush. Within seconds, students were scrambling toward the exit.

Soraya pushed through the dispersing crowd, eyes narrow with accusation. "You said you weren't auditioning."

Annouie brushed past her without slowing, ignoring the glares.

She hit the creaky staircase at a near run, pelting down the carpeted stairs and into the open air of a cloud-dark afternoon.

Digging her phone from the depths of her bag, she fired off a message as she crossed the quadrangle.

Did you know the audition was invite-only?

It wouldn't surprise her if Anderson had deliberately left out that important detail—treating her like an initiate, goading her into the impossible—it was all part of his process.

She dropped onto the sandstone wall opposite the cherry blossom tree, swung her legs over, and crossed her feet.

The air smelled of flowers and fresh-cut grass, laced with that earthy scent that came before the rain. She glanced toward the West Tower. Shadows stretched across the lawn as the wind picked up and thunderheads massed behind the building.

Her phone buzzed.

She rolled her eyes. Whatever Anderson sent back, it would be a glib brush-off.

Relax. If I know Antony Meyer-Edwards,
you're a shoo-in.

Her thumbs moved fast.

That's not an answer.

She glared at her screen, waiting.

Nothing.

Annoyed, she shoved the phone away.

The wind was stronger now, tugging at her hair and shirt, shaking the branches overhead.

The square had emptied: the line outside the admissions office was gone. The quadrangle stood eerily silent beneath the darkening sky.

The first raindrops hit the sandstone wall.

A final gust of wind sent the petals spiraling as the storm broke.

Annouie stood and bolted for the archway as the downpour began in earnest.

"Annouie Bach?"

A pale-skinned intern appeared out of nowhere, soaked and breathless. He thrust a folded note toward her, his voice barely audible over the rain.

She opened it.

Judith's cramped script flowed across the page.

Annouie's brow furrowed. "This is a mistake," she muttered. "This should say Studio One, not Dr. Pasolini's office."

A private meeting with Judith could only mean one thing—bad news.

The intern shook his head. "No mistake. Dr. Pasolini wants to see you in her office."

Annouie sighed. The weight of disappointment settled like a stone in her chest. Tucking the note into her pocket, she followed him inside.

* * *

Judith's office was tucked at the end of the corridor. Annouie paused at the nameplate: *Dr. Judith Pasolini*—a name spoken with equal parts reverence and trepidation by most undergrads.

She rapped twice on the smooth wooden surface before stepping inside.

"Good. Let's get started," Judith said, gesturing toward one of the chairs opposite her large desk.

Annouie closed the door, crossed the room, and slid into the nearest seat, her gaze sweeping the space.

The office was as imposing as its occupant. A full-sized nineteenth-century fortepiano dominated the room. Filing cabinets lined the walls. Artifacts crowded the space between the stone-mullioned windows, lending the space a scholar's gravitas.

Judith settled into her chair and opened a manila folder.

"Mr. Meyer-Edwards insisted you be placed on the audition list."

She exhaled sharply, her tone edged with irritation.

Annouie clenched her left fist under the desk and sent up a silent prayer of thanks.

Judith's steely blue gaze locked on her. "Antony Meyer-Edwards often gets what he wants, regardless of the rules." She sighed. "But I'm not convinced studying under him is in your best interests."

She glanced down at the folder. "I have someone else in mind—"

Annouie's stomach hollowed out. "But if he picked me—"

Judith silenced her with a look. "Yes. Rules are rules, as he reminded me. So I'm obligated to offer you this."

She slid a document across the desk.

Annouie turned it around and scanned the text before reading aloud: "I promise to attend all scheduled lectures, provide doctor's certificates for any absences, and maintain a strictly professional relationship with all members of staff, including Antony Meyer-Edwards."

Her brow furrowed. "Is everyone being asked to sign one of these?"

"Only students studying under Mr. Meyer-Edwards."

Annouie grabbed a pen from the desk and signed her name at the bottom. "So—just me."

Judith tore off a Post-it and scribbled something in tight, angular script. "Just you."

She handed over the note. "His address. And a word of warning—"

Annouie gazed down at the paper.

"You'll find him charismatic, brilliant—and quite maddening. Try not to piss him off."

Chapter Eleven

Nicholas Hope was having an ordinary day—until a speeding Fiat knocked him off his bike.

The collision could have been worse. The impact launched him into the air at a textbook forty-five-degree angle. He soared over the hood in a perfect parabolic arc, was airborne for three whole seconds, then crashed onto the asphalt a few feet away.

He rolled, momentum carrying him up onto his feet in a motion so fluid it looked intentional. Then he staggered in circles until the stabbing pain in his left leg dulled just shy of excruciating.

Traffic ground to a halt. A bystander retrieved his mangled bike.

Meanwhile, the Fiat driver—a woman of Asian descent with long, straight hair and what one witness would later describe as "the eyes of a snake"—checked briefly to confirm he was still alive. Then she floored it, disappearing without a backward glance.

Nicholas slumped onto the gutter's edge and gazed up into the stormy sky.

The bystander stepped forward with the broken bike and offered to call the police.

Nicholas waved him off. He pulled out his phone—miraculously intact—and sent a quick message:

Will be late. Don't leave without me.

He shoved it back into his pocket and limped up the road, wheeling the battered bike beside him.

By the time the long hand hit the hour, Nicholas was already staggering through the front doors of Victoria House. He stashed the bike in the print room and made his way to his desk—a solid mahogany centerpiece in the foyer.

He dropped into his high-backed chair, flipped through his diary—

—and groaned.

Sir James had canceled all his afternoon appointments. Again.

The front doors rattled as another bus rolled up to the curb. The furrow between Nicholas's brows deepened. If Sir James had cleared his schedule, there was only one explanation: the MP was going to see his lawyer.

About his son.

A warm trickle drew his attention downward. Blood was soaking through his left pant leg in uneven patches. He stood with a wince and limped back to the print room, leaving a dotted trail across the carpet.

The first-aid cabinet sat above the kitchenette sink. He yanked it down, dug out antiseptic, bandages, and tweezers. Perched on the counter's edge, he went to work.

Gravel mixed with blood as he picked the debris free. He wrapped the leg tightly, secured the bandage, and dumped the waste in the bin.

Behind him, the printer whirred to life, spitting out a fresh report.

Nicholas limped over to retrieve it.

Weekly Financial Analysis—Mr. Gibson Junior—Activities and Consequences.

Using a forensic accountant to track the MP's son's spending was an obscene waste of money. Not that Sir James ever read the report—he preferred a verbal summary. And even then, he only wanted to know how much the boy had burned through that week.

The floor trembled as another double-decker hissed to a stop outside.

"Nic!" Sir James bellowed. "For God's sake, where are you?"

Nicholas straightened his tie and forced himself to walk without limping, though pain flared with every step.

"I'm right here, sir," he said, sweeping into the office.

Sir James Gibson slouched in an antique Chesterfield captain's chair. It groaned beneath his weight, providing a weird counterpoint to the silk vest straining at the buttons. He jabbed a thick finger at the newspaper sprawled across his desk.

The headline screamed:

THE BAYSIDE RIPPER MURDERS AGAIN

"What do you make of this?"

Nicholas leaned closer, pretending to study the deck beneath the headline.

"Oh dear," he said.

The MP growled. "Is that all you've got?"

Nicholas straightened. "Oops. He's done it again?"

Sir James huffed, lips twitching toward a grimace. "Is that what I'm paying you the big bucks for? Quips?"

"Not so big," Nicholas murmured. "Which reminds me—it's been six months since my last pay review."

The MP waved a hand. "Yes, yes. Haven't forgotten. Send Maria a memo. How much this time? Ten? Twenty?"

Nicholas didn't blink. "Fifty."

"Fifty!" the MP barked—but after a moment's consideration, relented. "Fine. Fifty. But you're going to work for it."

"Don't I always," Nicholas muttered. Then more audibly, "Thank you, sir. Will that be all?"

Sir James shoved the newspaper across the desk. "No. I want you to find out more about this man they brought in. The electorate's in an uproar. I've got little old ladies ringing me at all hours of the night demanding answers. They want to know what the Minister for Police is doing about it."

His eyes narrowed to reptilian slits.

"What am *I* doing about it?"

Nicholas pursed his lips, waiting for an answer.

"Right. That's what I thought," Sir James snapped. "So here's what you're going to do. Find out who he is, where he came from, and whether he's our man."

"I understand the police have already ruled that out," Nicholas said.

The MP sighed. "Has he got a name?"

"Many, I believe."

"What's that supposed to mean?"

"It's one of those hyphenated affairs. But the authorities haven't released it to the public."

Sir James scowled. "We're not the public. Go flash your credentials and find out who he is—and why he's not our man."

"I'll get the details and put a report on your desk."

"I don't want a report. Get me someone's head. His head, if you have to. You've no idea how militant these old dears get when riled up."

"I'm on it."

"And Nic?"

Nicholas paused in the doorway. "Yes?"

Sir James pushed his glasses up his nose. "After you're done at the precinct, go to the morgue. Emil will be waiting."

"Emil?"

"Dr. Thorpe. Old friend. Bit of a crackpot, but says he's got DNA this time. I want to know: does it belong to this man with many names? Does it belong to someone else? And if either of the above applies—what are the police doing about it?"

* * *

Nicholas Hope arrived at the police station precisely five minutes after two, stepping into the media room just as DCI Dunbier was wrapping up his opening remarks. As usual, the Detective Chief Inspector managed to say a lot about nothing, and the killer—the Bayside Ripper—remained as enigmatic as ever.

At a quarter past the hour, Nicholas slipped out the back. The clamor of journalists faded behind him.

Let the profilers theorize all they liked—about the Ripper's childhood trauma, his compulsions to mutilate, his "signature". None of it had brought them any closer to catching him. The only tangible lead was the hope that this time, he'd left behind DNA.

Outside, the storm from earlier had given way to bright afternoon sun. He crossed the lot, his left calf throbbing with every step, a sharp reminder of the morning's collision.

Five minutes later, he pulled up outside a squat gray building. The sign above the glass doors read:

City Forensics Unit

A tall, stooped man met him at reception and introduced himself as Usman Malik, Thorpe's assistant. He led Nicholas to the fourth floor, where he was instructed to don the regulation plastic coveralls, boots, and a cap.

Malik reappeared and guided him into the autopsy suite, where the forensic pathologist was waiting.

Dr. Thorpe was short and round, with a worn face, and the hangdog eyes of a basset hound. Two detectives in similar protective gear stood nearby. Thorpe gestured to them.

"Detectives Ratcliffe and Saunders."

Ratcliffe was striking, with sharp eyes and a stance that suggested she considered herself smarter than everyone in the room. Saunders, by contrast, looked suitably large and stupid.

Thorpe toddled toward the back of the suite, and they followed. Malik trailed behind, visibly nervous in the confined space.

Nicholas noted Malik's unusually long lashes—oddly beautiful, shimmering against the sheen of sweat on his face. If not for the fear in his eyes, he would have been quite striking.

At the rear of the suite, a single gurney stood beneath a harsh fluorescent light.

Thorpe pulled back the pale blue sheet.

Nicholas inhaled sharply.

He drew out his notebook and pen, his breath catching as he glanced down again.

Bronze hair. Early thirties. Stunning.

No doubt.

It was her.

Thorpe's voice cut through the silence. "As you can see, the subject suffered blunt force injuries to the neck. Here . . . and here."

Nicholas leaned in, feigning focus. His pen moved mechanically across the page.

"Asphyxiation is the probable cause of death," Thorpe continued, "evidenced by the petechial hemorrhaging in the skin and conjunctiva."

"Are those finger marks?" Ratcliffe asked, her voice sharpening.

Thorpe nodded. "Indeed. Though these nail marks here—poor dear—are likely self-inflicted. There's evidence she broke free of her restraints and fought hard to pry his hands from her neck."

"Oh? I thought—" Nicholas cut himself off, nausea rising.

He straightened his spine and forced a breath as Malik's eyes fixed on him—wide, watchful.

Thorpe's smile broadened, oblivious. "We may be able to recover skin cells from her neck. If we're lucky, we can DNA-type the material and match it to the suspect."

Nicholas forced out the words. "Really? You can do that?"

Saunders smirked.

"Oh, yes," Thorpe said, beaming. "Provided his DNA's on file."

Nicholas's throat tightened. It was truly terrifying what modern forensics could do with a single strand of hair, a few blood cells, a trace of saliva.

He snapped the notebook shut. "Then let's hope the suspect's already in the system."

The book disappeared beneath his coveralls as he edged toward the door.

"But there's more," Thorpe called after him.

"I'm sure there is."

"I haven't told you about the finger contusions, and how his thumb—"

Nicholas waved him off. "I'm certain the officers will find it most illuminating." Then, more urgently: "I'll find my own way out."

He didn't wait for a reply.

* * *

Nicholas collided with the changing room door, muttering under his breath. He blundered inside, already peeling off the suffocating plastic coveralls. His boots hit the floor with a thud as he bent double, breath coming fast and shallow.

A wave of nausea overtook him. He stumbled into the first stall and threw up. The retching left him shuddering, his body convulsing as he backed out and turned to the mirror.

Sara. Damn you. Just couldn't let it go.

His reflection was pale and clammy, bronze hair disheveled, spit clinging to his chin like a grim reminder. Grimacing, he grabbed a handful of paper towels and scrubbed at his mouth just as his phone buzzed from his pocket.

His hands shook as he fumbled it free.

"Where the hell are you, boy?" Sir James barked. "I was expecting you over an hour ago."

Nicholas propped the phone against the counter and kept wiping his face. "I was doing what you asked."

Sir James's tone sharpened. "Remind me again what that was."

"The morgue," Nicholas bit out, his stomach twisting again. "Digging up whatever I could so you can reassure your constituents you're doing something." He pressed a hand to his stomach.

"Hmph!" Sir James grunted. "Leave it. No reason to run yourself ragged. The boys in blue will sort it. Any leads?"

Nicholas leaned over the sink, bracing himself against the edge. "None whatsoever."

"Typical," Sir James muttered. "Never mind. There's always tomorrow. Now get over here. Doncaster's off running errands, and someone needs to drive me to that exhibition thing."

Nicholas frowned. "Thought you weren't going?"

"Changed my mind."

"Can't you order a taxi?"

"I could," Sir James snapped, tone dripping with condescension. "But why, when I'm paying you a small fortune?"

Nicholas clenched his jaw, biting back the response he wanted to give.

"What was that?"

"I said I'll be there in twenty, sir."

"Make it fifteen. And lose whatever the hell suit you're wearing. I want you in something more urbane." A pause. "Oh, and did you get the information I wanted?"

Nicholas's grip tightened on the sink. "Thought you said it could wait until tomorrow."

"Changed my mind. Now get over here. You can fill me in on the way."

The line went dead.

Nicholas exhaled slowly. *Just you wait, Gibson.*

He dabbed at his mouth again, straightened, pushed thoughts of Sara from his mind, and left the room.

* * *

Malik was loitering just outside the door.

"Dr. Thorpe was concerned," he began, his voice high-pitched and jittery. He extended a stack of typewritten pages toward Nicholas. "He thought this might be helpful, seeing as you're not staying for the full presentation."

"That was very considerate of Dr. Thorpe."

Malik gave a crooked smile. "Emil can be thoughtful. When it suits him. Most of the time, he chooses not to be." He giggled nervously, teeth flashing. "I probably shouldn't have said that."

Without warning, he pivoted and scurried off down the corridor.

Nicholas glanced at the pages, his brow furrowing as he skimmed the dense text. Strings of technical gibberish—nucleotide sequences, alleles—swam before his eyes.

Cat saliva?

What the hell was Thorpe doing with feline DNA?

"What does cat saliva have to do with the murder?" he called.

Malik slid to a halt, backtracked toward Nicholas, and peered at the pages.

"To perform a forensic DNA analysis," he began, "DNA is first extracted from a sample. This one was taken from a cat. Even a nanogram is enough to provide good data. In this case, we're hoping to match it to an existing sample in the DNA index."

Nicholas's grip on the pages tightened. "But what's the connection between the cat and the killer?"

Malik offered a faint smile. "The owner had a cat. Detective Saunders was bitten by the animal the night of the murder. Some bright spark in forensics thought the perpetrator might've been bitten too."

"But you don't agree?"

Malik shrugged, glancing around as if someone might be listening. "It's unlikely. Even if we identify a sample, it won't help unless the suspect's DNA is already in the database. The Ripper's been careful so far. I doubt he's on file."

He hesitated, then reached into his breast pocket and produced a card. His pupils dilated slightly as he made eye contact for the first time. "Ring me anytime—night or day—if you have more questions. I'm happy to help."

His gaze dropped as he handed over the card, tension still humming in the air between them.

Nicholas nodded. "Thanks."

Malik offered a tight smile, then turned and fled, his footsteps echoing down the hallway.

* * *

Nicholas rode the elevator to the yellow-level garage, his thoughts still tangled from the strange exchange upstairs. The ding of the doors barely registered. He stepped off, blinking rapidly as he strode toward the Bentley.

Halfway down the second aisle, he came to an abrupt stop.

Sara was dead.

But—

If he found the man who'd fathered them . . .

He pulled out his phone, hesitated, then keyed in the number from Malik's card. It rang four times before the doctor picked up.

"Dr. Malik? This might seem unorthodox," he began, "but I have a personal request." He paused before forging ahead. "I never knew my father—he was a military man. If I gave you a sample of DNA, could you run a check against your databases? See if there's a match? Of course, I'd compensate you for your time."

His tongue darted over his lower lip. He was skirting ethical boundaries, but he didn't care.

A muffled cough came through the line, followed by Malik's whispered reply. "Can't talk now. Emil's watching. Send the sample. Mark it for my attention. Can't promise this week—maybe early next. If you're willing to wait."

A strange flutter stirred in Nicholas's chest, like a bird testing its wings.

"Call me later," Malik added. "We'll discuss the rest then."

The line went dead.

Nicholas stared at the phone, then slipped it back into his pocket and continued toward the Bentley.

The fluttering sensation grew—warm and unfamiliar: *hope.*

A long shot—but he couldn't stop the joy rising through his chest like sunlight breaking through a storm.

Malik was a genius with DNA typing.

If anybody could find a match, it was him.

Nicholas opened the car door and slid inside, a rare smile spreading over his face as his thoughts, at last, took flight.

Chapter Twelve

Antony Meyer-Edwards rushed over the threshold of 112 Thomas Street, slipping on a brown A4 envelope shoved under the door. He caught himself with a curse and bent to retrieve it, frowning at the stamp on the back: *Hogan & Ryan Legal Services.*

He tore the package open and shook the contents onto the hall table. A dog-clipped sheaf of papers spilled out—thick enough to make his stomach tighten. On top was a handwritten note on crisp, white stationery.

> *Please sign and return at your earliest convenience. I've made an appointment with a life coach and counselor. Her card is included, should you have any additional questions.*
> *—Shari Vanamali*

Antony scoffed, kicked the door shut, and strode through to the kitchen, card and papers in hand.

He dropped the documents on the counter, set his phone to speaker, and dialed before disappearing into the walk-in pantry.

The ringtone filled the silence as he rummaged among jars and bottles.

When he returned, he held a bottle of brandy in one hand and a balloon glass in the other. He cracked the seal and poured without ceremony.

The last twelve hours hadn't been the worst in his life—

But they came close.

The line connected with a sharp click.

"Shari Vanamali speaking."

Antony downed half the glass in one smooth gulp. "Is it true?" he asked, resetting the bottle with a hollow thud.

"Mr. Meyer-Edwards. You've heard the good news, I take it."

He shrugged, though she couldn't see him. "Depends on your perspective. Tell me I don't have to go to rehab."

Her pause was brief. "You have to go. The dean was one hundred percent non-negotiable on that point."

Antony sighed and refilled his glass.

"You don't sound pleased."

He snorted, lifting the card—perfumed, overly elegant . . . a waste of his time.

"A therapist? Seriously?"

"The dean considers you an asset to the conservatory, despite your . . . extracurricular activities. But he was clear—while the press love you now, they'll be watching your progress. This is damage control. The right steps, the right spin, and you come out looking like a reformed hero on the road to redemption."

"On the road to somewhere," Antony muttered, draining the second glass and pouring a third.

The phone crackled. "This is a great opportunity to market yourself more favorably."

He eyed the card again—last thing he needed was a rehab counselor. "Do I have to see this Dr. Chin?"

"Absolutely. Your first appointment's this afternoon. She's already on her way."

He froze, glass halfway to his lips. "She's *what*?"

"She rescheduled to fit you," Shari replied. "So no complaints."

Antony swore under his breath. "And what about my schedule?"

"You have nothing until four."

His fingers tightened around the glass. "Not that you asked."

He moved to end the call, finger hovering above the red icon, when Shari's voice burst through the speaker again.

"Oh—one more thing. When can I expect the certificate?"

"Certificate?"

"The one you promised Thibault Messier."

Antony's jaw slackened. "He still wants proof?"

The bottle hovered in midair. Abandoning the glass, he drank straight from the neck.

A knock sounded at the front door.

He looked heavenward, resisting the urge to hurl the bottle. Of course the good doctor was right on time.

"Sure," he said, emptying the bottle with a final, defiant swig. "I'll get it to you first thing tomorrow morning."

* * *

Annouie grinned as she flattened the gas pedal to the floor. Andre's sleek Porsche surged forward, cutting through traffic with the ease of a predator through a school of fish. The fact that he'd entrusted her with the car still felt surreal.

At the next intersection, she adjusted the bespoke Prada sunglasses, tapping the arm to activate the interface. Oria2's crisp voice filled her ear:

"Take the next left and continue for thirteen hundred feet. There is a small parking lot at the bottom of the hill. Satellite tracking indicates one vacant space."

Annouie smirked as she spun the wheel, guiding the car down the narrow street to a tight cul-de-sac outside the conservatory gates. Sure enough, a single space remained.

She slid the Carrera into it, cut the engine, and sank back into the buttery Napa leather.

Number 112 stood about halfway up the hill—a sagging, semi-detached relic of a house that screamed neglect.

Shouldering her bag, she stepped out and slung the strap across her chest. The tree-lined path stretched before her, dappled sunlight fighting with shadow for a place on the cracked pavement.

She strode toward it.

Spying on Meyer-Edwards in his natural habitat—tracking his movements, logging his visitors, tailing him when necessary? Easy. Delivering her findings to Anderson? Even easier. But the best part?

She was back in the program, like the expulsion had never happened.

She paused at the rusted iron gate, tilting her head at the sad-looking three-story structure cowering in the overgrown garden.

Pasolini had called it "charming".

It wasn't charming. It was a hovel.

Paint peeled from the architraves, and the balcony's wrought iron flaked in strips of oxidized green. One of the front door panes had been partially boarded up. A wild Geisha Girl shrub clawed at the crumbling façade. The entire structure looked ready to dissolve back into the earth.

Annouie swore under her breath and shoved the gate open.

The flagstones were uneven, weeds pushing through the cracks. She picked her way forward, scanning her surroundings. A leaf blower buzzed somewhere up the street, its mechanical whine slicing through the stillness.

At the porch, she climbed four steps. Her chest tightened as she raised her hand and knocked. The sound was loud, intrusive.

The leaf blower fell silent.

She waited, ears straining.

No footsteps. No voices. No shuffling.

She tried the doorknob.

It gave with a groan of corroded hinges, grating over the sill like nails down a chalkboard. The sound echoed as she stepped inside.

She dropped her bag on a wobbly hall table, in front of a dusty amphora—beside which, curiously, sat a pile of unopened mail and a wad of banknotes.

The floorboards creaked underfoot as she ventured farther in.

"Mr. Meyer-Edwards?" she called, starting up the stairs. Her hand slid along the gritty banister. The house was eerily still. The silence sharpened her unease.

Near the top, she heard it—the rhythmic squeak of springs, coming from behind the first closed door.

"Yes. That's it. Keep the pressure up. It's about to slide back in."

Her eyes narrowed. Then widened as a long, very male moan drifted into the hall.

She grimaced.

Another pervert.

She stepped back, stumbled, her heel catching on the edge of the stairs. She flailed, grabbing at the newel post. Her knees hit the floor with a crack.

The groaning stopped.

A rustle of movement followed, and the bedroom door flew open.

Meyer-Edwards appeared on the landing, chest heaving slightly. Shirtless. Sweatpants slung low on his hips, revealing the sharp cut of his obliques.

Annouie's gaze dipped before she caught herself. For a privileged white man who'd supposedly squandered his career, he was improbably fit. His torso was a map of lean muscle and old scars—pale lines standing out against his skin like battle trophies.

And there—over his right pectoral—was the tattoo. A lotus. Jagged petals. Sharp as glass.

Before she could study it further, he turned, grabbed a shirt and pulled it over his head. The thin fabric clung, accenting rather than concealing his musculature. She tore her gaze away, composing her features just as he turned.

"Ah, the student has arrived. And right on time, I might add." He raised his voice toward the room behind him. "Forgive me, Doctor. I entirely forgot I had another appointment. We'll need to finish up."

"I didn't hear you knock," he said, one brow lifting. His gaze was dark. Assessing.

Annouie pushed herself to her feet, brushing off her knees. "Guess you were too busy to hear it."

A pause stretched between them. The air thickened with challenge.

Finally, Meyer-Edwards nodded toward the staircase. "Perhaps you could wait in the front room while the doctor and I conclude our business."

Annouie turned away, muttering under her breath. "Rumors must've been true after all."

Her voice bounced off the hard surfaces, echoing through the house.

A dark laugh followed. "Oh, yes. Except for the one about the ballerina and the jet ski. That one's pure fiction."

She glanced over her shoulder just in time to see him disappear into the bedroom.

As her foot hit the last step, his voice drifted after her:

"Do you think you can fit me in later this week, Doctor? I haven't had this sort of movement in months."

* * *

Antony tugged at the buttons of his shirt, fastening them with quick, practiced movements. He yanked a tie from the closet and looped it around his neck as he strode onto the landing.

Below, the student lingered by the front door, ignoring his instructions to wait in the front room.

Bach stood out like a blood-red diamond in a sea of white pebbles. The oversized designer sunglasses only sharpened her air of defiance. Her fingers played with the strap of her handbag—a subtle, repetitive motion that was somehow both innocent and provocative. He began to imagine where those hands might linger—then caught himself.

She'd been expelled. For serious misconduct.

But he couldn't shake the sound she'd coaxed from the old Studio One instrument. Her flawless command. Her ability to perform under pressure. It begged the question: a student so clearly gifted—what had she done to get herself kicked out?

Dr. Chin sidled up beside him, her gaze sliding down to the girl with thinly veiled curiosity.

"That's your student?" she murmured. Her snakelike eyes gleamed with surprise. "Not what I was expecting."

Chin's attention remained fixed on Bach, who either hadn't noticed or didn't care she was being scrutinized.

Chin was tiny, Asian. But there was a ruthless sharpness in the way she moved, in every clipped word. Her long black hair shimmered in the afternoon light. Her upturned, kohl-rimmed eyes were cold and calculating. And in the hollow of her throat, a diamond the size of a thumbnail sat suspended on a twisted chain of gold.

He shrugged. Bach wasn't what he'd expected either. "She's repeating third year. Very bad business. No idea why they let her back in."

He gestured toward the stairs. "Shall we?"

Chin swept past him, skirts trailing behind her like a shadow. At the bottom, she handed him her card, her sultry voice breaking the tension.

"Call me if your shoulder gives you trouble again."

Antony dropped the card beside the amphora. "I will."

She cast one last glance at Bach before slipping out the door.

Antony kicked it shut. The bang reverberated through the quiet house.

He leaned toward the mirror above the console, adjusting his tie with deliberate care. His fingers worked the silk with slow precision as he watched her in the glass.

She stood in the hallway, head tilted, peering down the corridor toward the kitchen.

When he turned, her attention snapped to him, one brow arched —a silent challenge.

"Please," he said, gesturing at the front reception room. "We'll work in here. Also, you might want to lose the shades. And just so we're clear—" his voice took on a dark edge, "—that wasn't a request."

She removed them.

Her cool, blue gaze locked onto his, unsettling in its intensity—as if she were peeling back every layer, exposing the darkest corners of him.

He suppressed the urge to clench his fists and followed her into the room.

* * *

Janine Chin slipped the earpiece into place as she jogged downhill. Her mark's voice crackled through the tiny speaker—low, resonant, unguarded. A slow smile curled across her glossy red lips. The hallway bug was transmitting at full strength.

A quick recon of the house had turned up nothing. If Antony Meyer-Edwards had the Rebrisi manuscript, he'd hidden it well.

She aimed her fob at the Fiat parked at the bottom of the narrow street. The car chirped, and she climbed in, one hand searching her bag for her phone as the earpiece fed her the conversation unfolding in the front room.

Bach.

Chin's mind raced. Annouie Bach—Anderson's golden girl. The one she'd left for dead.

She grimaced. Bach was a new variable.

Chin hated variables.

She leaned into the headrest and tapped the screen to dial.

Time to break the bad news to Sir James.

He wasn't going to like it.

Chapter Thirteen

Sir James Gibson pressed the handset to his ear, his lips twitching as a deep, female voice purred through the speaker.

"Sir James, darling."

He let out a low chuckle. "Hello, Doctor."

Nicholas had done a thorough background check on the Chinese woman. She came highly recommended—a specialist in fixing problems, the kind that required discretion and a ruthless hand.

She sighed—a sound that sent a delicious shiver sliding up his spine. An alluring creature with a reputation for violence. Just the sort of combination to set his blood roaring.

"You received my terms?" she drawled, the hum of a car engine rising in the background.

Sir James lifted a sheet of paper from his desk, brow furrowing as he scanned it. "Not quite what we agreed, is it?"

She scoffed, voice laced with disdain. "You'll note a clause covering the inclusion of any additional fees reasonably incurred. The appraisal was not as straightforward as expected."

He leaned back, the leather creaking beneath him. "I see." His fingers tapped his chin. "But you've completed the appraisal now?"

"It's exquisite work. My man was quite impressed," she said, the rhythmic tick of an indicator audible in the background.

Sir James allowed himself a smile, already envisioning his latest acquisition—and the secret that would soon be his. His fingers moved deftly over his keyboard, slipping through logins and layered security prompts. Anticipation settled like aged Scotch, warming him from the inside out.

"Rebrisi is one of the greats," he murmured.

Chin's laugh slithered through the line. "Ah, but you do realize—it's not a Rebrisi original."

He froze, smile sliding from his face. "What?"

"It's a fake. Brilliant to be sure. But still a copy."

The words hissed like steam.

"A forgery?" he growled, suspicion already flaring beneath his skin. "Know who did it?"

"No. My expert was baffled, too. Seems we have a new player on the board."

The phrase landed like a trigger. His gaze shifted to the photo on his desk—an outrageously handsome young man with a dangerous glint in his eye.

Sir James's jaw tightened. The boy was reckless. Too reckless.

He exhaled slowly, forcing his voice back to its usual measured tone.

"I'll see that your invoice is settled."

Chin's voice softened. Almost placating. "It really is beautiful work. Most appraisers would've been fooled."

"I'm not paying you for compliments," he snapped. "Any progress on that other matter?"

A pause. He imagined Chin's sculpted brows arching in mock surprise—nothing rattled the woman.

"Oh, yes. The manuscript. That's why I called."

His voice dropped to a low rumble. "And?"

"I'm certain Aguirre sent it to Meyer-Edwards."

Sir James closed his eyes, letting the weight of the information settle.

"Then we need to recover both items—before they fall into the wrong hands."

"Any particular hands I should be aware of?" she asked, curiosity dripping through the line.

"Let's refer to them as my competitors," Sir James said—and hung up.

His gaze lingered on the photo of Timothy.

Time to teach the boy a lesson he wouldn't soon forget.

He stood, smoothing the line of his suit. Something shifted in the corner of his eye.

He turned sharply—and flinched.

Nicholas Hope had materialized beside him.

"You were about to call," Hope said.

Sir James steadied himself on the back of his chair. "How the blazes do you do that?"

Hope's expression remained impassive. "It's my job to anticipate your every move." He lifted a folder. "And to deliver these. You requested them."

Sir James waved the reports away. "Later. First, call the bank." The time for indulgence was over. "Freeze my son's credit cards. Let him remember who pays the bills."

Hope's granite façade wavered. "Does this mean the preview is off?"

Sir James laughed—quiet, scornful. "Certainly not. Gabriella's promised me a private viewing of the new acquisition. And trust me, if you knew what it was, you'd understand—hell itself couldn't keep me away."

Chapter Fourteen

Antony disappeared into the back of the house and returned moments later, a small plastic bin tucked under one arm. Striding to the piano, he swept the papers into it, placed it by the door, and turned to Bach.

She dropped her bag and prowled toward the piano. Bending slightly, she angled her head to read the gilt-edged name above the keys.

"Chickering," she breathed with a hint of awe. "You know how rare these are?"

"Are they?" He crossed to the battered drinks trolley. Lifting a wide-shouldered bottle, he poured a generous measure of Scotch into a tumbler.

"Want one?"

Her focus stayed fixed on the instrument. "No."

He raised his glass, watching her across the rim. "Why don't you take it for a spin?"

She ran her long fingers over the keys instead of answering. Antony froze mid-sip, pulse quickening. She wasn't just attractive—she was breathtaking.

She tilted her head, a waterfall of hair spilling over one shoulder —as if to prove the point. "I beg your pardon?"

Christ, get a grip.

He forced his attention back to the task.

He tossed back his drink, setting the glass down harder than intended.

"Sit. Play whatever you want," he said, gesturing at the stool. "It's all a bit impromptu, I realize, but I can't decide whether to start you on CPE's essay or something more challenging, like the Liszt treatise." His voice thickened on the last word, rough and strained.

She laughed. "You mean the lost treatise? You're not suggesting you have it?"

That laugh—a sound that crawled inside, weakening his resolve. Time to stop this. He pinched the bridge of his nose and gestured sharply at the piano. "Just play."

With a shrug, she circled the instrument, fingers skimming the keys. Every nerve in his body tautened. When she finally settled onto the stool, she took her time adjusting the height, lowering her feet to the pedals, stretching her neck. Sweat prickled at his collar.

As she fussed, his gaze darted around the room. Dust-coated books lined the shelves, the floor was filthy, the windowsills were no better. The place was a disaster—not ideal for impressing a woman.

Shit. Another reflex thought.

She shifted, and the stool's legs screeched against the boards. Ordinarily, he'd have winced, but he was too distracted by her long legs now displayed to advantage. He resisted the urge to throw himself out the window and instead, slumped onto the lowest rung of the library ladder.

He feigned nonchalance, lacing his fingers together, as Judith's words repeated like a drumbeat in his head.

Line in the sand. Line in the sand. Line in the sand.

Bach poised her hands over the keys, and just as he thought he could take no more, she struck the keys—full-bodied and fierce.

That sound—

The air left his lungs in a rush.

She pounded the notes with an almost double tap, her left hand picking out the bass while the treble soared, distinct and controlled. The technique was unmistakable—she had to be one of Aguirre's.

"Stop."

She pulled her hands away, cool gaze locking on him as he climbed the ladder. At the top, his fingers skimmed the dusty spines, stopping on the large, unbound volume he'd hidden between thicker tomes only hours earlier.

"Knew I had this somewhere," he muttered, easing it free.

Clambering down, he dropped to the floor, face flushed. Dust danced in the air as he blew across the book's surface.

"Tell me what you think of this," he said, handing it to her.

A small test—a prompt only a former member of Alberto Aguirre's inner circle could pass.

She glanced at the manuscript, brow furrowing. The front cover, title page, frontispiece, and contents were gone. No acknowledgments. No date. Just dense, typewritten text with erratic, handwritten annotations.

"It's in French," she said, flipping to the first chapter.

Was she serious?

"You'll begin with this," he said, lowering his voice. "Don't tell anyone I gave it to you."

He studied her. No flicker of recognition. No micro-expressions.

She turned the manuscript over slowly, inspecting it with detached curiosity. "This wasn't written by you." She flipped through the pages, lingering over a particularly dense passage. "How did you come by it?"

"My brother acquired it in New York. Private auction. A birthday gift."

A lie. Jack never sent gifts—not for Christmas, graduation, and certainly not for a birthday.

Alberto Aguirre sent it.

Her gaze flicked to the top of the bookcase. "Do you always stash valuable manuscripts up there?"

He shrugged. "Pretty sure it's not valuable. Although my brother thinks it's Liszt's lost treatise."

She scoffed softly. "It's not the treatise."

"You're certain?"

Her lips curled faintly. "You'd hardly be giving it to me if it was."

He couldn't help the dry chuckle. "True. It's a hoax. A convincing one, though—and an excellent read."

He gestured toward the Chesterfield, still buried beneath a clutter of papers and cartons. "Shall we?"

She raised a brow. "Shall we what?"

"Discuss how this is going to work. Clear a spot if you need to."

Without warning, he strode from the room. When he returned, his arms were full of books.

She hadn't moved.

He brushed past her and dumped the stack on the piano stool. Then, with an air of resignation, he began clearing the Chesterfield, relocating the mess to an antique desk by the window. He reached for the stack, then hesitated. His hand hovered.

"My grandmother passed away," he said.

A beat.

And then another.

"She was ill for a long time. The place fell apart."

Then, as if that explained everything, he took the manuscript from her and replaced it with a heavy volume.

"Read this first."

"'*The Art of Practicing the Piano*'," she read aloud.

"Undoing your bad habits begins there," he said, handing her another.

She arched a brow. "I don't have any bad habits."

"We'll start with how you practice," he said, ignoring her. "Forget what you think you know. It's wrong." He paused. "How do I know, you ask?" He grinned. "I know because ninety-nine percent of what is taught is wrong." He handed her a third book. "Read these. Then come back."

Her expression darkened. "I thought we were beginning today?"

"We have. You're reading."

She stared at the books stacked in her arms. "You're serious?"

"Entirely. Read. Ponder. Return. No practicing."

"No practicing?"

His mouth twitched. "Correct. You'll understand soon enough. When you're done, there'll be a quiz."

"Quiz?"

"I'll be here. Just knock and enter."

"That's it?"

"Or use the key under the stone cat by the Geisha Girl if I'm not. I usually turn up within an hour. And I'm never longer than a day."

They stood in silence. Then, without a word, she shoved the books into her bag and strode through the door.

Antony watched her go, hands in his pockets. Only when the door clicked shut did he release the breath he hadn't realized he'd been holding.

Better this way—cut her loose now, before his feelings took hold.

But the thud in his chest told him it was already too late.

* * *

Annouie shifted her bag to the other shoulder, her stride lengthening as she marched downhill.

Loading her up with reading material? Calling it a *lesson*? Clearly a tactic to frustrate her. But why? He'd gone out of his way to push her onto the audition list—and now he wanted her to quit before they'd even begun?

She hadn't been made. So what had changed?

She flung the bag and books into the passenger seat of the Carrera and slid behind the wheel. The sunglasses snapped into place. The earpiece followed with a quick tap.

She exhaled once, slow and sharp.

Fine.

So be it.

If he wanted to play games—

She could play games.

"Oria, are we receiving?"

The AI's voice came through crisp and clear. "Strong signal from the reception room. But I'm detecting interference near the RF transmitter outside the bedroom."

"Another listening device?"

"You're not the only one surveilling Antony Meyer-Edwards."

Of course. The Chinese woman. Something about her had struck a nerve.

Too bad for her. Annouie already had the manuscript.

Reaching into her bag, Annouie pulled out the treatise as shifting shadows flitted across the Carrera's hood. Meyer-Edwards had been so busy shoving books into her arms, he hadn't noticed her slip this one into the pile.

Did he really not realize what he had?

She flipped through the opening pages, fingers grazing the textured paper. Tiny knots brushed her skin—a tactile signature of its woven construction. Old. Very old.

The typeset text suggested early nineteenth-century. It could easily be Liszt's lost treatise. But—

No.

Still—it was remarkable.

Not just a convincing forgery—

A masterpiece.

"Could you scan this document and tell me who created it, Oria?" she asked, leaning back into the seat.

"Certainly," the AI replied. "It is one of three pieces by the artist

Gabriel Rebrisi. Informally known as Rebrisi's manuscript, its proper name is *The Second Element*."

"What's its official status?"

"Stolen."

A sly smile crept across her face.

One down. Two to go.

Chapter Fifteen

Timothy Gibson lingered in the shadows of the gallery's main exhibition hall, watching Gabriella Fonteyn pace before the giant mural of pop princess Suki Rey. She moved with a sharp, restless energy, her whippet-thin frame accentuated by the sleek black ponytail that swished like a sword when she turned. Her Eastern European features were striking—Cleopatra eyes rimmed in deepest navy, ivory cheekbones, sumptuous plum-colored lips.

Timothy dropped his gaze to his iPhone, pulse hammering. Sweat beaded at the base of his neck, trickled down his back, and gathered beneath his arms until he felt like he was slow-cooking in his own juices.

Why wasn't the transaction going through?

He stabbed at the display again. The phone kept replaying the same message: the account was temporarily frozen.

He drew in a staggered breath and glanced toward the preparations on the main floor. The hook was baited. The buyers would be circling by midnight. All he needed was that one bite. Once the deal closed, his financial woes would vanish—and he could disappear into the sunset.

If he held it together that long.

Around him, the workmen were packing up. Plastic sheets rolled away. Ladders collapsed. Toolboxes snapped shut. Gabriella barked orders in rapid-fire Romanian, her ponytail slashing. She was a live wire, her energy lighting up the space—but even she couldn't outshine the mural affixed to the wall behind her.

Timothy stepped from the shadows, masking his unease with studied nonchalance.

"Was she a difficult subject?" Gabriella asked without turning. Her nose twitched, as if she could smell the fear on him.

"No more than most of my clients," he said, hands buried in the pockets of his coveralls. He hesitated. "I might need a small favor."

She ignored him, gaze fixed on the mural. "Your knife work is extraordinary," she said. "I love how you've blended these more painterly fragments." She gestured toward Suki's half-lidded eyes—inviting, aloof.

He forced a shrug. "Picked that up during my time in the East." Then, quieter: "Can I borrow your credit card?"

Gabriella scoffed as she stepped closer to the mural. "The cigarette is absurd."

"Please."

Gabriella chuffed, turning to him at last. She pulled a card from her bag and handed it over.

Timothy keyed in the numbers, shooting nervous glances as she returned to studying the painting—a vivid likeness he'd spent months perfecting inside his Green Point studio. Gabriella was right: the cigarette dangling from Suki's mouth was ridiculous.

The knot in his stomach unclenched as the transfer finally went through.

Gabriella tilted her head. "I forgot to mention—a journalist was meant to interview you at four."

He checked his watch. "It's four-thirty."

"Exactly," she said with a smirk. "Which is why I said 'was'." She turned sharply, pivoting like a ballerina. "I'm calling her. I'll tell her it's off."

Timothy stepped into the full glare of the spotlights. "Wait. What's her name?"

Gabriella flicked her tongue over her bottom lip. "Sara Miles."

His cheek twitched. "Sara Miles?" he asked, a slight tremor in his voice.

"That's what I said."

Late to an appointment? Unease curled in his gut.

Gabriella beckoned, scrolling on her phone. "Perhaps I was hasty. She writes such nice things about you. Listen to this." She paused. "'Most brilliant painter to emerge from the East End in decades. His work has a volcanic energy that emanates from the canvas like it's about to explode'." Gabriella snorted. "And yet, I hear she's quite the bitch." Her eyes narrowed. "You slept with her, didn't you?"

Timothy paled. "Why would you say that?"

Gabriella's mouth twisted. "How many women do you think call each day begging for private sittings with the city's most handsome artist?"

He shrugged, eyes darting.

"Relax. As long as they're willing to pay, I don't care. But Sara Miles? She ruins careers." Suspicion laced her tone. "What does she want with you?"

"I don't know," he lied.

Gabriella tutted. "She's going to be trouble. Mark my words." She stepped closer. "By the way—will Sir James be attending tonight?"

He rolled his eyes. "Who knows? Said he wasn't, but he never misses a photo op."

She grunted. "I hope he brings that good-looking PA." Then, abruptly, she pointed to the workmen. "No. Not there. Over there."

Timothy barely heard her. "Sara's never late," he murmured.

"There's a first time for everything," Gabriella said. "I told her you're busy. If she comes now, I'll turn her away."

Timothy frowned. "Weren't you going to call her office?"

Gabriella waved him off and dialed. Her voice dropped into clipped, cool tones. When she finished, her face was oddly tense.

"Strange," she said. "She didn't show for work today. No one knows where she is. Not answering her phone either."

Before he could reply, the maudlin opening of *The Godfather* cut through the air. Timothy flinched, fumbling his phone from his pocket. As he answered, he cast Gabriella a tight smile.

"I have to take this," he said, retreating.

She waved him off. "Go. I'll handle the rest." She turned and resumed barking orders, her voice echoing through the cavernous space.

With dread pooling in his stomach, he slipped into the shadows.

* * *

Sir James stalked the length of his office, steps heavy and deliberate. He paused by the landline, his fist clenched as his voice erupted.

"At first, I thought it had to be someone else—someone new with the same exceptional ability. Because not even *you* could be that stupid."

Timothy's voice filtered through the speaker, hesitant and strained. "You have nothing to worry about. I've been careful. After tonight, I'm giving it all up."

Sir James halted mid-stride, his expression darkening. A leopard didn't change its spots. The boy was fibbing again. He sank into the captain's chair, pinching the bridge of his nose to stave off the headache building behind his eyes.

"Don't lie to me, boy. Do you even comprehend what will happen if you're caught? And I'm not talking about the police. These men will *kill* you—for swindling them—but only after they've spent hours *torturing* you."

"I'm not going to get caught," Timothy said, voice wavering but resolute.

"That's right," Sir James snapped. "Because as of this moment, you're done. You're going to deactivate those black-market auction sites."

A crackling silence echoed through the line. Then: "It might be a bit late for that."

Sir James stiffened. "Let me guess—tonight's preview is a front?"

"It's a front," Timothy admitted, almost sheepishly.

"Who's the buyer?"

"Buyers," Timothy corrected. "Gabriella's meeting both at the gallery tonight."

Sir James dragged a hand down his face. "Sweet Jesus. How many fakes have you made besides the box?"

"Wait—you know about the box?"

Sir James froze, jaw clenched. A long pause. Then a slow exhale, nearly silent.

"So it's true."

Before Timothy could lie again, Sir James slammed the handset into its cradle. Papers fluttered across the desk. He leaned back, breath ragged, fury burning behind his eyes.

He had one option.

Clean up the mess himself.

His gaze swept the room. The vein at his temple pulsed. He reached for the handset again—fingers stiff with resolve. Then his eyes caught on Dr. Chin's invoice, half-buried in the mess.

A slow smile curled his lips.

His PA was good. But he didn't need a scalpel.

He needed a sword.

Straightening his tie, he picked up the phone and dialed.

Dr. Chin answered on the second ring, her sultry voice coiling through him—hot and exhilarating.

"Hello, my dear," he began, suddenly all charm. "Me again. Tell me—how do you feel about attending an art preview tonight?"

* * *

Dr. Janine Chin ended the call and exhaled through her nose, rolling her head side to side to ease the tension coiled at the base of her neck. She strolled to the wide windows of her seventh-floor serviced apartment at the Dorset and studied her naked reflection in the glass.

Working for Sir James—especially against her employer's interests—was proving more complicated than expected.

But the pay made it worthwhile.

The view alone was priceless.

The city sprawled below, glittering and serene—a far cry from the grimy dives she usually called home when on assignment for Security and Risk.

A ping cut through her thoughts. She turned, retrieved her phone from the bedside table, her movements unhurried. The MP's message blinked onto the screen—blueprints, access codes, instructions for infiltrating the gallery.

Smirking, she sauntered into the walk-in closet. Two floors above, John Chrysler Anderson, her handler—likely still believed she was holed up in the dingy hotel he'd booked for her.

The thought almost made her laugh. Little did he know his most loyal asset had been flipped by Sir James Gibson.

And he never would. Once this mission was over, she was in the wind. No trails. No ties.

Janine sighed, running her fingers over the gowns Sir James had sent over—high fashion, all of it. Elegant. Expensive. Impractical.

She frowned. Crawl spaces and rooftop access didn't exactly pair with *couture*.

Sir James was nothing if not dramatic. Loud. Flamboyant to a fault.

He loved the spotlight.

She fingered the blood-red diamond hanging at her throat. And he loved her, too—in his own selfish, theatrical way.

It had been his idea to use Anderson's resources. A simple snatch-and-grab: first, Rebrisi's box, plucked from the police evidence lockup

—too bad it turned out to be a fake. Then the manuscript, which she was certain Meyer-Edwards still possessed.

And now—the *Venus*.

Her gaze shifted back to the designer dresses. Gorgeous. Useless.

She reached instead for a pair of dark pants, a form-fitting sweater, boots, a tac vest, and a ski mask.

Now *this* was proper attire for the party Sir James had planned.

Chapter Sixteen

The rumble of engines drew Annouie's attention from the manuscript. She set it aside, turning just as a convoy of law enforcement vehicles rounded the corner at the far end of the street.

Pushing the Oria2 SmartSpecs higher on her nose, she tracked the movement, every sense on alert.

A standard cruiser led the procession, followed by two police vans and an unmarked sedan bringing up the rear. The lead car took a sharp left onto Thomas Street, the rest trailing in formation. As they neared Number 112, the convoy slowed, veering toward the curb.

The sedan and the first van split off. The sedan coasted another thirty feet before executing a crisp three-point turn, then rolled back down the hill to idle beneath a leafy elm. Engine running. The second van parked farther up.

Shimmering heat waves distorted the late afternoon light as car doors thudded open in unison.

Two plainclothes officers stepped out of the sedan.

Annouie's breath hitched.

She slid lower in her seat, ducking below the windshield. Her pulse ticked faster.

Detective Saunders buttoned his jacket, the brief flash of a hip holster catching the sun. He rounded the car to meet Katrine Ratcliffe, whose ponytail swished like a metronome as they moved toward the front gate. She walked with deliberate swagger—a bloodhound closing in.

From her vantage, Annouie watched them mount the path, several uniformed officers falling in behind.

She yanked out her phone, snapped a picture of the vehicles, and sent it to Anderson with a brief caption.

"Oria, get me everything from the front room—now. If they take Meyer-Edwards—"

A tightness curled in her gut.

"—I'm out the two hundred grand."

* * *

Antony climbed the library ladder, fingers sweeping the top shelf until they brushed something familiar. He grunted softly and tugged free a manila A4 envelope wedged between two leather-bound volumes.

Undoing the strings with care, he slid out a large photograph. The edges were frayed, the colors bleached by time—but the memory it captured remained vivid.

Aguirre stood at the center of the shot, slight and wiry, his weathered face etched by years under a South American sun. His expression, typically stern, hovered just shy of a smile—the rare, transformative kind that erased decades in an instant. That smile had once lit a fire in Antony, made him believe he could reach the impossible.

Antony exhaled, gaze lingering on his mentor's face. He almost missed the old goat—the lectures, gruff praise, even the blistering critiques. Then his focus shifted to a younger version of himself, standing just behind Aguirre—shoulders square, pride radiating off him. Before the world got in. Before the fall. Before Craiova.

A shadow crossed Antony's face, hardening his features.

Seven years. That's how long it'd been since Aguirre had abandoned him to rot in a Romanian prison. The wound had scabbed, but never healed. Not really. Not beneath the layers of cynicism and sarcasm he wore like armor.

A sudden knock at the front door jolted him. The sound cracked through the room, sharp and unexpected.

Adrenaline surged. He shoved the photo back into the envelope, returned it to its hiding place, and descended the ladder.

* * *

"I'll do the talking this time," Saunders said, lifting his hand from the door.

"What a dump," Katrine muttered, her gaze skimming the sagging wicker rocker and boarded-up sidelight.

Saunders leaned in, squinting through the frosted pane. He stepped back as the door swung open.

Meyer-Edwards stood framed by the doorway, a phone pressed to his ear.

"Officers," he said, lowering the phone slightly. "I was on my way out."

Saunders held up a sheaf of documents. "We have a search and seizure warrant," he said, his voice clipped.

Meyer-Edwards dropped the phone to his side, eyes narrowing. "For what?"

Saunders unfurled the warrant with bureaucratic flair. "All items pertaining to the deceased, all items belonging to the deceased—"

"In English," Meyer-Edwards snapped.

Saunders rolled the document closed. "We're here for all electronic items, including that phone." He nodded toward the phone in Meyer-Edwards's hand.

Before he could react, Saunders plucked it away and slid it into an evidence bag with a practiced flick.

"You've got to be kidding," Meyer-Edwards sputtered.

"Not in the slightest," Saunders said, striding inside.

Meyer-Edwards wheeled after him. "I need that phone. I have a meeting."

Saunders didn't look back.

Katrine crossed the threshold, offering him a smile with no warmth. "We're not detaining you. Once we're done, you'll get an itemized list."

"I'm not leaving you alone here to go through my things."

She clapped him lightly on the upper arm. "Then make yourself comfortable," she said sweetly. "We won't be long."

* * *

For the next hour, the police moved methodically through the Thomas Street house, their presence drawing a growing crowd. Neighbors gathered at windows and leaned over fences, phones poised to capture every humiliating moment.

By the time the officers began filing out—arms laden with boxes—the afternoon heat had peaked, thickening the air with a suffocating weight.

Antony leaned against the brick wall by the door, his gaze distant. Across the road, more phones angled his way, documenting his crumpled appearance. He gave a limp wave, the last of his self-control slipping away.

This circus would be on the evening news. No doubt Judith would be calling—except he no longer had a phone to take the call.

With a final slam, the van doors shut, sealing away his belongings.

Behind him, the staircase groaned. He turned, scowl deepening. Detective Ratcliffe descended without apology, a sheet of paper in one hand and a bright, almost gleeful smile on her face.

"This is everything we're taking," she said.

He scanned the list, lips curling. "At least you left the kitchen sink. When do I get this back?"

She shrugged. "Could be three months. Sometimes longer."

"Seriously?" His voice sharpened.

Ratcliffe slipped on her sunglasses, already turning toward Saunders. He stood in quiet conference with the uniformed officers by the van.

Antony folded his arms and watched her go.

A moment later, both detectives climbed into the black sedan. The engine growled. The car pulled away.

Antony was left standing alone in the heat.

Gradually, the neighbors receded indoors, the last police vehicle rumbling away down the street. A hush returned—broken only by birdsong, delicate and mocking.

He lingered in the doorway, scratching at the stubble along his jaw. The motion slowed as cold realization took hold.

He pushed off the wall and rushed inside.

The house had been a mess before. Now it was a catastrophe. Papers, books, and personal items lay strewn across the floor, as if a hurricane had swept through.

Antony stepped over the debris, scanning for the manuscript, plotting a course to the sofa.

Kneeling, he searched beneath it. Dust. Crumbs. Nothing.

He swept the surrounding floor—still nothing.

Yanking the inventory list from his back pocket, he skimmed the entries. No mention of a book.

He sank back on his heels, exhaling hard.

They probably hadn't taken it—but the doubt still gnawed.

The grandfather clock ticked behind him, its pendulum a cold metronome. Trouble pressed in from every direction. He'd betrayed Deluca. Lost Rebrisi's manuscript. And now—just hours into his first day—he'd violated almost every undertaking he'd made to the dean.

Possession of illegal drugs might be forgivable—eccentricity came with the territory. But being linked to a murder?

That was a scandal he couldn't outrun.

He grimaced, dragging both hands through his hair. He could handle Deluca's fury—it wasn't like the mobster could have him killed.

And the manuscript? It would resurface. It had to. Beneath the sofa. In an evidence bag. Or—God help him—on some black-market auction site.

But an inquiry?

There was no outrunning that. A full-panel hearing at the conservatory loomed, and his reputation—already battered—was about to be eviscerated.

If Messier was on the panel, he might as well resign now.

Antony's shoulders sagged. He dropped his head into his hands.

The headlines were already forming in his mind.

By nightfall, his career would be in tatters.

And this time, there would be no coming back.

Chapter Seventeen

Dahlia House loomed above its neighbors on Harborside Road, an imposing mansion that overlooked the harbor.

Calling it a "house" was an understatement of epic proportions; it was a monument to opulence. Imported Italian tiles gleamed underfoot, while hand-carved wooden columns flanked the entrance to the reception room—a testament to early-twentieth-century Art Deco craftsmanship.

Annouie pulled into the sloping driveway just before six, the Carrera's tires crunching over the gravel. Across the harbor, yachts strained against their moorings, bobbing in the evening swell. For a moment, she was back in Kiel—Isidore at the helm of his latest acquisition, the wind whipping his hair, while John Chrysler Anderson sketched exotic locales in the air from a deck chair.

She blinked the memory away and stepped from the car. A sharp wind gusted off the water, biting through her jacket. She folded her arms and hurried to the front steps.

As she reached for the keypad, the door clicked open. Andre stood silhouetted in the foyer, his expression taut with relief and frustration.

"You're an hour late," he said, shoulders dropping with a sharp exhale. "Next time, send a text. You have no idea what it does to me when you don't show."

Without warning, he pulled her into a hug, the door slamming shut behind them. His grip was fierce, the heat from his body stifling.

"All right, all right," Annouie said, pushing away. "This isn't Bogotá, Andre. Sometimes late is just late."

He studied her, his gaze hard to meet. "Maybe. But I'll never unsee you lying in that alley. Humor me. Let me know."

"Sure. But if all goes to plan, this is my last job."

He grimaced. "Retiring won't be easy."

She shrugged. "Anderson won't have a choice."

"You're underestimating him."

"I'm not. That's why we have Plan B."

He sighed sharply and ushered her up the stairs. "Which is why we need to move. Paul's expecting us at six."

They climbed three flights. At the top-level landing, Andre overtook her and strode to the reinforced ballistic door at the corridor's end.

Crouching at the keypad, he shielded the numbers.

"Five, Six, Four, Three," Annouie muttered in a loud stage whisper.

Andre scowled as he tapped in the final digit. "One of these days."

"What? You'll change it?"

A metallic clunk echoed. The maglock disengaged with a low grind of steel on steel. As the heavy door opened, Andre's irritation melted into pride.

The room was a black-hat masterpiece.

Ceiling-high open-frame racks of humming servers and routers lined the walls. Workbenches cluttered with half-empty cardboard boxes, Ziploc bags of wires and microchips, and tangled cable ties hinted at both abandoned and ongoing projects. Screwdrivers, pliers, and magnifying lenses gleamed beneath overhead lights. The air was sharp with the scent of soldering metal and scorched plastic.

Andre had turned the entire fourth floor into his personal tactical ops center.

He sidestepped Annouie and dropped into a plush executive chair at the head of a long, metal-framed conference table. A semicircle of curved monitors flickered before him, streaming code, surveillance feeds, and encrypted data.

The mechanical keyboard clacked as his fingers flew.

Annouie sauntered over and perched on a stool. She pulled the manuscript from her bag and slid it across the table.

Andre kept typing as the upload began, but when his gaze landed on the book, his fingers froze.

"Where did you get this?" he asked, grabbing it, eyes gleaming.

Annouie grinned. "Would you believe Meyer-Edwards gave it to me?"

He gaped. "You're kidding? This has to be what Anderson's after."

"That would be my guess."

"Tell me you haven't told him about it?"

She scoffed. "Of course not."

He turned back to the right-hand monitor and resumed typing, lines of Python code cascading down the screen.

The stool squealed as Annouie rolled to the edge of the table. "What about the *Venus*? Has Oria found a way in?"

"Still working on it."

"Security?"

"Heat and motion sensors," Andre said, without looking up. "The painting's probably tagged, too. But since you won't be touching anything, not a problem. Your job is to get eyes on it. Oria handles the rest." He held out his hand. "Specs."

Annouie handed over the Prada glasses. He plugged them into his system, opened a new window, and began typing. Data scrolled rapidly across the screen.

"You'll be using the Oria2 update at the preview. Glasses for general use—contacts for those more intimate moments. And one more thing—" He spun in his seat. "Paul scored us some press badges. You're a journalist with *The Tribune*. So we're gonna lose the dumpster chic." He flicked her sleeve. "Upload will take ten minutes. Plenty of time to make you over."

Annouie groaned as he yanked her from the stool.

Makeovers were the worst.

He dragged her down to the first floor and shoved her into the master bedroom. Golden light spilled through French doors, warm and slanted. A long balcony overlooked the marina. Yawls, sloops, and ketches rose and fell on the swell.

Leaning against the doorframe, Annouie took it in. For a moment, she imagined her life without Anderson—no danger, no debt.

No Isidore in prison.

She sighed and shook herself free of the fantasy just as Andre reappeared with what looked like a child's dress.

He tossed it to her. "Squeeze into that."

She held it at arm's length. It was absurdly small.

"Hey, don't look at me like that. It's a dual-purpose marvel. Looks scandalous, but . . ."

She rolled her eyes, kicked off her pants, and struggled out of her blouse. In her underwear, she gave the dress one last skeptical glance—then yanked it on.

The stretchy fabric clung like a second skin, moving seamlessly as she stretched. She turned toward the mirror.

Her breath caught. The dress didn't just flatter—it transformed.

"Gibson's a dead man."

Andre chuckled. "Hold still."

He swept up her hair with practiced ease and secured it in place with two delicate sticks shaped like flower sprays.

Annouie tilted her head. "Beautiful. Family heirloom?"

"No," he said, with a wistful tone. "Titanium. If you're in a tight spot, they double as weapons." He gestured at a pair of sky-high heels at the foot of the bed. "Put those on."

She eyed them. "Dual purpose, too?"

"No. But I'm sure you'll find a way to weaponize them."

She slipped them on and stalked across the room, testing their limits. A breeze coiled around her as she moved.

They looked incredible. But there was no way she'd be scaling walls in them.

Andre gave an appreciative whistle. "Now, if I weren't gay . . ." He trailed off with a grin, then caught sight of his own reflection.

Frowning, he whipped off his T-shirt, pitched it into the hamper, and grabbed a neon paisley button-down. He shrugged it on and buttoned it halfway, flipping his pink hair.

"Too conservative?"

Annouie smirked. "Yeah. But you'll make it work."

* * *

Antony rummaged through the pantry at the back of the kitchen, the dim light from a naked bulb swinging overhead casting frantic shadows across the shelves. They danced with his rising frustration, each flicker mocking his effort.

After several minutes—and a string of curses—he let out a bark of triumph and emerged clutching a dusty fixed line phone unit.

Judith's priority had always been clear: protect the conservatory's reputation at all costs. Yes, Antony's global connections and prodigious talent made him essential to her vision of elevating their international prestige. But she'd also warned him—explicitly—about courting negative press. Becoming the prime suspect in a murder investigation was very much *not* the brand.

He sighed and glanced at the morning paper still lying open on the kitchen table. Suki Rey's stippled portrait stared back at him, a limp cigarette dangling from her mouth.

It was the cigarette that did it.

There was only one thing the press loved more than a corpse.

Scandal.

Hunkering beside the ancient telecom outlet, he jammed the RJ-11 connector into the socket and offered up a silent prayer as he powered the unit on. The odds of the service still being active were near zero.

But the console blinked to life. A backlog of condolence messages flickered across the screen.

"Some other time," he muttered, lifting the handset. A dial tone purred in his ear. Promising.

Without hesitation, he punched in the first number that came to mind.

Jack Vallone answered on the fifth ring. "Sorry. It appears you've dialed the wrong number—"

"It's Antony." His voice echoed across the cold tiles. "I'm coming to the preview."

A pause. Then: "I knew you'd change your mind."

"I'm not changing my mind," Antony said, eyes scanning the chaos the police had left in their wake. "I'm making a scene. So whatever you've got planned—make it *count*."

Before Jack could respond, he hung up.

Then strode into the hallway, already calculating how best to charm and scandalize the city's elite.

* * *

Ten minutes later, dressed in a *Savile Row* suit and a crimson silk tie, Antony descended the stairs at speed. His polished shoes struck the floorboards with staccato precision as he swept through the foyer and reached for the brass doorknob.

He had thirty minutes to hit the red carpet and make that scene.

Grinning, he straightened his jacket and raked a hand through his hair. Drawing attention was his forte.

Then the landline trilled.

He froze mid-step, a curse catching in his throat. Slowly, he backtracked to the kitchen. The phone sat on the tiny table, blinking with urgency. He snatched up the receiver.

"Hello?"

A woman with a thick accent answered. "Am I speaking with Mr. Meyer-Edwards?"

His grip slackened. Telemarketer? "I don't have time—"

"I'm from the Accademia. I am . . . I was Maestro Aguirre's personal assistant."

He straightened. "Was?"

"You are Mr. Meyer-Edwards?"

"Yes. What's happened to Alberto?"

A breath of relief pulsed through the line. "Oh, thank God. I wasn't sure this number still worked. It's the only one we had on file."

His fingers tightened around the handset. "Is he alright?"

A muffled sob crackled through the line. "Oh, sir—" The sobs came harder now. "Maestro Aguirre was shot last month."

Antony's blood turned cold. "And I'm only hearing about this now? Where is he?"

A beat—taut with doom. "The Maestro passed away this morning."

He sank into the wooden chair. "He's dead?"

"Passed away," she repeated gently. "Which is why I'm calling. In his will, he left you one item. A manuscript. But it wasn't among his belongings. We were hoping . . . Has anything arrived from—"

Antony stood in a single fluid motion, every nerve ending prickling.

"You're not with the Accademia," he said softly.

There was a click.

The line went dead.

He stared at the receiver for a moment before lowering it, his pulse drumming in his ears.

He'd almost been duped. Had almost tipped his hand.

He was getting soft.

If Alberto Aguirre had been on death's door, he should have known. He *would* have known.

He crossed the room to the door, steps slow and deliberate.

Rebrisi was not his concern.

He paused, inhaled deeply. The air tasted sharp. He shook his head. No time for Aguirre's manipulations.

Tonight, he was giving the performance of his life. No script. No safety net. Just a desperate hope that fate owed him.

His hand closed around the doorknob. Fate. He sent up a quick prayer—just in case someone was listening.

Then, spine straight, breath steady, he stepped into the night.

Chapter Eighteen

The Fonteyn Gallery heaved its blocky five stories into the wet night, rain pelting its narrow rear windows with relentless fury. A heritage-listed site, its front façade on the main street dripped with neoclassical pretentiousness—Doric capitals, colonnaded portico, the whole shebang. But around back, it was just another industrial block in a row of aging warehouses.

Andre's Carrera crawled along the lower road behind the building. At the edge, a brick wall hemmed the asphalt from a steep drop to the pebbled beach below. Beyond that, the river glimmered under the half-hearted flicker of a streetlamp.

He rolled the car over a curb-cut beside a neighboring warehouse and killed the engine. For a moment, the silence held—until the world filtered back in: the hammering of rain on the hardtop, the low growl of the river below.

He glanced at Annouie. "Last chance to back out."

Her brow arched.

A normal-looking door opened beside a massive roll-up at the gallery's rear.

Annouie slid from the passenger seat, her gaze flicking to the entrance as a blond man emerged.

"He looks pissed."

Andre exhaled. "Yep. That's Paul."

They crossed the slick cement, climbing the short flight of stairs to the landing, where rain sheeted off the awning.

"I was expecting you ten minutes ago," Paul snapped, voice low but sharp. "I had to make all sorts of excuses."

"Can we do this inside?" Andre replied coolly.

Paul exhaled, irritated, and stepped aside. They slipped past him into the loading dock, water pooling at their feet.

"You've no idea how hard it was to get away—and then you're late. I was supposed to be back on the floor five minutes ago." He thrust a badge at Andre and stalked off.

Andre sighed and handed the lanyard to Annouie.

She eyed it and frowned. "Nobody's going to believe I'm Tom Masters."

Andre shrugged. "If anyone asks, wing it. No one checks these things anyway. Comms ready?"

She slipped in her earpiece. "Ready."

"I'll find a closet to set up in. You do your usual—strut, look stunning, blow off anyone who hits on you. Except Gibson. Reel him in."

"You sure he will?"

"I'd stake my life on it," Andre said, casting a glance at her dress.

* * *

Nicholas angled the Bentley into a tight spot three hundred feet up the street, his eyes fixed on the bumper of the car behind.

Sir James cleared his throat.

Nicholas ignored him.

The sound came again.

Leather creaked as Nicholas finally turned. He knew all of Sir James's throat-clearings.

The man was about to bail.

Perfect. Take him home. Double back. Sneak into the Rose Chambers Room. Confirm authenticity.

The rasping sound came a third time.

"I'll write a press release," Nicholas said, reaching for the ignition, a slow smile curling his lips. "Let them know something came up—"

A firm hand settled on his shoulder.

"No." Sir James sighed. "This can't be put off. I need to confront Timothy about that fake *Venus* in the Rose Chambers Room."

Nicholas stilled, mind scrambling. *Fake?*

Sir James leaned forward, leather groaning beneath him. "You're the art recovery expert. Surely you've heard the rumors."

He had. But Sir James didn't need to know that. Nicholas turned slightly, keeping his expression neutral. "Rumors?"

Sir James rolled his eyes. "Don't insult me. The goddamn *Venus* is back in play. Let me put you out of your misery—Timothy painted the one in the Rose Chambers Room."

Nicholas exhaled quietly. Another dead end.

Sir James checked his watch. "Not that it'll be there much longer," he added with a smirk. "I've got someone on the inside taking care of it as we speak."

Nicholas shoved the door open and stepped onto the slick pavement, frustration cutting deep.

The door slammed shut behind him. He rounded the Bentley just as a sharp gust yanked the passenger side door open.

Sir James stepped onto the curb with a grunt. "Now, here's the plan—you keep Gabriella Fonteyn distracted."

Nicholas stopped. "Why me?"

"Because I'm not her type, and someone needs to keep her away from the Rose Chambers Room until my man has finished the job."

Nicholas sighed. Gabriella Fonteyn was insufferable.

Sir James waved at a couple approaching the porte-cochère, then leaned in. "I know what you're thinking—she's a menace. Keep her busy for the next half hour, and I'll give you tomorrow morning off."

Nicholas groaned but fell in behind Sir James as he swept through the grand foyer, politician's smile already in place, greeting press and VIPs alike with effortless charm.

* * *

Antony Meyer-Edwards had the cab pull behind a line of town cars beneath the covered entrance. He stepped out, shoving a hundred through the cabbie's window without waiting for change, and inhaled the sharp scent of rain.

He turned toward the gallery.

Spotlights bathed the colonnaded portico in harsh light. A banner hung over the doorway. Celebrities, scholars, and art-world figures snaked up the sandstone steps toward the hubbub inside.

On either side, paparazzi jostled at the ropes, cameras snapping. A fresh surge came as Suki Rey stepped from a town car. The pop princess barely paused before sweeping up the stairs, photographers surging after her like a breaking wave.

Antony exhaled. Now or never.

He took the steps two at a time, weaving through the crowd. Wind gusted. The line bottlenecked at the glass doors—and Suki halted at the top for another photo op, her back arching as cameras zeroed in on her.

Someone pushed back. She wobbled.

Antony lunged and caught her before she could fall. A thousand flashes went off, freezing the moment in a burst of white light.

Suki blinked up at him, eyes wide with surprise. Antony gave her a measured smile, aware that the cameras were devouring every angle.

"What's your name?" she asked, breathless and perfectly pitched for the crowd.

"Antony Meyer-Edwards," he said, voice smooth, carrying cleanly above the wind and rain.

She placed a manicured hand on his arm. "Well, Antony Meyer-Edwards—I don't have an escort this evening. Would you do the honors?"

The press locked onto him. His face—and name—would be everywhere by morning, and he'd be a tabloid darling for all the right reasons.

Half-baked plans were often the best—more room for improvisation. And for fate to lend a hand. Nothing short of murder charges would make Judith dismiss him now.

Though at the rate his week was going, that wasn't off the table.

He grinned, extending his arm. "Delighted."

They swept inside together.

As Antony vanished with Suki into the throng, Jack Vallone emerged from the shadows at the foot of the steps, watching the press trail after them. He hesitated—then turned and slipped along the front of the building, disappearing down a side alley.

* * *

Timothy Gibson positioned himself in the main exhibition hall, greeting guests and handing out catalogs while tallying the number of players in attendance.

Suki arrived half an hour late—on the arm of the infamous Antony Meyer-Edwards. A storm of flashbulbs lit up the sky behind them. As she sauntered past, her eyes narrowed in disdain—still stinging, no doubt, over the way he'd dumped her. Her attention shifted at once to the larger-than-life nudes adorning the walls, her disinterest palpable.

She needn't have bothered. He couldn't have cared less.

His gaze swept the room. They were all here.

Even his father.

Sir James stood before the mural, scowling, his PA looking stonier than usual. That pompous American entrepreneur, John Chrysler Anderson, had shown up, too.

Timothy suppressed a grin. They'd come because of the rumor.

The whispers seeded on the dark web had done their job—word had spread that the Rebrisi *Venus* had resurfaced and was on display in the Rose Chambers Room. He'd dropped that tidbit into a dozen chatrooms. Nothing worked quite like gossip. Now all he had to do was wait for the Gray Cat to take the bait.

The legendary spook was more myth than man. No one knew what the Gray Cat looked like—but that was about to change.

He watched the players, rating each one out of ten.

Antony Meyer-Edwards? Zero. Too flamboyant. Too visible. If that man was the Gray Cat, then Timothy was the King of Sweden.

John Chrysler Anderson? A two, at best. Tall, arrogant, notorious in the antiquities world for questionable methods. A slim possibility.

Gabriella glided toward Anderson, tablet in one hand, taloned fingers grazing his sleeve. She gushed over him, coaxing him into another bid. A minute later, she slipped away and closed in on Timothy like a heat-seeking missile.

"Loves it," she murmured. "Just made another bid." She slid the tablet toward him.

Timothy kept his expression neutral as he handed her his drink. Inside, he was reveling. The figures were better than expected. He scrolled with a swipe of his finger—Gabriella was a genius.

She snatched the tablet away as Anderson abruptly changed direction and headed for them.

"Ms. Fonteyn. A word?"

Gabriella turned to Timothy, brows waggling. "Would you excuse us?" She passed his glass to a waiter and glided off.

A blur of cotton-candy pink.

Timothy stiffened. Turned.

His pulse ticked up.

The waiter.

He scanned the room. Gabriella was already huddled with Anderson. His father—gone. Hope—melting into the shadows.

Timothy slipped into the long hallway, trailing the pink-haired waiter toward the kitchens.

The clamor of voices and clinking of crockery grew louder as he pushed through the doors. The back-of-house was a maelstrom of movement, fragrance, and sound. A hotplate flared, flames extinguished beneath a heavy metal lid. Slipping through the chaos, Timothy hovered near the hors d'oeuvres.

The pink-haired Eurasian man had made his way to the back of the room. A woman accosted him—began jabbing him in the chest.

Timothy gave a satisfied grunt.

Andre Landvik.

IT royalty turned rogue. A black hat hacker with ties to the city's underworld. Presumably here for the *Venus,* too.

Timothy frowned. For a fleeting second, he considered the possibility—was Landvik the Gray Cat?

He nearly laughed aloud. Preposterous. Landvik was a complication, sure. And certainly skilled. But he wasn't the Cat.

His gaze shifted to the woman.

She was shouting now—sharp, furious. Too young to be the Gray Cat. And far too memorable.

His breath caught

More than memorable.

One of the most arresting women he'd ever seen.

To call her beautiful was like calling the wind breezy. He stared, jaw slack—like being sucker punched.

She pirouetted on a stiletto and stormed across the room. Timothy shrank back into the cold room as she swept past.

Cream skin. Honey-gold hair shimmering like liquid light. A rush of inspiration—and something darker—swept over him.

She was perfect.

He could already see it: the pigments, the knife, the brush. Capturing her essence.

But as she vanished, a different desire took root.

Not to paint her.

To possess her.

Women came to him. He didn't chase. But this one—too delicious to resist.

He ran a hand through his hair, caught between reverie and the urge to hunt.

Then—

He slipped from the room in pursuit.

Chapter Nineteen

Katrine Ratcliffe gazed down at her remaining tasks: reports, financial sheets, logbook entries. All waiting to be finalized, itemized, amended.

But tonight—they could wait.

She blinked at the screen, her mind racing through next steps. Widening the net, as Shiruku suggested, had changed everything. She had a working theory now—a modus operandi—and it revolved around Timothy Gibson and a lost masterpiece called *The Three Elements*.

A heavy footfall echoed from the doorway of Greg Dunbier's office. She turned, bracing. The Detective Chief Inspector beckoned.

She yanked her jacket from the back of the chair and shrugged into it, glancing at her watch. Two minutes past seven. With a sigh, she trudged the twenty feet of vinyl separating her desk from Dunbier's doorway.

"I was leaving," she muttered.

His gaze sharpened beneath wiry brows. "Let's talk." He turned and stalked into his office.

Katrine followed. She sank into the nearest chair, steeling herself for the reaming she knew was coming.

Dunbier grinned. Under the fluorescent lighting, the flash of white looked almost sinister.

"DNA results just came in. We got a match—Peter Darby."

Her breath caught. She steadied herself. "Has it been verified?"

"Confirmed through CODIS. Double-checked by the lab."

She exhaled hard. "Do we have probable cause for an arrest?"

He shook his head. "Not yet. The match won't hold on its own—we need something concrete. Physical evidence. Eyewitness. Something to tie him directly to the crime."

He leaned in, voice low and firm. "I first crossed paths with Darby twenty years ago. Kid was sullen. Wouldn't meet your eye. But sharp—too sharp."

The chair groaned as he shifted. "His foster mother was a known offender. Violent. Police were called out—neighbors heard her screaming threats. Turns out, she'd beaten the boy badly. He escaped next door. When officers got there, she was unconscious—strung out on something. While she was out, the kid hacked off her hair. Almost scalped her."

Dunbier's face darkened. "Weeks later, neighbors reported a stench. The boy hadn't been to school. Cops did a welfare check—found her dead in bed. Strangled. Blood everywhere—at least a month old. Sound familiar?"

Katrine stiffened, a knot winding tight in her gut. "What happened to Darby?"

"Removed by Child Services. Rehomed. But three weeks later, he vanished. Paperwork says he went to his father—but the address was bogus."

Katrine inched forward. "Darby's our killer?"

Dunbier gave a grim nod. "Head to Lomanville. Talk to Dr. Addison—the attending at the time. Pull Darby's files. Biological parents. Foster placements. We need to find him. Fast."

* * *

As Gabriella Fonteyn emerged on the far side of the room, Nicholas Hope ducked into the long corridor leading to the kitchens, moving with quiet urgency.

The scent of sizzling meat and slow-simmering sauces enveloped him as he burst through the doors. The air was thick with heat and movement. Flames hissed, metal clashed, knives flashed under bright lights—a symphony of precision and pressure. It was more than food prep. It was art. Kinetic. Raw. More alive than anything hanging in the gallery beyond.

A flicker of motion caught his eye.

Gibson Junior slithered into the cold room, gaze locked on a couple mid-argument.

Nicholas turned. His mouth twitched.

Andre Landvik.

Tall. Sharp-eyed. Eurasian. Posture squared in challenge, eyes gleaming with cool intelligence. A reformed black hat, now consulting to the police.

If the whispers on the dark web held even a sliver of truth, Landvik had built something—an AI capable of slicing through military-grade encryption, mapping vulnerabilities, and harvesting intelligence at an unprecedented scale.

"Nic?"

Sir James's voice cracked down the corridor—sharp, imperious.

Nicholas exhaled slowly, masking his irritation beneath a blank veneer. He turned, shoulders drawn in ever so slightly, and strode back toward the main room, where Sir James prowled like a caged beast.

For now, he would play the dutiful PA.

But the day would come when Sir James learned who was truly in control.

* * *

Annouie adjusted her press badge as she wove between a sea of tailored suits and cocktail dresses. The exhibition hall gleamed—polished wood floors, black leather lounges, cool concrete walls. Every plaque and companion piece had been meticulously arranged to exude value, reinforced by the wealthy clientele posturing before the seven main works on display.

She stationed herself before one of Gibson's lesser-known works, plucking a champagne flute from a passing tray. She sipped, cataloging every movement in the room, waiting for Gibson to track her down.

Across the hall, Suki Rey posed in front of her oversized likeness while her security team hovered at a discreet but vigilant distance. Their attention, however, was locked on the man at the pop princess's side.

Suki tilted her face toward him, letting the press feast on the moment. Camera flashes caught her slow, deliberate blink—a well-practiced move. The man responded on cue, slinging an arm around her waist and flashing a brilliant smile.

Annouie exhaled sharply. Less than three hours ago, he'd thrown her out of Thomas Street with an armful of books. Now, here Meyer-Edwards was, playing the celebrity whore.

Suki laughed—painted lips stretching over pointed white teeth. Meyer-Edwards's gaze swept the room, then caught on Annouie.

A flicker of surprise—no more than a glitch.

She raised her glass in acknowledgment, savoring his discomfort, and drained it in one go.

To his credit, he recovered quickly, resuming his polished performance as he pulled Suki closer.

Annouie stepped back—and collided with something solid.

John Chrysler Anderson.

He leaned in, voice smooth, dark, and far too close. "Come with me."

His grip on her elbow was firm, guiding her into an adjoining room.

The walls were an aggressive lime green. The enormous nude of Suki Rey—reclined before a green silk backdrop—practically vibrated off the canvas.

Anderson's breath warmed her ear. "Change of plan. Aguirre sent Meyer-Edwards an envelope from the Accademia in Rome. Find it. Bring it to me at the Dorset."

"What about the manuscript?" she asked, pulse quickening.

"No longer your assignment." He paused, voice dropping. "Just get me the envelope by COB tomorrow—and I'll bump your fee to three hundred grand."

Andre's voice crackled in her ear. "Fish swimming your way."

Anderson stepped back as Fonteyn swept into the space, all cool command. "Mr. Anderson, I've been looking for you everywhere."

Annouie eased into the background.

"Keep moving south," Andre said. "Small room to your rear."

She slipped through the corridor.

The room was small. Intimate. She sank onto a nearby sofa.

"Gibson's thirty seconds out," Andre said. "Quick test before he arrives."

She leaned toward the painting's description and read aloud. "'In this work, Gibson captures the essence of the subject through his unique use of gouache, ink, and acrylic—'"

"Contact from the rear," Andre interrupted.

Annouie rose, smoothing her dress, and strolled toward another portrait—an old man in shirtsleeves, face weathered from years in the sun. Her chest tightened. Whatever else he was, Gibson was a master. She moved on. A woman kneeling in her garden. A tattooed man gripping a long-necked bottle, resignation in his eyes.

Circling back toward the large canvas near the entrance, she knew Gibson was watching now. Silent. Predatory.

The floorboards barely creaked as he entered.

She feigned deep concentration, brow furrowed as she studied the painting: a woman sprawled in a La-Z-Boy, feet up, head dominating the bottom-right quadrant. *Newport Princess*. Oil on linen. The knife work was meticulous. The colors jagged and raw.

The air shifted as he stepped beside her. A soft clearing of the throat.

She turned. Met his gaze. Gasped—just enough to feed his ego.

"It's one of my favorites too," he said, eyes on the painting.

Timothy Gibson was lean, muscular, pale. His nose had a sculpted elegance, unlike the usual misshapen lumps men carried. Truth be told, he was startling—like one of his paintings. But it wasn't just his aesthetics—it was the lack of care. The way he held her gaze. The unhurried smile. Even the set of his brow was sensuous. Her gaze dropped to his mouth—also full of invitation.

Twenty-two years of age, she would've guessed. His dossier said twenty-eight.

He extended a hand. "Timothy Gibson."

Annouie glanced at her badge. "I'm . . ." She frowned.

He moved closer. "Let me read it for you." A beat. "Now, that's interesting."

"What is?"

"Tom Masters. From *The Tribune*."

Annouie gasped. "Really? That explains the strange looks. Not that Tom's bad to look at. I suppose that means he's wearing my badge." She laughed, completely freestyling. "Oh, dear. He'll be livid."

Gibson's grin widened. "He might be more than that. This is invitation-only. Everyone's vetted. Gabriella's orders."

"So, you're hired security? Checking credentials?" She dove into her bag, rifling around theatrically.

He laughed, gesturing at the walls. "Hardly. I'm the artist."

She feigned surprise. "But you're so handsome."

Gibson smiled. "They're not mutually exclusive, you know."

"Pretty people don't usually work hard for their fame. But these—"

"You think I'm pretty?"

She eyed him coolly. "You know you are."

He rubbed his chin, studying her. It was unsettling.

"I can't find the right word for you. Pretty. Beautiful. Gorgeous. None of them do you justice. You're like a Van Gogh: every stroke bursting with life, yet something strains beneath the surface. *'Haunting'* is overused, but that's what you are."

She snorted. "That's your best pickup line?"

He shrugged. "I don't usually have to ask. And if I were, believe me, you'd know—but I never mix business with pleasure."

"Now that's disappointing." She turned to go.

He stepped in front of her. "But if you're not Tom Masters, that would change things."

"We've established I'm not."

"I meant—if you weren't a journalist."

"What else would I be?"

She lifted her chin. Met his gaze. His eyes were green. Like the sea.

He laughed. "I don't know. Why don't we find out together?"

"Cheesy," she said, brushing past.

"That's not what I meant."

She paused, pivoting.

"I meant—it would make things simpler."

Her mouth quirked. "How?"

"I wouldn't have to break my own rules."

She stepped closer, softened her voice to a husk. "Break them."

Her hand slipped into his.

His breath hitched. Then—his hands found her waist, drawing her close.

He lowered his face—

Clicking heels. Voices. A man and a woman.

Annouie broke away as Gabriella Fonteyn swept in with a distinguished man on her arm.

"Timothy, look who I found lurking by the Suki Rey mural?"

"I wouldn't exactly call it *lurking*," the man said.

Fonteyn laughed. "Of course you were, Sir James."

Gibson moved close, his lips grazing Annouie's ear. "Back entrance. First left. Service elevator to the ground floor." He pressed a key card into her hand. "If anyone asks—you're looking for the bathroom. Five minutes."

"Make it three," Annouie whispered, already backing away.

Fonteyn's eyes narrowed. "A *date*?"

Gibson shrugged. "She's looking for the bathroom. Ask for her life story when she returns."

"Is she on the list?"

"Probably not."

"I said no invite, no entry."

"Come on, Gabriella. She's my date."

Annouie slipped through the door and ran—four-inch heels be damned.

* * *

Dr. Chin crawled through the network of catwalks and rigging above the Rose Chambers Room, her phone—displaying the gallery blueprints—secured to a magnetic neck mount. Below, the space lay still.

Her tech guy had already hacked the hallway feed and disabled the motion and heat sensors covering the rigging and the room. The main doors were primed—if she needed a fast exit, she'd have it.

The *Venus* was tagged. All she had to do was cut the canvas from the frame.

She rose onto the balls of her feet, slid the phone inside her vest, and scanned the room below. Silent. Waiting.

She rigged her pulley system, clipped in, and began her descent.

Chapter Twenty

"I've got Gibson's key card," Annouie said, waving it as she rushed down the corridor.

Andre exhaled sharply. "That'll get you to the fourth floor." He grabbed her hand. "But it won't get you inside." He pressed a gel fingerprint over the end of her finger. "This will."

"And the voiceprint?"

"Oria's working on it."

Annouie stepped inside the elevator and swiped. The doors bumped shut, and it began its ascent.

She slid the Oria2 SmartSpecs on as the elevator slowed. A maze of red, blue, and green hotspots appeared on her HUD, marking camera positions, sensors, exits.

"I've switched to the prerecorded feeds. You're clear to approach," Andre said as the doors parted.

She slipped forward, the sky-high heels whisper-quiet on the carpet.

She pressed her gel-coated finger to the reader beside the Rose Chambers Room doors. A voice crackled from the wall speaker.

"Hello, Ms. Fonteyn. Please repeat the phrase: *Two, three, zero, nine. Your place or mine?*"

Fonteyn's voice issued from the tiny speaker embedded in the arm of the SmartSpecs.

"Try again," flashed on the security display.

"Recalibrating," Andre muttered.

Fonteyn's voice lisped through the speaker again. This time, an audible click sounded, and the doors swung open.

"I'm in," Annouie said, stepping inside.

"Hold. Something's wrong," Andre barked.

Too late.

The doors boomed shut. Overhead, a pair of boots disappeared into the rigging. Below, an empty frame swung on its wires.

An Asian woman peered down from the catwalk, dark eyes flashing with glee.

"My tech guy just triggered an intruder alert. You've got about a minute. Good luck." She sprinted along the metal walkway, hoisted herself up a ladder, and vanished into the roof.

Annouie whirled. Pressed her finger to the reader.

No response.

She yanked on the handles. Sealed. Her pulse kicked up. No exits. No plan. No time.

"I'm locked in."

"Give me a minute," Andre rasped.

"I've got less than forty seconds."

A crack of thunder rattled the roof overhead. "I'll try the reader again."

"Waste of time. Security breach protocol locks down all exits. Guards are seconds away. Suggest you improvise."

"What about an emergency reboot?"

"Not an option. Your best bet is finding a way into the ceiling cavity."

Fifteen seconds.

She scanned the room. No ladders. No shelves. No way up.

The ding of the elevator echoed through the room.

Andre swore. "Six hostiles inbound. I can trigger some alarms, but—"

Ten seconds.

A fire alarm blared through the gallery.

"Dammit. Still three heading your way. If you can't get up into the ceiling, your only option is to surrender."

* * *

The doors to the Rose Chambers Room burst open. Three uniformed security guards stormed inside, breaking left and right, tasers drawn.

A long, upturned sofa teetered in the corner—rocked—then crashed onto its side.

The guards halted, glancing up.

Fifteen feet above, two titanium hairpins jutted from the wall like pitons. At the base of the wall: a pair of abandoned Louis Vuitton heels.

The nearest guard thumbed his radio. "This is Two. Perp's in the roof cavity. He'll likely head—"

The other man pointed at the heels.

"Correction. She'll likely head toward the back of the building." A pause, then, "Defining features: no shoes. Watch for movement in the ceiling grid."

* * *

Annouie scrambled up the ladder, hands slick with sweat, the thud of boots echoing faintly below. Thunder cracked overhead—the storm closing fast, its fury matching the thrumming in her chest.

Chin had vanished into the darkness above.

Annouie followed, scaling a second ladder into the gallery's upper levels.

The narrow space beneath the roof offered a brief reprieve. She paused, orienting herself.

Her original plan—walking out the front doors? No longer an option. New plan?

Wing it.

She tapped the SmartSpecs. A red dot marked her position within the gallery's network of catwalks and ladders.

To her south—the loading dock.

She crawled forward. "Making my way to the back. I'll need a big distraction when I get there."

"Copy that."

Annouie paused above a utility cupboard. Sliding a ceiling tile aside, she peered into the darkness.

Another crack of thunder rattled the structure.

Then—the HUD froze.

She tapped the SmartSpecs. "Oria?"

White noise hissed.

"Andre?"

Earpiece dead.

Annouie kicked out the tile and dropped into the cupboard, landing with a muffled thud. The darkness swallowed her. Static hissed softly in her ear.

Boots pounded past.

"Systems are down," someone yelled nearby. "Emergency lighting only!"

She edged to the door and pressed her ear against the wood. The footfalls faded, and she cracked it open.

The corridor was dim. The camera above the open fire door exit —dark.

She slipped into the hallway, angling for the fire exit—a straight shot to the building's side.

But as she stepped over the threshold—

Smack. The thud of rubber on concrete. Sharp. Close.

A figure tore up the stairwell—moving at phenomenal speed.

Tall. Lean. Bronze hair catching the emergency lights as he surged upward. He rounded the landing in a blur, thigh muscles flexing beneath tailored slacks. His hand shifted just enough to reveal the outline of a holstered gun.

Shit.

Annouie spun and bolted. Her bare feet pounded the carpet.

"Oria?" She tapped the SmartSpecs. Still dead. No AI. No comms.

She glanced back—the man burst through the fire door.

She veered into the main stairwell.

Confined space. No cover. Maximum vulnerability.

A chill slid down her spine. Bogotá. The alley. The fatal funnel.

She crushed the memory and ran harder.

But it wouldn't be enough.

She was fast. But he was faster.

* * *

Nicholas Hope plunged down the stairwell, eyes locked on his quarry. No mere thief. She was fast, fluid, fearless—moving with the precision of a trained operative.

She veered through an open doorway. His hand twitched toward his gun.

He stayed the impulse. Too many questions.

Ones he couldn't answer.

He leaned into the turn, quadriceps burning as he chased her down a wide service corridor.

Another doorway.

Then—nothing.

He slowed, sweeping the space. Corners. Shadows. Every blind angle of the dimly lit passage.

She was gone.

Methodically, he cleared the nearest rooms.

A closet—crammed with cleaning supplies.

A laundry room—the low hum of a washing machine jarringly mundane amid the tension.

Back in the hallway, he paused. Shadow clung thick between the exit and the wall. Improbable—but not impossible.

He moved forward, steps measured, the click of his soles loud against the concrete.

The gun at his hip sat heavy. Waiting.

A door slammed in the distance. Urgent shouts followed.

Nicholas froze. Calculated. Then pivoted—

And strode toward the noise.

* * *

Annouie froze as the man halted mid-stride, breath catching.

His eyes narrowed, scanning the dark.

Her muscles locked. He couldn't see her—not completely. But he was close. Too close.

Footsteps pounded. Voices rose outside. He hesitated. Exhaled sharply. Then flung the door wide—and disappeared through it.

She waited. Counted three slow breaths. Then chimneyed down, legs trembling, palms burning from the rough walls. She landed softly, chest heaving.

Fingers shaking, she tapped her earpiece. Nothing. Either Andre had been forced to move, or the storm was killing his signal.

Her last instruction echoed in her mind: *Making my way to the back.*

She steeled herself—then slipped through the stairwell door, angling south.

* * *

Outside, beneath a battered aluminum awning, Dr. Janine Chin groaned and rolled onto her side. Rain slashed down, pooling in slick rivulets around her. She sat up slowly, disoriented, blinking against the sting of water streaming into her eyes.

The last thing she remembered: slipping out the gallery's fire door, the *Venus* strapped to her back. Then—something dark and hulking, dropping from above. A brutal impact. Concrete biting into her spine. A flash of pain—then nothing.

The *Venus*.

Her fingers groped instinctively for the cardboard tube.

Gone.

Her stomach clenched.

As if on cue, her phone buzzed in her pocket. She hissed, rubbing at her bruised cheek as she struggled upright. Rain hammered down, blurring the screen.

Sir James.

She snarled. She was in no mood for his pompous lecturing.

Swiping the screen, she snapped, "What?"

"My, my. Someone's in a mood." His amused drawl slithered through the speaker. "Did you get the *Venus*?"

Janine stalked through the torrential downpour. "It's gone. Someone jumped me in the alley." She braced for the inevitable barrage.

Three. Two.

A sharp inhale.

"Excellent," he said, smugness curling every syllable.

Janine froze mid-step, blinking against the rain. "Excellent?"

A low chuckle. "I don't know why you're being so prickly, Doctor. You carried out the assignment to a *T*."

Her brow furrowed. "I botched the job."

"Far from it, my dear. Now, listen carefully. I have a new assignment for you."

She prowled toward the curb, rain hammering her shoulders, her grip tightening on the phone.

"Another task?" she hissed.

"Jack Vallone was sighted earlier this evening. I'm sending you an address." Her phone buzzed with a fresh text. "Find him. Track him. If I'm right—he'll lead us straight to the box."

The line went dead.

Janine lowered the phone, blinking rain from her lashes.

Irritating. Smug. Full of himself.

But he paid well. And until she had enough to walk away, Janine would jump as high as he asked.

For now.

Chapter Twenty-One

Timothy Gibson stared at the empty frame as security bustled in and out, their radios crackling. The elevator chimed at regular intervals, signaling a constant stream of arrivals. Outside, Gabriella paced the corridor like a caged panther, ready to pounce. The gallery was in full lockdown. The press, their appetite stoked by the chaos, remained corralled in the lobby. Rumors were already circulating that someone from Art Recovery was on-site.

"Sir?" A guard approached cautiously, tablet in hand. "We managed to reboot the system. We've been reviewing the feed. A woman entered the Rose Chambers Room just prior to the shutdown."

Timothy's brow furrowed as the guard angled the screen toward him. The grainy footage showed a black-clad thief vanishing into the rigging. A moment later, a second figure entered—the woman calling herself *Tom*.

He rubbed his jaw. "Have you identified her?"

"Not yet. But we think they were working together. Her partner must have cut her loose and escaped during the blackout."

Timothy's gaze sharpened. "What makes you think they were working together?"

Before the guard could answer, Gabriella swept into the room, phone clenched in one hand, eyes darting between the empty frame and the staff swarming around it.

"I'll have to call insurance, the broker, and then the goddamn police," she snapped, already dialing. She pressed the phone to her ear and resumed pacing, fury in every step.

Timothy barely looked up. His attention stayed on the frame, the torn edges of the canvas stark beneath the overhead lighting. "Tell everyone it was a false alarm," he said, his voice oddly calm. "You forgot the painting was at the lab for last-minute testing."

Gabriella froze. "Excuse me?"

He met her incredulous stare with cool indifference.

"Testing?" she repeated, eyeing the vacant frame. Then her eyes narrowed—not in disbelief, but in grudging respect. After a beat, she nodded, a sly smile forming.

She turned, lifting the phone again. "False alarm," she said, then snapped it shut. Her gaze swung back to him, hardening. "And what about this woman?"

"Irrelevant," he said with a shrug.

Gabriella's eyes gleamed. "Irrelevant? You introduced her as your date!"

"I did," he said, unbothered. "And I'm telling you—she didn't steal the painting."

Without waiting for further protest, he pivoted and strode to the door.

Gabriella followed, her voice low and sharp. "You can't just walk off."

"I need some air."

He pushed through the knot of guards at the entrance and made for the elevator. The guard known as "One" peeled away and stepped to Gabriella's side.

"Should we continue the search, Ms. Fonteyn?" His voice was low but carried clearly down the corridor.

Gabriella didn't hesitate. "Of course. Radio me the moment you find her."

As the elevator closed, Timothy's phone buzzed. A new message, routed through the dark web. His lips quirked. The chaos was unfolding exactly as planned—the thief had cracked the hidden instructions.

He flipped open the phone, scanned the message, and dialed the attached number. A man answered on the second ring.

As the elevator descended, Timothy pressed for intel on the operative known as the Gray Cat. The answers were slippery, cagey. He doubted this was *the* Gray Cat—but whoever the man was, he had access to the manuscript.

Perfect.

Stepping out into the lobby, Timothy made his offer: a private viewing of the *Venus*—the *real* one—in exchange for a look at the manuscript. His tone was businesslike, but his thoughts were racing.

One touch.

That's all it took. With his eidetic memory, he could replicate it exactly.

He ended the call, snapped the phone shut, and fished a packet of cigarettes from his jacket pocket.

Almost a perfect evening.

Only one thing left to do—find *Tom*.

Gabriella was right: the woman was still inside. He could feel her presence. Her voice. Her smirk.

The insult of her escape.

He grinned—a reckoning went without saying.

Outside, the rain had stopped. The air hung thick and damp. Timothy lit a cigarette and took a long, slow drag, the ember flaring in the dark. The door rattled shut behind him as he stepped into the night, savoring the thought of what he'd do to her once he had her.

* * *

Annouie crept to the end of the corridor, every sense sharp as a blade. The door ahead led to a narrow balcony overlooking the loading dock. To her left—a service elevator. To her right—a railing boxed in the edge. Beyond it—a fifteen-foot drop.

She peered over. Two guards loitered behind the parked trucks, covering the elevator and the main dock entrance. Off to the side, partially obscured by pallets and towering shelves, sat the fire door.

Two options: head back inside and risk another run-in with the bronze-haired predator, or find a way down.

Her gut clenched. Option one was a nonstarter.

Moving quickly, she secured the balcony door, jamming a shard of metal into the keyhole. Then slid down to sit against it, breath catching. She tapped her earpiece.

"Andre?"

Only static.

Footsteps. Muffled on the other side of the door. The handle rattled.

"Locked," a man's voice said. A pause. Whispering. Then—

"You have her?" Gabriella Fonteyn, sharp as glass.

"Pinned behind the door," the man replied. "Three and Four have the exits covered. No way off this balcony without a parachute."

"What are you waiting for? Breach," Fonteyn snapped.

Something heavy slammed the door.

"It's holding," came the reply. "We'll need something bigger."

"Then go get it."

Annouie scrambled to the edge. Fifteen feet below, a stack of pallets—cardboard boxes shrink-wrapped and gleaming—waited like a lifeline. Small landing zone. Minimal momentum. Risk factor: high.

Another crash. Metal groaned.

Her breath turned shallow. Time was running out.

Backing up to the elevator, she centered herself. Three steady breaths. On the third, she launched—sprinting straight for the rail.

Her hands struck the cold metal. She vaulted, twisting midair. Time fractured.

She landed on the boxes with a thud and a jolt—knees screaming, spine rattling.

She skidded down the wrap-slick sides, dropped the final few feet, and landed catlike on the concrete.

The guards near the trucks continued their watch undisturbed.

Then—

The door burst off its hinges.

They froze, heads snapping upward.

Above, Fonteyn emerged onto the balcony, her men in tow. "Well?" she barked. "Find her. That painting must be recovered at all costs."

She spun and vanished through the ruined doorway.

Annouie darted behind the pallet stack, heart hammering, shoulder pressed to the cold plastic wrap. The guards began to fan out, moving between the towering shelves—cardboard, printing paper, sealed chemical drums.

The fire door lay just beyond the next row.

Footsteps thudded closer.

She ducked into the shadows, crouching low, fingertips brushing the cool floor.

A sudden pop crackled in her earpiece.

Andre's voice burst through—low, urgent. "Annouie, what's your status?"

She dove under a shelf as one of the guards—"Three"—veered toward her.

"Pinned in the loading dock," she whispered. "Four guards closing in. Thirty seconds, max. What the hell happened?"

"The upgrade glitched."

A shadow swept across the floor beside her. She froze, heart thumping. Another slid in from the other side—converging fast.

From across the bay, Gabriella's voice rang out—taunting, amused. "Come now, darling. You're only drawing this out."

Annouie rasped into her mic. "Now would be a really good time to do something."

"Hold tight. Just a few more seconds."

The shadows grew. Sweat trickled down her neck. Her pulse drummed in her ears. Reflections wavered in the plexiglass boxes ahead. She rose onto the balls of her feet, every muscle coiled for flight.

Then—

A burst of static. Andre's voice: "We are go!"

The roll-up door screeched as it began to rise.

The guards spun in unison. Their shadows vanished as they jogged toward the noise, tasers drawn.

A low growl echoed near the trucks—then an engine roared to life.

"She's getting away!" Gabriella shrieked, her voice ricocheting through the dock.

Andre came back, cool and crisp. "Fire door, two aisles over—right side. It leads out. Head to Wilson and Broke. I'll pick you up in five."

Annouie didn't wait. She rolled out, sprinted low, adrenaline surging as she tore toward the door.

* * *

Timothy Gibson strolled casually to the back of the building, the faint slap of the river against the seawall a steady beat to his steps. He turned down the narrow accessway between the gallery and the adjacent structure, sneakers scuffing against the cracked pavement.

A shadowy doorway beckoned. He leaned against the dented steel, the cool brick at his back grounding him. Flicking the butt of his cigarette to the ground, he pulled out another. His lighter hissed. The flame caught, briefly illuminating his face and the wall behind him.

He inhaled, the ember pulsing orange. Smoke curled from his lips into the chill night air. His mind wasn't on the guards or the loading dock.

Just her.

Tom.

Ash drifted from his cigarette. He closed his eyes. The tip glowed brighter for a moment, his arousal stirring low and sharp.

"Who are you, Tom?" he murmured. The words vanished into the dark.

He replayed the moment:

The back room.

That dress.

The almost-kiss—

His eyes snapped open.

The tip hovered at his lips, the pieces falling into place.

A trap.

His lips curled. A sharp laugh escaped, quick and clean.

Not a journalist. A spy. A rival in the hunt for Rebrisi's *Three Elements.*

Maybe she was the Gray Cat after all.

Desire coiled through him, hungry and taut. The manuscript would be his by morning.

But tonight—

Tonight, she was the prize.

His eyes narrowed, scanning the alley. The cigarette burned low.

He dropped it—crushed it—

Then the fire door slammed open.

And Tom burst through it.

* * *

Annouie barreled through the doorway, bare feet slapping against the concrete. She leapt down the short flight of steps and surged off the last one, stride lengthening as she sprinted for the street.

Just as her momentum built, a man stepped out of the shadows.

She dropped low, instinctively rolling to clear him—but he moved faster, redirecting her momentum to flip her over the low dividing wall.

A hand clamped over her mouth, silencing her as he hauled her into the recessed doorway of the neighboring property.

"Not a word," he whispered, pulling her tight.

Annouie twisted to glare up at him. "You?"

Gibson grinned. "I believe we agreed to meet in three."

The fire door slammed open. Gabriella and her security detail crowded onto the small landing.

Gibson yanked Annouie deeper into the shadows as Gabriella's gaze raked the narrow passage.

"We'll find her," a guard said.

Gabriella waved him off. "Don't bother. She's gone." She spun and stalked back inside, the door groaning shut behind her.

Rain began to fall again—steady, cold. Gibson's breath warmed the back of Annouie's neck. He wasn't in a hurry to let her go. In fact —he seemed to enjoy spooning her in the dark.

"You can let go now."

Gibson's brow lifted, amused, as he released her. "You're a spy, aren't you, Tom?" Playful tone. Calculating eyes.

She scoffed and stepped toward the edge of the doorway.

"I'll take that as a yes." He shook a cigarette loose and lit it with a flick. The tip flared in the rain-soaked dark. "Can I have your real name at least? 'Tom' feels so impersonal."

She huffed a laugh.

"I'm serious." He took a long drag, exhaling smoke in a lazy stream. "It's only fair."

She tilted her head, studying him. He wasn't rattled. Not even after losing the *Venus*. Odds were good it was a fake.

"It's Annouie."

The cigarette paused midair. He dropped it. The ember hissed out on the wet ground.

"Lovely," he murmured. "Here's the thing, Annouie—I've got a decision to make."

He leaned close, voice conspiratorial. "My *Venus* has been stolen, which is . . . problematic. A couple of buyers are anxious to view it. My agent wants blood—specifically yours. But I'm willing to let all that slide if you do me one little favor."

"A favor?"

"One you can't refuse." He flashed a grin. "A client's coming tomorrow. He expects to view the *Venus*."

She arched a brow. "Which you no longer have."

"Precisely."

She glanced up the street, eyeing the Carrera parked in shadow.

"What exactly do you expect me to do?"

He gave her a once-over, eyes gleaming. "You're nimble on your feet. I want you to put it back."

She laughed, short and incredulous. "Put back what? Surely not the original?"

His smirk widened. "You catch on fast."

"You're saying you have it?"

His grin turned enigmatic. "Come for a ride. I'll tell you everything."

Her eyes narrowed. "Where?"

"My place."

She scoffed. The man was practically neon with transparency. But if he knew where the real *Venus* was . . .

She shrugged. "Fine. Your place." She glanced down at her feet. "But first—give me two seconds."

Before he could respond, she vanished up the street. A minute later, she returned with a large leather tote and a pair of sneakers.

"Lead the way."

Gibson guided her down a narrow staircase to the riverbank. The tide was turning, water licking at the embankment.

They veered onto a riverside path toward a pontoon where an inflatable boat bobbed in the current.

Annouie stopped short. "That's a boat."

"A rigid inflatable boat," he replied, untying the bowline and jumping aboard.

Before he could offer a hand, she leapt in beside him.

Gibson's grin returned as he started the motor. The outboard roared to life, and the RIB slipped from the dock, carving through the dark water toward the open river.

Chapter Twenty-Two

The door snicked shut behind Andre as he followed Paul out of the storeroom. Paul didn't wait—he strode off, chest tight with indignation, vanishing into the kitchen.

Andre straightened his uniform, ran a hand through his hair, and took a steadying breath. Echoes of hurried footsteps and muffled voices pulled him down the corridor toward the exhibition hall.

As he emerged—still wiping the tears from his eyes—chaos greeted him. Guests huddled in uneasy groups while guards swarmed in and out of the room. Reporters scribbled, recording every scandalous moment.

A waiter buzzed past, balancing a tray of clinking glasses. Andre stopped him.

"What's going on?"

The man paused, brows lifting. "Where have you been?"

Andre tugged on his name tag. "Uh—"

"Never mind." The man waved him off, lowering his voice conspiratorially. "It was nothing. False alarm. Apparently Gabriella forgot she sent the painting out for testing. Security's pissed. Guests are bailing. The press?" He rolled his eyes. "They're eating it up."

Andre blinked. "False alarm?"

"Yep. Thankfully no cops, but still a total circus. Anyway, I've got work to do before I can put this shitshow behind me." He disappeared into the crowd, leaving Andre to absorb it all.

The tension in the room was palpable. Gabriella stood at the center of it, flanked by security. She gesticulated wildly as the press leaned in, jotting down every word with predatory glee.

Andre turned away, fingers flying over his phone.

What's your twenty?

Seconds ticked by. No response. He typed again:

Did you make it to Wilson and Broke?

Still nothing. He started drifting toward the nearest exit, eyes flicking between his screen and the room—until a gruff, commanding voice cut through the din.

Sir James Gibson.

The MP for Haynes stood with his hands on his hips, berating a younger man.

Andre froze.

He knew of Nicholas Hope—Sir James's personal assistant and a former art recovery specialist. But it wasn't the PA's résumé that caught Andre's attention.

The man was aesthetically perfect. Symmetrical features, chiseled lines, and an effortless poise that sent Andre's pulse skittering.

"You were supposed to keep her busy," Sir James snapped, jabbing a finger at Hope's chest. "Damn woman wouldn't leave me alone. Fortunately, the power went out, and some idiot crashed the preview. Still, this doesn't mean you're off the hook."

Nicholas stared at the far wall, his expression unreadable. "I'm sorry, sir. Must have been something I ate."

The politician waved a dismissive hand. "Well, spilt milk and all that. Let's make our excuses and get out of here before someone decides to do a strip search or something equally embarrassing."

Sir James swept toward the exit, brushing past reporters with a brusque, "No comment. My office opens at eight. Good night."

Then, under his breath: "Get the car."

"I've organised a cab," Nicholas replied.

Sir James stiffened as if bracing for a fight—but instead of the expected tirade, he spun on his heel and vanished into the crowd.

The moment he was gone, Nicholas straightened. His shoulders squared, his chin lifted, and a cool confidence settled over him like a second skin.

His gaze settled on Andre. He adjusted his jacket and crossed the room with unhurried grace, extending a hand.

"Nicholas Hope. PA to Sir James Gibson."

Andre took it without hesitation. "I know who you are."

Hope arched a brow. "Journalist?"

"Waiter."

Hope's lips twitched—almost betraying a smile. "Better career prospects." His eyes drifted over the pastel pink hair. "Hope I'm not being too forward—but . . . you seem familiar?"

Andre shrugged. "I consult to the police."

Hope's brows lifted. "Not about waiting, I presume."

Andre laughed. "About technology."

Hope turned, scanning the room's scattered clusters and lingering energy from the lockdown. He flashed a quick smile.

"So . . . this is a cover? Intriguing."

Andre's phone buzzed. He glanced down:

> Change of plans. En route to Green Point.
> Will text further details upon arrival.

Relief washed over him.

Hope's smile widened. "Say, do you feel like grabbing a drink? After the night I've had, I need something stronger than champagne."

Andre hesitated, slipping the phone into his pocket. "Yeah. Why not? I was supposed to meet someone, but she just canceled."

"She?" Hope's eyes flickered with something unreadable.

"A friend," Andre clarified.

Hope's full smile returned. "In that case, there's a bar around the corner—great ambience, excellent liquor."

Andre nodded. "Sounds perfect. Give me two seconds to finish up in the kitchen."

A faint smirk played across Hope's lips. "Of course. I'll be waiting."

* * *

Rain hammered the sidewalk beyond the gallery's main entrance as Antony wrestled Suki Rey into the back of her limousine. She clung to him like a drowning woman, her arms locked around his neck in a desperate bid to drag him in with her. Cameras flashed, capturing every angle of the chaos.

"Join me, Antony darling," she purred, voice thick with drink and mischief. "The night hasn't even begun."

He sighed, peeling her off and easing her into the back seat. The idea of drinking away his sorrows with the pop princess had its appeal—but not tonight.

"Some other time," he said, stepping back and slamming the door.

He walked to the driver's open window and leaned in, voice low. "Make sure she gets inside safely. She's had a bit too much."

Sliding a couple of hundreds into the man's hand, Antony gave a quick nod and stepped away.

The limo pulled out of the porte-cochère, its sleek form disappearing down the rain-slicked street. Overhead, lightning forked through the clouds, illuminating the drenched cityscape. Thunder followed a few seconds later, low and rolling.

Behind him, the muffled buzz of the dwindling crowd turned to startled cries.

Antony tugged up his collar and lowered his head.

As he started down the pavement, a familiar figure brushed past him. The contact was brief but unmistakable. A folded slip of paper—pressed into his palm.

Their eyes met.

Jack gave a subtle shake of his head, then melted into the rain.

Antony's fist tightened around the note as he continued toward the taxi stand. Wind howled, snatching garbage from the gutter and hurling it across the sidewalk.

Sliding into the back of the nearest cab, he unfolded the damp paper. Ink bled into the loops of hurried handwriting, but the address was clear enough.

He leaned forward, voice steady despite the pounding in his chest. "Corner of Victoria Park and Albert Street, please."

The driver nodded and pulled into traffic.

Antony sat back, the note crumpled in his fist, his mind already racing ahead.

* * *

Half an hour later, Antony stepped out at the Victoria Park intersection, rain drumming on the cracked pavement. He paid the driver in cash, tugged his jacket tighter, and set off toward the park.

By the time he emerged on the other side, the rain had soaked through to his undershirt. He kept moving, the blur of red taillights, neon signs, and headlights bleeding together in his periphery. Ahead, Saint Martin's Road bustled despite the weather. He ducked between umbrella-wielding pedestrians, the wind driving the rain into his face like needles.

Under a shopfront awning, he paused to wipe the water from his eyes. Across the road, the silhouette of the cathedral loomed above the street, its spire veiled in mist. A flight of stone steps cut into the hillside drew his gaze upward to the oak branches arching overhead like sentinels.

He crossed the road and took the stairs to the top.

A graveled path led to a colonnaded façade. A figure in a cassock stood beneath one of the arches, rough-hewn features and stocky frame unmistakable.

Without a word, Jack turned and disappeared inside.

Antony followed, gravel crunching underfoot as he hurried to catch him.

The faint murmur of voices greeted Antony as he entered the cathedral, his footsteps echoing down the nave. Jack led him through the narthex, past the towering piers supporting the organ loft.

Near the front, a small group gathered around a battered grand piano. A younger man jabbed at the keys with one finger, cueing the tenors. It might have been Palestrina—though it was so badly mangled, it was hard to tell.

Antony scoffed under his breath.

The pianist's head snapped up, a scowl creasing his brow. The tenors kept singing, oblivious.

With a sharp clap of his hands, the singing stopped. Antony offered the ceiling a look of mock gratitude and kept walking, ignoring the hostile gaze burning between his shoulder blades.

Jack led him through the transept and down a narrow spiral staircase. The air cooled with each step. Stone walls grew rougher. Shadows thickened. The light dimmed.

At the base of the steps, an enormous oak door swung open without a sound, revealing a vast, cavernous chamber. Crypts lined the walls, their damp surfaces slick with condensation.

Antony made a face. "Seriously?"

Jack silenced him with a raised finger and continued across the chamber. His cassock whispered over stone as he passed through a narrow archway. Several small rooms branched off the corridor beyond. He entered the last.

Antony followed and shut the door behind them.

The room was spartan—just a cot, a chair, and the faint tang of damp stone and decay.

"This is where you've been hiding?" Antony asked, sinking into the chair.

Jack gave the door a final glance, then turned. "Did you bring the manuscript?"

Antony leaned back, the chair creaking. "No."

Jack's smile vanished. "Why not?"

"I no longer have it."

"What's that supposed to mean?"

Antony crossed his legs, steepled his fingers, and assumed his most infuriatingly calm expression. "It means today's been one hell of a day. I misplaced it."

Jack's mouth fell open. "You lost it?"

"Technically, yes. But no. It's in one of three places. First option: my front room, which looks like a bomb went off, thanks to the police and their murder investigation. Second: the evidence lockup, if they were idiotic enough to grab it." He hesitated. "Third—and most likely —I may have loaned it to a student."

Jack stared. "Why would you loan it to a student?"

"It was an accident. As I said—it's been a day."

But then he pictured Bach's defiant grin, the way she raised her glass like it was a toast.

To chaos. To trouble. To him.

A big, deliberate fuck you.

Was it really an accident?

Jack slumped onto the cot. The springs groaned. "Fine," he muttered, dragging a hand down his face. "We'll deal with your student in a minute. Right now, there's something you need to see."

Antony's gaze sharpened. "What?"

Jack stood, his cassock brushing the floor as he moved toward the door. "Follow me."

Chapter Twenty-Three

The roar from the outboard echoed off the walls of the bridge as the tender passed beneath, bow cleaving through the inky water.

Annouie sat in the stern, rereading her hastily typed text.

> Change of plan involves finding out what Gibson knows about the Three Elements. Don't expect me home tonight.

The boat picked up speed, the wind whipping her hair behind her. Annouie gripped the seat and shivered, silently cursing herself for not grabbing the oversized hoodie from the front seat of the Carrera. The skin-tight, multi-purpose dress, while perfect for catching Gibson's eye, was utterly useless against the night chill.

Perfect for him. Useless for her. She might've landed her mark, but now she was paying the price.

Ten minutes later, the tender veered toward a graveled shore. Gibson cut the engine, and the boat glided into the shallows. He leapt out, splashing through the water, and dragged the inflatable to land.

The moon hung low, spilling a ribbon of silver across the waves. Gibson secured the boat and turned to her, extending his hand.

She hesitated, the moment hanging awkwardly between them. Then she grasped his hand and jumped down onto the pebbled shore. Her sneakers crunched against the gravel as she followed him past the looming warehouses perched above the sea wall.

"My place is a few blocks over," Gibson said, climbing a wooden staircase embedded in the wall.

She followed him up to the street above and along two blocks before he descended a winding ramp to the sublevel of a modest, four-story brick building. In the corner of the dimly lit underground garage, an old bird-cage elevator stood waiting. Gibson strolled over and punched the call button.

The doors rattled open. Annouie tightened her grip on her tote. Inside was a small arsenal: flex-cuffs, a charged taser, a 1.5-ounce bottle of ketamine, and a loaded syringe. If it came to it, she was ready to pry answers out of him.

He winked—oblivious that his evening was heading in a different direction than the one planned—and stepped into the elevator.

The wink worked better than it should have. She ignored the heated prickle along her skin and followed him in.

The elevator groaned and shuddered to the fourth floor. The doors scraped open—

Annouie barked out a laugh of surprise. A sprawling loft.

Long floor-to-ceiling windows lined the far wall, showcasing the city's glittering skyline. Recycled pine floorboards gleamed under a thick varnish, while rows of decorative bricks rose into the rafters. The renovation struck a tasteful balance between old-world charm and modern functionality.

Not quite the sex lair she'd been expecting.

Her gaze swept the room, pausing on an ornate Japanese room divider partially obscuring a carved bedframe. Gibson's eyes followed her as she strolled toward the kitchen island, slipping her phone from her bag as she perched on a stool.

A message from Andre lit up her screen:

Tell me you didn't go home with that casanova!

She thumbed a quick reply.

We're discussing a business opportunity.

What sort of business?

Gibson kicked off his shoes. "Coffee?"

Her lips curved despite herself. She nodded, swiveling to take in the rest of the room.

Easels stood scattered across the studio, displaying works at various stages of completion. A workbench overflowed with brushes, empty jars, and bottles of cleaning fluid. But it was the canvas nailed to the back wall that caught her attention: the penciled-in form of a semi-naked woman stretched across a chaise longue, rendered against a burnt sienna ground.

Annouie slid off the stool, drawn to it. Unlike the stylized Suki Rey portraits, this subject seemed unaware she was being observed.

"Girlfriend?" she asked as Gibson slipped in beside her.

He shrugged. "We had a thing." His voice was clipped as he turned and gestured toward the kitchen. "Come."

Gibson's orbit was dangerously easy to fall into. Annouie kept her distance—just enough to remind him—and herself—who was in control.

Back at the island, he grabbed a tablet, swiping and typing furiously. "I'm ordering two long blacks from the cafe downstairs. Shouldn't take long."

His tone shifted, brisk and business-like. "Let's get down to it. My client is coming first thing tomorrow to see the *Venus*."

Annouie whistled. "That's quite the dilemma, seeing as someone stole it this evening."

He nodded. "Precisely. I'll be spending most of the night creating a new copy." His voice dropped, expression darkening. "The curing process alone takes several hours."

The buzzer rang, breaking the tension. Gibson slid off the stool and strode barefoot to the intercom, his footsteps echoing.

She watched him go, her gaze snagging on the sculpted lines of his body, the muscles shifting beneath his shirt. *Ugh.* She straightened her back.

"Fortunately, I have an eidetic memory," he said, glancing over his shoulder with a wry smile. "I should be able to knock out a few copies without any trouble at all."

Her brow furrowed. "Eidetic? So all you have to do is *see* the original?"

His eyes glinted with mischief. "And touch it. But yeah, that's the general idea."

She nodded slowly, mind racing. *Touch it. Feel it.* That's how he was doing it.

Which meant—

He had the real *Venus.*

* * *

Andre Landvik sat frozen at the café table, heart skipping madly, as Nicholas Hope rose from his seat.

"Think about it—and give me a call," Hope said, striding for the exit.

Andre's gaze shifted at last, tracking the man as he deployed his black umbrella and stepped out. Rain bounced harmlessly off the taut fabric as he disappeared up the street, leaving Andre to replay their conversation—and that kiss.

He touched his lips, recalling the light, insistent pressure of Hope's mouth.

His phone buzzed against the table, snapping him out of his thoughts. He let it ring out, exhaling a long, slow breath. He'd spent nearly an hour talking about himself—and learned almost nothing about Hope. Somehow, Hope had turned the whole conversation inside out, leaving Andre both impressed and irritated.

The bartender's voice cut through his thoughts. "We're closing, mate."

Andre glanced around. The stools were stacked. Two young staffers bustled—one mopping, the other flipping chairs onto tables.

He dropped a few bills on the table and stood, pulling his jacket tighter as he headed for the door.

Outside, the rain had eased to a thin drizzle, but the air was cold. He tucked his chin into his collar and walked the empty street, fingers brushing the edge of the business card in his pocket. Beneath a streetlamp, he paused and pulled it out.

The card was a study in understatement:

Nicholas Hope
Private Secretary to Sir James Gibson

The script was clean, elegant—much like the man himself. Andre flipped it. Hope had written his phone number in neat, precise handwriting.

Andre pulled out his phone. His fingers hovered, then moved—each press heavier than the last. The call rang a few times before it dropped to voicemail.

"It's Andre," he said after the tone. "Thanks for listening tonight. But . . . I need to clarify—I'm not looking for anything new right now. It's too soon. I hope you understand."

The words hung in the air as he ended the call. No sooner had he pocketed the phone than it buzzed again.

Annouie.

> Venus still in play. Don't worry. Have a backup plan. You're going to love it.

Typical. Annouie always had a backup plan—one that usually led to chaos.

His grip tightened on his phone.

Are you still with Gibson?

No reply.

Annouie. Are you with Gibson?

Still nothing.

Her silence was confirmation enough. Andre swore under his breath and shoved the phone into his jacket. Things always got messy when Annouie went off-script. And Annouie always went off-script.

He found the Carrera, parked in shadow just as he'd left it. Sliding behind the wheel, he gunned the engine and peeled onto the slick road, tires hissing over the wet asphalt.

Time to brace for whatever fallout Annouie was about to leave in her wake.

* * *

Annouie pushed the Samsung Flip aside and drummed her fingers on the marble. Gibson emerged from behind the screen in baggy denim overalls, straps hanging loose against his bare, toned chest.

She fought the urge to stare.

"What now?" she asked, keeping her tone carefully casual.

He snapped the straps into place and beckoned her toward the large easel behind his worktable. He set a half-finished portrait on the floor, rummaging through a stack of stretched canvases until he found the one he was after.

"Is this it?" she asked, stepping in. The brushwork was flawless. For a moment, she was impressed—until the word *COPY* flashed across her Smart-contacts display. She took a step back. "A copy."

Gibson gave a stiff nod. "Yes. Almost perfect. But not enough to impress the client coming tomorrow." He removed the painting, propped it face-in against the wall, and replaced it with a blank canvas.

He squeezed paint onto a glass palette. A slow smile crept across his face as he picked up a wide brush, dabbed it in linseed oil and mixed pigments with practiced ease. The swish of the bristles against canvas filled the loft as he began blocking in the background.

He moved quickly—fluid, deliberate. From time to time, his brow furrowed as he swapped brushes or stepped back to study the emerging composition. His biceps flexed with each squeeze of a paint tube, the physicality of his work oddly hypnotic. As the painting took shape, his pace grew frenzied, his focus absolute.

Annouie sank onto the chaise longue at the center of his studio. The exhaustion of the day—and the night before—pulled at her. She stretched out, resting her head against the padded armrest. Then it hit her: this wasn't just a chaise. It was the infamous sex chair.

However—

The stool creaked as Gibson leaned around the canvas, frowning in frustration.

It was obvious: sex was the last thing on his mind.

"Something's not right," he muttered, setting the brush aside and stepping back. His fingers stroked his chin. "The pigment—it's not warm enough."

He pulled the painting down, rifled through the stack again, and selected another blank canvas. "This needs to be precise if we want the buyer to believe it's the real thing."

Even scowling, he was distractingly beautiful.

Annouie watched as he started over, his focus absolute. His intensity was intoxicating. She let her eyes drift shut—then snapped them open.

A glint of gold.

She turned toward the Japanese screen separating the sleeping quarters from the studio. Curiosity prickled.

Sliding off the chaise, she crept toward it, checking to make sure Gibson was still immersed in his work. The first panel depicted a black cat gazing up into a Japanese maple, a golden canary perched in its branches. In the second, the cat frolicked beneath a cascade of petals. In the third, it sat in the tree, eyes fixed on the moon.

The artistry held her for a beat. Behind her, Gibson changed brushes, unaware.

Her gaze drifted past the screen to the bed—solid wood, intricately carved. The headboard doubled as a bookshelf—its rows crammed with volumes of varying heights and colors.

Slipping into the sleeping area, she circled the bed. The rumpled sheets hinted at a restless night. On the bedside table sat an ashtray, a half-smoked cigarette perched on the rim. The scent—spicy, aromatic—still lingered.

She bent to inspect it—and that's when she saw it.

An ancient-looking chest sat tucked beside the bed, its lid carved with low relief symbols. She brushed her fingers along the edge and found a concealed lock. A twist, a gentle push—and a satisfying click.

She eased the lid open and propped it against the wall.

On top, a green silk dress lay coiled like a secret. She brushed it aside. Beneath were several rolled canvases.

Annouie carried them to the bed, unrolling each with care. Her breath hitched. A Cézanne. A Vermeer. A Renoir. And finally—her eyes traced the luminous brushwork—the Rebrisi *Venus*.

"I think I'm done."

Gibson's voice rang from across the room, followed by the splash of a brush hitting turpentine.

Annouie leapt into motion, rolling the canvases and tucking them back into the chest. The lid thudded shut. She scrambled across the bed, grabbing the cigarette stub.

She held it up as Gibson stepped into view, barefoot. "Holding out on me?" she teased.

His brow quirked as he dried his hands on a rag. "Didn't think you were the type."

She dropped the cigarette into the ashtray, slid off the bed, and strolled toward him.

He stepped back, wary. "What's with the look?"

She shrugged as she passed. "Didn't think you were the type to make assumptions."

His laugh was low, amused. He followed her back to the easel. She circled to the front of the canvas, studying the new copy. Gibson stepped in behind her, hands gliding to her waist, his body radiating heat.

She ignored his closeness. "This is good."

"Surprised?"

She met his gaze. "No."

His lips curved. "Good. Because there's something I've been wanting to ask you."

Her brow arched. "So ask."

He dropped his voice to a whisper. "How'd you end up doing what you do?"

The question hit like a punch. Flashbulb memories: the embassy official's apologies, a dingy café, Anderson's fingers tightening on her shoulder, the smell of bratwurst and fear.

Her throat closed.

She pulled away without a word, returning to the chaise. Her face gave nothing away.

Gibson sighed. "Okay. I get it. You're not supposed to talk about it."

He grabbed another brush and returned to the canvas, his movements sharper now. The silence hung heavy in the air.

Finally, he stepped back. "I think it's almost there."

She stood and crossed the floor. "I thought you said *almost* wasn't good enough."

"Correct," he said, wiping his brow. "But it will be—once we bake it."

"Bake?"

He grinned, lifting the canvas from the easel. "Four hours in the oven. Then no one'll know the difference."

Without waiting, he crossed to the wide glass doors. Pressing down the brass handles, he swung them open.

A cool breeze swept in. Annouie sighed, the chill reviving her. She followed him onto the terrace.

At the far corner, he yanked open the lid of a sleek pizza oven, its steel hood glinting.

"The beauty of modern pizza ovens," he called, "is that they're perfect for aging paint."

She watched, amused and skeptical. He slid the canvas inside. The lid clanged shut. He adjusted the controls with practiced ease.

"It's all about temperature and time," he added, throwing her a look.

She shrugged. "You're the expert."

"I am." He stepped back from the oven, grinning. "Now—how about one of my special cigarettes while we wait? Or am I making assumptions again?"

Chapter Twenty-Four

Antony followed Jack out of the tiny cell and into the crypt room—but instead of heading for the church above, Jack approached an alcove at the far end and pushed on the wall. A section swung open, revealing a hidden passage.

Jack clicked on a red penlight, its narrow beam slicing through the darkness.

"This isn't creepy at all," Antony muttered, trailing him down a steep, shadowy staircase.

Jack's voice echoed softly ahead. "The catacombs spread out beneath the old city. Some tunnels are mapped and open to tourists. Others, like this one, aren't."

Antony's shoes scuffed over the dusty floor.

"Don't worry." Jack gave a breathy laugh. "City engineers might've skipped these tunnels, but I didn't. Every passage, twist and turn—it's in my head."

They walked in silence until the corridor widened into a large room. The penlight swept across stone walls lined with shelves. A desk stood at the center, cables snaking from a desk lamp across the floor. Jack flipped the switch.

Nothing happened.

"You might want to replace that bulb," Antony quipped.

Jack ignored him, directing the penlight toward the canvas stretched across the desk. "Look closely." He lifted the lamp, bathing the paintwork in UV light. A string of numbers glowed to life—like landing lights on an airstrip.

Antony leaned in. "What is that?"

"Phosphorescence," Jack said. "Certain additives glow when exposed to radiation. Rebrisi was a master at embedding cryptic messages."

"I know what phosphorescence is," Antony said, voice sharpening. "But what do the numbers mean?"

"If this were the original, they'd point to the next clue in the manuscript. Which would then help us unlock the box. But this is a fake—and we're still missing the second and third pieces."

Antony straightened. "You're saying the forger's left us a message?"

Jack gave a pleased nod.

Antony studied the digits, his frown deepening. "Is this an *onion* URL?"

"Yeah. Takes you to a dark website," Jack said. "Gibson has the original *Venus*. He's talented—new on the scene, but naïve. He thinks the Gray Cat can get him the manuscript. He wants to meet."

Antony's face hardened. "The *who*?"

"A freelance specialist. Clandestine ops. Used to be the best. Mostly myth now. My guess: someone put him in the ground—or he's rotting in jail."

A cold prickle slithered down Antony's spine. Images—gray cinder block walls, iron doors, a frozen yard. He forced the memories down.

"And how does this help us?"

Jack's mouth twisted into a smirk. "I contacted Gibson. Posed as the Gray Cat."

Antony scoffed. "Gibson must be truly naïve if he bought that."

"No," Jack said, unbothered by the interruption. "I was the insurance consultant the banks brought in after a Gray Cat heist. I studied his methods. I know him better than he knows himself." Jack's smile was thin. "Wasn't hard to convince Gibson I'm the real deal."

Antony rubbed his jaw. "And the plan is to steal his *Venus*?"

"Pretty much. But the only way I get close is if I have the manuscript." He gave Antony a pointed look. "So call your student."

Antony checked his watch. His mouth tightened. "It's late. She won't answer."

Jack blinked. "She?"

Antony let the question hang as he dialed. The call rang out, then kicked to voicemail.

He spoke smoothly, polished veneer slipping into place. "My dear. Hope I didn't wake you. Your presence is required—112 Thomas Street. Eight sharp. Bring the manuscript. I trust you've done some reading. We'll start with the quiz."

He snapped the phone shut. "Done. You'll have your *damn* manuscript by eight tomorrow morning."

* * *

The rooftop patio stretched thirty feet from the French doors to a low parapet that framed the city skyline. Timothy Gibson's outdoor area was as curated as his forgeries: pencil pines in ochre pots, verbena and rosemary perfuming the night, lavender, and gardenia nodding in a gentle breeze. In the far corner, the pizza oven smoldered, smoke trailing faintly from its chimney.

Annouie slumped at the wrought-iron table, head pillowed on her arms. Her phone buzzed. Groaning, she dragged it closer.

Meyer-Edwards's voice oozed from the speaker—smug, imperious, infuriating. Each word grated like sandpaper on wood. A *quiz. Seriously?* She toyed with sending him a one-fingered emoji, decided on a long, deliberate drag on her cigarette instead, blowing smoke into the night, along with her irritation.

She set down the phone and stared at the skyline—jagged silhouette, city lights blinking back with indifference.

Gibson was still stonewalling about the *Three Elements*.

Maybe another joint would loosen his tongue—

"I would advise against smoking any more of those."

Oria's voice purred through her earpiece.

Annouie stiffened. *Mind-reading now?* It was more than creepy—it was invasive. She took another drag out of spite.

A ping—this time from the pizza oven.

Gibson stepped onto the terrace, oven mitt in hand, bare chest visible beneath the loose denim overalls. Heat coiled low in her belly—unwelcome, distracting.

He slid the canvas onto the table with a flourish. "Just like the real thing, don't you think?"

She exhaled. "But without the cheese." Even if it was a fake, the execution was flawless.

"It's not finished yet." He sat, joint already between his fingers. "Needs time to cure."

A curl flopped into his eyes. He brushed it away with a careless flick of his wrist.

She stared—flushed, lightheaded, her inhibitions loosening.

Probably the THC.

"So, what now?"

His gaze lingered. "We go to bed."

He stubbed out the joint and stood.

"To sleep?"

He shrugged. "If you want. But I'd prefer to spend the time fucking."

Her cigarette slipped onto the chair, ember dying.

"And the no-mixing-business-with-pleasure rule?"

"Doesn't apply to you."

He was already close, heat rolling off him. He pulled her to her feet and pressed her against the wall.

She didn't resist.

When he kissed her—soft and sure—Anderson's number one rule clanged like a warning: *Never bed the enemy.*

His lips moved lower, inexorably, to her collarbone.

"This is a bad idea," she murmured.

His mouth pressed harder. Tongue tracing heat. Teeth grazing like a promise.

"Bedding Gibson *is* a bad idea, Agent Bach," Oria hissed in her ear. "The mission is—"

Annouie flicked the bud from her ear. It hit the floorboards with a dry *tap-tap*—just as his hands found the hem of her dress. Fabric pooled. Her bra snapped open. His thumbs—

Her fingers curled into his hair.

"And that," Gibson murmured, "is why this feels so. Damn. Good."

Her lips parted. His tongue glided in. The straps unbuckled. His coveralls puddled at his feet.

He swept her up, carried her inside. Lowered her onto the chaise. Pressed into her—solid, warm, insistent.

Their breath tangled. A low moan escaped her lips. The chair groaned beneath them.

Outside, the river murmured beneath tolling church bells. Inside, their rhythm quickened—sharp, feral, inevitable.

Crescendo.

Accelerando.

Climax.

Then silence—soft, spent—and the hum of the city reclaiming the night.

* * *

Church bells chimed across the river as a man moved to the book-lined walls of his dim office. Drawing a slim, red penlight from his pocket, he tugged a volume forward. A muted click echoed, and the bookcase swung out on hidden rails, revealing a hidden passage.

Slipping inside, he twisted an ornate brass sconce. With a quiet groan, the Murphy door shut behind him, sealing out the world. The air was damp, the space tight. Every breath tasted of stone-rot. He waited, eyes adjusting to the gloom, then started down the steps to the catacombs.

A corridor sloped into blackness, the gritty floor shifting beneath his shoes—until it opened on a vault. The beam of his penlight swept alcoves full of lead coffins: silent witnesses to centuries of secrets. Sometimes, in the stillness, he spoke to them.

Several tunnels radiated from the vault. He chose the left-hand spur, pace quickening. More alcoves. More coffins. Far off, the river's rumble pulsed through the walls.

Another chamber. To the left, a passage dipped toward a wharf—his discreet escape route—but not tonight.

He pressed on, downhill again, into a square room directly beneath the Courts of Justice.

At its center—an original John Ruskin desk and a high-backed Thomas Chippendale chair, treasures he had ferried here piece by piece. An Art Deco lamp, a Rolodex, and crumbling stacks of newspapers completed the subterranean study.

On the far wall, a corkboard bristled with pins and string. He sat, the Chippendale creaking, and let the hush settle over him like a shroud.

Julia hadn't been his first kill—war had taught him that skill—but she was the first to leave a bruise of remorse. *Pretty woman,* he thought. *Too curious. Asked questions she shouldn't have. Saw things that should have remained unseen.*

Her death had been necessary. But staging it? Watching her blood pool across that floor had soured his stomach. Such a crime against beauty.

He rose and added a new peg. *Sara Miles.*

String snaked from her name to the museum, the gallery, the Belmont Beach house—each line drawn tighter than the last. *Working both sides,* he scrawled in felt-tip, jaw flexing.

She'd blindsided him—gone behind his back, brought in her own experts. Killing her had been both necessary *and* satisfying. She'd been too close to solving the puzzle box. And then, infuriatingly, she'd sent it away—before he could stop her.

Four pins now: the agent, the public relations manager, the dealer, the journalist. But his very first kill? Still undiscovered.

He twirled a sleek penknife between his fingers, the blade catching the lamp's wan glow.

Ping.

The vibration shattered the tomb-quiet. He swiped his screen:

Lost target. Awaiting further instructions.

His large thumbs moved with surprising precision.

Remain in place. Watch. Wait. When he arrives—text me.

He leaned back, tapping the knife against the armrest—*click, click, click.*

Even if the man talked, mercy wasn't on the table. He'd peel the truth from his living flesh, sliver by sliver—then silence him for good.

Some secrets stayed buried only one way: *You cut down everyone reckless enough to dig for them.*

Chapter Twenty-Five

The morning after the storm, a body washed ashore on a secluded strip of sand known as Wilkins Beach, forty miles east.

Until then, the storm damage had dominated the news cycle. That changed when a local fisherman found the body wedged grotesquely inside the splintered husk of a tree. He snapped a photo and posted it on Facebook. Within minutes, the image spread like wildfire through the village.

Buoyed by likes and comments, the fisherman uploaded more photos to the local news site. By six a.m., Wilkins Beach was swarming with reporters. He basked in his viral fame while they scrambled for sound bites and dramatic angles.

The police were late, as usual, arriving closer to seven—well after a sizable crowd had gathered. Officers pushed through gawkers, and on sighting the body, reached for their radios.

By 7:30, rolls of tape cordoned off the beach. Crime-scene techs, gloved and silent, began combing through the wreckage: rotting tree trunks, garbage, dead fish. All of it sifted, cataloged, bagged.

Speculation rippled through the crowd.

"Been adrift a week," one young officer said, loud enough to earn himself reassignment to crowd control.

It took until 7:45 to pry the corpse from the tree's mangled embrace. A makeshift stretcher bore it to a hastily erected tent. Initial guesses put the time of death at two to three weeks—but closer inspection raised doubts. While crows had pecked out the eyes, lips, and cheeks, the rest remained shockingly intact, as if it had only just been placed there.

Unease settled over the investigators. Debate flared. Then someone thought to call Dr. Emil Thorpe.

The mention of a body in a tree at Wilkins Beach had Thorpe out of bed within minutes. By 7:55, without his usual complaints, he boarded Sir James Gibson's private helicopter and braced for the one-hour flight to the coast.

Chapter Twenty-Six

Annouie shifted on the silken pillow, her gut already telling her what her gaze was slowly confirming—she'd slept with the enemy.

A glance under the sheets confirmed another grim fact. She was still naked.

She sat up, silk pooling at her waist. She squinted at her smartwatch. Just after eight—later than planned. She continued to stare, her mind already on edge.

Gibson stirred, a wayward curl flopping over his outrageously handsome face. He cracked a lazy smile, stretching like a cat, his body unapologetically displayed.

"Good morning," he murmured, voice smooth as honey.

Heat crawled up her throat—a toxic mix of regret and fury. She forced it down. "This is the part where I deny all knowledge of what happened between us last night."

Gibson chuckled as she slipped out of bed, the floorboards shockingly cold beneath her bare feet. She could blame the weed. The alcohol. Pretend she remembered nothing. But the truth clung to her skin—raw, stubborn. Every vivid detail—the way he'd touched her, undone her, wrecked her—was burned there.

She dropped to her knees, yanking up the bed skirt in search of her dress.

"You're enjoying this, aren't you?" she snapped when his laughter followed her.

"Immensely," he admitted, leaning on one elbow to watch her.

Her head snapped up. "This isn't me."

"No," he said, grin maddening. "That fierce, unstoppable woman I couldn't get enough of? That was you."

She stood. He was sprawled across the bed, his gaze raking over her body with a hunger that was both unsettling and electric.

She scanned the room. "Where's my dress?"

His grin stretched, infuriatingly unrepentant. "Bathroom, beside the vanity. Right where you tossed it—dramatically, if I recall."

She started to leave, but his voice dropped, quieter now. "Those scars . . . below your collarbone. Gunshot wounds?"

She didn't answer, steadying her breath as she strode into the adjoining room.

The bathroom was cool, mercifully quiet. Her dress lay in a crumpled heap by the vanity.

She grabbed it, catching her reflection in the mirror. The scars—three neat, raised lines where the 9mm rounds had torn through her—stood stark against her skin.

She turned away, pulling the dress over her head, hiding them—and the memory of that alley—beneath the fabric. She rubbed at her smudged eyeliner, ran her fingers through her disheveled hair.

"Stay a little longer," Gibson called.

"Can't." She twisted her hair into a loose bun, already moving. "I've got a gallery to break into, your fake Rebrisi to stage, and a lesson with Herr Meyer-Edwards."

"You're posing as a student?" His tone softened in surprise.

She stepped out, eyes scanning for her bag. "It's not a cover. It's what I am."

He sat up, more alert now. "You must've been young when they recruited you."

Her answer came too fast. "Old enough."

Meant to ring like iron. Instead, the words wavered—brittle, unsteady.

Frustrated, she redirected. "Handbag?"

His grin returned—sharp, unapologetic. "Probably on the chaise," he said. "Where things got really out of hand before you dragged me in here." His eyes glinted. "Why don't we meet for dinner? Come back here. Revisit what happened over there." He chinned toward the rest of the apartment, his smirk impossible to ignore.

She sniffed. "Thought you were a one-night kind of guy."

"You're being evasive."

"Just calling it like I see it."

She slung the tote over her shoulder, spine straight—heart fluttering.

No time for regret. She still had two hundred grand to collect.

* * *

Antony stood on the wisteria-shrouded back patio of 112 Thomas Street. Light filtered through the trees lining the narrow yard, dappling the grass in shifting patterns. Birds flitted between overhanging boughs, chittering and restless, some alighting briefly on the hedged retaining wall or the sunlit tiles. Where the light struck the sandy conglomerate, it shimmered with the promise of late summer.

Bach was a no-show.

He checked his watch—*past eight.* A growl rumbled low in his throat as he retreated to the cool shadows of the kitchen.

He tapped out a terse message to Jack:

She's not coming. Better cancel Gibson.

Just as he hit send, a sharp knock rang out at the front door. Outside, the birds fell silent.

The knock came again—louder, more insistent. It echoed down the narrow hallway.

Antony leaned over the marble-topped island, thumbs flying:

Belay that.

A silhouette flickered behind the frosted sidelight—a small figure, poised and motionless.

He moistened his lips and rounded the island in a shuffle-jog. The floorboards groaned underfoot, an atonal countermelody to the tension prickling up his spine. Pausing at the mirror, he raked a hand through his hair and straightened his collar.

The third knock landed like a gavel.

Scowling, he threw the door open. "Finally, you show up—"

Instead of an exquisite blonde, Dr. Chin stood rigid on the top step. Her dirt-brown eyes were hard as flint, her brows drawn tight. The belt of her coat cinched her angular figure, severe and spare.

She gave him a once-over—cool, unfazed, calculating.

Antony blinked. Frustration pulsed beneath his skin. "My apologies," he said stiffly. "That was meant for someone else."

His phone buzzed. Jack's reply flashed and vanished.

Chin sniffed, her disdain palpable. "Poor girl," she rasped.

She bent to collect a case, the motion parting her coat to reveal a short skirt, dark stockings—and the unmistakable flash of a garter. Dropping the bag by the staircase, she swept inside like she owned the place.

Antony shut the door with force. "Yes. By all means. Do come in."

Dr. Chin strutted into the kitchen, her gaze sweeping the room with clinical precision. She paused on the walk-in pantry behind the island, tutting sharply before perching on one of the wooden barstools. Her coat hitched slightly, revealing more of her stockinged legs—and the garter. She pulled a prescription pad from her oversized bag and clicked her pen.

"Your lawyer said you need a certificate," she said, scribbling briskly. She tore the page free and handed it to him. "Give her this. Dr. Pasolini also called this morning. She wants an update on your rehab."

Antony barely glanced at the page, his focus elsewhere. "Forgive me. Can we do this another time?"

His phone buzzed again. A preview flashed:

> Canceling isn't an option. I need that manuscript. NOW.

Time was slipping through his fingers. The hearing was set for eleven. Jack was breathing down his neck. He had no bandwidth for a therapy session.

He dropped his gaze to his trembling hands.

"You're wound tighter than a cobra," Chin said, her voice dripping with smoky warmth. "I have something that can help you relax."

She rummaged in her bag and dropped a Ziplock of dark, crumpled leaves on the counter.

Antony recoiled. "I can't take that. I'm being drug tested."

"It's medicinal tea. An old Chinese remedy, handed down from mother to daughter over centuries." Her tone was low and silken. "Completely harmless. It'll quiet your thoughts. Settle your body."

He eyed the bag, doubtful. "This is supposed to calm me?"

She leaned closer, voice soft and conspiratorial. "Dr. Pasolini trusts me completely. She wants you to trust me, too. And she's expecting progress—progress I'll be reporting."

Her perfectly arched brow lifted. The implication was clear.

Another buzz:

> I've rescheduled. Meeting at twelve. En route to yours. Produce the manuscript or I'll go after your student myself.

Antony's jaw tightened. Jack was on the move. The clock was ticking. As usual, disaster was only a heartbeat away.

"Fine," he muttered, snatching the bag off the counter. "Let's make this quick."

Chapter Twenty-Seven

The sun hovered low on the horizon. Andre stepped out of Dahlia House, sliding on his new sunglasses. He flipped up his hood and took the steps two at a time, sneakers striking the pavement in a quick staccato—but the rhythm did nothing to calm his thoughts.

By the time he reached the street's end, he'd imagined every worst-case scenario—getting the call, going to the morgue, pulling back the thin blue sheet to reveal Annouie Bach's pallid, lifeless body.

Even in the morning warmth, a shiver ran through him. Was she still with Gibson? Heading to class? Asleep in that crumbling warehouse she called home?

Focus. She'd check in when ready—like a cat, on her own terms.

The harbor came into view—a frenzy of choppy, foam-tipped waves. He shoved the thoughts aside and picked up his pace.

Halfway to the intersection, the base of his neck prickled.

"You have a tail," Oria chirped in his ear.

"How far back?"

"A hundred feet. Male, six-two, bronze hair, navy suit. He's stopped to look in a window."

"You tapped his comms?"

"Of course."

A faint smirk tugged at his lips. "Any hits?"

"Nicholas Hope. Art Recovery."

Andre stumbled, pulse quickening. "The guy from last night?"

"He's operating under non-official cover—nothing formal, no badge, just watching."

His jaw tightened. "And you're sure it's him?"

"He's liaising with the Art Crime Division. Requesting expanded TECHINT protocols—digital surveillance, comms intercepts, predictive modelling. On you."

"Me?"

"Yes. Claims your consulting gig's a front. Says you're the architect behind Gibson's black-market operation."

A dry laugh escaped Andre. "Please. If I were running it, Art Recovery wouldn't even know it existed."

"The director seems to agree. Hope's request for additional assets was denied. He's been ordered to observe only—to avoid interfering with other jurisdictions. Specifically, DOJ operations."

Andre paused outside a Thai takeaway, his reflection warped in the glass.

"So, if he makes a move, it's off-book?"

"Correct," Oria replied, tone cool and detached. "He'd be disobeying a direct order."

A smile crept across Andre's face.

The door jingled as he stepped inside. The scent of spices and sizzling oil wrapped around him like a warm greeting. Conversation hummed. Plates clattered—

And behind his ribs, something sparked: anticipation, bright and sharp.

The morning rush was in full swing. The clang of plates from the kitchen clashed with the ding of the door and the rhythm of the cash register.

Andre joined the end of the line, his gaze flicking to the blackboard menu, then the intersection beyond the window. The lights cycled—red to green, then amber.

"Mr. Andre?"

A girl's voice pulled him back. Petite, Asian, her hands deftly loading pastries into a paper bag.

"Sorry, it took so long—it's busy this morning."

His mouth quirked. "Because you make the best pastries in town."

The bell jingled. Two more students squeezed into the line. She handed over the bag, her gaze flicking past his shoulder.

"No Mr. Paul today?"

His smile faltered. "Not today."

Her expression softened. "Too bad," she said, and turned to the next order.

Andre threaded his way through the crowded shop, the din fading as he entered the long corridor at the back. He followed its dogleg past the restrooms and slipped out the side door.

A gust of wind whipped along the alley, flinging the first drops of rain against his hood. Overhead, clouds churned. Pedestrians scrambled. Umbrellas snapped open.

He pressed on, a faint unease niggling at the back of his mind as he circled back to the main street. His lips tingled—a ghostly reminder of last night's kiss.

He shoved the memory aside. Paused at the corner. Counted.

Then right on schedule, Nicholas Hope burst through the shop door.

Even from a distance, the man's lack of composure was obvious—hair in his face, shoulders tense. The cool, professional façade was slipping.

Andre slid his phone from his pocket, tapping the screen and feigning immersion as he closed the distance. The traffic lights changed. Vehicles surged. A train clattered faintly in the distance.

Three. Two.

He collided with Hope.

"Watch where you're going!" he snapped, scowling. He stepped back—then, right on cue, he froze, his expression melting into wide-eyed surprise.

"As I live and breathe. Nicholas Hope?"

Hope blinked. "Andre?"

Andre pressed a hand to his cheek in mock astonishment. "My God, it *is* you!" He grazed his lips theatrically. "And to think—I was just thinking about you." He lifted the paper bag. "Have you had breakfast? These pastries are divine. I was going home to sulk." He rolled his eyes. "But since you're here, you should join me."

Hope's brows lifted sardonically. "To sulk?"

Andre snorted. "Of course not. Go grab us some coffees. I'll wait." He slouched against the bus shelter, already scrolling his phone.

Hope hesitated—then disappeared back inside.

Andre tapped his earpiece. "Is he sending messages?"

"Oh, yes," Oria replied. "He's in a panic."

Andre thumbed his screen. His last text remained unread. He frowned. Hit dial.

It rang twice, then kicked to voicemail.

"For God's sake, Annouie, would it kill you to pick up occasionally?" He pinched the bridge of his nose, exhaling. "When you get this, I'll be home. If not, let yourself in—but stay out of the OC. I've changed the password, so you won't have much choice."

He paused, then added, "If you *do* need to wander—but again, please don't—and somehow crack my password—which you *won't*—the updated Oria is ready. Just text me to say you're alive."

A beat.

"I don't trust Gibson. And we'll be discussing him—"

Another beat.

"When. You. Finally. Check. In."

His easy smile returned as Hope reappeared, a plastic bag in one hand.

"Let's go," Andre said, already walking. "I'm this way."

* * *

Andre stooped over the electronic keypad and tapped in his code. The lock clicked softly.

Beside him, Nicholas Hope shifted on the tiled landing—posture loose, feet shuffling—seemingly casual. But Andre caught the flick of his gaze: scanning the harbor, the street, the house. Clocking access points. Calculating escape routes.

He smothered a grin. He'd have done the same.

"Welcome to my humble abode," he said, pushing the door open.

Hope's eyes roved the wide hallway, pausing on the polished marble and ornate moldings—before drifting to the contents of the front reception room. Priceless paintings, sculptures and artifacts filled the space. Meticulously curated. Devoid of warmth. The room was a monument to his lonely childhood—a museum of neglect.

"This must be worth—" Hope began.

"Squillions," Andre cut in, derailing the question. "Kitchen's this way."

They passed through the living area where a massive modular lounge faced an oversized LCD panel. Tangled cords and gaming controllers littered the space. It was as if the front of the house belonged to someone else entirely.

A staircase took them to the subfloor.

The kitchen spanned the entire level, radiating sleek functionality. Warm wood cabinetry softened the sterility of poured concrete countertops. Narrow, monastic windows filtered in silvery light. The effect was modern, trendy—and deceptively welcoming.

A sideboard lined one wall. At the room's center, a large table stood set, as if waiting for guests.

Hope shrugged off his jacket and sank into one of the velvet chairs.

Andre retrieved a cutting board, arranged the pastries with meticulous care, and placed them on the table. Then he sat—calm expectation sliding into place like a well-worn mask.

Hope pulled the coffees from the plastic bag, slid one across to Andre, and cradled the other. He sipped—shoulders relaxing, eyes still sharp. Even now, he was casing the place.

Andre crossed one leg over the other and regarded him across the rim of his cup. "So, tell me," he said, pausing just long enough to let the tension bite, "do you honestly think I'd get into bed with Timothy Gibson?"

Coffee exploded from Hope's mouth, spraying his pristine white shirt.

"Christ!" he choked, grabbing a napkin. "Knew I'd been made."

Andre's lips curved into a grin.

Not the cool, calculating response he'd been expecting—

But it would do.

Chapter Twenty-Eight

Annouie perched on the gallery's parapet, her shadow beginning to shorten as the sun climbed higher. A faint vibration at her hip interrupted her thoughts. She slipped off the wall and retrieved her phone.

A text.

From Meyer-Edwards.

The message scrolled across the bottom of her Smart-contact lens.

Oria's voice purred through her earbud. "Do you wish to reply?"

"Later," Annouie murmured.

The rooftop stretched around her—minimal cover save for the rooftop fire exit. The security camera mounted above the door rotated back and forth—covering 120 degrees of arc, four seconds per pass, pausing briefly at each endpoint. Annouie dropped low, contemplating her approach.

Another ping.

A second message scrolled across the lens.

Oria spoke again, a hint of reproach in her tone. "Mr. Meyer-

Edwards is becoming agitated with your lack of response. Do you wish to—"

"Later," Annouie repeated, cutting the AI off.

She adjusted the strap of her pack and crept forward, angling toward the access point. Timing was everything. She tracked the camera's movement, then darted forward as the lens swept away.

At the door, she set her pack down and removed a compact, motorised pan-tilt device—a programmable gimbal—along with a burner phone. Powering on the phone, she mounted it to the gimbal and queued a seamless loop of footage showing an empty rooftop.

Carefully, she attached the gimbal's magnetic base just below the camera's line of sight. Using her primary phone, she synced the gimbal's pan speed and arc to mirror the camera's. The illusion would be flawless.

Satisfied, she turned her attention to the door.

The deadbolt was heavy-duty, but she was prepared. As the faint hum of the camera filled the air, she pulled out a tension wrench and a pair of picks. Kneeling, she inserted the wrench into the bottom of the keyhole and applied light, steady pressure. Too much, and the pins wouldn't set; too little, and it was wasted effort.

One by one, she teased the pins into place. A soft click signaled progress.

She increased the tension, turning the lock until it yielded with a faint metallic scrape. The door swung inward.

Annouie eased inside, pulling the door closed behind her.

The stairwell was dim, the air tinged with glue and paint thinner. She adjusted her earbud and descended the first flight, sneakers whispering over the dusty surface.

On the landing, she activated the 3D schematic overlay on her Smart-contacts. The dynamic map, updated in real-time via Oria's tap on the gallery's security systems, lit up in sharp detail. Six red dots moved on various floors; two remained in the ground-floor command center.

Her target: the Rose Chambers Room on the fourth floor. Oria's job: disable the motion, proximity, and infrared sensors before she arrived.

Hunkering beside a maintenance panel, Annouie withdrew a multi-tool. She unscrewed the bolts, catching each in her gloved hand. Panel off, she peered into the dark recess.

A narrow passage led into the ceiling's cavity. She snugged her pack to her back and hoisted herself inside.

The crawlspace opened into a lattice of catwalks and ladders above the gallery. Emergency lights bathed the void in an eerie red.

At 8:40, the sensors in the Rose Chambers Room went dark.

One red dot lingered outside the doors—a guard nearing the end of his patrol. Annouie climbed a ladder, feet precise and silent, as his radio crackled to life.

"Control for Unit Three."

"Go for Control."

"Gibson inbound. ETA five mikes. Report to the main entrance for escort."

"Copy. En route."

The red dot moved. She waited. When his footfalls could no longer be heard, she moved.

Across the catwalk, quick and quiet. She secured a grappling hook to a steel beam, gave the line two firm tugs, and dropped—descending hand-over-hand into the room below.

She landed with a soft thud. Detached the hook.

Sliding her bag off her back, she crossed to the vandalised frame. From her belt, she unclipped a penknife and began stripping away the damaged remnants of canvas. Staples hit the bin with metallic pings.

Frame bare, she stretched the replacement canvas taut. The staple gun emerged. She winced at each snap as she fired staples into the frame.

Once done, she rehung the piece.

And paused.

Those luminous colours. The transparency of the layers. The small imperfection in the upper right corner.

Even she had to admit—hiding the original Rebrisi *Venus* in plain sight was inspired.

Her HUD flashed: the red spot was returning.

She reattached the grappling line and hauled herself back up just as the doors jerked open.

The guard stepped inside, flashlight slicing the shadows. He swept the room, stopping in front of the painting.

"No. Nothing to report," he said into his radio. "Must be noise from next door's renovations."

He turned. Paused. "Hang on."

He stepped closer, eyes narrowing.

"Control, this is Three," he said. "The painting's back."

"Say again?"

"The *Venus*. It's back on the wall."

A pause before Control's voice returned.

"Hold your position. Gibson's here."

Annouie froze, muscles coiled tight.

The radio crackled. "Stand down. Gibson's confirmed its return. Nice of him to let us know."

"Copy that."

"Shall I proceed to reception?"

"Negative. Stay put. Gibson's on his way up. Meet him at the elevator."

Three lingered, staring at the *Venus* like it might speak. Then, finally, he turned and left.

Annouie exhaled slowly. Her HUD flashed again—more texts.

Could wait no longer. Back soon. Study those books. Quiz moved forward.

Failure to answer all questions correctly = F.

Failure to show up = F.

Failure to reply to my texts again = F.

She bit back a curse, crawling through the rigging toward the exit.

She might've smoked too much weed, slept with the enemy, and helped a con-artist—but there was one thing she would not let happen today:

That arrogant prick was *not* failing her.

No. He wouldn't—

Adrenaline surged as she tore through the passageways.

Because—somehow—she was going to beat him at his own game.

* * *

Antony flung the tie around his neck, his thoughts tangling in frustration as he strode from the bathroom. Bach thought she could ghost him?

He straightened his cuffs, irritation simmering beneath his groomed exterior. Now wasn't the time to address her insolence—

Later.

When he had the upper hand.

When he had time to make her squirm. *Really* squirm.

He tapped at his phone, fingers flying:

Going to be late.

With a swipe, the message vanished into the ether. He only hoped Shari was as good as she claimed.

Her reply came almost instantly:

How late?

He exhaled sharply, thumbs hammering:

Stall until I arrive.

Phone and wallet disappeared into his back pocket. Jacket—grabbed. He bolted down the internal staircase of 112 Thomas Street, knotting his tie one-handed. The front door slammed behind him, its heavy bang cutting through the quiet street.

No time to waste.

He vaulted the iron fence and sprinted uphill, weaving through the early-morning shadows.

* * *

Barely half an hour later, Annouie stood at the foot of Andre's driveway, cold morning air biting at her skin. She gazed up at the house, running through the next steps of her plan—

Get the manuscript. Go to Thomas Street. Cheat my way through Meyer-Edwards's test.

She climbed the stone steps and knocked. Silence. Her gaze shifted to the keypad beside the door. Brushing her fingers across the keys, she felt for the telltale sheen of wear, the faint residue from repeated use. Guessing the right combination took seconds. With a soft click, the lock disengaged, and the door swung open.

"Good morning, Ms. Bach."

Annouie nearly dropped her phone, catching it midair as her pulse spiked. "Shit."

"Please repeat the request," lisped a disembodied voice from a speaker above the door.

"Oria?"

"Actually, I am Oria3—a new and improved version of my former self," the voice replied, oozing smugness. "And you are Annouie Bach, friend and work colleague."

Annouie exhaled sharply, slipping her phone into her pocket. "Where's Andre?"

"In the kitchen with Nicholas Hope from the Art Crimes Division," Oria replied cheerfully.

Annouie blinked. "With *who*?"

"Agent Nicholas Hope."

Agent? The word hung in the air. "Andre's being investigated?"

"Agent Hope believes Andre assisted Timothy Gibson in the Gartner Haus heist two years ago. He was attempting to gather intelligence; however, Andre jumped him in the street."

A familiar unease prickled at the base of Annouie's skull. Typical Andre. Always dancing on the edge of legality.

"Is Hope right?"

"No. Andre had nothing to do with that heist."

Below, a cupboard door slammed. Metal clattered against porcelain.

"I despise the man," Andre's indignant voice floated up the stairwell. "It'll be a cold day in hell before I work for him in any capacity."

A sharper, unfamiliar voice answered. "Then why were you at the preview?"

"Andre left instructions for you to wait in the front room," Oria said, cutting over the voices below.

Annouie lingered, tempted to eavesdrop, but the persistent buzz of her phone snapped her back to the present. Meyer-Edwards was getting antsy.

She crept up the second flight of stairs, her steps silent on the carpeted treads, and hurried to the Kevlar-reinforced ballistic door at the end of the hall.

Just as she reached for the keypad, Oria's voice filled the hallway. "I've informed Andre of your arrival. He said not to let you into the OC. He'll meet you in the front reception room as soon as he's done with Agent Hope. Please return now."

"Sure," Annouie muttered, punching in Andre's passcode. Access denied. A surprised huff escaped her.

He'd actually changed it.

Stooping, she keyed in a few alternate combinations until the lock disengaged with a satisfying *thunk*. The door whirred open.

She grinned: Andre was such a creature of habit.

Inside, the dimly lit room was a mix of shifting light, cooling fans, blinking drives, and soft alerts. The manuscript lay exactly where she'd left it. She padded across the smooth floorboards and perched on the desk.

Beside Andre's keyboard sat the new Oria3 prototype—sleeker, more streamlined than its predecessor. She slipped them on, the device settling snugly over her ears, and spread the manuscript across her lap.

The dense pages brimmed with diagrams, technical notes, and detailed explanations—but it was the spidery handwriting in the margins that caught her eye.

Frowning, she leaned in, squinting at the illegible scrawl.

"Oria," she murmured, "can you read this back?"

Oria's voice purred. "'After the key reaches the bed, the hand's downward motion must be stopped. There is a brief application of force to the finger. This force must be removed immediately to attain complete relaxation.'"

Annouie flipped to the next page. Oria resumed reading.

"Just the heads-up," Annouie interrupted.

The room fell quiet as Oria projected the translated text onto her retina.

Rebrisi's insights were extraordinary. Every paragraph revealed techniques that bridged art and science. Page after page, she sank deeper, totally engrossed as time slipped away.

Her phone buzzed.

"You have an incoming call," Oria said.

"Ignore it."

"It's Antony Meyer-Edwards."

Her brow furrowed. "Definitely ignore it."

Moments later, her phone quivered again.

"A text?" she asked.

"He's trying to get your attention," Oria responded gleefully. "Single sentence. 'Where the fuck are you?' Shall I reply?"

Annouie sighed. "Sure. Tell him I'm running late—I'll be there in thirty."

As Oria fell silent, Annouie studied the manuscript. "Oria, do you have access to *The Art of Playing the Piano*?"

"Of course."

"What about CPE's treatise *On the True Art of Playing Keyboard Instruments*?"

"Absolutely."

Annouie slid the manuscript into her tote, grinning as the shape of her plan snapped into focus. She slipped off the desk and stepped into the hallway.

Stairs groaned below. Voices floated up the stairwell.

"You could've just asked—without all the games," Andre's voice echoed.

"I wanted to be sure," Hope replied, smooth as polished glass.

Annouie edged closer to the banister and peered down. The moment she saw Hope, her breath hitched. Bronze hair. Chiseled features. The cool, clinical poise.

The man from the gallery. The one with the gun.

"You're a known black hat," Hope said, tone measured.

Andre, unbothered, pulled his phone. "*Former* black hat," he corrected, dialing.

Annouie's phone began to buzz. She declined the call with a swipe, pulse quickening.

Andre peered into the front room, brows knitting. "Of course. When does she ever do what I ask?" he muttered, bounding for the stairs.

Hope followed, eyes scanning his surroundings like a hunter.

But by the time they reached the second staircase, Annouie was already slipping over the balcony railing, shimmying down the trellis. The rough wood snagged her shirt, but she didn't stop. Her sneakers hit the garden bed below with a thud.

At the end of the drive, she glanced back. No one was in sight.

She shoved the manuscript deeper into her bag and bolted for the street corner, heartbeat steady despite the adrenaline coursing through her veins.

But as she rounded it, the image of Hope's face returned—calm, sharp, predatory.

An agent with his own deadly agenda—if the gun was anything to go by.

And now, he had entered Andre's orbit.

Chapter Twenty-Nine

Nicholas frowned as Landvik tapped his password, fingers flying with practiced ease.

The lock clicked. Landvik straightened and pushed the heavy door open. "Brace yourself. This is more than an office setup."

Four of Nicholas's five senses were hit at once—flashing LEDs, the acrid tang of overheated solder joints, glue and scorched plastic, stifling heat, and a cacophony of chirps and squeaks.

He followed Landvik into the room, eyes scanning the chaos: the server racks humming against the wall, conduit strung haphazardly above picture rails, tangled wiring coiling like vines, the LED monitors blinking across a wide console. Beyond it all, the floor-to-ceiling windows offered an uninterrupted view of the harbor.

Landvik dropped his messenger bag on the table and eased into a high-backed executive chair behind the sprawling workstation. He gestured broadly, palms up.

"Welcome to my operations center—where I engage exclusively in ethical hacking for my clients. You're welcome to audit my logs, my client list, anything that'll convince you I had nothing to do with the Gartner Haus heist."

Nicholas pulled up a nearby stool and lowered himself onto it. His pulse ticked just above sixty. Slightly elevated. He focused on his breathing—slow inhale, measured exhale.

What came next had to be precise.

No wasted words.

"Putting you under surveillance was a ruse."

Landvik's brow arched, a flicker of surprise cracking his cool exterior.

Nicholas placed both hands on the desk and leaned in. "Truth is—I want to hire you."

Landvik blinked. "Come again?"

"I never knew my father," Nicholas said, voice low. "Not even his name. My mother took that to the grave. All she ever told me was that he shipped out to the Middle East."

Landvik's skepticism wavered, curiosity beginning to surface.

Nicholas pressed on, the edge of something raw—something real—creeping into his voice. "You built an AI that can find patterns in chaos. It can sift through the noise, mine meaning, draw lines no human can. It can process every piece of data ever generated and extrapolate, interpolate—postulate."

He hesitated—just for a beat.

"Please, I need to know what happened to him."

* * *

The H175 Airbus throttled back, its twin engines winding down as it swept low over the city. Below, Emil spotted the squat, four-story police station wedged into the dense urban grid. Four blocks away, the helipad atop the medical examiner's building slid into view.

The pilot flared the aircraft expertly, aligning the skids with the center of the pad. With a subtle dip of the collective control, the chopper settled onto the tarmac.

Rotor wash buffeted him as he climbed out, the noise deafening but familiar. He crouched instinctively, moving quickly across the helipad toward the access door, where a staffer waved him inside.

In the elevator, Emil tugged at his jacket, smoothing its creases. His reflection stared back from the polished doors—grim, determined. The car descended, and his thoughts fell into a rhythm.

Review the findings. Confirm the cause of death. Draft the press release. That should do it.

The doors parted on the second floor. He detoured via the staff lounge for his second coffee of the day, the bitter heat steadying him as he pushed through the double doors of the autopsy suite.

Usman was already waiting, clutching his clipboard like a shield.

Moments later, the technicians wheeled in a flatbed. The shrouded body lay motionless beneath a blue sheet.

A faint flicker of excitement lit Emil's otherwise impassive face. He sipped his coffee, standing back as the body was transferred to the autopsy table.

Usman and his assistant bustled, rolling in carts stacked with dissecting kits, CT and MRI scanners, microscopes, gas spectrometers. Under the surgical lights, scalpels and forceps gleamed; high-resolution binocular loupes stood ready.

Emil drained his mug, rolled his lips together, and strode into the washroom. As he scrubbed his hands, his thoughts drifted to the press conference ahead. The media would be ravenous. But for now, his focus was here.

He dried his hands meticulously, then suited up—impervious gown, double gloves, surgical cap, face shield.

Ready, he stepped back into the suite and approached the table.

"Let's begin."

Usman pulled back the sheet and adjusted the light. Discoloration around the nail beds. Evidence of prolonged decomposition. The body's preservation was remarkable, but molecular breakdown tests would narrow the time of death.

Emil examined the chest for the expected signs of trauma—the entry wound of a .30 hunting round.

But the skin was smooth. Intact.

His breath caught.

He tilted the skull gently, already suspecting what he would find. Two small entry wounds punctured the occipital bone. Stippling confirmed it—9 mm rounds, fired at close range. No exit wounds.

Emil stepped back, peeling off his gloves with a snap.

His lips trembled.

Daniel had lied.

He stumbled into the glass-fronted office adjoining the suite, slammed the door, and yanked the blinds shut. Collapsing into the chair behind the desk, he snatched out his phone, hands slick with sweat as he dialed.

No answer.

Just the voicemail beep.

He leaned in, his voice a rasp.

"It's Emil. I've run initial tests on the body from Wilkins Beach." He mopped his brow, breath ragged. "You told me it was a hunting accident."

A pause. His eyes scanned the office.

"It's murder, Daniel. And you know it. There's no way I can cover this up."

He ended the call, staring at the screen in disbelief.

The room felt smaller. Airless. The truth pressing in from all sides.

Nearly twenty-five years ago, he and his best friend had buried the real Sir James Gibson beneath a tree in a remote clearing.

Now, a freak storm had unearthed it—dragging up the corpse, the lies, and the fraud they'd buried.

The world would soon learn the truth: Sir James Gibson was an impostor. The man using his name was Daniel Parrish, a low-level thug hired to kill him.

The timing was too diabolical to be chance. It was the sort of thing only God could orchestrate with such devastating precision.

Sweat slicked the back of Emil's neck. He traced a cross over his forehead, heart, stomach, and shoulders—a ritual he hadn't performed in years.

The truth was coming.

Unstoppable.

Cold.

But not today.

He turned to his keyboard, fingers flying.

Each word of the press release was carefully measured, each phrase a veiled lie. If he was lucky, it might buy them a few more days.

* * *

In the adjoining office, Dr. Usman Malik scowled at the closed blinds separating him from Emil.

A sharp ping from his computer cut through the silence. He leaned forward, pulse quickening as he nudged the mouse, the alert expanding onto his screen.

He gasped.

The results were there—clear, irrefutable. He read them twice, his eyes widening with every line.

Then he stood, peeling off his gloves and protective eyewear, discarding them on his workstation without ceremony. He yanked off his surgical cap and stuffed it into his pocket as he strode from the office, through the suite, past the gleaming tools and the quiet hum of machines.

He didn't slow.

At the far end of the floor, away from prying eyes and ears, Usman slipped his phone from his coat and dialed the number etched into memory.

Hope's.

The call rang once, then dropped to voicemail—unsurprising. Men like Hope rarely picked up. But unlike Emil, Usman didn't hang up. He waited for the final beep, patient, hopeful.

For the first time in years, the leverage was his.

The pieces were falling into place—and this time, no one was going to steal his moment from him.

As the beep faded, he lifted the phone to his lips, voice dropping to a conspiratorial murmur.

"This is Dr. Malik. I have big news for you—about the John Doe recovered from Wilkins Beach."

He paused, letting the silence settle like a stone dropped in still water.

His eyes drifted toward the autopsy suite. Then—

"His name is Sir James Gibson."

Chapter Thirty

Traffic on the bridge was at a standstill. Antony checked his watch, then craned his neck toward the bus window. Nothing moved. Accident? Roadworks? Didn't matter—he couldn't afford to wait.

He sprang from his seat and shouldered his way to the doors, ignoring the irritated glances. He jabbed the stop button. The doors hissed open, and he stepped onto the pavement, steam rising through the soles of his shoes.

Another glance at his watch. Shari had managed to adjourn the hearing for an hour, but the judge wouldn't tolerate another delay.

Antony broke into a run, weaving through the pedestrian crush.

By the time he staggered through the iron gates of the Courts of Justice, his lungs burned, and his tie hung askew. He yanked it straight, smoothed his jacket, and ran a hand through his damp hair as he approached the Gothic façade.

Reporters swarmed the courtyard. Cameras swung in his direction.

"Mr. Meyer-Edwards! Any comment on the allegations in Ms. Miles's article?"

Antony kept moving, jaw set. A microphone was thrust into his face. The reporters didn't care whether he spoke or not; they were here to spin their narrative, regardless. Snippets floated through the din:

". . . a close-lipped Mr. Meyer-Edwards arrived at court this morning . . ."

". . . sources confirm a witness was taken in for questioning . . ."

". . . with Ms. Miles's tragic death, what other secrets might he be hiding . . ."

He pushed through the arched doorway into the cool interior. Long lines stretched from the security checkpoints.

Suppressing a groan, he joined the shortest, emptying his pockets into a plastic tray: phone, keys, wallet. The tray disappeared into the machine. As he stepped through the scanner, a sharp shriek rang out.

"Step aside, sir," a guard said.

Antony raised his arms. A handheld wand skimmed over him. No further alarms.

"You're good to go," the guard said.

He snatched up his belongings and rushed into the great hall.

The space hummed—solicitors in tailored suits rolled carry-ons behind them, murmuring to clients, junior associates, and police officers. Antony made for the elevators at the rear, heart pounding.

Two plainclothes officers leaned against the wall nearby, badges visible. Casual posture. Sharp eyes. One of them—sandy-haired, flat, cold stare—locked onto him instantly.

DCI Greg Dunbier. Relentless. Sharp. Desperate for a break in the Ripper case.

Antony didn't miss the flicker of recognition—the hard, appraising glare.

"Mr. Meyer-Edwards," he said.

Antony dropped his gaze to his phone and moved to the opposite side of the elevator.

The doors opened. The crowd surged in.

Dunbier followed, positioning himself too close.

"Quite a splash you've made in the headlines this morning," he growled, breath warm against the base of Antony's neck

Antony stared at the floor numbers, jaw clenched.

A buzz sounded. Dunbier shifted, pulling out his phone.

"Dunbier," he answered, voice crisp.

Antony resisted the urge to step away.

"Just arrived," Dunbier said. "Should be a formality—judge signs off, we hit the location." A beat. "Recall Ratcliffe. If she pushes back, tell her I want her in the room with him."

At the second floor, most passengers disembarked. Only Antony and the two officers remained. His grip tightened around his phone.

At the third floor, a clerk stepped in, breaking the tension. Antony exhaled, but his posture remained taut as the elevator resumed its climb.

By the time they reached the fourth floor, sweat soaked his undershirt.

"Excuse me," he muttered, squeezing past the clerk.

He strode down the corridor, pace quickening.

The floor was a maze: courtrooms, interview rooms, chambers, offices, long tables, bathrooms, and a line of benches against the wall, most of them occupied. He scanned each door, looking for Courtroom 4.

At the end of the hall, a pinboard displayed a list of hearings. He strode up to it, eyes scanning until he found it.

Meyer-Edwards v. State—10:00 a.m.

"Antony!"

He whirled. A small woman dropped a lever-arch file onto a table with a thud. Dark-skinned. Bespectacled. Navy suit. Starched blouse.

Shari Vanamali.

"I've got some documents for you to sign," she said, pulling papers from a plastic sleeve. Fluorescent sticky notes jutted from the margins like battlefield flags. She tapped a page with her pen. "This confirms you agree to their terms. Sign here."

Antony stepped up, tension riding his spine. "And this won't be recorded as a conviction?" he asked, taking the pen.

"As long as you stick to the conditions."

He hesitated. "Fine. If this makes it all go away, I'll stick to anything." He signed, then handed back the pen.

Shari tucked the pages back into the sleeve. "Excellent. I'll pass this to the prosecution. With any luck, it'll go before the judge today."

"And that's it? No more court appearances?"

She paused. "If the judge decides it's the best course."

Antony's jaw tensed. "*If?*"

Shari opened her mouth, but a voice cut through the corridor.

"In the matter of the State versus Antony Meyer-Edwards."

Antony turned toward the courtroom door. An attendant stood in the doorway, clipboard in hand.

His pulse spiked. He looked back at Shari. She squeezed his arm.

"Don't worry," she said, not quite meeting his eyes. "This is all going to be *absolutely* fine."

* * *

At first glance, the village of Lomanville looked like a relic from a bygone era the modern world had quietly abandoned.

Katrine grimaced and set her third cup of burnt general store coffee on the cruiser's dashboard. Through the windshield, she eyed Dr. Addison's home—a three-story brick building with ivy creeping up its walls.

Beside her, Saunders snored softly.

She gave him a sharp nudge. "Wake up."

He jolted upright, blinking like a startled rabbit. "Huh? What?"

"We're here."

Saunders squinted out the window. "Where's here?"

"Addison's."

Katrine slid on her sunglasses and stepped out into the crisp morning air. As Saunders yawned and stretched, she pulled out her phone and dialed. Predictably, the call kicked to voicemail.

She pinched the bridge of her nose as the automated message droned on, then exhaled sharply at the beep.

"Annouie. I know it's early, but would it kill you to pick up once in a while?" A pause. She softened her tone. "Look, something came up. I hate doing this—but I can't make breakfast."

She ended the call with a frustrated jab at the screen and shoved the phone into her jacket pocket.

Annouie had always had a rebellious streak, but since returning from Frankfurt—

Something was off.

Katrine joined Saunders on the garden path. The navy-blue door creaked open at their knock, revealing a round-faced man in a cardigan and wire-rimmed glasses.

"Dr. Addison?" Katrine flipped open her badge. "Bayside Police. We spoke earlier on the phone about a cold case."

Addison blinked slowly and adjusted his glasses. "Ah, yes. Peter Darby. Come in."

He led them into a wood-paneled office and settled into a leather chair behind an oversized desk. Turning to the computer, he began typing with slow, deliberate keystrokes.

"My memory's not what it used to be," he said, "but I kept detailed notes. My receptionist digitized everything—she's better with computers than I am." He tapped the screen. "Should be here somewhere."

"Mind if I take a look?"

Addison shifted aside, and Katrine slid into the chair, fingers flying over the keyboard.

"I kept diaries for every year I worked at the hospital," he said. "Would've been twenty years ago, the night Child Services brought young Darby in." He pointed. "Try that folder."

She opened it and began to scroll.

"There was a rumor he ran off to the coast, looking for his real mother," Addison added, rubbing his chin.

"Her name?"

"Should be in the file."

Katrine's eyes locked on the screen. "Here. Maeve Darby." She scribbled the name into her notebook and clicked on an attached photo. A striking woman appeared—amber eyes, hair the color of burnished gold.

"She was institutionalized," Addison said. "Severe psychotic break. Claimed Peter's father wasn't really his father—insisted he was some sort of impostor."

Katrine exhaled. "Says here she died six months after Peter disappeared."

Addison nodded. "Overdose."

Katrine paused, pen hovering. "And Peter was taken into care?"

Addison's expression darkened. "His foster carer, Mrs. Banks, had a reputation for cruelty. There weren't many options. The placement was supposed to be temporary."

"And Mrs. Banks—she's the one who was murdered?"

His lips thinned. "Brutally."

Katrine scrolled further, her pulse ticking up. Nothing on Peter Darby after the murder. The trail ended there. She closed the folder.

"You wouldn't happen to know where he went next?"

Addison's gaze drifted. For a moment, he seemed lost in thought. Then his eyes cleared.

"They placed him with Deirdre Jones."

Katrine straightened. "Does she live locally?"

He nodded. "About a half-hour from here."

* * *

As Katrine and Saunders exited the house, a low buzz issued from his pocket. He pulled out his phone and pressed it to his ear.

"Saunders here." His voice cut through the quiet as they descended the winding garden path.

"We were about to follow up on a lead," he said, his tone shifting as he listened. "Roger that. I'll let her know."

He snapped the phone shut, jaw tight. "Chief wants us back at HQ. ASAP. Cyber's about to pull in Shiruku. He wants you there for the interview."

Katrine muttered a curse. "And Mrs. Jones?"

Saunders shrugged. "Orders."

She spun on her heel, fists clenched. "Did he actually say 'ASAP'?"

He nodded.

She kicked a loose rock, sending it skittering across the pavement. Without another word, she stalked to the cruiser, yanked open the door, and climbed in, gripping the steering wheel until her knuckles turned white.

Shiruku was an invaluable source. Dunbier was making a big mistake.

For a long moment, she stared through the windshield, thoughts spiraling.

Then, with a sharp intake of breath, she rammed the keys into the ignition and gunned the engine. The cruiser roared to life.

She threw the car into reverse, tires squealing. It lurched backward. A hard shift to drive. Foot to the floor. The cruiser leapt forward.

Gravel sprayed behind them as she tore toward the village limits.

Orders were orders. But loyalty mattered too. Somehow, she had to find a way to keep her promise to Shiruku—and make damn sure it didn't cost her the case.

Chapter Thirty-One

"You said it was a mere formality!"

Antony Meyer-Edwards slumped against the back of the elevator as the doors bumped shut and the car began its descent to the ground floor of the Courts of Justice.

Shari shifted beside him, her grip tightening on the handle of her wheeled briefcase. "In all fairness, I didn't know about the Sara Miles article."

Antony's head snapped up. His voice sharpened. "Yes. About that. How the hell does a dead woman drop an exposé on the exact day of my hearing?"

The one he'd carefully deleted.

Shari clicked her tongue. "Come on, Antony. Breathe. It's not all bad."

"Isn't it? This was supposed to go away. You heard the judge—he's making an example of me because of that article. It's everywhere. Have you heard what they're saying? Organized crime. Murder. Espionage. Wait until Judith gets wind of it." He tugged at his hair, voice dipping to a whisper. "I'm finished."

"Don't be so melodramatic," Shari said, tone crisp. "Beg her for a second chance."

"This was my second chance."

She shrugged. "Still better than doing time, isn't it?"

Antony paled. "Didn't you hear him? He's making an example of me. What makes you think he won't put me behind bars?"

Another shrug. Cool. Unbothered. "That's highly unlikely."

The elevator shuddered to a halt. The floor indicator dinged. The doors slid open onto a bustling lobby.

Antony stepped out first, scanning the space. "Where's the exit?"

A few lawyers glanced up. A security officer frowned. Noise was building at the far end.

Shari hustled after him, her briefcase clattering over the tiles.

The background hubbub swelled.

Antony froze. His gaze snapped to the arched wooden doors. Beyond them, a rising cacophony: questions, shouted names, phones held aloft, a mob pressing forward.

"Perhaps we should take the back exit," Shari said, tugging at his sleeve.

He shook her off. "What the hell is going on out there?"

Before she could stop him, he stepped forward—and the doors burst open.

"There he is!" someone shouted, pointing straight at him.

"Oh, God!" Antony turned and ran.

The reporters surged after him, voices echoing through the hall.

"Where did you say that back door was?" he called, grabbing Shari's arm and dragging her with him.

Shari pointed, breathless. "This way!"

"So this isn't all bad?" he snapped as they sprinted down the corridor.

"No. Trust me," she shot back, heels clacking, briefcase jerking behind her. "This is nothing compared to what I usually deal with."

They tore past the courtroom café, scrambled up a narrow flight of stairs, veered left—and burst through the back exit, gasping.

* * *

Outside, the grandeur of the Courts of Justice loomed even from the rear. Sandstone columns and high-relief carvings framed the walled-off courtyard, a stark contrast to the grimy alley beyond the iron gates.

Antony and Shari rushed through, her briefcase rattling over the uneven path. Once clear, she came to a stop, breath rasping. She flicked a stray strand of hair from her face and pressed her phone to her ear.

Pacing in tight circles, she spoke in hushed tones. Then slid the phone away.

"Judith is sending a car. It'll be here in a few minutes."

Antony's brow creased. "I don't like the sound of that."

Shari extended her hand—suddenly all business, the urgency gone from her voice. "Well, Mr. Meyer-Edwards, I wish you luck with the next step."

He blinked. "I'm being fired?"

She drew a slow breath. "No. But this is where we part ways."

His throat dried. "I *am* being fired."

Shari's voice softened. "All I can say is there's more in play than meets the eye. The partners feel—that with the media focus on the Sara Miles article—you'll need someone more . . . qualified."

His voice grew wary. "Define 'qualified'?"

Shari shook her head. "More qualified than me."

A sleek gray Mercedes EQS glided to a stop outside the gates.

"This must be her," Shari said, nodding toward the car.

The driver stepped onto the road, circled around, and opened the back. Someone was already inside.

"Mr. Edwards?"

Antony hesitated, cast a final glance at Shari, then strode toward the car.

"It's Meyer-Edwards," he muttered as he slid in. The leather groaned beneath him.

Across from him, a lanky man with curly brown hair turned and gave a sheepish grin. "Surprise." He held up his hands. "Now, before you start yelling, just hear me out—

"Mackie," Antony growled.

Then lunged.

His fist smashed into Mackie's nose with a wet thud. Blood spurted. Mackie's head slammed back against the headrest.

Groaning, he clutched his face. "Stop being so emotional. Put your fists away," he mumbled through the blood. "We just got a ping on Rebrisi's *Third Element*—and you're the only one who can go after it."

* * *

Annouie sifted through a thousand plausible excuses as she marched uphill toward 112 Thomas Street. So she was late? Meyer-Edwards had given her next to no notice after telling her to "take her time". What kind of mixed message was that? And quizzing her without a moment to prep?

He had a nerve.

She halted on the footpath and looked up at the house. It loomed in the midday heat, shabby and still. Bracing herself, she stepped over the low fence.

In the distance, traffic rumbled along the main road, the low thrum vibrating through her shoes. She rapped on the weathered door, knuckles brushing cracked paint.

Silence.

She stepped back, scanning the façade.

Bees droned lazily around the stone cat tucked in the weeds below the veranda.

Crouching, she felt beneath the sculpture, fingers skimming its base. No key.

She exhaled, pulled her lock-pick set from her bag, and knelt at the door. The L-rake slid into the keyhole. A scrape, some rocking, a twitch. The pins settled, and the door clicked open.

She eased across the sill. "Mr. Meyer-Edwards?"

Her voice echoed up the stairs and down the hall.

Nothing. No creaking springs. No groans. Or the impatient clicking of his shoes. Just the tired bones of the house settling into their foundations.

She shut the door behind her, dropping her bag by the reception room.

She tapped her earpiece. "Oria." A faint whir tickled her ear as the AI awakened.

She stepped into the front room and froze.

Overturned drawers. Papers strewn across every surface. Books lying haphazardly on the floor. The place looked like it'd been hit by a tornado.

It would take hours—days—to sift through this mess.

Annouie sank onto the lowest rung of the library ladder and tapped her earpiece.

"Oria, I'm looking for an envelope. From Italy. Might have the Accademia's address on it."

The AI scanned the room in rapid bursts.

Annouie moved quickly, sifting through the detritus of bills, notices, old letters. No blips. No pings.

And no envelope.

She exhaled sharply. Think.

If I were Meyer-Edwards . . .

Her gaze lifted.

Smiling, she climbed the ladder. Nestled between two oversized volumes sat an A4 envelope. She tugged it free. On the back: *Accademia Nazionale di Santa Cecilia.*

Heart ticking faster, she scrambled down and settled on the floor. Anderson had pulled her off the manuscript for this?

She shook the contents loose: photos, letters, a folded page.

Unfolding it, she scanned it.

A will.

But most surprising—Aguirre had left everything to Meyer-

Edwards.

Annouie scoffed. Impossible. The emotionally distant maestro had never shown affection. Not for anyone.

Something didn't add up.

She leafed through the photographs—most of Meyer-Edwards. Laughing. Smiling. Toasting friends in sunlit cafés.

Not the man she knew.

She set them aside and skimmed the clippings. Awards. Reviews. Then—a headline: *Music student killed in road accident.*

Sophie Muxlow.

Something twisted in her gut. Curiosity went to war with her conscience—a surprisingly short struggle—before she pushed the article aside.

She calmed her thoughts, gaze drifting. Then she saw it. A staff photo. Aguirre sat beside Meyer-Edwards—young, bright-eyed—one arm draped around his protégé. The other—around another man, lanky, curly-haired, too-wide smile.

A note was tucked behind it. Slanted scrawl.

To the best of us. It has been an utter joy to watch the pair of you grow into the caring, generous men you've become.

A shadow flitted past the front window. Roof rivets strained. A footstep landed on the veranda.

Annouie's pulse spiked.

She shoved the photo and note into the envelope and rose.

A knock echoed through the foyer.

Bag slung over her chest, she darted for the staircase, taking the steps two at a time. The master bedroom loomed ahead.

Clothes littered the floor. Drawers hung open. An empty Scotch bottle lay tipped on the bedside table.

And before her—an oversized window, overlooking the neighbor's roof.

From below: "Tony? Are you here?"

The voice was low, slightly rough—uncannily close to Meyer-Edwards's voice.

"Jesus, Tony, you better not be sleeping."

Annouie bolted the door. Jammed a chair under the handle. Not a perfect barrier—but it would buy a few seconds.

She pried the window open. The frame shrieked. Paint flaked.

She leaned out.

Tiled roof. Not ideal.

Footsteps creaked on the landing. Rattling at the door. "Tony! Don't be an ass. Open up."

Buzz.

She glanced at her phone.

> I'm in Judith's office, pleading your case. Messier's filed a complaint. Show cause hearing at 4:00. If you do nothing else today, be there. Both our futures depend on it.

Her jaw tensed. Perfect timing. She fired a message to Anderson:

> Envelope acquired. Meeting you at Dorset tonight—but only if you call Judith Pasolini and fix this hearing nonsense.

The door began to splinter.

Annouie sprang onto the sill, hands gripping the frame. The tiles shimmered in the heat.

Buzz.

> What hearing nonsense?

She jabbed at her phone:

> Work it out. I'm about to jump out a window.

Send.

The door exploded inward.

* * *

Jack Vallone stumbled into the room, gaze locking on the figure halfway out the bedroom window. He lunged, hand out.

"Got you!"

His fingers closed around the end of her ponytail. He yanked hard.

They crashed to the floor in a heap. Jack rolled clear and scrambled upright, ready to pin her.

Too late.

She rocked back onto her shoulders and snapped upright like a coiled spring.

"What the—"

She turned and bolted, monkey-vaulting through the window. She landed on the roof like a cat—sure-footed, fluid—barely breaking stride.

She raced across the roof.

Jack rushed to the window.

Gone.

He leaned out just in time to catch a flash of her dark-blonde ponytail vanishing over the edge.

"Well, I'll be damned!" he muttered.

He pulled back from the sill, sweeping the room with a practiced eye. To anyone else, it would've looked like a break-in. Clothes everywhere. Drawers half-open. A mess.

Jack knew better.

He crossed to the bedside table, pulled open the drawer. Socks. Lighters. Antony's Rolex. Still there. Credit cards, too. And—a thick wad of hundreds.

All untouched.

His frown deepened as he headed downstairs. Whoever she was, she hadn't come for the cash—or anything obvious.

The front reception room was worse. Papers scattered. Overturned furniture. Dust still in the air. But nothing vital missing.

Then he saw it.

Near the door. Buried in the mess. Old. Coverless. Lying face down. Jack froze. Crossed the room. Crouched.

The manuscript.

The one Antony supposedly gave to his student.

As he lifted it, something slipped from between the pages. He caught it midair.

A key. Long-stemmed. Ornate. A brass tag dangled from the bow. Stamped in old block type:

Haynes Park Real Estate
112 Bent Street

Jack blinked. Then smiled.

"Well, what are the odds?" he murmured, slipping the key into his pocket.

If Antony's little ninja had found the manuscript . . . Chances were, she wasn't far from the *Venus*.

Or the box.

And now—

Thanks to her key—

Neither was he.

Chapter Thirty-Two

The bullpen buzzed with activity—voices rising, keyboards clacking. From the far corner, a stream of profanity flowed without pause. A knot of bearded officers in tactical rigs huddled around the coffee machine, pants stamped with Cybercrime Operations Group insignia, heads shaking dolefully.

Katrine caught snippets as she crossed the floor, Saunders close on her heels—the Shiruku raid had gone sideways.

Dunbier's voice boomed from his glass-fronted office.

As they entered, the DCI slammed the phone down hard enough to rattle his desk. "Damn!"

"Raid was a bust?" Saunders asked, deadpan.

Dunbier glared. "Spoofed IP addresses—whatever the hell that means." He dragged a hand down his face and exhaled sharply. "The Cyber boys kicked in the door. Scared the shit out of a lad doing laundry in his kitchen sink."

Katrine stepped in front of the desk.

Dunbier's gaze snapped up. His tone shifted. "Good. You're here. Heard you might've dug up a lead."

She sat. "That's what I wanted to—"

He cut her off with a wave. "Later. Something more urgent just dropped."

He leaned forward, chair groaning beneath his 220-lb frame. "We've got intel Sara Miles was seeing Timothy Gibson at the time of her death. You know what that means?" His voice dropped. "You're gonna pay him a visit."

Katrine's brows rose. "I get to question Gibson?"

Dunbier nodded. "Tread softly. Sir James will swoop the second we screw up. I don't want him crying foul before we even start."

Katrine straightened. "I won't screw up, Chief."

"Exactly. Which is why you're on it." He nodded, thumb stroking his chin. "With Junior's weakness for pretty women, it should be a piece of cake."

Her eyes narrowed. "You're sending me because I'm pretty?"

Dunbier huffed. "Oh, come on, Ratcliffe. You know how this works. Your good looks are an asset. Flatter him. Use your feminine wiles. I don't care how—just get him talking."

Katrine stood, lips curling. "Pretty," she muttered.

Dunbier cleared his throat. "One more thing."

She paused, jaw flexing.

"When you're done with Gibson, help bring in Shiruku. He's a clean operator—in and out, without a trace. Sitting on intel nobody else has—not even Cyber." He paused, cocking a brow. "They think we might be dealing with Landvik."

"It's not Landvik."

Dunbier's eyes narrowed. "You sound awfully sure. You holding something back?"

She shrugged. "Call it a hunch."

"I don't do hunches. We deal in hard evidence. That's how we get results. Now get moving. And take Saunders. Wong and Perkins are already in situ in case Gibson takes a stroll."

Katrine nodded and followed Saunders into the bullpen. Her gaze flicked toward the Cyber Ops team still clustered by the coffee machine—high-tech cowboys full of swagger and jargon. No way in hell she was handing them her asset.

"Be with you in two," she said, veering toward her desk.

She shrugged on her jacket and reached for her bag. Her eyes snagged on the blinking notification at the top of her screen.

One new message.

She dropped into her chair and logged into the secure end-to-end chat.

The message was brief:

> SHIRUKU: `FYI - Nicholas Hope, PA to Sir James Gibson (aka Timothy Gibson's father), is Art Crimes. His PA role's a cover. Not sure how it fits—yet. But I'm certain the murders are tied to the hunt for Rebrisis's Three Elements.`

Katrine sat back. Art Recovery encryption was military-grade. Unbreachable. Only someone with Landvik's skills could've cracked it. Maybe Cyber weren't so far off after all.

The thud of boots on linoleum drew her attention. Saunders was closing in.

Her fingers flew as she typed:

> RATCLIFFE: `Is Gibson our perp?`

The hacker replied instantly:

> SHIRUKU: `No. But he's hunting the manuscript. Track him—and you might find Sara's killer.`

Seconds left.

> RATCLIFFE: Do you know why he's looking for the pieces?

A pause. The cursor blinked. Nothing.

> RATCLIFFE: Is that you, Landvik?

Still nothing.

Katrine flicked her mouse, activating the screensaver, and turned just as Saunders reached her desk.

"Ready?" he asked.

She stood, holstering her Glock. Its weight settled on her hip.

"To take down Gibson?" Her brow arched. "Yeah. I'm ready."

Chapter Thirty-Three

It was just after two when Annouie stepped off the train at Green Point. She slipped down the station stairs, hood low, matching the pace of commuters surging toward the exit.

Oria had queued a stack of notifications since her last check-in. Scrolling, she skimmed the list as she walked.

She stopped.

Second-to-last alert.

Big red flag.

She'd been routing her traffic through a proxy—a router owned by a student across the street.

Cyber Ops had raided his apartment.

Annouie exhaled slowly.

Not the immunity Katrine had promised.

Hands buried in her pockets, she picked up speed.

Gibson's street came into view—and with it, an unmarked sedan parked opposite the entrance.

She passed close enough to clock them in a shopfront window: two-man surveillance, low-tier.

Driver: Asian, late twenties, finishing a sub sandwich.

Passenger: Caucasian, early thirties, licking sauce from his fingers.

Half-empty coffee tray on the dash.

Watch-and-report. Not here to kick doors.

Her stomach tightened. One team in sight—

She reached the corner, ducked into a doorway, and scanned the upper levels of the building opposite for the flash of a scope, movement behind glass.

Nothing.

Just the sedan.

A service lane dog-legged behind Gibson's building—narrow, empty, full of shadow.

Halfway along, she looked up.

Fourth floor. Third window from the left—bathroom—still propped open.

Perfect.

She checked her watch—still time before the Studio One hearing.

Eyes scanning the brickwork, she cataloged ledges, drainpipes, mortar seams—anything that might offer a hand or foothold.

She backed up. Visualized her approach. Then—

Ran. Six strides. Straight at the wall.

She planted her foot and exploded upward. Fingers caught the first ledge; knee slammed in for leverage. Using cracks and jutting stone, she free soloed up the face of the building. At the open window, she hung by her fingertips, swung twice, then slid through the gap, dropping soundlessly onto the cold tile.

Voices drifted from the main room.

* * *

Gabriella paced across the apartment floor in short, sharp strides, her heels clicking against the wood. She stopped in front of the unfinished canvas—yet another of Timothy Gibson's fleeting bedroom conquests.

She scoffed softly and spun away.

Timothy remained at his easel, brush in hand, completely absorbed.

"Your buyer was most pleased," Gabriella said. A calculated opening, meant to grab his attention.

His brush swept across the canvas with steady precision. "Of course."

Her smile tightened. "His expert confirmed it's the real thing. No doubt about it."

The brushstrokes didn't falter. "Of course."

Her patience frayed. "I wasn't sure I could trust you—but when Nicholas Hope confirmed its provenance, I felt reassured."

That got a reaction. Timothy stilled, brush hovering midair. "Nicholas Hope?"

A flicker of triumph crossed Gabriella's face. "Didn't I tell you? Sir James sent him."

Timothy lowered the brush, reached for a cloth, and wiped his hands. His expression darkened. "You did not."

Gabriella's lips curved into a feline smile. "Nicholas has quite the eye. He noticed a deliberate imperfection in the upper-right corner. Signature Rebrisi. I missed it—but when the lab examined it, they confirmed it. Rebrisi always left his mark."

Timothy tossed the rag aside, movements sharp, dismissive. He turned back to the canvas, staring at it with a distant expression. "A slight imperfection?" he murmured. He dipped his brush in vermilion.

Gabriella's smile faltered. He wasn't even listening. His focus had returned to the subject captured on the canvas—a woman curled beneath his rumpled sheets, relaxed, open, disarmingly vulnerable.

Gabriella rolled her eyes. Snatching up her coat, she stalked to the elevator, kitten heels clicking. She hammered the call button, lips twisting in frustration.

She whirled, half-expecting a retort.

Nothing.

Timothy remained fully absorbed, leaning in, brush moving with surprising tenderness.

The sharp buzz of the lobby intercom shattered the quiet. Gabriella jumped.

Timothy looked up. He dropped his brush into a pot of turpentine with a faint clink, then spun the easel toward the wall, concealing the painting. Crossing the floor, he snatched the handset from its cradle.

"Thank God!" His voice trembled with relief and anxiety. "You should've called. I've been half out of my mind wondering if I'd offended you."

A pause. His expression shifted as he listened. A crease formed between his brows, deepening by the second.

"My apologies. I thought you were someone else." His voice tightened. "Of course, officer. Come right up. We're on the fourth floor."

He replaced the handset and turned to Gabriella, face ashen.

"You'd better stay. The police are on their way up. They want to talk to both of us."

* * *

Annouie slipped into the bedroom, her movements masked by the rattle of the rickety elevator groaning its way to the fourth floor. She moved quickly—unfastening the strap on her bag and pulling out the rolled painting.

Dropping to her knees in front of the chest, her fingers worked deftly, finding the catch as the elevator doors shuddered open and voices echoed through the loft.

She flipped the lid. Inside, the silk dress and stolen canvases lay in a heap. She shoved them aside and buried the copy of the *Venus* at the bottom—right where the original had rested just hours earlier.

Gibson's mellow drawl drifted in from the other room, followed by Gabriella's clipped European cadence. Then a third voice cut in—firmer, unmistakable.

Annouie froze. Unease coiled in her chest.

She turned toward the Japanese screen, angling her head to catch the words. Every instinct screamed: *Get out.* But instinct was like fear —and Anderson had taught her to master both.

She slid closer, pressing her ear to the painted surface.

* * *

"Timothy Gibson?"

The blonde woman's voice cut through the loft as she and her taller, broader partner stepped from the elevator. She flashed her badge with brisk precision and strode forward. He followed, eyes sweeping the space.

Her cool, blue gaze landed on Timothy. She appeared utterly unaffected by his good looks, which both puzzled and unsettled him.

Gabriella perched on the edge of the chaise longue, silent but watchful.

The detective's attention slid to the worktable where incense burned in a shallow dish—an attempt to mask the lingering scent of cannabis. Worse, a lace bra lay in plain sight on the wooden floorboards.

The man's brow twitched in mild amusement. The blonde detective leaned sideways, angling for a view beyond the Japanese screen.

Timothy stepped between her and the partition, forcing a polite smile. "How can I help you, Detective?"

She straightened and produced a small notebook. "Detective Ratcliffe. My partner, Detective Saunders. We have a few questions about Sara Miles."

A flicker of unease tightened Timothy's chest. He forced a sigh. "I've already spoken to the police. We were meant to meet at four. She never showed. My agent called her office—no one had heard from her."

Ratcliffe's pen moved across the pristine pages of her notebook. "When did you last see her?"

"Two weeks ago."

"Where did you first meet?"

He exhaled slowly—lying was an art. "At the State Gallery. She was reviewing the Egyptian collection." He dropped his gaze, feigning discomfort. "I was there for personal reasons."

Ratcliffe tilted her head. "And those reasons were?"

"I'd prefer not to say."

A brief nod. "Where were you two nights ago?"

Timothy froze—*in bed with Sara.* "I'm not sure."

"It would help if you could remember."

Gabriella rose, voice smooth and cool. "He was with me." She glided closer. "We were preparing his exhibition."

Ratcliffe lifted a brow. "Your name?"

"Gabriella Fonteyn—Mr. Gibson's agent. On the night in question, we stayed late at the gallery, then ate at Sunny Side Up on Epps Road. Staff will confirm."

Ratcliffe's lips thinned. Her gaze dropped to the bra on the floor. She strode over, crouched, and lifted it with the tip of her pen.

"What are you doing?" Timothy snapped.

She ignored him. "Yours?" she asked Gabriella.

Gabriella laughed, a sharp, humorless sound. "Good God, no."

Ratcliffe twirled the bra. "High-grade lace. Precision boning. Only one designer makes pieces like this."

Timothy rubbed his temples. "Detective, I've been up all night. Can we get to the point?"

Ratcliffe closed her notebook. "You saw Sara Miles two weeks ago—at the State Gallery. And afterward?"

Timothy's confidence faltered. He glanced at Gabriella, the color draining from his face. "We came back here," he admitted.

"You were lovers?" Ratcliffe asked.

He hesitated. Gabriella stiffened, jaw tight.

Timothy swallowed. "One thing led to another. You know how it is—drinks, laughter—"

Gabriella hissed, voice icy. "I knew it."

Ratcliffe's tone didn't change. "Is that a yes?"

He gave a curt nod.

Beside the kitchen counter, Saunders cleared his throat. "Mind if I use the restroom? We've been on the go all afternoon."

Timothy gestured. "Behind the screen."

Saunders nodded and disappeared into the bedroom.

Chapter Thirty-Four

Annouie dove under the bed, dragging her backpack with her. The front flap popped open, spilling the contents across the floorboards. Heart pounding, she shoved them back inside and crawled deeper into the shadows just as Saunders entered the room.

The floor whined as he crossed to the bedside table. Drawers scraped open. He rummaged through them methodically. A half-smoked joint rested on the lip of an ashtray. He picked it up, sniffed, and returned it with a wry grin.

Then, he sat.

The mattress sagged under his weight. Springs groaned—just inches from her head.

Annouie bit her lip, breath shallow.

The bed creaked again. He stood. The tension in her chest eased—until he crouched beside the chest.

He lifted the lid.

The silk dress rustled. The rolled canvases whispered.

Her breath caught.

If he turned—even slightly—it was over.

The seconds dragged. Her left foot began to cramp. She clenched her jaw and bore it.

Then: a soft thud as the lid closed.

He stood, knees cracking. He moved toward the bathroom, boots thudding against the tiles. A tuneless whistle floated back.

The toilet flushed.

At last, he left.

Annouie lowered her forehead to the cool floorboards and exhaled. She lay still, heart slowing—then wriggled out from under the bed.

She slung her backpack over one shoulder and slipped into the bathroom.

She had one leg over the windowsill—

"Forgot my phone," Saunders called out.

Her stomach twisted. She slithered over the edge, landing lightly on the narrow ledge outside. The backpack dragged at her shoulders like an anchor as she edged toward the stormwater pipes at the building's corner.

A scrape echoed behind her.

She pressed against the brickwork.

Saunders's head emerged through the window. He scanned the alley below, then the roofline above.

She didn't move.

Didn't breathe.

Sweat beaded on her forehead. One drop slid into her eye, stinging.

She didn't blink.

Seconds stretched. Her muscles burned. Gravity dragged with a cold, uncaring weight.

Then—an irritated huff.

A pigeon landed on the sill beside Saunders. He swatted it away with a flick of his hand.

His gaze lingered, then—

He retreated.

A thud—rubber on tile.

Gone.

Annouie exhaled, slow and quiet.

Adjusting her pack, she swung over the edge, and—legs quivering—began her descent to the pavement below.

* * *

Ratcliffe flicked through her notebook. "Just a few more questions, then we'll be out of your hair."

"Ask away," Timothy said, his voice straining around the edges.

Her face remained unreadable. "Did you know Julia Morecroft?"

"Yes."

"Sleep with her?"

He nodded.

"What about Rita Holmes?"

Another nod.

Gabriella slid in beside him, her tone sharp. "Surely, he's not a suspect?"

Ratcliffe snapped her notebook shut. "No. We can account for Mr. Gibson's movements on the nights in question. Perks of being so high-profile, I guess." She let the implication hang. "But we think there's a connection—possibly involving stolen art." Her eyes gleamed.

"Stolen art?" Timothy asked, his brows knitting together as he feigned confusion.

Gabriella jumped in. "What about a stalker?"

Ratcliffe's tone remained cool. "That was our first thought. Disgruntled client. Past girlfriend. Obsessed fan." She turned a pointed look on Timothy.

He rubbed his temples. "What makes you think this has anything to do with art theft?"

Her gaze wandered the room. "We received information."

"About stolen art?"

She swished her ponytail. "Mind if we have a look around?"

Gabriella stepped forward. "Not without a warrant."

The corner of Ratcliffe's mouth lifted. "I can arrange one."

"Good. You get a warrant, and then you can look. Until then, my client is very busy. Auction to oversee. Exhibition to prepare." Gabriella gestured toward the elevator, all crisp finality.

"Look as much as you want," Timothy said.

Gabriella hissed under her breath.

The floorboards creaked as Saunders returned. He gave Ratcliffe a subtle nod.

Ratcliffe sauntered past Gabriella and stopped in front of an easel where a portrait faced the wall. She turned it—and gave a sharp exhale.

"Beautiful girl," she murmured, her voice carrying a slight husk.

Timothy nodded. Annouie was beautiful, alluring—and, he suspected, dangerous when the moment called for it.

"Girlfriend?" Ratcliffe asked, eyes still on the painting.

Timothy shrugged.

"The bra on the floor—hers?"

Another shrug

Her gaze sharpened. "You'd better give me her name."

"Why?"

Ratcliffe didn't blink. She flipped open her notebook, pen poised. "Because I don't want another body. Name?"

Timothy hesitated, distaste curling his lips. Giving names was unprofessional. He gave a half-shrug, narrowing his eyes in mock effort. "It might've been Anna. Or Annie. Possibly Annabelle."

Ratcliffe blinked once. "Real suave."

He offered a sheepish grin. "Occupational hazard."

Gabriella cut in, her voice clipped. "Mr. Gibson needs to get back to work now, if that's all?" She gestured toward the elevator.

Ratcliffe didn't move. She paced in front of the portrait, brow furrowed as if something about the image disturbed her. Pulling out her phone, she asked, "Would you mind if I took a photo?"

"Yes!" Gabriella hissed.

"No," Timothy said.

Snap. Ratcliffe shoved the phone into her back pocket, ignoring Gabriella's glare. She wandered to the workbench, fingers trailing over the wood, gaze drifting toward the Japanese screen.

"What's behind there?"

"The bedroom," Saunders offered.

Ratcliffe sighed and finally retreated. "Well, Mr. Gibson, Ms. Fonteyn. Thank you for your time." She handed Timothy a card. "If you think of anything that might help, don't hesitate to call."

As the elevator doors closed, Timothy flipped the card over.

The moment the cage disappeared from sight, Gabriella whirled on him. Her voice was low, tight. "She wasn't talking about the Gartner Haus heist, was she?"

Timothy ran a hand through his hair. "Of course she was."

"And those names she rattled off?"

"I meet a lot of women. You know that."

Gabriella's eyes narrowed, her voice turning steely. "You don't just meet them—you screw them. And now they're winding up dead."

Timothy exhaled. "It has to be a stalker."

"A stalker?" Gabriella scoffed. "This sort of exposure is not good for business, Timothy."

"Of course."

"And stop saying 'of course'. It's wearing thin." She jabbed the elevator button. "Dump this Anna-Annie-what-ever-her-name-is. We can't afford another corpse."

Timothy stared at his phone. The screen was blank. No reply from Annouie.

"Yeah," he muttered. His lips thinned to a grim line. "Somehow, I don't think that's going to be a problem."

* * *

Katrine Ratcliffe stepped onto the curb and beckoned Saunders, already striding briskly down the road.

"See anything?" she asked, lengthening her stride.

Saunders caught up in three long steps, easily matching her pace. "Half-smoked joint on the bedside table. Plastic cuffs in the top drawer. Other than that, nothing useful."

Katrine halted at the corner, eyes fixed on the nearby park. "I don't think Gibson's our perp. But whatever he's into is getting these women killed."

"So . . . wait and watch?" Saunders asked, uncertain.

She shook her head, gaze shifting to the river's dull shimmer. "No. If we wait, we risk another body."

"The girl he was with last night?"

Katrine's lips flattened into a hard line. "I've tried putting her under surveillance. But she's remarkably hard to track."

Saunders scoffed. "That's why you took the picture. You know who she is."

Katrine's smile was grim. "Gibson may be many things, but he's a gifted artist. The moment I saw that painting, I knew."

Her eyes darkened.

"And if I'm right . . . the Ripper's going to be the least of her problems."

Chapter Thirty-Five

Jack Vallone sat in the farthest aluminum chair, posture loose, attention wired. From the café's open-air terrace, he commanded an unbroken view of the derelict paper mill down the street, its rust-striped façade looming over the river.

The mill was a four-story monument to decay—jagged roofline, broken panes, streaks of oxidized iron. New townhouses and freshly painted warehouses crowded around it, but the mill refused gentrification, a fist raised in defiance.

Jack's fingers brushed the long-handled key in his jacket pocket—the trophy the nimble little thief had dropped. He rolled the metal between thumb and forefinger, a half-smile tugging at his mouth while he studied the ruin.

The café hummed. The espresso machine hissed steam; waitstaff darted between tables with wobbling trays. Jack lifted two fingers.

"Check."

The waitress nodded, wiped his table, her eyes skimming past without meeting his gaze.

He stretched, cat-slow. The sun hung low in the sky, smearing ribbons of gold across the river. The mill stayed stubbornly still—its silence beginning to chafe.

When the waitress returned with the bill, he dropped a few coins on the table. Rising, he tugged his cap low, slid on the sunglasses dangling from his open collar, and palmed the key. Its weight was a promise—of reclamation. Of retribution.

Then he stepped into the pedestrian flow, unhurried, invisible, drifting downstream toward the mill.

* * *

Inside the café, the waitress ducked into the cramped back room, the air thick with the scent of wilting produce and citrus cleaner. She took a long sip from her water bottle, wiped the sweat from her brow, and paused—eyes drifting to the *Ten Most Wanted* poster pinned to the wall.

She stepped closer, frowning. Someone had scrawled a cartoonish mustache on the burliest of the fugitives. She barely glanced at him. Her attention snagged on the man in the second row, far right.

The grin. The unruly curls. The sharp, watchful eyes.

Table Two.

Her stomach tightened.

Slowly, she lowered the bottle, set it aside, and pulled out her phone. Her gaze remained fixed on the poster as she dialed. *Should've been less handsome,* she thought. *Would've helped you disappear into the background better.*

The line connected.

She turned toward the door, pulse quickening.

"Hi. I think I just saw someone on your list."

* * *

By Annouie's count, she now possessed—if not physically, then in theory—two of Rebrisi's *Three Elements*.

The taxi dropped her at Haynes Park station, a single block from the old mill. The station clock was edging toward 3:30 p.m.

She shoved a fistful of notes through the driver's window, tugged a cap low over her eyes, and slung her bag across one shoulder. As she moved with the foot traffic, she cataloged faces, storefronts, vehicles—every threat vector.

A white egret landed on the edge of a pontoon; a lone fisherman in a sun-bleached cap threaded bait on a hook.

Normal. Ordinary. No alarms.

The ramp at the intersection fed her into a busy cross street. Students clustered at the lights—T-shirts, sneakers, backpacks. Ubiquitous. Expected.

Also clean.

She looped behind them, doubled back, and approached the mill from the far side. No cruisers, no unmarked sedans, no watchers on rooftops.

Her hand slipped into her bag to confirm what mattered. Seconds later her fingers stilled.

The manuscript was gone.

Jaw tight, she checked her watch. No time to run back to Thomas Street. She plunged both hands into the pack, hunting the small pouch that held her wallet, phone, and keys.

Also missing.

She ducked into the narrow alley between the mill and the warehouse next door, weaving past sagging cartons and splintered pallets. A row of plastic bins lined the base of the mill's crumbling wall. Thirteen feet above, a window gaped.

She dragged two bins into position, tipped one on its side, then backed up. Not perfect. Not safe.

It'd do.

Quick inhale. Long exhale. Go.

Foot on one, skip to two, push off three. Wall. Plant. Hands. Sill.

Momentum carried her the rest of the way.

She muscled through the opening and dropped to the dusty floor inside.

Light bled through the filthy panes, striping rows of shelving stacked with the mill's forgotten innards: cracked boxes, shrink-wrap, dented barrels. Dust lay thick. A carton of tarnished gym trophies caught the light. Next to it: a Smith & Wesson Model 36. *Chief's Special.* Isidore's favorite. The sight of it stirred an unwelcome pang of despair. She pivoted toward the storage room door.

The building murmured—iron skeleton flexing, river slapping the foundation, pigeons cooing in the rafters.

At the long wooden table, she unlatched her bag, unclipped the cardboard tube, and shook out Gibson's second forged *Venus*.

It'd been a bad day for losing things: the manuscript, her phone, wallet, ID. She ran a silent inventory—she still had cash, spare IDs, and a drawer of burners. Manageable.

The real *Venus* hung at the gallery, secure as if it were locked in a vault. Once the heat died down, she'd swap it for the duplicate. But first: the box. And the damn manuscript.

Which meant returning to 112 Thomas Street.

A pungent tang drifted through the air—dust, rat droppings, river rot . . . and something else. She stilled. Sniffed. Another scent teased the air. She sniffed again: bergamot, lavender, sandalwood, citrus, musk.

Aftershave.

In the kitchen.

She crossed the floor, boards groaning, and found an upside-down mug in the sink, her missing key propped beside the tap. The kettle was still warm.

She refilled it. Brewed an instant coffee. Carried the mug to the grand piano in the far corner.

La Belle Dame stood on a makeshift riser before the last floor-to-ceiling window. She cleared the debris, sat on the tufted bench, and lifted the lid.

If Meyer-Edwards thought she wasn't going to practice—

Her fingers hit the keys. The sound rolled back, full and resonant despite dust and age.

She struck the chord again, repeating it with increasing force. The instrument responded: a sweet, sonorous sound that cut through the briny air.

The shifting harmonies filled the void, masking the soft clanging as her intruder tiptoed down the industrial staircase behind the kitchen.

* * *

Jack Vallone kept to the shadows, his movements near-silent—save for a faint metallic scrape.

His eyes locked on the table.

The *Venus* stared back.

Goddamn. The little ninja had done it—she'd already secured the original.

Admiration flickered, quick and involuntary. Then his expression hardened.

He moved across the floor, eyes fixed on the woman at the piano. She hadn't noticed him—the music cloaked the space in a deceptive warmth, full of pathos, yearning.

He reached beneath his jacket and pulled out a retractable rod.

Sometimes, finesse wasn't part of the job. If she refused to talk—he'd beat the location of the box out of her.

Chapter Thirty-Six

The pigeons in the rafters fell silent. The hairs on the back of Annouie's neck lifted. Even the river seemed to hush.

She stopped playing. Her fingers hovered as the last notes faded. Rolling the lid shut, she slid off the bench and turned.

Jack Vallone stood ten feet away, telescoping bo in hand, arms loose but ready.

She took a long sip from her mug, studying him. Under the hoodie and cargo pants, he likely hid a wiry, dangerous strength. The way he moved—casual but coiled—told her he was fast.

He offered a roguish smile, but the staff in his hand betrayed him. He wasn't here to talk.

Her eyes flicked to the piano lid, cluttered with potential weapons. Any one of them could knock him senseless.

She smiled into her mug and sipped again.

His face twitched, misunderstanding her composure for hesitation. The rod snapped to its full six feet.

He lunged.

She tossed the mug.

It smashed into his nose with a crunch, coffee spraying. He staggered, cursing, as she vaulted the piano and vanished behind it.

The bo slammed down a breath later, gouging the lacquer.

She gasped—genuine dismay. "That's a priceless antique, you Philistine."

Crouching, she scanned for a weapon. Masonry, wood, old fittings. Her gaze caught on the industrial broom. She grabbed it, stomped the bristled head off, and kicked the stick into her hands.

By the time Vallone rounded the piano—spinning his staff with unnecessary flair—she was ready.

Rule #1: *Study your enemy.*

His chest swelled with confidence. Grin on his face—wide and cocky.

Overconfident. Sloppy.

He struck fast, slashing down. She parried. The crack of graphite on wood echoed.

Vallone bulled forward, leaning into her space, brute strength against her makeshift defense, hands reaching for her weapon.

Rule #2: There are no fair fights in the field.

She pivoted, driving her elbow into his throat. He staggered back, gasping.

Reset. Grip. Breathe.

He cleared his throat, chuckled. "Too trained for Deluca. Too polished for Security and Risk. Not bureaucratic enough for DOJ." His eyes glinted. "So who are you?"

He spun the staff, showboating—then launched into a flurry of sweeps and jabs. All muscle, little finesse. Keeping her on the defensive. Parry. Block. Deflect. The broomstick groaned.

"So little ninja—gonna tell me who you work for?"

She caught the tell—feint high, sweep low. She leapt; he missed. Just. As he raised the bo again, she caught the end, yanked, and punched his nose.

Cartilage crunched.

He reeled, blood flowing from his nostrils. Still—he shook his head and grinned.

"Dirty," he rasped. "We're doing dirty, then."

He dropped low, and the staff whistled beneath her boots. She sprang off the wall, twisted mid-air, leg snapping out. A hook kick to the chest.

He crashed to the floor, rolled, staggered upright.

Still grinning.

Resilient. She had to give him that. But that was all he was getting.

She leapt again, drove her boot into the back of his knee. He hit the hardwood floor with a crack.

She circled, broomstick high.

"Who do you work for?" he asked again, rasping.

She didn't answer. "How did you find me?"

He pushed to his feet, mouth quirking. "The manuscript."

Her grip slackened. "You have it?"

Rule #3: Keep emotion out of the ring.

He surged forward, shoulder-checking her into the dining table. Air shot from her lungs. Pain lanced through her chest. She gripped the table's edge. Glanced at the kitchen clock.

He was wasting her time.

He twirled his staff, circling.

She sighed. He wasn't going to quit.

He struck. Check. Twist. Counter.

She had to end this.

She swung—drove the broomstick into his solar plexus. He doubled over. She pivoted, snapping it across his shoulder. He hit the floor, hard.

She raised the broomstick again. Vallone grunted, one hand slapping the floor.

"You don't get to tap out," she snapped.

"Not tapping out," he wheezed, a grin breaking through the strain.

Then he swept her legs.

The ground rushed up. She hit hard, broomstick skittering from her grip.

Rule #4. Never lose control of your weapon.

He pinned her wrists, breath ragged. Flashed a grin through the blood trailing from his nose.

She could almost hear Anderson's soft, amused laughter in her ear. *Physical advantage doesn't mean you've lost.*

"All's fair in love and war, right, love?"

She stilled. Let her gaze soften. "Indeed," she purred. "Which is why I'm willing to make you a deal."

He laughed, grip beginning to loosen. "I'm calling the shots."

Her smile sharpened. "Are you? Because that *Venus* on the table? It's a fake."

Rule #5: Never take your eyes off your opponent.

His gaze flicked to the painting.

She bridged, hooked his leg, flipped him.

He hit hard.

She rolled, snatched the broomstick, and cracked him across the jaw.

His head snapped back, eyes rolling. He slumped to the floor. Lights out.

Annouie exhaled, tossed the staff aside, and staggered up.

"Keep your eyes on the hands," she muttered. "The mouth always lies."

She dragged his limp body to the kitchen, fished a burner from a drawer, and dialed.

"Need a favor," she rasped.

"What?" Andre's sleepy voice echoed through the line.

"I've got an intruder. We fought. He's out cold. I need you to babysit."

A sharp intake of breath. "Did you say he's out cold?"

"Focus. Can you babysit?"

"Call the police. They'll put him in a cell."

She dropped her voice. "He's not that kind of intruder. He's after the Rebrisi. We need to question him. But I have a hearing in thirty minutes."

Long pause. Then: "Fine. Leave the front door open."

"Thanks. I owe you."

"And for the love of God, truss him up properly this time. No repeat of Jakarta."

She rolled her eyes and ended the call.

She rummaged through a drawer. Returned with zip ties.

Vallone was beginning to stir.

She crouched. Grabbed his arms. Wrapped them around the column. Cinched his wrists tight.

He moaned.

"Harden up. You did the break and enter."

She patted him down. Her fingers brushed something bulky beneath his sweater. She tugged it free.

Her heart skipped.

The manuscript.

She tucked it quickly beneath her hoodie.

He blinked, gaze sharpening. "You can't leave me like this," he growled.

She slid onto a barstool and grabbed a deck of Post-it notes. She scribbled, tore the note free, and slapped it on his forehead.

"Oh, but I can," she said.

"Don't think I won't tell the police who you are."

"Good thing they're not coming."

She adjusted her bag, snugged the manuscript tight to her chest. "Don't worry, I won't be long. Then we'll talk terms."

His cursing echoed as she jogged for the exit. In the glass, she caught her reflection—dirty jeans, torn hoodie.

She shook her head. Out of time.

She hit the pavement running, manuscript scraping her ribs.

One war down.

Another looming.

Chapter Thirty-Seven

Light spilled through Dahlia House's open balcony doors, gilding the polished floor. Beyond the railing, the waves kept time, a steady slap-slap against the harbor wall, echoing the quick beat in Nicholas Hope's veins.

Flat on Landvik's bed, he slid his phone beneath the silk sheet and eyed the new notification: a voicemail from Usman Malik.

Intriguing.

On the balcony, Landvik paced, voice low and urgent. Nicholas was certain hidden mics and cameras tracked his every breath.

But he pressed play anyway.

Malik's monotone murmured from the tiny speaker. "We've identified the Wilkin's Beach John Doe. Sir James Gibson is a—"

From the balcony came stray fragments of Landvik's call: *Intruder . . . Police . . . Jakarta.*

Then a single, unexpected word hooked his attention: *Rebrisi.*

He paused the message, a slow smile curling his lips.

Sliding the phone aside, he peeled a translucent gel dot from inside the case—a micro-transmitter no bigger than a fingernail. Landvik wasn't the only one with toys.

The balcony doors whispered shut; sunlight framed Landvik's flushed face and mussed pink hair.

"Problem?" Nicholas asked, stretching beneath the sheet.

Landvik snatched the T-shirt draped over the cheval mirror. "The usual client drama." He yanked the shirt over a lean torso, his irritation palpable.

Nicholas clocked the tension. He sat up, winced. Pain arced through his lower back, a souvenir from yesterday.

"I understand. Sir James lives for drama."

He rolled from the bed and recovered his boxers. Landvik, half-dressed, hesitated by the footboard, Jimmy Choo high-tops in hand. "See you after work?" The question was soft, almost shy.

Nicholas paused long enough to hold his gaze. "I'd like that."

Landvik perched on the edge of the mattress. "I know a place." His eyes—warm, trusting, nothing like the cold operator described in police dossiers—tracked Nicholas with something like canine hope.

Something brittle cracked in Nicholas's chest. He managed a smile that almost touched his eyes. "Text me the address."

He turned, shrugging into his coffee-stained shirt. Flinging his tie around his neck, he reached for the polished wingtips beneath the bed. "I'm sure your police consulting will be fascinating," he said.

And your AI even more so.

Landvik drummed his fingers on the bed. "And you can tell me what it's like working for Sir James."

A waking nightmare. Nicholas tightened his tie. The hollowness yawned wide inside him—familiar, endless, oddly comforting. Regret, though—that was new. A future with Landvik? Impossible . . . yet the thought clung, refusing to die.

"Six o'clock?" he asked, stooping to lace the wingtips.

Landvik laughed. "Sure. I'll make myself available."

Nicholas straightened, slid across the mattress, and caught Landvik by the nape. The kiss he laid on him was hard, decisive—surprisingly possessive. He pressed the gel transmitter behind Landvik's ear. But instead of pulling away, he deepened the kiss, fingers curling in that ridiculous pink hair, tasting a possibility that would never be.

Business, he reminded himself. *Only business.*

* * *

The minute hand on the central tower clock crept toward four, and the bells began their tolling. The sound reverberated through the air as Annouie slipped in the Oria2 Smart-contacts and earpiece, her steps quickening along the cloistered walkway. She darted through the archway, the chimes marking her progress.

By the time she reached the first-floor landing, the final chime was fading. She skidded to a halt and smoothed her hair back.

The door to Studio One creaked open, sunlight spilling into the corridor. Its warmth vanished as Judith emerged. Her gaze dropped to Annouie's dirty hoodie and ripped jeans, mouth curling downward.

"Follow me," she said, and turned.

Studio One was empty—save for Meyer-Edwards, slouched against the grand, his expression unreadable.

Annouie slowed, scanning the room. "I thought the whole board would be in attendance—"

Judith waved her off. "There's been a change of plans—the dean is on his way."

Her pulse quickened. No board. Just the dean. That couldn't be good. "Why?"

Judith almost smiled. "He wants to share some good news. Specifically, about you."

Meyer-Edwards arched a brow. "Really?"

Judith's eyes narrowed. "Yes, really, Antony. So don't wander off."

She left without waiting for a reply.

Meyer-Edwards pushed off the piano and perched on the desk. "Sit."

Annouie hesitated, then dropped into the chair. "What's going on?"

His mouth tightened. "How would I know?"

"You're on the board," she said, leaning forward. Her voice lowered. "But if it's good news . . . that means I'm not fired, right?"

He shook his head. "No. It means I'm not fired. You still have to pass my quiz." He raised a brow. "Where's my manuscript?"

Annouie gave him a look. "What manuscript?"

She reached into her backpack and pulled out a small stack of books, setting them beside him.

"The large, unbound volume you claimed wasn't the Liszt treatise. Remember?" His scowl deepened as he glanced at the titles.

She shrugged. "It's not here."

"I can see that," he said, snatching the top book and flipping it open.

"'Playing arpeggios at speed is much the same as playing chords at speed'," he read, then shot her a pointed look. "What comes next? Verbatim."

Annouie blinked. "You can't be serious?"

"Do I look like I'm joking?" His voice dropped to a low growl. Word-for-word or it's a fail."

She stroked her ear, buying time. "Could you repeat the question?"

He gave her a wolfish smile. "Take as long as you need."

The words scrolled before her eyes. She steadied her breathing and read aloud: "'Just as you would play the chord with a single downward motion, play all notes of the chord as if carried by that single impetus'."

He frowned and flipped to another page. "'Follow the note mentally as it reaches the key bed'. What comes next?"

The data feed responded seamlessly. "'Being hyperaware of each note is the key to absolute control'."

He flipped deeper into the book. "'When you can focus your mind on both hands at the same time—'"

"'Which is an impossibility'," she cut in. "'Regardless, you will have mastered the essence of independence'."

He snapped the book shut. "How?"

She raised a brow. "A little more context, please?"

"I'm not quoting. I'm asking how you memorized a two-hundred-page volume. That's not possible." He dropped the book onto the table with a thud.

"So you admit you set me up to fail?"

His eyes flashed. He leaned forward, a retort forming.

The door burst open, and Judith entered, followed by a tall, lanky man. Deep lines framed a too-wide smile. Despite the gauze stuffed in his swollen nose, Annouie recognized him instantly—the young man from Aguirre's photo.

Judith beamed. "Allow me to introduce the Dean of Studies, Professor Robert Mackie."

The dean extended his hand, voice nasal. "Please excuse my appearance. Bit of a mishap with a car door this morning." His grip lingered. "I've heard great things about you."

"Thank you," Annouie said, politely extricating her hand.

Mackie turned to Meyer-Edwards with unsettling bonhomie. "Good work the other night. The reviews were excellent. Always a bonus for the conservatory."

Meyer-Edwards frowned but said nothing.

Mackie strolled to the Steinway, his shiny wingtips clicking on the floor. He pivoted sharply, hands raised as if about to conduct an invisible orchestra.

"You're probably wondering why I gathered you both here." Even through the gauze, his glee was unmistakable.

Annouie braced herself.

"Judith's been in touch with one of our benefactors," he continued. "He wants to send a student to Rome next semester." Mackie clasped his hands. "Ms. Bach is the ideal candidate."

"How?" Meyer-Edwards asked.

Mackie's grin sharpened. "How indeed. Ms. Bach is an . . . asset.

But we can't play favorites. So she'll compete for the Bernard Smith Scholarship. Like everyone else."

"That's barely six weeks away," Meyer-Edwards said. "How am I supposed to prepare her in time?"

"Judith assures me Ms. Bach is up to the challenge."

"I have a tight schedule," Meyer-Edwards snapped. "I couldn't possibly—"

A shadow passed over Mackie's face. "I spoke with legal today. They're confident the matter that went before Justice Hargreaves today can be . . . resolved. With a few undertakings." His smile returned. "How does that sound, Tony? Think you can move a few things around?"

Meyer-Edwards's nostrils flared. "Our legal team?"

"They're very good at making things disappear," Mackie said.

A long silence followed.

Meyer-Edwards's chest rose and fell. "I suppose I could reschedule." A sneer tugged at his lip. "Sir."

Mackie's grin snapped back into place. "Knew you'd see it my way."

He dropped into a metal chair, dragged out his phone, and waved them off. "Now off you go. I have calls to make. No more chitchat."

He turned his attention to the phone. "Ah, Charles," he crooned, already performing for his next audience.

Meyer-Edwards tapped Annouie's shoulder. "Outside. Now."

They exited, the doors swinging shut behind them.

Annouie turned to Meyer-Edwards. "Huge amounts of subtext going on back there. Care to read me in?"

He kept walking. "No idea what you're talking about. Focus on the fact neither of us has been fired. Now. You heard him. We need to prep. My place. One hour."

She cleared her throat. "Can't."

He stopped. "That wasn't a request, Bach."

"I know. But I really can't. Tomorrow afternoon?"

His eyes narrowed. "What's so important it can't wait?"

She laughed dryly. "You know. Unreasonable boss. Excessive demands."

He gave her an assessing look, eyes flicking over her hoodie and ripped jeans. After a long pause, he sighed. "Fine. Tomorrow morning. Ten-thirty sharp." He stressed the last four syllables.

Then, with a sardonic lift of his brow, "And this time, don't keep me waiting. Maybe take a bath. Change into something clean. Honestly, Bach—you look like you spent the afternoon cage-fighting."

Chapter Thirty-Eight

"Absolutely. Rebrisi's *Three Elements* will be ready for pickup by tomorrow afternoon."

Timothy resisted the urge to shudder as Luigi Deluca —mobster and heir apparent to the Deluca crime family throne— finally hung up. Sliding the phone into his back pocket, he crossed the studio floor and stopped in front of the easel.

His latest attempt at the *Venus* stared back at him.

Beside it, on the desk, sat the finished copy of Rebrisi's *Third Element*—the puzzle box. All he needed now was the manuscript.

His attention returned to the box, a faint smile tugging at his lips.

Sourcing the rare African blackwood had been a nightmare, but his second attempt? A quiet triumph. Unlike his first flawed version, this one was perfect—carved from a single block, inlaid with mother-of-pearl, seamless and keyless. It gleamed in the light, its coffin-like shape unsettling.

He'd even found a gaudy, fake red diamond in the back of an op shop. For authenticity.

Lifting the box, he gave it a gentle shake.

A distinct rattle echoed from within.

Perfect.

Only one problem remained: the manuscript. His contact had failed to show.

Deluca wanted pristine copies of all three elements. But without first touching the original, Timothy was stalled. Near enough wasn't an option. Not with Deluca. The man demanded perfection.

The theme from *The Godfather* blared from his phone, slicing through his thoughts. He pulled his phone and swiped, his voice low and frayed. "What?"

"Is that how you greet your father?" Sir James's disapproval was palpable, even through the line.

Timothy knuckled the fatigue from his eyes. "Sorry. It's been a rough week."

"Well, it's about to get rougher."

Timothy straightened, breath stilling.

"We're going to talk about your allowance."

Timothy slumped against the edge of the desk, glancing again at the puzzle box. Deluca wasn't known for his patience.

"I'm busy," he muttered.

"I'm standing outside."

"You don't mean *outside*-outside?"

"I do. Now get out of bed and let me in."

Timothy closed his eyes. Of course. The old bastard would choose now—when everything was spiraling out of control.

He moved toward the birdcage elevator, muttering as he pressed the intercom button to release the downstairs security door.

"Sure. Why not. What's one more disaster?"

* * *

Sir James swept in, shrugging off his coat and draping it over the end of the chaise longue. His sharp gaze roamed the apartment, settling on the display of unfinished works hanging against the far wall. For an instant, Timothy thought he saw a flicker of pride in his father's eyes.

It didn't last.

Sir James moved from piece to piece, muttering under his breath as the furrow in his brow deepened.

"Self-indulgent." Step to his right. "Contrived." Another step. "Mediocre." "Stale." "Bland."

He reached the last piece—a canvas turned to face the wall—and paused. With deliberate care, he rotated it into the light. His expression shifted, his contempt lifting ever so slightly

"Now this shows promise," he said, voice losing some of its usual edge.

Timothy slid in beside him. "That one's personal."

"Personal?" Sir James studied the portrait more closely. His eyes sharpened. "That's the woman from the preview. The journalist." He turned, voice edged with suspicion. "You slept with her?"

Heat crept up Timothy's neck. He nudged Sir James toward the kitchen, trying to steer him away.

Sir James didn't budge. He stared at the painting, rubbing his chin. "This isn't your usual style. It's more . . ." He trailed off, assessing. "Intimate."

Then he laughed—sharp, surprised. "My womanizing son . . . smitten."

Timothy scoffed. "Don't be ridiculous." He sighed, lowering his voice. "Why are you really here . . . Dad?" The word landed strangely in his mouth.

Sir James moved to the worktable and dropped onto a stool, shoving a bottle of turpentine aside. From his coat, he pulled a manila folder and flicked it open. At the top was an invoice—the figure at the bottom circled in confrontational red ink.

He jabbed a finger at it. "Care to explain?"

Timothy leaned closer. "An accounting error?"

"And this?" Sir James flipped the page. Flipped again. Over and over.

At the end of the stack, he leaned back, arms folded, stool groaning beneath him. "Where's it all going?"

Timothy's face paled. "Where's what going?"

"Your allowance. You're not paying your creditors. It's going somewhere. I'm assuming you're paying someone off. A usurer?"

The word hit like a slap.

"Well, I . . ." Timothy floundered, mouth suddenly dry. "Perhaps if—"

Sir James cut him off with a glare. "So that's an affirmative. Next question: how much?"

Timothy glanced at the vein pulsing in his father's temple. "It's not simply a matter of how much—"

"Right." Sir James's eyes narrowed to slits. "You're in over your head. Who's the usurer?"

Timothy hesitated, then shrugged. "A local group. Luigi Deluca runs them."

Sir James recoiled. "Deluca!"

Timothy raised his hands. "I know how it looks. At least, on paper."

Sir James stabbed a finger at the stack of invoices. "And in reality?"

Timothy gave a thin smile. "Yes. It's bad. No denying that." He inhaled slowly, shifting his tone. "But I have a plan to fix it. You don't need to worry about bailing me out."

He desperately needed that manuscript.

Sir James sneered. "I wasn't intending to."

Perversely, the tightness in Timothy's chest loosened. This was well-traveled ground—Sir James always opened with a refusal. Like a chess opening.

Now came the performance.

"You . . . weren't?"

Sir James laced his fingers together, faux-casual. "Why would I? You have a plan."

Timothy's pulse quickened. Time to pitch.

The trick was to confess enough—sound contrite without revealing the full extent of his indiscretions. Appeal to Sir James's non-existent paternal instincts while baiting his professional interest. It was a delicate balance: too much honesty would kill the deal, too little would provoke suspicion.

He smiled boyishly. "The truth is, I've racked up a few debts. But I've been working hard to dig myself out. Just yesterday, I sold the Suki Rey mural. And I've got another piece headed to auction—should fetch quite a bit."

Sir James barked a laugh. "Even if you sold a Suki Rey every day for a year, it wouldn't touch what you owe. And Deluca isn't going to wait."

Timothy sighed wistfully, the picture of subdued regret. "Exactly. Which is why I diversified. I've been commissioned to produce a set of copies. They'll cover the debt—and then some."

"Counterfeits?"

Timothy grinned. "Precisely. But wait—there's more."

Sliding off the stool, he led Sir James to the rear wall. Under the studio lights, the Rebrisi box gleamed. Beside it lay a lone *Venus* copy.

He frowned. Yesterday, there'd been three.

He shrugged off the unease, grabbing the remaining canvas and laying it on the desk beside the box. Slipping the loupes around his neck, he gestured for Sir James to take a closer look.

"These are copies?" Sir James asked, voice skeptical.

Timothy nodded. "Deluca agreed to erase my debt if I deliver flawless reproductions of Rebrisi's *Three Elements*."

Sir James frowned. "I see two."

"Exactly." Timothy's jaw clenched. "But if I can get my hands on the manuscript."

Sir James's brows shot up. "How?"

"I have a contact," Timothy said, voice lowering conspiratorially.

Sir James studied the *Venus* reproduction copy. "These are good. Too good. You must have touched the originals to produce this level of quality." He turned, eyes widening. "The *Venus* was lost during the Gartner Haus heist."

Timothy smirked.

"That was you?"

The smirk spread. "Want to see it?"

"You're not keeping it here," Sir James said, aghast.

"Oh, it's safe," Timothy replied. "And by safe, I mean it's hidden where nobody would think to look."

He led Sir James to the partitioned-off bedroom, knelt at the old chest, and released the lock. The lid creaked open.

Sir James peered in. "Doesn't look very safe."

Timothy ignored him, pushing aside a jade emerald gown, and retrieved the rolled canvas from the bottom. He spread it across the unmade bed.

Sir James's gaze swept over the work. "How do I know this isn't a fake?"

Timothy pointed. "Look at the top right corner. A slight imperfection—proof of its authenticity."

Sir James squinted. "I see nothing."

"It's there," Timothy insisted, leaning in. "A small—"

The words died.

He yanked the loupes from around his neck. Bent over the canvas.

The blood drained from his face.

He straightened, breath shallow.

Then bolted.

He tore back into the studio, skidding to a halt where the other copies had been.

Not misplaced. Gone.

Dread pooled in his stomach.

It couldn't be. Annouie was too young. But—she'd been recruited as a child.

His hands trembled.

The Gray Cat.

Slowly, he turned back toward Sir James, forcing composure onto his face.

"Yes," he said smoothly, despite the chill sliding down his spine. "Gabriella hosted a private showing yesterday. The client brought an expert. We needed the original in place. It's hanging in the Rose Chambers Room. You could say—" He swallowed hard. "It's hiding in plain sight."

The lie tasted bitter.

She'd played him. Got him high. Stolen his *Venus*.

He'd lured the Gray Cat to the gallery—and she'd come.

Worse—he'd fallen for her, like a besotted schoolboy.

Sir James's phone buzzed, shattering the moment. He checked the screen, scowled, and pointed. "Stay put. When I'm done with this call, we're going to talk."

As he stepped away, voice already rising, Timothy turned to the window.

Somewhere out there, the Gray Cat was laughing.

She'd made a fool of him.

But this wasn't over.

He'd hunt her down—

And when he did . . .

* * *

Emil couldn't conceal his concern as the phone rang on. For once, the heavens seemed to agree with him—Sir James picked up on the fifth ring instead of letting it go to voicemail, as he usually did.

"I've identified the body," Emil blurted, not giving Sir James a chance to cut in. "It took time, and some very clever cross-referencing—"

"Is it James?" Sir James interrupted, derailing the explanation before it could gain traction.

Emil swallowed the rest of his sentence. The pause that followed was taut. He sniffed and glanced through the glass wall of his office.

In the adjoining lab, Usman Malik hovered over the cadaver, gloved hands moving with clinical precision. The man was a nightmare in scrubs—methodical, relentless. Emil lowered his voice.

"Yes."

A heavy silence hung on the line.

Then Sir James cleared his throat. "Anybody else know?"

Emil's gaze tracked Usman as he moved to his computer, already tapping commands—running searches, refining queries, pulling threads. The man never stopped.

"No," Emil said.

"Then keep it that way."

"How am I supposed to do that?" Emil snapped, his voice rising despite himself.

"By doing nothing unless I tell you otherwise." Sir James's voice cut like glass—cold, sharp, dangerous.

Emil's grip tightened on the receiver. "Don't you think—"

"If this gets out, we're in the wind. But that's a big *if*. I'm counting on you to make sure that doesn't happen."

Emil nodded even though Sir James couldn't see him.

"Sit tight. Say nothing. Do nothing."

"But—"

The line went dead.

* * *

Timothy slipped away from the window.

Sir James paced the length of the kitchen island, his shoes clicking against the floorboards.

With a sharp exhale, he ended the call and strode for the birdcage elevator, brows drawn like thunderheads.

"I'll be back to sort this out. Don't do anything while I'm gone," he barked, voice ricocheting through the loft.

Timothy dipped his head politely, though his thoughts were raging elsewhere.

Sir James slammed the call button with his fist. "I mean it. Don't try to handle this yourself."

The elevator doors slid open. He stepped inside and blocked them from closing with one meaty hand. "But there's one condition—we're tracking down the manuscript together."

Before Timothy could argue, the doors closed, and the cage began its descent to the garage.

The knot in Timothy's chest didn't loosen.

It twisted. Hardened. Until finally, it became something else.

Fury.

The West End's most handsome portrait artist. The mastermind behind the Gartner Haus heist. Untouchable until now.

And he'd been seduced, robbed and ghosted in the space of a single night.

By the Gray Cat.

His fists clenched. When he found her—

And therein lay the problem.

He knew nothing about her.

A humming sound sliced through his spiraling thoughts. Faint. Insistent. Not from the kitchen. Not from the studio.

He turned toward the bedroom, every muscle wired with tension.

The sound grew louder as he entered. He dropped beside the bed and scanned the shadows beneath.

There—nestled in the dark—a woman's clutch handbag. Vibrating.

He yanked it free and upended it onto the floor.

Annouie's Samsung Flip tumbled out, sliding across the hardwood, still buzzing.

He snatched it up and slid his finger across the screen. *Locked.*

Cursing, he tossed it back into the bag.

He scanned the rest: lipstick, a set of picks, tweezers, painkillers, and a notepad.

One by one, he shoved them back inside, his movements growing rougher—until his hand closed on a sheaf of papers.

He drew it out. Flipped through it.

An appeal. Affidavits. His breath hitched.

A prisoner in a Romanian jail.

He rocked back on his heels, a wicked smile curling his lips.

Of course. He should've seen it sooner. But now—he knew who to call: the scheming forensic accountant who'd helped put Isidore Bach behind bars.

Finding her wasn't a matter of *if* anymore—

But *when.*

Chapter Thirty-Nine

Jack Vallone strained at his plastic cuffs. Six months with a paramilitary outfit in Africa, another six sweating on a dig in Saqqara—he'd earned his professor stripes the hard way. A little thing like being forced to hug a cheap Doric column wasn't going to hold him.

The ties bit deep; his temper flared. He drew a slow breath, focused. Flexion of the thumbs. Dislocation. Key to a clean escape. Gritting his teeth, he popped the joints.

Three seconds later, he was free.

He staggered upright, muttering a string of curses as he snapped his thumbs back into place—a sickening crack, a jolt of pain.

The thought of lying in wait for Antony's student was tempting. She'd tied him to a knockoff column. Maybe she needed a lesson in classical architecture—and pain.

But he didn't have time.

He needed to move. Find the other elements—before Deluca did.

He patted his jacket—

And groaned. Of course the bloody manuscript was gone.

He dragged a hand through his hair in sheer despair.

No *Venus*. No manuscript. But he still had the delivery docket from Sara's desk. All he had to do—

A faint scuff broke the silence.

He froze. Tracked the sound—a subtle scrape against the front doors.

Back already?

A slow, savage grin curled his lips. He still owed her pain.

He slid off the stool and slipped into the shadows of the storage room as the door creaked inward.

* * *

Andre Landvik was finally making his move on the mill.

Nicholas Hope eased into a chair beneath the awning of Dominic's Café. His overwatch position was near perfect—clear line of sight to the mill's front doors and partial visibility on the right flank.

Over the past half hour, it had become clear that Landvik was running an embarrassingly shoddy surveillance detection route. He'd arrived just before the hour, bought a bag of chips at the takeaway, then wandered into the park. There, he sprawled on a bench, fed the gulls, and lobbed the brown paper wrapper into a bin. From there: a lazy loop along the river path, a detour into a convenience store, and two minutes later, he emerged with a carton of milk.

Nicholas smirked. A world-class hacker with no tradecraft.

Landvik crossed the street and disappeared into the building.

Nicholas's smile deepened. No matter how clever Landvik was, the skin-colored transmitter ensured he was traceable.

A petite, dark-haired waitress swooped in, pad at the ready. She smiled brightly and pulled a pencil from behind her ear.

"Ready to order?"

* * *

Andre slipped through the mill doors and locked them behind him. Padding quietly into the main room, he reached behind his ear and peeled off the skin-colored tracker. The micro-transmitter adhered like a second layer of skin—seamless, state-of-the-art, and virtually RF silent.

He studied it for a moment, his brow lifting in grudging respect. Hope had access to some seriously impressive tech.

Then he dropped the device into a vase on the kitchen counter.

Beside the vase, zip ties lay scattered. Dusty footprints traced a path from the mezzanine to the dining area, looping past the piano and returning into the storage room beyond. The cloying scent of aftershave still clung to the air—sharp, intrusive, territorial.

Andre shrugged off his backpack and let it thud onto the bench. Sliding onto a stool, he pulled out his phone and typed a quick message.

Your intruder's gone.

Setting the phone aside, he retrieved his laptop, flipped it open, and logged in. Four camera feeds flickered onto the screen.

Camera One: exterior front door.

Camera Two: mezzanine approach.

Camera Three: dining room.

Camera Four: kitchen.

He scrubbed Camera Four back thirty minutes. Fingers dancing over the keys, he scanned the timeline.

There—Annouie dragging Vallone into the kitchen by the ankles.

He hit play.

The next few minutes unfolded in real time: Annouie exiting the frame, Vallone straining against his restraints, face taut with concentration. A grimace. The pop of dislocated thumbs. Then the wince as he snapped them back into place. His head jerked toward the door—then he darted out of view.

Andre switched to Camera One. Fast-forwarded. The exterior feed showed nothing—just the pavement outside undisturbed.

He hesitated, fingers hovering over the keyboard. A faint prickle crawled up the back of his neck.

Then, without warning, Jack Vallone stepped through the storage room door, squinting over the sights of a Smith & Wesson Model 36.

Andre sighed and raised both hands in surrender.

"And, of course," he muttered dryly, "you never left the building."

* * *

Nicholas frowned at his phone. The bug wasn't transmitting.

His mind churned, sifting through the short list of reasons: interference, shielding, hardware failure. Or—

Removal.

A tight knot twisted in his gut as the waitress reappeared, setting down a flat white and a plate stacked with two scones, thick with jam and cream.

He took a bite, barely registering the taste. The bug was state-of-the-art—virtually undetectable.

No way Landvik found it.

He reloaded the app, eyes fixed on the spinning wheel. Across the street, the arched door of the mill remained shut. Landvik was still inside. But for how long?

Nicholas set his cup down. He couldn't risk losing the hacker. He stood—

Then froze.

Three hundred feet up the street, dark figures emerged from the alleyway shadows—tactical gear, quiet steps, methodical precision.

Special Ops.

He sank slowly back into his chair, lifting the second scone. Across the street, officers stacked up on either side of the mill's doors, weapons held at the low ready.

Nicholas chewed thoughtfully, a faint smile tugging at his lips. *Let's see you get out of this one, Landvik.*

* * *

Vallone paced the wooden floor of the mill's converted kitchen, revolver swinging loosely in his hand.

"I must say, I didn't expect to find Andre Landvik on the end of that little ninja's leash. What's the deal? Is she DOJ as well?"

Andre blinked, feigning surprise. "Beg your pardon?"

Vallone stopped dead, fixing him with a cold stare. "Don't play cute with me. I know who you really work for."

"The police?" Andre tapped the arm of his SmartSpecs, pulling up Vallone's rap sheet. Number Four on the Police Most Wanted list had a mile-long history of forgery, theft, and armed breaking and entering.

But not murder.

Still, the way Vallone was waving that gun around didn't inspire confidence. Accidents had a way of happening.

"I'm on a tight deadline and I need answers," Vallone growled, grip tightening on the revolver. "So, I'm going to do whatever it takes to get them."

Andre lowered his hands. "Just tell me what you want. My rates are reasonable."

Vallone laughed, waving the Smith & Wesson at the computer. "Nuh-uh. This one's pro bono."

Andre shrugged and tugged at the laptop's lower edge. It squealed across the stone benchtop as he angled it away from Vallone.

On the external feed, the street outside the mill came into focus. A dark shape moved near the left side. He toggled the camera. More figures—stacking up on the right.

His Crime Stoppers app was blinking an alert.

Andre exhaled. Things were about to tip sideways.

Especially for Vallone.

The ex-con eased onto the stool beside him, oblivious. "Can you track an item that left Belmont Beach by courier a few days ago?"

Andre rested his fingers on the keyboard. "I'll need an address, date and time." His gaze flicked to the revolver. "I also work a lot faster if I'm not being threatened."

Vallone hesitated, then gave a rueful smile and tucked the gun into his waistband. "An item—suspected to be the Rebrisi puzzle box —was picked up by boat from 112 Belmont Heights Road around ten p.m. on the twenty-fifth. The courier was Delivery By Water Courier Services."

Andre arched a brow and launched a terminal window. He initiated a scan, probing the DBWCS network for open ports. A flick of his wrist. Custom script. Infiltration via an exposed SSH service.

"You found the puzzle box?" His voice stayed smooth, but his pulse quickened.

Out of the corner of his eye, he watched the tactical team shift into formation outside.

Vallone leaned in. "Not yet," he admitted, voice slippery. "But I'll make you a deal." He nodded at the screen. "Help me get the box, and I won't out the both of you to John Chrysler Anderson."

Andre glanced up. A bemused look flickered across his face before he returned to the screen. He pivoted through the internal network, escalated privileges, and modified firewall rules, clearing a path to the central security database. "That's a fascinating proposition."

Vallone edged closer. "You don't believe me? I consulted for DOJ during the ransomware clean-up they brought you in for. I've worked for Anderson, too. And believe me—he'd be real pissed if he knew he had a couple of DOJ agents working deep cover inside his organization. I hear bits of Enrico Sanchez are still missing."

Andre tapped at his keyboard, securing root access.

"I have no idea what you're talking about," he murmured, bypassing encryption protocols. "I don't work for Anderson."

The pigeons had gone quiet in the rafters. Andre suppressed the urge to swallow and invoked a series of iptables flush commands, clearing firewall chains. He was deep inside the network now. One clean SQL dump. And bingo. Full access to the records.

Vallone smirked. "Andre Landvik. DOJ asset. MIT prodigy. Deep cover black hat. That's you, isn't it?"

Andre ignored him, eyes on the code. But his pulse was thumping like a jackhammer.

Every word Vallone spat was going to be picked up by Annouie's surveillance system.

He triggered the custom script to scrub the drives. No time to edit. Just wipe and move.

"That's quite a story you're spinning," he said, glancing at the Camera One feed.

Outside, the group leader raised a gloved hand.

The stack tensed on either side of the door.

Even the pigeons held their breath.

Andre slammed his laptop shut, slipped it away, and slung the bag across his chest. "Thanks for the address. I'll take it from here."

Three.

Vallone's hand twitched toward his gun. "Where do you think you're going?"

Two.

Andre raised both hands in mock surrender, his expression bored. "Nowhere. There's no warrant for my arrest."

The doors exploded inward.

"POLICE! HANDS IN THE AIR!"

Tactical officers stormed through the breach.

Vallone's eyes went wide. "Shit!" He bolted for the storage room, slamming the door shut behind him.

Andre sighed, raising his hands higher as officers surged into the kitchen. "For the record," he said, deadpan, "I was cooperating."

One of them shoved him to his knees, zip ties locking around his wrists.

Andre winced.

Not how he'd planned to spend his afternoon.

Or his evening.

One thing was certain: he wouldn't be meeting Hope for dinner.

But he suspected the PA already knew that.

Chapter Forty

Nicholas drained the last dregs of his tea as the tactical team flooded through the warehouse doors three hundred feet away, up the street. He snagged the waitress by the elbow as she darted past.

"Any idea what's going on?" he asked, voice casual, though he doubted she knew anything. Still, people often knew more than they realized.

She bent close, her breath warm against his ear as she cupped her hand to whisper, "Jack Vallone went into that building two hours ago. I ID'ed him and rang the Crime Stoppers hotline." Her lips curled into a smirk as she straightened, satisfaction glowing on her face.

Nicholas's mouth tightened into a silent "oh" as she darted away with his dirty dishes, a strut in her step.

Vallone.

Another player on the board.

He rose slowly and unbuttoned his jacket, making sure his credentials were clearly visible. Dropping a few coins on the table, he let his hand slide to his hip. His fingers traced the familiar outline of his Sig Sauer P226, snug in its paddle holster.

With his weapon close, Nicholas stepped off the curb and crossed the street—into the unfolding chaos.

* * *

A small crowd had already gathered at the roped-off perimeter. Nicholas ducked under the barricade and strode toward the building.

"You can't be here, sir."

An officer stepped into his path near the main doors. Nicholas clocked him instantly—the operations commander. He lifted his lanyard, letting the man scan his credentials.

The officer blinked, gaze narrowing. "You work for the Minister for Police?" He gave Nicholas a quick once-over.

Nicholas nodded and dropped the lanyard against his chest. He retrieved a notepad and pen from his jacket. "His PA. He sent me as soon as he heard. Wants to be kept in the loop." He poised his pen. "Vallone's still on the premises, I assume."

The OC's brow furrowed. "No. Squirted the second we breached."

A commotion drew their attention—two officers emerged carrying a large laptop, a water-cooled chassis, and a black gear bag. Nicholas stepped aside as they passed, watching them load the equipment into a white van parked across the street.

"Anyone else inside?" His pen hovered midair.

The officer leaned in. "Vallone had a Eurasian man at gunpoint. He's been escorted to the station. Real compliant."

Nicholas's gaze drifted toward the southern end of the warehouse. "This Vallone's hide-out?"

The OC shook his head. "We don't think so. Neighbors report a woman's been squatting here. We've issued an alert, but the description's vague. Hopefully, the guy we brought in can shed more light."

Nicholas handed over a business card. "Keep me posted. Sir James will want a full report once you've spoken to him." He gestured toward the mezzanine. "Mind if I have a look around?"

The officer shrugged. "There's not much left to see but go ahead. Just remember—anything you find goes through chain of custody."

Nicholas nodded and snapped his notebook shut. He stepped deeper into the mill.

The building was little more than a husk—iron girders, concrete, and half-built partitions. Pigeon droppings streaked the floor. A metal staircase led to the upper floor. At the south end, behind a partially constructed dividing wall, a grand piano loomed on its riser, framed by the windows. Beyond the glass, a narrow wharf jutted into the river.

As he turned, two officers clattered down the stairs carrying a box of hardware between them. Another pair emerged from the kitchen, voices low as they swept the storage room.

"All clear," one of them called.

"Okay. Let's wrap this up. Muster outside. Dunbier's crew will be here in fifteen." The OC gestured sharply, and his team filed out through the shattered doors. He surveyed the scene, shaking his head. "Better notify the owner, too."

As the last officer exited, Nicholas crouched and began his sweep.

The distinctive tread patterns of Alt-Berg boots—standard for the tac team—were easy to trace. He followed them to the staircase, around the kitchen island, and into the storage room. But two other sets caught his eye. One was familiar. Jimmy Choo high-tops. Landvik's. Clean, narrow, clustered around the kitchen.

The other was heavier. Army surplus combat boots.

Nicholas studied the treads. The combat boots had traversed the stairs and ended in the storage room.

He rose and climbed the stairs, the metal steps clanging under his weight.

Upstairs, a new mattress lay on a rusted iron frame. The sheets had that pristine, just-out-of-the-packet look. Soft. High thread count. Definitely a woman.

His gaze slid to the desk by the balcony: a curved monitor, racing mouse, compact keyboard. The rack was empty—drives stripped clean.

A hacker's rig. Advanced. Portable. Not government-issue. Something more niche.

Shiruku's lair? The black hat hacker had been making a lot of noise lately.

Sir James would want eyes on her. But Nicholas had other plans.

He descended the stairs just as his phone began to buzz. He answered with a thumb-swipe.

"Sir James?"

"Why haven't you been answering your phone?" the politician growled.

Nicholas stepped into the storage room, drawing his weapon on instinct as he scanned the corners.

"Didn't Maria tell you? I have a stomach bug. Been vomiting all day. It's highly contagious."

He sliced the room—clearing corners like it was a drill. Empty. Still, something about the air caught him: briny, faint decay, and a familiar undertone he recognized but couldn't place.

He moved to a shelf. A cardboard box overflowed with trophies. He pulled one free.

Annouie Bach, Junior Gymnastics Champion.

He dropped it back and kept moving.

A blur of motion startled him—a rat skittered across the floor.

He grunted and turned his focus to the walls. Knocked lightly, listening for a tell-tale resonance.

Sir James rumbled in his ear. "Contagious or not, get your ass back here. The shit's about to hit the fan."

Nicholas crossed to the far wall and kept knocking.

"Maria's prepping a list of things I need—"

"Did I mention I'm contagious?" Nicholas quipped. He worked methodically, rapping his knuckles against the bricks.

Then—a hollow response. His lips almost twitched into a smile.

Fingertips gliding, he felt for the seam.

"What do I care? Wear a mask."

A click. An exhale of air. Part of the wall swung inward.

He pulled out a red penlight and raised it high. The beam cut into the dark, revealing stairs descending below the mill.

"You'll have to excuse me, sir. I'm about to be sick again." He ended the call before Sir James could reply.

Phone pocketed. Gun ready.

Nicholas stepped into the dark, wingtips tapping faintly against the stone.

* * *

Jack Vallone emerged from the sewer tunnel a mile south of the River Street mill. He climbed the embankment and dropped onto the concrete path, breathing hard.

He could've sworn he'd heard footsteps behind him—but now, only the sound of his own ragged breath filled the air.

He straightened, shook off the unease, and followed the path down to the pebbled shore, boots crunching over gravel.

A small boat lay beached sixty feet away.

He picked his way toward it.

Behind him, the sewer grate creaked. A figure stepped from the tunnel's mouth.

Jack crouched behind the gunwale, body taut with tension.

Nicholas Hope.

Hope scanned the beach, eyes sweeping. Then—without hesitation—he squelched off in the opposite direction.

Jack bared his teeth as he watched him recede into the distance.

Not his first tango with Hope.

He climbed back up to the path and followed it to the top of the grade.

His breathing steadied. He began to hum.

He choked off the tune as a petite Asian woman appeared silently on the path ahead.

She smiled—white teeth gleaming.

Jack reached for his weapon.

She spun, delivering a sharp kick to his chest. He slammed into the wall. His gun tumbled down the embankment.

He fumbled for the folding knife strapped to his thigh.

She struck again—open palm to the throat.

His airway collapsed. The blade clattered onto the path. He dropped to the ground, gasping like a fish.

She crouched beside him, perfectly calm.

"Are we done?" she asked, tilting her head. "Because my employer would like a word."

* * *

Jack Vallone had no idea how much time had passed since the woman shoved him, bound and gagged, into the trunk of her car.

For one brief moment, he'd blinked up at the night sky as the lid lifted—three seconds, maybe less—before someone put his lights out. After that, nothing.

Until now.

He tried to lift his hand—a reflex—only to realize he couldn't. A cold spike of fear shot through him. Other hand—useless. Legs—dead weight. Throat—silent.

Not even a croak.

Panic surged, sharp and suffocating. He strained, willing himself to move, but his body refused to obey.

Then—something skittered past his cheek.

A whisper of movement. A tickling sensation.

Chittering followed.

Bile burned his throat as the creature scurried away. A rat.

If he could've screamed, he would have.

The air was stale. The distant rumble of the river thrummed through the stone walls. Cold seeped into his bones.

Was the paralysis temporary?

A finger twitched. Then another. With an effort, he forced his right eye open. Then the left. He blinked.

Again.

Blackness swallowed him whole.

Panic twisted through his gut. Blind? Buried? Already dead? Until—shadows, dim and grainy, took shape. The subterranean room bled in—gray and ghostly.

He was lying on a slab of cold rock. Around him, coffin-filled alcoves loomed.

A preparation room.

An uneasy tickle crept down his throat. He coughed. The sound rolled back at him. He coughed again. Louder. The echo stretched on and on.

He was in the catacombs.

At least one thing was in his favour—he knew the tunnels beneath the city like the back of his hand. He just needed a starting point.

As if in answer, a deep vibration rumbled through the chamber. The stone beneath him trembled—for nearly a minute—then fell still.

Water. The murmur of pedestrian traffic. And now—the unmistakable grind of the bridge rising.

Jack smiled. There were only a few places along the riverbank where all three aligned.

Before he could pinpoint his exact location, footsteps echoed down the passage to his left. Soft. Measured.

They halted.

A sharp scent—coffee—curled through the air.

Then something pierced the side of his neck.

Heat flooded his veins. Sensation roared back. His lips tingled. His fingers twitched. A bulb flared above him.

The naked light swung lazily, casting jagged shadows across the domed ceiling and the bone-filled alcoves.

"Good evening, Mr. Vallone."

A face swam into view, eclipsing the bulb.

"My name is Sir James Gibson. Perhaps you've heard of me. Not that it matters. All you need do is answer my questions—truthfully—and this will go well. If you don't . . ." He grinned. "There will be excruciating pain."

Jack's pulse hammered in his ears.

"The drug you were just injected with," Sir James continued, "amplifies the pain centers of your brain."

Jack's throat was dry. He swallowed hard. "Whatever it is, I don't have it."

Sir James chuckled. "Oh, we know. But you know who does. A name, Mr. Vallone. That's all we want."

A shadow shifted behind him. The Asian woman from the alley stepped forward, snapping on a pair of surgical gloves.

"Meet Dr. Chin," Sir James said, his voice bright with anticipation. "She's going to help you remember."

Chapter Forty-One

The first thing Annouie noticed as she stepped into the Dorset's foyer was the low murmur of voices. The second was the sheer opulence.

Set in one of the city's most exclusive districts, the hotel was pure ritz: gleaming surfaces, gaudy chandeliers, overstuffed sofas parked in alcoves.

But beneath the surface, it was seedy as hell.

Exactly the kind of place Anderson favored for city business.

She kept moving, keeping the restaurant hubbub to her left, and headed for the bank of elevators. A tap on the middle call button, a soft chime, and the doors slid open.

While the car climbed to the seventh floor, she glanced at Meyer-Edwards's envelope peeking from her tote. Her chest tightened—a twinge of guilt. She forced it aside. Getting Isidore out of Craiova mattered more than a prima donna's ego.

The elevator dinged, and the doors parted.

She stepped into the corridor. Room 712 was second from the end.

She rapped twice. The security chain rattled. The door opened, revealing a wall of a man dressed in a black silk suit. Anderson's sentry.

He tapped his earpiece. "Ms. Bach's here."

Raucous sports commentary echoed down the penthouse hall. Although Anderson was only thirty feet away, the guard stepped forward, palms out for a pat-down.

Annouie vaulted the hallway console, landed lightly, and—without breaking stride—sprinted for the lounge.

The guard's hands closed on empty air. "Hey—"

She skidded to a stop in front of Anderson and flung the envelope onto the glass coffee table.

"At ease, Greg," Anderson said, waving the bruiser off and thumbing his TV remote to mute. He picked up the envelope, raising his brows. "All here?"

"Of course."

He tipped the contents onto the table, paused at the photo, and smiled. "Good. Very good."

From a leather satchel beneath the coffee table, he produced a thick legal folder. He signed page two, dated it, and slid the packet across.

Annouie skimmed the fine print.

No more lies. No more deceptions.

Satisfied, she stowed the papers in her bag.

Anderson leaned back. "The balance is in your account—though after finalizing your contract, there wasn't much left."

Her brow knitted. "There should've been plenty—"

He sighed. "Early termination clause. Directors insisted."

"What clause?"

Anderson rubbed his chin, his five o'clock shadow edging into the first stages of a beard. "Should've read the fine print."

She stepped closer. "It wasn't there."

The guard's hand twitched toward his taser.

"Relax," she said. Then to Anderson: "I need that money."

He offered a bland smile. "Sure. Call me. Good operatives are hard to find." A business card skated across the glass.

Annouie eyed it with disgust. "I'd rather sleep on the street."

"Your call." He raised his glass and unmuted the game. "Oh—heard Special Ops raided the mill on River Street this afternoon."

Crowd noise roared from the screen.

Annouie froze. Raided?

Of course. They were probably there for Vallone. And she'd asked Andre—

She didn't finish the thought. She spun and strode for the door.

* * *

Annouie stepped outside the Dorset and was instantly swept into the rush-hour exodus. Office workers streamed from high-rise buildings, their soft leather wingtips, brogues, pumps, and sneakers pounding the sidewalk as they funneled toward the train station.

She slipped free, vaulted the retaining wall between the station and the park, and followed the winding path downhill. Plane trees arched overhead, the air thick with the scent of rotting fruit. Indigo faded to black. Lamps flickered to life along the foreshore.

She followed the path for another mile, then stopped.

She tapped her earpiece.

"Oria, safe house status?"

"Taped off. Under surveillance."

Her stomach tightened—River Street was burned.

"And Andre?"

"In custody."

She squeezed her eyes shut—no money, no home, and now no friend.

A hollow ache spread through her chest as she glanced down at her bag. She had one last card to play.

The manuscript.

Settling onto a park bench, she slipped her phone from her back pocket and opened an end-to-end encrypted chat.

She typed quickly:

> ANNOUIE: `I can get you the manuscript.`

Gibson's reply popped up seconds later:

> GIBSON: `Where's my Venus?`

She skipped the question. Straight to business.

> ANNOUIE: `Want it or not?`

The river lapped against the wall, each ripple stretching into the night.

> GIBSON: `Name your price.`

She typed. The number was obscene.

A heartbeat later:

> GIBSON: `I want to see it.`

She laughed aloud.

> ANNOUIE: `Not a chance.`

> GIBSON: `I need proof. Send a pic.`

She laid the manuscript flat, stood, snapped a photo, and hit send.

Then waited.

Her heart thudded.

Silence stretched like a held breath.

> ANNOUIE: Do we have a deal? Yes or no?

The seconds dragged. The river lapped. Her grip tightened around the phone.

Then:

> GIBSON: *Yes.*

Her fingers flew:

> ANNOUIE: Wire the funds.

His reply was instant:

> GIBSON: I want to meet.

She scoffed. No way in hell was she meeting with Gibson.

> ANNOUIE: No.

> GIBSON: Then the deal's off.

She swore softly.

> ANNOUIE: When?

> GIBSON: Tonight. Midnight. My place.

She grimaced. Not without Andre to back her up.

> ANNOUIE: Can't. Make it two tomorrow.

> GIBSON: I'm on a deadline. Noon's the latest I can do.

Her jaw clenched.

> ANNOUIE: `Fine. Noon.`

She exited the chat. Resumed walking.

Her thoughts churned. *Bring Andre in. Skip class. Deliver the manuscript.*

Bailing Andre out wouldn't be simple. Not this time. Not without knowing what went down at the mill.

"Oria, replay Camera Two footage from four-thirty to five-thirty p.m. at double speed."

"I am unable to process your request," the AI replied.

"Why?"

"The drives have been securely wiped."

Of course. Perimeter breach protocols. Andre would've executed a zero-trust data purge—overwriting active logs, encrypting volatile memory, and triggering a secure erase command on local and remote servers.

She blew out a long breath, tension easing. Andre always had her back.

But she needed him now more than ever.

"Authenticate override. Route through backup node."

"Specify target," the AI prompted.

"Camera Five." She rattled off the IP address—for the webcam behind the kitchen clock. "Reconstruct the data stream and run the query again."

A panoramic view materialised in her display—Andre and Vallone at the kitchen island. The audio was pristine. Every word isolated from the background noise.

At the five-minute mark, her pulse stuttered.

"Stop. Roll back thirty seconds. Playback at normal speed."

Vallone's words filled her ear, each accusation a hammer to her chest.

Andre. A double agent.

Looking back, the red flags were undeniable—the off-books Tier-One trauma facility in Bogotá. Taking out that little worm in Jakarta before he could pull the trigger. Magically conjuring mission-critical tech, always at a moment's notice.

The pattern of access was too clean. His ability to redirect intelligence flows too convenient. The delayed reports, subtle diversions—just enough to avoid detection.

None of it was coincidence. It was planned and executed with ruthless precision.

Andre Landvik hadn't just played her. He'd run her like an asset.

A sharp ache bloomed beneath her ribs, widening, spiraling downward—until the slap of water against brick snapped her back.

A boat churned upriver.

Delivery by Water Courier Services.

The web address jolted her into sharp focus.

She shouldered her bag and hurried back to the main thoroughfare. Wading against the tide of foot traffic, she pushed through the crowd until she spotted a department store.

Inside, she grabbed an envelope, a burner, and a notepad. Then she ducked into the changing rooms at the rear.

Store music trickled from the ceiling as she shut the cubicle door.

She tore the packaging from the burner phone and powered it on.

Pulling up the courier's website, she filled out the form.

Enough time to attend classes, meet with Gibson, and find a way inside the mill before it was delivered.

She pulled a pen and scribbled quickly on the notepad, tore off the page, and shoved it into the package.

Then she hesitated.

Removed the Oria2 SmartSpecs.

Without them, there was no Shiruku. No second chances. No cheating Meyer-Edwards.

But loose ends were dangerous—especially with a deep-cover operative like Andre Landvik.

Her fingers curled around the specs one last time. Then she dropped them into the envelope and sealed it.

She stood, strode for the checkout, paid, and exited through the glass doors.

Pedestrian traffic still clogged the sidewalk. She walked to the corner, carrying the envelope like an offering. Once the courier took receipt, there would be no going back. The last thread tying her to a life she never chose would be severed for good.

Chapter Forty-Two

Katrine Ratcliffe jogged up the steps of her fourth-floor walk-up, keys digging into her palm. She kicked off her boots and headed straight to the kitchen.

Annouie was still incommunicado—which meant she was keeping secrets. *Again.*

Katrine sighed and yanked open the fridge. Her fingers skimmed the long-necked bottles, the cool glass anchoring her frayed thoughts. A few drinks to take the edge off while she worked. She grabbed the chardonnay, kicked the door shut, and padded down the narrow hallway toward the living room.

She slumped onto the sofa, pulled her laptop across the glass-topped coffee table, and twisted off the chardonnay cap. She took a long swig as the device ran through its two-factor authentication sequence.

The law enforcement network login screen flickered to life. She entered her credentials, gaze drifting to the idle VPN chat window in the corner.

Shiruku had gone dark.

Not a good sign.

The loading wheel vanished, revealing the National Art Recovery database's landing page. Katrine hunched over the keyboard and began entering her queries.

For two hours, she sifted through siloed data—cross-referencing registries, police records, intelligence feeds. The process was painstaking. Shiruku's AI could've scraped, collated, and synthesized it in minutes.

Another swig. The bottle was nearly empty—and that edge hadn't dulled.

She never should've gone to Dunbier about the black hat.

Katrine scanned through her handwritten notes. Nicholas Hope had kept to the shadows for most of his life, his name surfacing only two years ago in political circles. His bio was as clinical as the man himself: graduated *summa cum laude* in criminology, immediately recruited by Art Recovery.

A newsreel of Sir James Gibson's election victory played in a side panel. Katrine clicked it.

Hope stood beside him—preternaturally still, a controlled presence, perfectly curated.

Sir James launched into his speech. Katrine double-clicked on the playback speed. He immediately began chipmunking through the rest of his spiel.

". . . been a bit wild after my return from the Middle East . . . the investigation was the turning point. I went off to Cambridge. Straightened myself out. Went into law."

Katrine swiped to the next clip.

Hope stepped up to the lectern.

She leaned in, propping her chin on her knuckles.

Undeniably handsome, infuriatingly inscrutable. And yet—she could sense it. Something wild, barely contained, simmering just beneath the surface.

Indicators. Tells.

He was hiding something.

Hope's voice carried through her speakers—smooth, even.

"I was an analyst, working in art recovery—that's how I met Sir James. We were tracking the Rebrisi manuscript, and our intel pointed to a rogue operator known as the Gray Cat. Sir James's firm got involved. He took a particular interest in my work. When he decided to run for office, I joined him as his campaign manager."

Katrine eased back, fingers tapping lightly against her keyboard. The niggle at the base of her skull sharpened. Shiruku had been hinting at a connection between The Bayside Ripper and the lost Rebrisi works.

She set the bottle aside and reached for the keyboard—

The intercom buzzed. A sharp, jarring intrusion.

Her hands froze. She glanced at the wall clock.

Much too late for visitors.

She slid off the sofa and moved to the door, pressing her eye to the peephole.

Detective Kyle Saunders stood outside, bouncing from foot to foot. Raw energy crackled off him.

She unlatched the chain and pulled the door open. "Something on your mind, Detective?"

Saunders didn't answer—just shouldered past her.

"I know how to flush out The Bayside Ripper."

She heeled the door shut and followed him into the living room.

His gaze snagged on the bottle of wine. He picked it up with a smirk. "Seriously, Ratcliffe? Chardonnay? You got anything stronger?"

She shrugged. "Depends. Tell me how we get our perp, and I'll bring out the Scotch."

He dropped onto her sofa, elbows on knees. "We beat the bushes."

She scoffed. "That's it?"

He snatched her pen and started scribbling on her notepad. "These murders are tied to Timothy Gibson, but he's got an iron-clad alibi. CCTV places him miles away from each scene at the estimated times of death. No way he could've done it." He tapped the pad, eyes sharpening. "What if it's not one killer, but a team—covering their tracks by making it look like the work of a lone psychopath?"

The sofa creaked as Saunders leaned forward. "And if it is—what are they trying to hide?" He flipped the pen between his fingers. "I did some digging. Gibson's been shopping Rebrisi's *Venus* on the dark web—the same painting stolen in the Gartner Haus heist two years ago."

Katrine stilled.

She reached for the Scotch and two tumblers, setting them on the table. "What's your plan for flushing out these bad actors?"

Saunders grinned. "Lean on everybody in Gibson's orbit and see who cracks."

She unstoppered the bottle and poured two fingers into each glass. "Like the PA?"

"Yeah, the PA. One of us goes overt—lets him know we're watching. The other stays covert. When someone starts twitching, we know we're onto something." He grabbed one of the glasses and knocked it back.

Katrine refilled it, her mind already working the angles. Hope was Art Recovery—not a career criminal. But if they wanted a window into Gibson's black-market operations, the man who knew everything—the PA—was the best place to start.

She rolled her tumbler between her fingers, watching the amber liquid catch the light. Then, with a decisive nod, she set it down.

"All right. I'm in. Tomorrow morning. Seven-thirty. That coffeehouse on Chapel Road." Her gaze locked onto his. "We go over the plan, then hit his office before eight."

Saunders grabbed the bottle and poured the last of the Scotch into his glass. He swirled it, considering.

Then, a slow, wolfish grin spread across his face.

"Can't wait to put the wind up that preppy, privileged bastard. Guy's never had dirt under his nails." He drained the glass and set it down with a soft clink. "Reckon he'll run like a fox—then the real fun begins."

Chapter Forty-Three

As early-morning traffic crawled along Chapel Road, Nicholas Hope took the front steps of Victoria House two at a time. He paused at the door, patting down his pockets for his key.

Across the street, a bus hissed into its stop, commuters spilling from the front and middle exits in a sluggish tide. It idled for another thirty seconds, belched exhaust, then groaned back into motion. Nicholas jammed the key into the lock, twisted, and entered.

Straight to the desk. Hit play. Set the answering service to speaker. Then into the print room.

The messages played, filling the foyer. He sorted them mentally—flagging anything that might impact Sir James's re-election bid.

The printer whirred. Pages spewed into the tray. He snatched them, already ticking more items off his to-do list.

The final message stopped him cold.

Usman Malik.

"I ran further tests. Your DNA flagged a match almost immediately. I had to double-check the figures, but there's no denying it—the Wilkin's Beach John Doe is your father."

The printouts slipped from Nicholas's hands.

He retraced his steps, approaching the answering machine like it might bite.

"But that's not all. I expanded the search—cross-referenced military personnel records through CODIS and DoD databases. That's when I got a hit. John Doe has a name. James Gibson. Given he was murdered, it's strange he was never reported missing."

Cold dread curled in Nicholas's gut.

Not strange at all.

He'd suspected it all along—Sir James Gibson was an impostor.

He snatched a pen, scribbled down the number, and punched it into the keypad.

Two rings.

Then—

"Dr. Malik."

Nicholas steadied his breath, tamping down the white-hot rage crawling beneath his skin.

"It's Nicholas Hope. I'm returning your—"

"Sir James Gibson is an impostor," Malik blurted.

Nicholas's hand tightened on the desk's edge. His voice, when it came, was low—stripped of warmth. "Listen carefully, Malik. I'm on my way. Stay put. Speak to no one. Not even Thorpe. This stays between us."

A beat.

Then, Malik's sharp exhale. "I understand."

Nicholas hung up, turned abruptly on his heel, and bolted for the bike in the print room.

* * *

Detective Ratcliffe wiped her boots on the mat outside Victoria House and knocked. No answer. She pushed the door open and stepped into the foyer.

Empty.

A dull thump from the kitchenette gave Nicholas Hope away. She followed the sound and poked her head through the doorway.

Hope was crouched beside a bicycle, fingers smeared with grease. He grunted when she stepped into view.

"Nicholas Hope?"

The chain slipped through his fingers and hit the floor with a metallic clatter. He exhaled, pushed the bike back against the wall, and grabbed a towel to wipe his hands. "I was on my way out."

She extended a hand. "We met at the morgue."

He kept wiping. After a few beats, she let her hand drop.

"I have some questions about the Gartner Haus heist."

He tossed the towel aside and dragged a distracted hand through his bronze hair. His gaze flicked from the bike to Katrine.

"I only have a few minutes."

"That's all I need."

Exhaling, he ushered her out of the kitchenette and into the office, nodding toward the chair opposite his desk.

She sat. Waited.

He still looked like the preternaturally cool PA from the newsreel —but the glance toward the front doors and the slow, measured breath told a different story.

"How can I help?"

"You worked for Art Recovery?"

He leaned over his landline and pressed the call button. A woman bustled into the foyer.

"Ah, Mr. Hope. I thought you were going out?"

His shoulders lifted in a casual shrug. "I am—as soon as my taxi arrives. Would you mind calling one for me? And—" He glanced at Katrine, brow arched. "Grab me a coffee. Something for the detective, too."

"I thought you only had minutes," Katrine said.

He smiled—a flicker of amusement. "It'll take the taxi at least twenty to get here."

She pulled out her notebook and flipped it open.

"Black, no sugar," she called as Maria disappeared into the kitchenette. The whine of a kettle filled the silence.

Hope's demeanor shifted. His voice dropped. "What do you want to know, Detective?"

"You were in charge of the Gartner Haus heist investigation."

Hope gave a half-smile. "Was. Before I accepted the role as Sir James's PA."

"Did Sir James know you were investigating his son?"

"I never asked, but I imagine he did."

A beat. She slid a folder across the desk.

"What do you make of these?"

He flipped through the documents—articles, journals, papers. Then, on the final page, he paused.

Sara Miles.

His fingers lingered. Then he pushed the folder back.

Maria returned, setting two well-worn mugs on the desk. "Will that be all, Mr. Hope?"

"Yes, Maria. Thank you."

She tottered away. Silence crept in. Katrine watched him closely. His expression hadn't changed—brow smooth, mouth relaxed—but she could sense it.

A deep, bone-weary sadness.

A door at the end of the corridor clicked shut. Hope leaned over his steaming mug. "I'm on a deadline, Detective. Let's cut to the chase—what specifically do you want to know?"

She slid another folder onto the desk. "This is Julia Morecroft." She slapped a crime scene photo down. "This is Rita Holmes." Another. "And this—" She placed the photo of Sara Miles last, watching his face. "—is Sara Miles."

He dragged the photo closer. Rubbed his eyes with the heels of his hands.

Not sadness.

Grief.

Katrine leaned closer. "Did you know any of these women?"

His eyes stayed on Sara's photo.

He blinked. "Yes. They were assisting with my investigations." He looked up. "You think there's a connection between the murders and the heist?"

"We're working that angle."

She paused, struck by the way his hair caught the light.

Bronze hair. Amber eyes. Patrician features.

"How well did you know Sara Miles?"

The stillness in his eyes. The brief pause before answering. Almost an admission.

"We spent time together. She had a particular interest in Rebrisi."

Hope was good at masking his emotions—but not good enough. She jotted a note in her book: *Hope and Miles have a history. Siblings?*

A ping from his computer broke the silence. Hope turned away, fingers skimming over his phone.

"Could I ask about the nature of her interest?" Katrine pressed.

Hope didn't look up. Instead, he hit the call button on his landline.

Maria reappeared.

He grabbed his jacket and shrugged it on. "Taxi's here. Let's pick this up later." He checked his watch. "Maria, find a time later this week and book the detective in."

Without waiting for a response, he strode to the front doors.

A taxi idled at the curb. Hope took the steps two at a time, cut along the path, and slid into the back.

Smooth exit, Katrine thought. But something had rattled him.

The moment the taxi pulled into traffic, a black Suburban executed a tight U-turn and tailed after it.

Katrine stepped outside, tapping her earpiece. "You catch all that?"

Saunders's voice crackled in her ear. "Five by five. Target acquired. Twelve car lengths back."

"Make it fifteen."

"Thought we were going for obvious."

"Don't want him too spooked."

As she headed down the stairs, her phone lit up. She tapped her earpiece again. "Ratcliffe."

"Dunbier here. Thought you'd want to know—Landvik was brought in for questioning last night. Currently cooling his heels in Interview Room Two."

Katrine's stride faltered. "Son of a—"

She broke into a run, sprinting for the unmarked cruiser up the street.

"I'll be there in twenty."

* * *

The second hand on the West Tower clock ticked relentlessly as Annouie strolled the cloistered walkway of the conservatory. Crossing the quadrangle, she exited on the north side, took the stairs two at a time, and sauntered down the corridor. At the end, she pushed through the back doors of the small lecture hall.

At the lectern, Thibault Messier surveyed his students with thinly veiled disdain as they filed in. Then he saw her.

His glare locked onto her. She ignored him, descending casually toward her usual seat halfway back from the stage.

Messier turned to his screen and began calling names.

"Adams? Bell? Brand?"

Annouie flipped open her laptop. A flagged email sat at the top of her inbox. *High priority*. She double-clicked.

"Jacobs? Jones? Nichols?"

The message exploded across her screen:

Some changes have been made to your program. Meet me in my office at nine to discuss.

"Thomas? Whyte? Zeigler?"

"Ms. Bach!"

Messier's voice cracked through the room like a whip.

Annouie glanced up. So did everyone else.

Messier tapped his screen. "Why aren't you on the roll? All third-year students are required to take advanced harmony and counterpoint. I can't grade you if you're not on the list."

She shrugged and shoved her laptop into her backpack, edging into the middle aisle.

"Ms. Bach!" Messier's glare burned into her.

She turned. "Hmm?"

"Where do you think you're going?"

"To find out why I'm not on the roll."

Messier gaped. "A less than ninety-five percent attendance rate will result in a fail. Did you not understand that?"

"I did," she replied. "Which is why I need to sort this out with Ms. Pasolini immediately. Once I do, I promise I'll be back."

Messier wasn't done. "I suppose you also forgot about the homework?"

Right on cue, nervous whispering flared like spotfires around the room.

". . . there was homework . . ."

". . . did you know about this . . ."

". . . but he didn't give us any warning . . ."

Annouie stifled the eye roll. Same old, same old—Messier's favorite trick: burying an obscure assignment deep in the portal where no one would find it.

She met his gaze. Gave a curt nod. "Uploaded last night, sir."

Chapter Forty-Four

Andre Landvik sipped his lukewarm espresso and stared at the blank gray wall. This was taking too long. The young officer was stalling—he was sure of it.

He glanced at his wrist, then caught himself. Right. No watch. The charging officer had taken it the night before, along with his belt and shoelaces.

He didn't need a watch to know he'd been sitting here for hours. At least they'd uncuffed him—a call from his lawyer had put an end to that. Too bad the man was tied up in court for the morning.

Andre exhaled slowly, stretching his fingers. He hated waiting.

He lifted the cup again and took another sip just as the interview room door swung open. An officer stepped through and slapped down his phone, earpiece, watch, wallet, backpack, the Oria2 Smart-Specs, and the messenger bag with *Version One Point One.*

Andre reached for the designer frames and shoved them onto his nose. He inserted the earpiece, pocketed the rest, and rose. The messenger bag went across his chest. He moved for the door.

"DCI Dunbier sends his apologies. Said it was all a misunderstanding," the officer said, following him into the hallway.

Andre flipped open his phone. Ran the tracker. The second pair of Oria2 SmartSpecs was on the move—heading downriver toward Harborside.

He exhaled, tension coiling low in his stomach. At least he could still track Annouie. But the signal was too smooth. Too clean. She should've checked in by now.

The officer struggled to match his stride as he powered down the corridor. "Is there anywhere I can drop you?" she asked.

Andre slung his bag over one shoulder and pushed through the doors into reception. "Kind of you," he said. "But I'll make my own way."

* * *

Katrine Ratcliffe rounded the corner, tires smoking, and floored the accelerator. The cruiser jumped the curb-cut and fishtailed into the station parking lot.

She tapped her earpiece as she climbed out. "Saunders, how's our bird?"

A burst of static. "I think I've been made. Almost lost him on Taylor and Firth. Just pulling into the medical examiner's now. Continue to tail?"

"Up the stakes. He knows he's being followed—now we engage. Shake him up. Find out what was so urgent he had to ditch me and sprint to the M.E.'s."

"I'll use Thorpe as cover."

"Good idea. I'm at the station—Landvik's in Interview Two."

She killed the call, sprinted for the door, flashed her card, and shoved it open, boots thudding as she shot down the hall.

The bullpen buzzed louder than usual. Staff clustered around the wall-mounted screen. A banner scrolled beneath the feed:

BREAKTHROUGH IN JOHN DOE CASE—M.E. BRIEFING 10 A.M.

She cut through the knot of uniforms and ducked into Dunbier's office.

He loomed behind his desk, sweat glistening at his brow, glaring at a uniformed officer standing at rigid attention.

"Had we known, sir—"

"Landvik still here?" Katrine asked.

Dunbier jerked a thumb. "Dismissed."

The officer turned and fled.

Katrine heeled the door shut and dropped into the nearest seat.

His lip curled. "DOJ called. Landvik is not to be detained, questioned, or inconvenienced in any way."

"Sorry. Did you say *inconvenienced*?" She rose halfway out of her seat. "That's—"

"Bullshit. I know." He rubbed a palm across his temple. "We've been told to stand down. That's it. No explanation. 'Need-to-know'. And apparently, we don't."

She sank back. "Landvik was with Vallone."

"And fifty meters from the Shiruku raid," he said. "It's fishy as hell. But the official story is—Vallone took him hostage."

"Meaning Landvik *is* Shiruku?"

"My read, yes. Unfortunately, DOJ shut us down before we could press him."

"What about CCTV?"

Dunbier swiveled his monitor. "Got this from a convenience store across the street. Vallone enters at 3:02. At 3:30, this woman walks past."

Grainy footage filled the screen. A figure in a cap, head down.

"Facial recog?"

"No. But watch."

He switched to a side-alley cam. The woman vaulted off a bin, scaled two stories, and slipped through an open window.

Katrine leaned closer. Froze the single semi-clear frame. Zoomed.

"Pixelated as hell," Dunbier muttered.

She kept her eyes on the screen. Something familiar about the woman's jawline—distinctive, stubborn.

"We ran checks on the building, too," he said.

"Let me guess—owned by a shell company buried behind three more, all offshore?"

"Got it in one."

He took the mouse, scrubbed forward. "She leaves at 4:15. Still camera-shy. Then—" He fast-forwarded. "Landvik arrives at 4:45."

Katrine straightened. Drew a slow breath. It wasn't hard to join the dots. "She's tied to Landvik. Might be our Shiruku. Want me to follow up?"

He nodded. "But do it quietly. DOJ's all over this." His brows drew together like thunderheads. "And I'm not starting a turf war."

* * *

Nicholas first noticed the black Suburban three minutes after leaving Victoria House. Given the surprise visit from Detective Ratcliffe, it was conceivable that the man tailing him was her larger, less intelligent partner.

He leaned forward. "Drive me around the suburbs until I say otherwise."

"Any particular route?" the cabbie asked.

"Wherever you like."

Ten minutes passed.

He angled his head toward the side mirror.

The Suburban was still there.

With a sigh, he tucked away his phone. He didn't have time for games.

"Take me to the City Forensics Unit."

The cab veered left, leaving behind the leafy sprawl of the suburbs and descending into the concrete mayhem of the industrial district. Warehouses blurred past. Nicholas sat in silence, ordering the chaos in his head.

It didn't seem possible. But the more he thought about his childhood—the foster homes, the social workers, his mother's delusions—the more Malik's discovery made sense.

And now—he was sure.

Sir James Gibson was an impostor. And, more than likely, a killer.

Nicholas's fingers drifted to the Sig Sauer P226 nestled snug in its holster.

Gibson would meet his fate soon. Just as soon as he took care of the doctor.

His face remained impassive as the cab pulled up outside the Medical Examiner's office—a squat, four-story building.

He climbed out, slid several crisp hundreds through the driver's window, and strode inside.

* * *

Emil shoved Usman toward the elevators, his voice rising. "Now is not the time to argue. Sir James is on his way."

He hammered the down button.

Usman's shoulders slumped. "But Emil . . . the John Doe. We should call the police."

"Stop talking and do as I say."

The elevator dinged.

The doors slid open—

Nicholas Hope stepped out, suppressed Sig Sauer P226 leveled at Emil's chest. "Hands up. I won't say it twice."

Emil snapped his mouth shut and raised his hands. Usman hesitated before lifting his own, his gaze flicking between Hope and the pistol—caught between horror and fascination.

Hope gestured with the gun. "Back inside."

They obeyed, retreating into the autopsy suite. The John Doe's body lay on the table in full view.

Hope chinned toward it. "That him?"

Usman nodded.

Thorpe stared at Hope as if seeing a ghost. "So it's true." He took a faltering step forward, eyes wide. "We thought you were dead."

"We?"

Emil stiffened. "Sir James."

Hope's lips lifted into a sneer, fingers tightening on the trigger. "You mean Daniel Parrish?"

"Who's Daniel Parrish?" Usman backed into a trolley, knocking a remote to the floor. The large flat screen opposite flickered to life.

A breaking news banner scrolled across the bottom: Gibson's PA son of murdered John Doe found at Wilkin's Beach.

Hope snatched up the remote and flicked through the channels. The story was everywhere.

"How the hell—" His gaze snapped to Usman. "You were supposed to keep this quiet."

Usman paled. "Wasn't me." His eyes darted to Emil.

Hope sighed. "You told Thorpe."

Usman gave a jerky nod.

Emil started inching away. "He's lying."

Hope's expression went blank. The polished PA vanished. What remained was hollow. Merciless. Lethal.

"I was very specific." His voice was chillingly calm. "No sharing."

Then—

He swung and squeezed the trigger.

Blood and brain tissue decorated the wall. Usman toppled, sightless eyes staring at the ceiling.

Emil screamed. Hope turned the gun on him, the suppressor still warm. For a moment, the only sound in the room was that of the droning newscasters.

Emil clamped a hand over his mouth, bile rising as a dark patch spread across his pants.

"Relax," Hope said, faintly amused. "I'm not going to shoot you." He tilted his head, studying him with predatory interest. "Yet."

Emil shrieked again—but this time, he turned and bolted into his office, slamming the door and locking it shut.

Chapter Forty-Five

A low murmur was the first thing Kyle Saunders registered as he slipped into the autopsy suite. Whispering voices. And then—

A muffled sob.

He stilled, listening. It came from the tiny glass-fronted office at the back of the room. Stepping around a gurney, he moved deeper inside.

Thorpe sat slumped at his desk, head in his hands, shoulders shaking.

Saunders barely spared him a glance before his eyes landed on the body on the table. He stopped cold.

The John Doe.

The corpse's chest had been split open, the ribs pulled apart and clamped in place with retractable metal claws. Where the organs should have been, there was only a hollow cavity. The missing parts lay neatly arranged on a steel tray beside him, dissected and cataloged.

Another sob cut through the silence.

Saunders turned—and slipped on something slick. His hand shot out, gripping the cold metal gurney to steady himself. He looked down.

Usman Malik's lifeless face stared up at him, eyes wide, sightless. A single bullet hole marked his forehead—small caliber, precise. Blood pooled beneath him, seeping into the cracks of the linoleum. Saunders crouched, angling for a better look. The exit wound had blown out the back of his skull, splattering brain matter across the wall and window.

Saunders pressed the push-to-talk button on his shoulder mic. "Dispatch, Saunders Five. Confirmed homicide. Male victim, approximate age thirties, gunshot wound to the head. Location: fourth floor, autopsy suite, ME building, John Evans Drive. Possible active shooter still on-site. Requesting immediate backup and EMS Code Three. Will provide updates."

He drew his Glock, keeping his finger indexed, and moved toward Thorpe's office.

Inside, Thorpe hunched over his desk. A hypodermic needle and a vial were arranged neatly in front of him. A tourniquet constricted his upper arm. He lifted the syringe with a trembling hand.

"Please. There's no need for this."

A figure stepped from the shadows, back to Saunders.

Saunders flattened against the wall, Glock raised. He edged closer.

The man turned just enough for a profile view.

Nicholas Hope.

Ratcliffe sure knew how to pick 'em.

Hope raised his weapon—a Sig Sauer P226 fitted with a suppressor.

Thorpe lifted his tear-streaked face. "I did what you asked," he rasped. "All the records have gone."

Hope's finger tightened on the trigger.

"Please. I can still be useful."

"Prove it."

Thorpe grabbed a handful of tissues, blew into them. "The DNA records—there's more you don't know. I can fill in the gaps. Surely you have questions."

"No questions." Hope's voice held a faint edge of disappointment. "Get writing. Then shoot up, or I'll do it for you. And if I do it, it won't be clean."

Tears welled. "The police will never believe it's suicide."

"Why not?" Hope pressed the barrel against Thorpe's temple. "You killed Malik. Then, in a fit of remorse, you blew your own brains out. What's hard about that?"

Thorpe's fingers scrabbled for paper. He grabbed a pen and began scrawling with a shaking hand.

"I could tell you what really happened to your mother," he said, pausing mid-scratch.

Hope stiffened. "I know what happened."

Thorpe glanced up, eyes calculating behind the tears. "Do you really, Peter?"

Hope's jaw clenched. "Don't call me that." His voice scraped on the last syllable.

"The medical certificate was forged—she didn't die of a drug overdose."

Hope's voice dropped to a whisper, low and lethal. "Get writing."

"She was murdered. Just like Sara Miles."

Hope's hand faltered, the gun beginning to lower. "How would you know?"

"I was there," Thorpe said. "I helped him cover it up. And then there was Dora Banks . . . remember her?"

Hope shook his head, confused. "Why would you—"

Saunders swung into the doorway, Glock aimed at Hope's center mass.

"Drop the gun."

Hope moved impossibly fast, snapping the gun up and firing through the doorway.

The first round shattered the window. The second pinged off the jamb. The third punched through the synthetic fibers of Saunders's pants, grazing his thigh before embedding in the floor.

Thorpe ripped the tourniquet from his arm and dropped to the ground, ducking beneath the desk.

Saunders somersaulted out of Hope's line of sight, pain lancing up his spine. He gritted his teeth, rolled onto his feet, pancaked against the wall.

The thin partition wouldn't stop Hope for long.

He dove right, sliding under a table milliseconds before rounds stitched the wall. Plaster dust filled the air. Saunders glanced down—his pants were wet with blood.

He shoved the pain down, crawling forward, Glock gripped tight.

Glass scraped underfoot. Saunders lined up the gun's sights on the windowsill.

A shadow wavered at the boundary between the office and the suite.

He exhaled to a beat of four, steadying his breath. As the figure edged closer, he squeezed the trigger, five pounds of pressure.

The report was deafening. Wood splintered. A grunt of surprise followed.

Saunders scurried backward, sliding beneath a gurney as Hope's arm appeared at the doorway. Bullets spat across the room, tearing into metal, linoleum, cupboards.

Saunders kept sliding, pressing himself into the corner.

Hope stepped into view, shoes crunching broken glass and mortar. Saunders rose to the balls of his feet.

Hope had to be nearly out of ammo.

Get out. Wait for backup.

The unmistakable click of a magazine dropping echoed.

Saunders bolted for the main exit.

Bullets snapped past. He swore—no one reloaded that fast.

Metal crashed as he hurtled past. Without breaking stride, he leapt into the corridor, rolled onto his back, and returned fire.

The slide locked open.

Empty.

He scrambled right, patting down his pockets.

Across the room, Hope stepped through the doors, gun raised. He pulled the trigger.

Click.

Again. *Click.*

Just the empty snap of a spent weapon.

He reached for the Walther PPS MS strapped to his ankle—then froze as the elevator pinged.

His head snapped up, eyes darting. Locked on the fire exit.

He pivoted—and bolted.

Saunders slammed the mag home, dropped the slide, fired. Again. Then again. Masonry exploded beside Hope's shoulder.

Hope didn't flinch. His gaze locked with Saunders's—cool, calculating. He raised a hand in a mocking salute.

Then vanished into the stairwell.

Saunders fired again—too late. The fire door hissed shut. He slammed a fist into the floor and swore as uniforms flooded the corridor.

"Shooter sighted. Fire exit. Semiautomatic confirmed." His voice barely carried over the thunder of boots.

"Alpha, with me. Bravo, cover the exits," the lead officer barked. Two peeled off into the stairwell.

Another ding.

A young officer stepped from the second elevator, eyes sweeping the chaos. She spotted Saunders, lifted her radio.

"Dispatch, Alpha Twelve. Ten thirty-six. One-eighty-seven in progress. Location Fourth Floor foyer, ME's building, John Evans Drive. Officer down. Shooter armed, on foot. Requesting Code Thirty backup. I repeat, Code Thirty, officer down."

Static burst from her comms.

"Copy, Alpha Twelve. All units be advised. Code Thirty in progress, one eighty-seven reported. EMS en route."

Police radio chatter filled the foyer.

She dropped to one knee, pulled trauma shears from her belt. With practiced speed, she cut away his pant leg. Relief crossed her face.

Bruising. Burn marks. Laceration of the epidermis and dermis.

"Only a graze," she said. "You'll live."

Saunders grunted, bracing the wall. "So, I'm good to go?"

She chuckled and shoved him back down. "Not so fast, buddy. EMS is en route. ETA less than five. You're not going anywhere."

Saunders sagged against the wall.

"Fine. But once I'm stitched up and cleared, I'm outta here."

* * *

As he descended to the ground floor, Nicholas Hope calculated the probability of escape.

Zero.

There was no scenario where he walked away from this. His rule of thumb in such situations: cooperate, gather intel, wait.

Escape was simply a matter of timing.

He pushed through the fire exit, hands raised, stepping into the blinding glare of tactical lights. A battalion of SWAT officers stood ready, rifles trained on him. Shouted commands cut through the air, but Hope kept his breath even, his movements slow.

He sank to his knees. Then onto his stomach. No sudden moves. Full submission.

Still, the thing within whispered: *Take the gun. Shoot them all.*

He silenced it.

Deliberately, he interlocked his fingers behind his head. Officers closed in, weapons at the low ready. They stripped him of the knife strapped to his calf. The tiny pistol at his ankle. His notebook.

They cuffed him. Hauled him to his feet.

A large, square-jawed officer stepped forward, badge flashing, and continued the farce by reading him his rights.

"Do you understand these rights as I've read them to you?"

Nicholas exhaled loudly.

The big officer shrugged. "Take him away."

As they marched him through the main doors of the building, he stumbled. His pant leg clung wetly to his calf.

Well, well. Detective Saunders had managed to wing him after all.

He hadn't noticed. Not surprising. Wasn't the first time he'd been shot.

Nor the first time he'd been on the wrong side of the tape.

Blue and red lightbars stuttered across the façade, bathing the building in a surreal glow. News crews crowded at the rope barricade. Cameras panned. Reporters scurried, murmuring into microphones.

He stumbled again as one of the officers shoved him toward the waiting van.

Camera flashes burst like fireworks, capturing the moment.

Instant celebrity.

Nicholas Hope was done.

Time to become someone else.

The van doors groaned open. His escorts guided him inside. He slid onto the cold metal bench. Vibrations hummed through the floor as the smaller officer crouched and chained him to the D-ring in the floor. The bigger man rapped twice on the wall—go time.

The van jolted backward.

Then slammed to a stop.

Before he could brace, it surged forward, pitching him sideways. The smaller officer grinned.

Nicholas righted himself, leaned back against cold steel, and closed his eyes.

Not the end. Just the eye of the storm.

* * *

Saunders struggled into the back of the ambulance and surrendered to the ministrations of the medical team, who immediately set to work—blood pressure monitor, antiseptic swabs, syringes.

Through the open doors, he spotted Ratcliffe crossing the tarmac. He called out. She veered toward him, tactical boots thudding.

"All this fuss over a little scratch," she said, climbing inside.

"I was shot, Ratcliffe," Saunders gritted out, as the medic jabbed a needle into his arm.

Her mouth curled into a grin. "Dunbier told me to give you grief."

"Why didn't he come do it himself?"

She shrugged. "You know Dunbier. Doesn't bother with the small stuff."

He flinched as the medic scrubbed the wound. "What's the word on Thorpe? Any movement?"

"Vanished. But he won't get far—we've got a BOLO out county-wide. Units are on it."

He blew out a slow breath. "Well, we just caught the break we needed. Hope completely lost it when Thorpe called him Peter."

He met her gaze, voice low.

"If Hope really is Darby, then odds are—we just pinned down the Bayside Ripper."

* * *

Emil waded through the stormwater drain, filthy water dragging at his legs. He emerged on the other side, scrambled up the slick bank, and collapsed into the long grass, chest heaving.

In the distance, blue and red lights flashed.

He wiped his brow, fumbled for his phone, and opened his email client. With trembling fingers, he began to type.

Dear Detective Saunders,

My apologies for not staying to personally confess my part in this dreadful drama. Attached is DNA evidence that supports what I am about to tell you.

To begin: Sir James Gibson was born Daniel Parrish. He assumed Sir James's identity—and I deeply regret aiding in that deception.

It began with the real Sir James's mother. She was terminally ill, with less than a year to live. We were about to deploy to the Middle East, but had a few days of leave remaining. We lied, telling her we'd been called up early. It seemed kinder.

During a hunting trip, Sir James was shot. Daniel claimed it was an accident, though I've since come to suspect otherwise. We should have reported it, but agreed on a story: that James died overseas.

We buried him near a creek, marked the grave with a rare black poplar tree, and left for the Middle East, believing Lady Gibson would have passed before we returned. Then we would confess. But she lived.

And to my horror, she believed Daniel was *James. They'd always looked alike—two peas in a pod—and Daniel played along. After her death, he convinced me there was no need to correct the lie.*

What we didn't know was that Sir James had fathered a child with a woman named Maeve Darby. The boy, Peter, was six. They lived in an apartment in Lomanville—presumably paid for by Sir James.

It all began to unravel when Maeve came to the estate, asking after James. She recognized Daniel immediately and threatened to go to the authorities.

Daniel tried to pay her off. She left with the boy. Soon after, she was institutionalized. The boy placed in foster care. Then he vanished. I fear Daniel had a hand in that, too.

When a body recently washed up inside a black poplar on Wilkins Beach, I knew it was Sir James. Dr. Malik's DNA tests confirmed it—and something else: the man known as Nicholas Hope is actually Peter Darby.

Sir James's son.

Until today, I had no idea Peter was still alive.

Emil added every major news feed and local law enforcement agency to the CC field. Then hit send.

A shaky exhale left him. The tension of the last few hours drained away, leaving him light, empty. He lay back in the grass, staring up at the sky.

Crickets chirped.

Frogs croaked.

He was free.

For the first time in decades, he drew in a full breath without the crush of guilt on his chest.

But freedom was fleeting.

He sat up.

Scrambled to the ridge.

Stared down at the sprawling city.

Why did it have to end?

Somewhere out there, *The Way* was anchored in a marina, tanks full, supplies loaded. If he knew Daniel, the bastard was ready to sail at a moment's notice.

All Emil had to do was reach it.

Which meant avoiding the police.

Avoiding Daniel.

And—at all costs—

Avoiding Nicholas Hope.

Chapter Forty-Six

Thibault Messier stormed up to Judith Pasolini's office door and banged loudly.

Judith's alto rumbled through the door. "Come in."

Thibault flung it open—and halted mid-stride.

His gaze flicked from Judith, seated behind her oversized executive desk, to the man opposite, a delicate teacup paused halfway to his lips.

Bach slouched in the only other chair, completely at ease. She caught his eye and winked.

How *dare* she!

White-hot indignation clawed up his throat.

With a soft clink, the man set the teacup gently on Judith's desk.

Thibault forced his face into a smile—tight, toothy, brittle. "Apologies for the intrusion, sir." He shut the door behind him. "But this is a matter of the utmost urgency."

Mackie exhaled, long-suffering. "If it's about the exemption—"

"It is," Thibault snapped. "Why wasn't I consulted? This is highly irregular. You can't just grant her an exemption without departmental input. There are *rules*."

Judith's chair creaked as she leaned forward. "In exceptional circumstances, the dean may exercise his powers of discretion."

"And I *do* have discretionary powers," Mackie added smoothly.

Thibault's face reddened. "But the rules. And—she was *rude*."

Bach straightened, one brow lifting in silent challenge.

Judith cast her a sidelong glance. "If that's the case, I'll speak with her."

Thibault seized on the offer. "Yes, yes. Very rude. She left without permission."

Judith folded her hands. "That was on me."

The dean stroked his chin, tone mild. "I see. Well, given her past performance and the tension between you two, I felt it was in everyone's best interest to grant the exemption. Meyer-Edwards will supervise from this point on."

Thibault's lip curled. "That charlatan shouldn't be supervising anyone—least of all a student. Have we all forgotten what happened to Sophie?"

The dean gave a slow, tired smile. "Then what do you propose?"

Thibault inhaled sharply, masking his relief. "We take the matter before the board. Bach is to attend all classes until a decision is made."

"You're suggesting a hearing?" Mackie asked.

"Yes," Thibault replied. "A hearing before all sitting board members—including myself—with a vote to resolve the matter."

Mackie turned to Judith. "Any objections?"

She shrugged. "It's your call."

Mackie looked to Bach. "Alright, then. Four-thirty this afternoon, Studio One. We'll convene, hear the arguments for and against, and reach a final decision."

* * *

Annouie sauntered down the staircase and yawned as she stepped out into the quadrangle. She found a spot near the cherry blossom and stretched out along the sandstone ponywall.

Her phone buzzed.

A string of messages from Gibson lit the screen, impatience bleeding through every line.

> GIBSON: `Can you make it by eleven?`

She thumbed a reply:

> ANNOUIE: `Why? We agreed twelve.`

His response came fast.

> GIBSON: `Let's say it's a matter of life and death.`

Evasive. Dramatic.

A chill prickled at her nape.

He was up to something.

She checked her watch.

> ANNOUIE: `I can't ditch class.`

> GIBSON: `I'll make it worth your while.`

She frowned, fingers hovering.

> ANNOUIE: `How?`

His next message dropped like a bomb: an offer of a sizable bonus.

Definitely up to something. She gnawed her lip. Clearing her debts was tempting.

Too tempting.

She jumped down from the wall and checked the time again.

> ANNOUIE: `Make it 11:30. Conservatory. Below the clocktower.`

She hit send, slung her backpack over one shoulder, and jogged down the avenue toward the main thoroughfare—already bracing for another unorthodox session with Meyer-Edwards.

* * *

A faint mewling filtered through the closed door of the master bedroom at 112 Thomas Street.

Antony rolled onto his back. The sun was already well above the chimney pots of the neighboring house.

With a muttered curse, he reached for his watch. Ten o'clock.

Kicking free of the sheets, he lurched upright, grabbed his pants and shirt from the back of a chair, and dressed at speed. He flung the door open and thundered down the staircase, each step creaking beneath him.

"Tib, Tib?" he called, voice echoing down the corridor.

The cat emerged, squeezing out from behind the console table. Antony exhaled.

"Ridiculous," he muttered, though his throat tightened. The cat stared back, low purr vibrating its chest.

In the kitchen, his new Motorola flip blinked. He grabbed it, scrolling through unread messages while shaking kibble into a bowl by the pantry door.

One message caught his eye—Jack. Time-stamped 3:00 a.m.

Got a lead. Meet me at the Pier. Ten thirty sharp. And bring the manuscript.

Antony swore. He didn't have the manuscript—and the pier was the last place he'd go for this sort of meeting.

Worse, Bach was due at 10:30.

Can't. Why don't we meet later?

He shoved the phone into his back pocket, grabbed his jacket, and strode for the front door.

Coffee. Newspaper. Cigarette.

He swung the door open.

A woman stood on the threshold.

"Doctor Chin? I was just on my way out."

Tears welled in her dirt-brown eyes, tracking through her makeup to the sharp edge of her pixie-like jaw.

She sniffed, stepped close, and pressed a palm to his chest. "Dear Antony. You must help me."

Before he could stop her, she pushed inside, heels clicking over the floorboards.

He scowled, heeled the door shut, and followed her into the front room.

She pointed at the sofa. "Sit."

He hesitated, unsettled by the shift in tone.

Her eyes glistened again. She waved a hand, voice trembling. "Please, my darling. We need to talk."

When he didn't move, she struck—viper-fast. He should've seen it coming.

She slammed him onto the sofa, then wrenched him down to the rug, twisting his arm behind his back with brutal precision. He recognized the expert wrist-twist. The speed. But the coward in him refused to believe it.

Her heels dug into his ribs as she straddled him.

Adrenaline surged. "What the hell—"

She snapped a pair of handcuffs around his wrists.

Hauling him upright, she shoved him onto the sofa.

He glared at her, incredulous. "This isn't funny."

She gave him a flat look and flopped into the chair opposite. "Where's the manuscript?"

Of course. Everyone wanted it. Why not his therapist too?

"Perhaps if you could be more specific?" he said through gritted teeth.

Chin slid off the chair and moved toward him, eyes gleaming. Her right hand slipped behind her back.

"I work for Luigi Deluca."

He rolled his eyes. Of course she did.

Without warning, she jabbed a loaded syringe into his neck.

He flinched. "Ow! What was that?"

She let the needle fall onto the coffee table. "Something to make you more compliant."

His heart stuttered. Whatever she'd used was already kicking in.

Chin knelt in front of him. "Now we're going to play a game."

He licked his lips, throat dry. "If it's truth or dare, I must warn you, I prefer dare."

Her smile barely moved. "This is a game of truth. The sodium thiopental will help you with that."

Antony scoffed, though his voice had lost its edge. "You know that stuff doesn't work."

"In small doses, true." She leaned in, breath warm against his cheek. "But in larger doses, you won't even think about lying to me."

She jabbed him again.

A loud knock broke the silence.

Chin drew back, grimacing. "I told them to wait."

Antony sagged into the cushions, head heavy, tongue thick. "Why don't we reschedule?"

The knock came again, louder.

"I said wait in the van," Chin shouted, her voice cracking.

Footsteps retreated.

She turned back, dragging a nail down his chest.

"Last chance. Tell me where it is—or this gets ugly."

"What?"

Her palm cracked across his cheek. His head snapped sideways. His skin flared with heat.

"Don't play the fool." Her voice dropped. "You know exactly what I'm talking about."

He turned his head slowly. "I thought you wanted to play."

Chin pushed off the sofa and paced, heels clicking over the boards. Then she spun, stalking toward him.

"All right. One more time—then I stop being polite. Rebrisi's manuscript. The one Aguirre sent you. Where is it?"

Antony shrugged. "No idea."

Her hand trembled. "You're lying."

He lifted his chin. "I wouldn't dream of lying to you."

Her expression hardened. She moved closer, face inches from his, breath laced with peppermint and strawberries.

"Fine. Here's how this works: you will tell me. Everybody does. The only question is how much it hurts before you do."

He gave a soft exhale. "This is going to hurt?"

She pulled back, cold eyes scanning him. "It won't take long to break a pretty boy like you."

She moved to her case. *Snap.* The lid lifted. She ran her fingers over the contents and turned, a pair of shears in her hands.

His breath hitched.

Kneeling before him, she smiled like a cat. "Luigi said not to touch your hands. But he didn't say anything about your feet."

She slipped off his shoe and sock. The cool air on his skin felt unnervingly intimate.

A door slammed.

A girl's voice called. "Mr. Meyer-Edwards?"

Antony shut his eyes. Bach's timing was abysmal.

He rolled his head toward Chin. Her face blurred, shifting in and out of focus.

"I'll tell you everything."

Her eyes lit with vicious glee. She set the shears down and stood.

"I can't touch your hands," she said. "But hers are fair game."

He strained against the cuffs, voice rising. "I just said I'll tell you everything."

Chin put her finger to her lips as she glided to the door. "Don't worry. At least you get to keep your toes—for now."

Chapter Forty-Seven

As Annouie stepped into the hallway, the whispering ceased. She froze, head tilted. Outside, wind hissed through the elms. She dropped her backpack on the kitchen bench and crept down the corridor.

"Mr. Meyer-Edwards?" Her voice echoed through the stillness.

A soft rustle—then a woman stepped into view from the front room, tugging the belt of a ridiculously short trench coat. Dark hair spilled over one shoulder as she cinched the knot tight.

Dr. Chin.

Then she struck—fast and lethal, like a predator.

Annouie steadied her breathing as sensory data poured in. Distance. Speed. Time to impact. By the time Chin launched off the floor, she was five moves ahead.

Sidestep the jab. The tang of lavender and verbena filled her nostrils as Chin's fist sliced through air. The smell of summer at its height.

Chin's body coiled for the uppercut. *Observe. Anticipate. Exploit.* Annouie met the strike with a crisp palm deflection—reflexive, precise. The sound cracked through the corridor as she followed with a double punch to the face. Chin staggered back, blinking.

But not for long.

Former MSS, Chin reset, spun, and lashed out with a horizontal elbow.

Anderson's voice echoed in Annouie's head: *defend and offend.* She slap-blocked, then hammered a fist into Chin's temple and drove a spear-hand thrust at her throat.

Chin backed up, coughing. She wiped her mouth and grinned. "You've learned a lot since Bogotá. As I recall, I left you to bleed out."

Annouie's chest tightened, scar tissue tugging beneath her collarbone. "Yeah. You did." She flexed her fingers, forcing a grin.

Chin prowled back and forth. She feinted left. Annouie held steady, her gaze flicking to the front room. Still no Meyer-Edwards.

Chin laughed. "Is that a little post-traumatic stress I see?"

Just another mind game. *Breathe. Think. Execute.*

Third pass. Chin struck again—heel snapping down in a reverse axe kick. Beautiful form. Timed to perfection. Completely devastating.

And predictable.

Annouie pivoted, blading her body out of range. Chin's foot crashed into a kitchen chair. Wood shrieked as it splintered.

Always play offence.

As Chin stumbled, Annouie struck—a roundhouse kick to the back of the leg. Chin slammed face-first into the brick wall. The wet crunch of cartilage echoed through the house. She staggered, groaning, one hand to her face. Blood streamed from her nose, snaking down her neck.

She tutted softly, smearing blood over her lower face and neck like war paint. Her glare—feral, venomous—promised pain. She raised both hands, bloodied and steady. A grim reminder: she didn't fear wet work.

Annouie jabbed toward her throat.

Chin lunged—uncoiling like a cobra—and swung, enamel jug clutched in her hand.

White light exploded behind Annouie's eyes. Pain arced through her skull. The kitchen tilted.

She dropped to her knees.

Chin discarded the jug and rose.

Annouie blinked. Vision blurred. Body listing sideways.

Chin loomed above her—blood-slicked and grinning. "You still have a lot to learn."

* * *

Antony shifted on the sofa, bare foot twitching as he glanced toward the foyer. The struggle had ceased—replaced by a grunt, wet and guttural. Then a slow, slithering noise across the floorboards.

Not good.

Chin undoubtedly had the upper hand. Which meant she'd be back—to finish the job.

He wiggled his toes. Losing them really wasn't on today's to-do list.

A glint caught his eye. Paperclips. A small pile on the side table.

Useful.

He rose, backing carefully toward the table. After several awkward tries, he pinched one between his third and fourth fingers. He bent the end. Levered it into the lock.

Click.

The left cuff sprang open. The right followed moments later.

He dropped the restraints onto the sofa and shook out his wrists.

Rustier than he'd like—but the muscle memory held.

He slipped off his remaining shoe. The tremors had gone, but his pulse hadn't got the memo—it thumped like a techno bassline as he crept toward the hall.

Breathe. Focus.

He eyed the staircase. He could run. Lock himself in the upstairs bathroom. Call the police.

A smart move. Sensible. What sane people did.

A harsh scrape—wood on tile—echoed down the hall.

Then a crash. Splintering wood.

Antony sucked in a breath.

And another.

He could do this.

Sane people.

He took a third breath—and bolted for the hallway.

* * *

Chin grunted as she slammed into the kitchen island.

Annouie flung the broken chair aside, chest heaving, and closed the distance.

Chin lunged, fingers clawing at the straps of Annouie's backpack. She yanked—and the bag burst open, contents scattering across the floor.

The Rebrisi manuscript landed with a heavy thud, pages fanning out.

Chin's eyes snapped wide.

Annouie was already pivoting, winding up for a roundhouse kick—

Meyer-Edwards burst from the front room and sprinted across the foyer.

Her foot clipped a barstool.

She stumbled.

All the distraction Chin needed.

She dove, rolled, scooped up the manuscript—and bolted for the hallway.

Annouie grabbed the landline from the counter, spun the cord and receiver like a flail and let it fly.

The cord snapped around Chin's leg mid-stride. She went down hard, sliding across the floorboards and slamming into the console table.

The amphora rocked on the edge, hung for a breath—then fell. It shattered on impact.

Chin groaned and dragged herself upright, blood streaking her face. She staggered for the door.

Annouie was already moving.

She sprinted, sprang off the wall to Chin's left, and dropped onto her back. Legs scissored around her torso. Using her momentum, she twisted—wrenching them both to the ground.

She locked her legs. Slid her arm beneath Chin's jaw. Cinched tight.

A blood choke.

Chin thrashed.

At twenty seconds, she flailed.

At twenty-two, she went limp.

Annouie let go, shoved her to the side.

Chin wouldn't be out for long.

Snatching up the manuscript, she climbed to her feet. Chin groaned—eyelids fluttering.

Annouie grabbed her by the ankles and dragged her into the front room.

The cuffs lay on the sofa.

She looped one around Chin's wrist, the other to the heater outlet.

Stepping back, she wiped her brow—palm streaked with blood. She staggered to the sideboard, grabbed a fistful of tissues, and pressed them against her temple.

"Meyer-Edwards?" she called, voice hoarse. "Are you still here?"

* * *

Antony edged toward the balustrade as Chin slammed into the console.

Common sense screamed at him—flee, slip out the beckoning bedroom window, run. But he didn't.

The amphora crashed to the ground, shattering into a thousand pieces. He barely flinched.

He was focused on Bach.

She sprinted up the wall at a dead run and launched herself into the air like an avenging Valkyrie. Her speed. Her control. Her sheer, relentless energy—breathtaking.

For a moment, he remembered what it felt like to be that invincible—before Craiova.

Post-traumatic stress. That was the official diagnosis—a convenient label for the way his hands shook.

That were no longer shaking.

He exhaled slowly and forced himself upright.

Maybe it was the last dregs of the sodium thiopental in his system. But he suspected it had more to do with something else.

Bach.

Ever since that impromptu audition in Studio One, she'd been pulling him closer to that invisible line in the sand—the one he'd drawn there. The one he swore he'd never cross.

And now—watching her choke Chin into unconsciousness with such cold resolve—

That line? Obliterated. Like it had never existed.

* * *

Annouie held no illusions about the man upstairs. If he had any self-preservation instincts left, he was gone. More likely, Meyer-Edwards was holed up in the bathroom with his phone—possibly calling the police.

Or his agent.

That left her with limited time to extract answers from Chin.

She squatted beside the unconscious woman and slapped her cheek. No response.

Annouie sat back on her heels. "You can cut the act. I know you're awake. Who sent you?"

Still nothing.

She stood. "Fine. Play it your way. You're an asset for hire—same as me. I'm guessing your client wants the *Three Elements*."

Chin's jaw twitched. Her lids snapped open, brown irises gleaming.

"I'll make you a deal."

Annouie raised a brow. "Seriously? You think you're in a position to bargain?"

Chin smiled—cool, faintly amused. "Give me the manuscript, and I won't tell Anderson you've had it all along."

Annouie pulled up a stool and sat across from her. "Tell who?"

Chin scoffed. "Darling, are we seriously going to do this?" She rolled her eyes. "All right, then. You work for Security and Risk. You're two million in debt. You could have paid it off years ago—but you won't do wet jobs." Her smile sharpened. "And since you asked—I work for Anderson."

A chill coiled in Annouie's chest.

Chin gave a low, throaty laugh. "Oh, Anderson. Tsk, tsk. He does love his games."

Annouie's gaze hardened. "You're lying."

Chin batted her lashes. "Am I?" Her smile turned syrupy. "So—what do you say? Hand over the manuscript, and I'll keep your secret."

Chapter Forty-Eight

"Answer the goddamn phone, Jack!"

Antony stole glances over the balustrade as the line rang. No answer. He scowled, left a clipped message, and shoved the phone into his back pocket.

The whine of the front gate drew his attention. The conversation in the front room continued, undisturbed—even as soft footfalls announced new arrivals.

Antony crept down the staircase, head tilted toward the rear of the house.

A long shadow stretched over the square of grass beyond the sun-baked tiles.

Front and back. Flanked.

Escape? Impossible.

Unless . . .

He flicked his gaze toward the master bedroom—then he bolted downstairs.

Bursting into the front room, he found Bach seated on a stool across from a handcuffed Chin.

He grabbed his shoes and turned to Bach.

"Some seriously bad people just showed up—front and back. Whatever you're discussing with my ex-therapist? Table it." He glanced at Chin. "By the way—you're fired."

Bach grabbed the backpack beside the piano and followed him into the hall.

Voices murmured beyond the front entrance as Antony crossed toward the staircase.

"Come on. We can escape through the bedroom window," he said, bounding up the stairs.

Bach veered toward the kitchen.

He spun around. "What the hell—"

She reappeared seconds later, clutching a large, coverless book.

His eyes narrowed. "I knew you had it."

She shrugged, sliding the manuscript into her pack.

A figure loomed beyond the sidelights. Even through the frosted pane, it was clear the man was carrying something long—and heavy. He wedged it into the doorframe. The wood groaned.

Bach pushed past Antony, lifting her brows. "Are you coming?"

Jaw tight, he followed.

By the time he reached the bedroom, she was already crouched on the sill, beckoning. He sprinted to the window and climbed out.

She moved across the tiles with feline grace—or the precision of a well-trained thief. The shingles creaked threateningly as he followed, his movements less graceful, less certain.

Below, the door gave way—wood splintering with a jagged crack.

Antony slipped.

He began sliding toward the edge. He flung his arms wide, arresting his fall. He blinked at a cloudless sky, chest heaving.

Smooth, Meyer-Edwards.

Four deep breaths later, he sat up, clutched both shoes, and pushed forward—chasing the now-distant figure vanishing across the rooftops.

* * *

Timothy Gibson cowered in the shadows, eyes fixed on the clock tower overhead. The minute hand slid past the hour.

Annouie was late.

He redialed her number. It rang twice, then diverted to voicemail. As he waited for the tone, his phone buzzed.

Incoming call.

He tapped the screen. Stewie Hewson's voice slithered through the speaker.

"Mr. Deluca has moved the timetable up."

Again?

Sweat prickled at Timothy's hairline. "I was just about to call you. There's been a slight delay with the manuscript."

He turned away as a group of students drifted past, their voices echoing through the cloistered walkway.

Stewie grunted. "No longer required. Just letting you know—Mr. Deluca's prepared to take possession of the first and third items this afternoon. Same price."

Timothy's breath caught. *No longer required?*

"What do you mean, no longer required?"

Stewie chuckled, the sound grating in Timothy's ears. "Mr. Deluca will be taking delivery of the *Second Element* very soon."

Timothy's chest hollowed out. *That cunning bitch.*

"I don't suppose you'd care to share the name of your new supplier?"

"Now what sort of businessman would I be, Mr. Gibson," Stewie drawled, "if I gave up a name like that?"

The line went dead.

Scowling, Timothy dialed Sir James. He wasn't looking forward to the call. To his relief, it went to voicemail.

Timothy lifted the phone. "My supplier bailed. She's dealing directly with Deluca. Handover's happening at Wharf 12—sometime after three this afternoon. Meet me there—if you're still interested."

* * *

Church bells tolled to the east, summoning the faithful to prayer as Antony and Annouie made their way uphill toward the junction of Thomas Street and Main Road.

A three-story hardware store loomed above the intersection, casting the street below in shadow. On the pavement, two dark shapes wavered. Moments later, Deluca's security men rounded the corner.

Antony grabbed Annouie's arm. "Not this way."

He spun her around and bolted downhill, shoes pounding the concrete.

At the base of the incline, a white van screeched to a halt, cutting off the cross street. Its side door slid open, and Deluca's head of security stepped out, flanked by three more men in dark suits.

"Mr. Deluca would like a word."

Antony took a step back, mentally running numbers.

Stewie? Slow on his feet.

The two racing downhill? Five seconds out.

The pavement crew?

Factor in Bach's talent for mayhem—

"I know what you're thinking," Stewie said in his slow, lugubrious drawl.

Antony arched a brow. "Pretty sure you don't."

Stewie shrugged. "It's not hard. You're wondering—is it worth making a run for it?"

He opened his jacket, revealing a sidearm. "But consider this."

Bach leaned close. Her breath grazed his ear.

"Play along."

Before he could protest, she turned and climbed into the van, settling on the bench seat like she owned it.

She patted the space beside her and smiled.

With a sigh, he followed her in.

Chapter Forty-Nine

Antony lay on his side, a canvas bag over his head, his hands bound behind his back. Every jolt of the van sent him sliding across the hard floor, the ride growing rougher with each pothole and speed hump.

The stench inside the bag was indescribable—an acrid tang that churned his stomach. He gagged, swallowing back the urge to retch as the van bumped over what felt like cobblestones, then lurched around a sharp corner.

Time crawled. Maybe twenty minutes had passed. Or thirty. Finally, the vehicle slowed, veering onto gravel. Tires crunched up a gentle slope before the van rolled to a stop. The engine idled while voices barked instructions outside. Then: a metallic whine—the unmistakable grind of a heavy gate sliding back.

The van moved again, swaying side to side as it slalomed up the drive.

Thirty seconds. A final turn. Then—stop.

"Annouie?" Antony croaked, shifting toward the vague form beside him. A boot landed hard against his ribs, knocking the air from his lungs. He wheezed and rolled away, doubled over.

The van's sliding door screeched open. Rough hands dragged him out, tore off the hood, and sliced through the flex-cuffs. His vision blurred, then cleared—

Luigi Deluca's three-story suburban fortress loomed before him.

Red-brick, garish and oversized, it rose above manicured lawns and a line of spruce that marked the outer perimeter. Behind that, a stone wall sealed off the estate. Antony stumbled as loose stones shifted beneath his feet.

Stewie appeared on the gravel apron.

"Move it. Mr. Deluca doesn't like to be kept waiting."

Behind him, the van revved, spitting pebbles as it started back down the drive.

"Wait—where's Bach?" Antony lunged after it.

Stewie caught him by the collar and hauled him back. "Mr. Deluca has other plans for the girl."

Antony's heart kicked against his ribs. "What plans?"

The double doors creaked open, and he was shoved inside.

The entrance hall screamed excess—gleaming marble floors, an ostentatious chandelier, a sweeping staircase curling toward the upper levels. Stewie marched him across the polished expanse, up the stairs, and down a carpeted hallway to a sitting room at the end. Two guards flanked the entrance.

"Mr. Deluca said to make yourself comfortable."

Antony stepped inside. The guards followed him in and took up positions against the far wall—silent sentinels with dead eyes.

He glanced at the clock above the fireplace. Almost one.

The room was as gaudy as the man who owned it. High ceilings. Ornate cornices. Too much polished wood. A grand marble mantel dominated the far wall—but the real draw was the drinks trolley.

He crossed to it. Reached for the Macallan. Paused.

His fingers were trembling.

He exhaled, long and slow. Not a panic tremor. Not this time. Just adrenaline.

He unstoppered the bottle. Started to swig—and stopped. If he was going to get Bach out of this, he'd need his head clear.

He replaced the stopper and set the bottle back.

He paced over the Persian rug, savoring its rich lustre, the clean taste of country air filling his lungs. As he inhaled and exhaled, he counted. Five minutes to bring the tremor down to a two. Before Craiova, it would've been zero.

He checked the clock again. The shorthand hovered near the hour.

On impulse, he veered toward the double doors. The bodyguards shifted, blocking his exit with blank stares. Antony gave them a rueful smile and returned to the hearth, resuming his circuit of the rug.

At the half-hour mark, Luigi finally appeared.

His bodyguards stepped aside as he swept into the room, entourage in tow. The guards closed ranks, eyes tracking their master as he settled on the sofa before the fireplace.

Luigi was a shade under six feet, with slicked-back hair, thick gray brows, and eyes dark and vivid. The two men flanking him wore the same gray suits as the guards and moved with ex-military precision.

Antony stopped pacing and strode toward him. "Was that Chinese woman necessary?"

All four bodyguards reached for the Colt 1911s at their hips.

Deluca waved them off. "At ease." He turned to Antony. "She's one of Anderson's. I hired him to solve a problem." He nodded toward the trolley. "Have a drink. Calm your nerves."

Antony ignored the offer. "Who the hell is Anderson?"

Deluca shrugged off his sports jacket and tossed it to a bodyguard. "He's handling the Vallone situation."

"He's the hit man?"

Deluca scoffed. "No. He's a businessman—like me. Runs Security and Risk. Doctor Chin does the hits."

"Which includes drugging and handcuffing me?"

"She wasn't going to hurt you."

Antony whirled. "She was seconds from cutting off my toes!"

Deluca swirled his drink and stared into the cold hearth. "Theater. You were never in real danger. But the girl you came in with . . ." He sipped, eyes glinting over the rim of his glass. "Who is she?"

Antony waved a hand. "A student I agreed to take on. No one important."

"I see." Deluca bared his teeth in a predatory smile. "Pretty girl."

Antony's jaw tightened. "Hadn't noticed."

Deluca's gaze lingered. He waved to the guards. "Leave us."

They filed out, the doors clicking shut behind them.

The silence thickened.

"What's going on?" Antony asked.

Deluca rolled his eyes. "Sit down. I'm not explaining while you prowl around like an overgrown housecat."

Antony dropped into the chair opposite.

Deluca poured two glasses of Scotch and handed one over. Antony eyed it, then downed it in a single gulp.

"At least we agree," Deluca said, sipping at a more leisurely pace, "that Scotch whisky is one of life's few remaining pleasures."

Antony slammed the glass down. The burn in his throat offered no comfort.

Somewhere in the mansion, a door opened and closed. A breeze drifted through the windows.

Deluca's expression darkened. "Did you meet with Vallone?"

"No."

"But you know where he is?"

"Still no."

The door opened. Antony stiffened as Dr. Chin sauntered in, blowing him a kiss as she slinked across the rug.

Deluca looked up. "Did she talk?"

Chin rested a hand on the back of Deluca's chair, long nails glinting. "Yes. I've sent the boys to retrieve it. We'll know soon if she was telling the truth."

"What about Anderson?"

"On his way."

"Have you moved to Phase Two?"

Chin shrugged. "We're waiting on Anderson."

Deluca scowled. "This is my operation. Anderson gets the girl when I'm finished with her—not before. Tell the boys to come in."

Chin tapped her comms and glided out.

Antony watched her go, then turned to Deluca. "What's Phase Two?"

Deluca stretched and stood. "Tell me where Vallone is, and we won't need to find out."

"I don't know."

"Have it your way." Deluca turned as the bodyguards re-entered. "Escort my nephew to the car."

Antony's voice sharpened. "What's Phase Two?"

Deluca gave a casual shrug. "While I told Doctor Chin not to hurt you, I said nothing about the girl."

* * *

A horn blast echoed through the rear windows of Warehouse 12. Annouie Bach stirred, her head heavy, neck slack.

The chair groaned beneath her as she cracked one eye open. Nothing had changed—except the slant of light from the high window above the loading dock.

Mid-afternoon.

By her rough estimate, she'd been duct-taped to the chair for at least two hours. In that time, she'd endured the usual: threats, questions, the evitable slapping around. It was routine. Predictable. They'd learned little. She'd learned plenty.

She slumped forward, peering through a curtain of tousled hair. Six goons milled about the warehouse, each with an M16 slung sloppily across the chest and a sidearm at the back.

At her twelve, One and Two sat at a fold-up table, chugging cola and swiping through TikTok. Three stood overwatch on the balcony outside the glass-walled office. Four and Five were hosing down the white van beside the load dock doors. And Six—a wiry man in an oversized jacket—swept the perimeter.

She flexed her wrists. There was slack in the tape. She began probing the back of the chair, fingers quickly finding the head of a screw half-loosened from its base.

A squeal of hinges froze her mid-movement. The dock door opened, flooding the warehouse with light. A figure stood silhouetted. The door slammed shut. Darkness returned.

Annouie let her head loll forward.

Heels clicked across the concrete. Moments later, Dr. Janine Chin emerged from the shadows.

"How long's she been like this?"

One stood hastily. "An hour."

"An hour's enough to soften most people." Chin circled the chair. "But this one's not most people."

Smart woman.

"Unfortunately," Chin said, spinning on her heel, "we're out of time. Deluca's on his way. Wake her."

Annouie strained her ears. A door creaked open at the rear. Male voices murmured, then faded. A bang. The splash of water. Then—footsteps. Closing fast.

She braced.

Five gallons of iced water crashed over her. She gasped, blinking through the torrent.

Chin's soft laughter rippled through the warehouse. She stepped closer. "There you are."

Her nails dug into Annouie's jaw, lifting her chin. Snake-like eyes narrowed, then flicked away in disappointment. She released her with a flick of her wrist and dropped into the chair opposite. Her silk coat rustled as she pulled a cigarette holder and lighter from its folds. She thumbed the striker, brought the cigarette to the flame. Sparks flew, followed by a hiss. She took a long drag, eyes fixed on Annouie across the glowing tip.

She snapped her fingers. "Bring the table."

A desk scraped into position. A toolbox followed—its metal lid clanking open to reveal a tray of gleaming tools.

A bamboo skewer caught the light. Its sharpened end glinted.

Annouie's mouth dried out.

"Release her right hand," Chin said, selecting the skewer.

Two peeled back the tape and pinned her hand flat to the table.

Chin leaned in, her smile thin. "You lied to us. Where is it?"

Annouie blinked. "Where's what?"

Chin's mouth twitched. She handed the skewer to One.

"Wait," Annouie gasped. "Are you talking about that ratty old book Meyer-Edwards gave me?"

One pressed her hand into the table and slid the skewer beneath her nail.

She screamed.

Chin's laughter chimed like glass as the echoes faded.

She handed over a second skewer. "Let's try again."

Annouie blew wet hair from her face. "Like I said before—I have no idea—"

The second skewer slid home. Her scream tore through the rafters.

Chin blew smoke into her face. "This can stop," she crooned. "All you have to do is tell me where it is."

Annouie's head sagged. Her voice was little more than a rasp. "I. Don't. Know."

Chin sighed, flicking ash onto the concrete. "Again."

The third skewer glinted briefly in the light.

Annouie's scream rose once more.

Chapter Fifty

"Zoom in," Andre said, pointing at the tiny figure entering the first-floor theater. He leaned toward the wall of monitors lining his operations center, brow furrowed as Oria enlarged the image.

It was Annouie.

He let out a pent-up sigh, one that had been simmering since morning. Returning to his desk, he scrubbed through the feed, fingers flying over the keys.

At 9:10 a.m., Annouie left the theater and crossed the quadrangle. She climbed the staircase and arrived at Judith Pasolini's office shortly after.

Her tradecraft was sloppy. *Too* sloppy.

Just after ten, she emerged. Andre switched to an exterior feed and tracked her down University Avenue. Traffic cams caught her crossing the main intersection. Another device picked her up outside the Davies Building. She ran down Old School Road, past engineering, and out the back gate.

He flipped to the gate camera just in time to catch her turning into Thomas Street. At 10:21, a neighbor's front-door cam showed her on the veranda of Number 112. She knocked.

Andre initiated a title search. The screen blinked. The house belonged to Sibilla Meyer-Edwards—wife of the late corporate lawyer, David Meyer-Edwards.

At 10:25, Annouie stepped off the porch and disappeared down the side path.

A black van pulled up at 10:40. Three men in suits disembarked. They knocked. At 10:43, they forced entry with a crowbar.

At 10:46, they left with a woman in tow.

Andre froze the frame and zoomed in.

Janine Chin. Former Ministry of State Security.

He sat back, chair hissing, and ruffled his pink hair as the server rack blinked quietly behind him.

"Oria, get me satellite footage of Number 112, Thomas Street. Time stamp: 10:25 this morning."

The center screen flickered, shifting to an aerial view of the neighborhood.

"Zoom in on the right side of the building."

The image tightened. A small figure slipped through the back entrance.

"Tighter."

He glanced at the time code. At 10:43, a man and woman emerged from the upper level and began crossing the rooftops. They dropped to street level via a fire escape.

"Stay with them."

Oria tracked the pair as they popped out onto Thomas Street several minutes later. Two men—likely hostiles—turned into the street and sprinted toward them. The pair reversed course, running downhill. At the bottom, a white van screeched to a halt. Four men jumped out, surrounding them.

After a tense stand-off, the man and woman climbed into the van. It peeled away.

Andre's jaw tightened. "Get me that van's destination."

Oria pulled up a live map of the Hills District. At its center stood an opulent estate—twenty thousand square feet of architectural excess.

"The van made a three-minute stop here at 12:45," Oria purred. On-screen, several figures disembarked. Then the van continued.

Andre frowned. "Where's Annouie?"

"Warehouse 12," Oria replied. "Arrival logged at 1:00 p.m. Three people disembarked—including Annouie Bach."

Andre spun his seat. "Who owns the warehouse?"

"A shell company. Tied to another shell company. Registered offshore. Held in a blind trust—"

"So—no names without a forensic accountant." He slung his tech bag over one shoulder, eyes drifting toward the Canon DSLR on the shelf. He grabbed it, checked the battery, and looped it around his neck.

Oria tutted. "I'd advise against going in on your own. Without Annouie Bach to assist, the probability of a successful infil is less than twenty percent."

"Fair point," he muttered with a smirk. "Guess we'll have to call in the cavalry. Be a dear, Oria—hack the police network and dispatch all units to Warehouse 12."

* * *

The hubbub in the bullpen was escalating. Katrine blocked out the scrolling headlines and yammering studio anchors as she dropped into her seat. Dragging the chair across the floor, she focused on the grainy footage from the mill, fingers flying over the keyboard as she applied filters.

From a distance—and with eyes half-closed—the figure on the back sill looked like Annouie Bach.

Katrine sighed. Maybe she just wanted it to be Annouie. People saw what they wanted to see. But Annouie Bach pulling a parkour move up the side of the building? The girl couldn't manage a pull-up, let alone haul herself through a window.

She shoved back from her desk and finally registered the commotion around her.

A crowd had gathered near the coffee station, all eyes fixed on the large wall-mounted monitor. Katrine got up and joined them. Every news channel was broadcasting the same story: the aftermath of the shootout at City Forensics. A snippet from Dr. Emil Thorpe's email scrolled across the bottom of the screen.

Dunbier emerged from his office, face gray under the fluorescents. He shouted above the din—no one listened. After a futile second attempt, he jammed two fingers in his mouth and let out a piercing whistle.

The room fell silent.

"Everyone. Briefing room. Now."

The bullpen surged, a tide of bodies funneling into the corridor.

Katrine elbowed her way through the bottleneck, claiming one of the last seats at the back. Dunbier tapped the electronic board. Someone dimmed the lights. A live newsroom feed lit up the screen. A polished anchor filled the frame.

"In breaking news, Nicholas Hope, personal assistant to Sir James Gibson, was arrested outside the Medical Examiner's office this afternoon," she announced. "This follows confirmation that the Wilkins Beach John Doe has been identified as Sir James Gibson."

The footage cut to Hope's arrest. A scrolling ticker revealed: *One doctor confirmed dead. Sir James's office unavailable for comment.*

Dunbier froze the screen. Sir James's image filled the frame.

"Here's where things stand," he began.

A new image replaced the feed—a close-up of Nicholas Hope.

"Hope's our shooter. He's in transit now. We'll have him here within the hour."

Click.

"Our second person of interest is Dr. Emil Thorpe. He fled the scene on foot." Another image appeared—grainy CCTV footage.

"This was taken at 2:32 p.m. Thorpe then boarded the 2:36 train to the city. Thanks to the seven thousand cameras installed across the transit network, we've got eyes on him. Officers are stationed at every stop. The second he steps off, we'll grab him."

The door opened. Saunders limped in.

"What about Thorpe's email?" he asked. "Every outlet's running it. Are we bringing Sir James in?"

A strained silence settled over the room.

Dunbier nodded. "We're verifying Thorpe's claims. Forensics are analyzing the data now. Once we confirm the facts, you'll be the first to know."

He scanned the crowd.

"Sir James is unreachable. We're assuming he's dodging the media. His office promises a statement this afternoon. Until then, I'm sending a team to Victoria House to manage the situation."

His gaze locked on the back row.

"Ratcliffe and Saunders. Stay back. Everyone else—back to work."

As the room cleared, Katrine pushed to the front.

"Head to Chapel Road," Dunbier said. "Disperse the media. Then start questioning the staff—anything on Hope, and everything on Sir James: habits, routines, known associates."

"So you think Thorpe's telling the truth?" she asked.

Dunbier's lips twitched into a grim smile. "Let's just say I have a hunch this John Doe mess ties into our Bayside Ripper case."

Saunders raised a brow. "Didn't think you believed in hunches, Chief."

Dunbier shrugged. "I'm making an exception."

* * *

As the wagon tore down the eight-lane freeway, Nicholas leaned his head against the wall. Sir James had taken everything—his father, his mother, the safety a child should never be forced to live without.

A final reckoning was inevitable. Which meant escape was, too.

Through half-lidded eyes, he studied the two officers seated across from him. Both wore standard-issue Glocks. He didn't need to check—cops in this unit carried hot. Risk came with the badge. The officer on the right, Mitchell, was disciplined and taciturn. His vocabulary consisted of two words: *affirmative* and *negative*. The one on the left, Fredericks, was the weak link—chatty, twitchy, and more interested in cracking jokes through the grille than watching the prisoner.

The cabin fell quiet, tires humming on the asphalt, until the radio crackled:

"Barnes Three, this is Dispatch. Suspected organized crime activity at Warehouse 12, Docklands Industrial. Confirm status?"

"Dispatch, Barnes Three. Copy. Any units on-site?"

"Affirmative. Tactical already deployed. Proceed to South Patterson and Fifth for perimeter support."

"Barnes Three to Dispatch. Acknowledged. En route."

The wagon rumbled forward. Fredericks leaned toward the grille, cap pushed back, eyes alight.

Nicholas worked a thin wire free from his belt buckle and slipped it into the lock of his left cuff. Twist. Click. The shackle sprang open.

"Warehouse 12, huh?" Fredericks said, leaning across Mitchell. "Those tac boys don't mess around. Bet it'll be total carnage down there."

Nicholas kept his gaze on a point just past Mitchell's ear, stepping mentally through the sequence: drop Fredericks, grab Glock, fire.

The vehicle slowed, rolling up to a red light. Nicholas stared at Mitchell. The officer met his gaze, expression flat and unreadable. Nicholas faced the windshield and counted down.

The radio flared again.

"Dispatch, Barnes Three. Active engagement at Warehouse 12. Shots fired. Two down. Requesting medics ASAP."

"Copy. Medics en route. Maintain position."

Fredericks leaned forward. "Well, I'll be—"

Nicholas exploded upward.

His right hand shot for the Glock. His left elbow smashed into Fredericks's skull. In the same motion, he fired through the holster. The gun kicked.

Mitchell screamed, half-rising, Nicholas ripped the pistol free and fired again. Headshot.

Red mist filled the interior.

Fredericks, dazed and slumping, never had a chance. Two quick shots—chest, then forehead.

Outside, the lights turned green. Horns blared.

The driver flung his door open, weapon drawn.

Nicholas kicked the rear doors, hit the asphalt, and dropped to a crouch.

The driver rounded the van, raised his pistol—

One shot to the back of the head. He crumpled like a marionette.

Drivers shrank below dashboard level. A surreal silence settled over the intersection.

Nicholas rifled through the dead man's pockets, pulled out a phone. Jabbed at the screen. Again. Then again. "Fuck." He flung it onto the road and climbed back into the wagon.

Traffic stacked up, occupants frozen, some filming, others calling emergency services.

Beyond caring, Nicholas found Mitchell's phone and dialed.

The call went straight to voicemail.

"You're a dead man, Parrish!" he snarled as dozens of cameras captured him.

One by one, he dragged the bodies from the van, dumping them onto the road. Blood darkened the bitumen.

He slid into the driver's seat, slammed the door, and floored the accelerator. The wagon lurched through the red light—there was no cross-traffic to stop him.

Within minutes, his name was trending:

#HighwayAssassin

#DeathInASuit

#WhatItTakesToPAForSirJames.

Nicholas didn't care. He had one mission:

Hunt down Sir James Gibson—and terminate him with extreme prejudice.

Chapter Fifty-One

The first scream cut through the air as Deluca's men dragged Antony from the car. The second came as they hauled him toward the warehouse—Luigi in front, his two-man detail flanking him like loyal hounds. The crime boss halted just outside, pausing as a third scream rose above the background hiss of traffic and the churn of the river.

He raised a heavy brow. "She's being stubborn."

Antony's fists clenched as they shoved him through the door and down a dim corridor. At the base of a staircase, Deluca veered off, heading toward the far end of the building. The guards prodded Antony forward, cajoling him up the stairs.

He stumbled past rows of cubicles—each fitted with computers, monitors, and phones. Some had been personalized: framed family portraits, clay figurines, a bronze Buddha. They pushed him to the front of the room, where windows overlooked the warehouse floor. Overhead, a lone camera blinked, its lens trained on him.

Deluca reappeared, striding through the door. He joined Antony at the glass, a flicker of satisfaction softening his face as he looked down at the loading bay.

"Phase Two is about to begin."

Below, Chin paced the concrete. Bach slumped in a rickety wooden chair, her right hand pinned to a table. Three bamboo sticks pierced her fingers—second, third, fourth. A bruise bloomed high on her cheekbone. Makeup could hide that. But her hand? Not a chance.

Antony's stomach twisted. His fingers curled, the promise of violence rising—

Not yet. There's still time.

He drew a slow breath, grounded himself, forced the urge down.

On the floor, Chin blew smoke into the air, her tone light, casual. "Tell us what you did with it, and this all stops."

Deluca glanced at the guard beside him. "She lied?"

Chin leaned closer to Bach. "Mr. Deluca's not a patient man. Best tell me what you did with it, eh?"

Bach didn't flinch. "I don't know what you're talking about."

Chin scoffed, tapping ash onto the concrete. "Liar."

She turned on her heel and walked to the back of the loading dock, murmuring into her earpiece.

Deluca muttered, brushing his fingers along his own. "We're wasting time. Move on."

Chin nodded then circled back toward Annouie.

Deluca peeled off his jacket and tossed it to the bodyguard. He turned to Antony. "We still need to discuss Vallone's whereabouts. Maybe after this little display, you'll be more forthcoming."

* * *

Chin droned on, smoke curling in the air. Annouie lifted her gaze to the window above. A shadowy figure stood pressed to the glass.

Antony Meyer-Edwards.

Friend or foe? She couldn't be sure.

Chin's lips twitched into a smirk. "You'll talk soon enough. Everyone does."

Annouie chuckled, dry and rasping through cracked lips. "If it gets you to stop whining, maybe I will."

The cigarette paused midair. Chin's expression darkened. With a sharp hiss, she grabbed another skewer, wood scraping across metal like nails on a chalkboard.

Annouie twisted her wrist, working the screw further out of its hole.

"You should hear yourself," she muttered. "Like a B-grade soap villain on a sugar crash."

Chin circled behind her, breath hot against her neck. "Let's see how cocky you are once Mr. Deluca finishes with you."

"Not cocky," Annouie said, eyes forward. "Just trying to survive your drivel."

Chin lunged, ramming the skewer beneath Annouie's fingernail.

Pain detonated through her hand. A scream tore from her throat, bouncing off the warehouse walls—masking the faint plink of the screw landing in her upturned palm.

Chin dragged a hand through her hair, sweeping it back into place. "Listen to me, you spoiled little rich girl," she sneered. "Anderson's put a two-million-dollar bounty on your head. That's right. Two million."

She leaned in, eyes gleaming. "I wouldn't want to be in your shoes—especially after what he did to Sanchez. I hear they still haven't found all of him."

Annouie's face remained impassive as she shifted the screw into position.

A door creaked open somewhere in the dark. She straightened as a heavyset man emerged from the shadows at the back of the warehouse, his silhouette looming larger with every step.

He glanced at the skewers. "Remove those."

Rolling up his sleeves, he flexed his thick fingers until the knuckles cracked. Then he turned to her.

"One more time, Petal. Where did you put the manuscript?"

* * *

Antony peered down at the unfolding drama. Luigi was on the floor. Chin hovered nearby. And Bach—well, she didn't look nearly as terrified as she should have.

Two options: leave her and run—or embrace his criminal heritage and get her out.

Leaving wasn't on the table. Not when just looking at her sent a rush of heat to his face, his chest—and frankly, other parts of his anatomy.

He sighed, rubbing his eyes.

Screw it. Time to stop pretending.

Brutality was in his blood.

He lunged for the desk, grabbed the bronze statue, and hurled it at the camera. As it arced through the air, he pivoted—his hand shooting out, spearing the nearest guard in the throat. As the man staggered, he drove a knee into his face. A wet crunch followed. The guard collapsed, face-planting.

Mob Basic Training.

Like riding a bike.

The second guard's gun had just cleared its holster when Antony's heel caught him in the jaw. He flew into a desk and dropped, out cold.

Alberto Aguirre's Secret Martial Arts Class for the Especially Talented.

Antony crouched, rifled beneath the guard's vest, and pulled out his phone. He grabbed the limp hand, pressed the thumb to the screen until it unlocked.

Then dialed.

One ring.

Two.

"Nine-one-one. What's your emergency?"

"There's a mafia shootout happening right now at Warehouse 12," he said, and hung up.

He darted into the next room. A bank of monitors glowed along the wall, each displaying grainy surveillance feeds. A lone operator sat at the console, fumbling for his radio, eyes locked on the snow-filled screen at the bottom.

Antony slipped behind him. Snaked an arm around his throat. Choked him out.

Bodyguard Essentials: The Art of Incapacitation.

He lowered him gently onto the desk, his gaze jumping to the center screen.

One of Chin's thugs loomed into view, reaching for an instrument tray. He lifted a pair of bolt cutters.

Antony's breath caught as the man angled them toward Bach's fifth finger.

He severed the feeds, grabbed the radio, and sprinted into the corridor.

* * *

Annouie opened her eyes and forced every shred of focus into steadying her breath.

The cutters gleamed beneath the fluorescent lighting as Goon Two widened the jaws, aligning them with her little finger. He looked to the heavyset man across from her, brows lifting in silent question.

Deluca lounged back, cigar balanced between two fingers. He took a slow drag, exhaling a pungent cloud into the air.

"Well, Petal," he said, reclining further. "Last chance to get this right. If I don't like the answer . . ." His gaze slid to the blades. "Goodbye, pinky."

The chair creaked as he leaned in. "Location. Now."

Annouie's fingers curled tighter around the screw hidden in her palm. One misstep—off by even a hundredth of a second—and her career as a musician . . . maybe her life . . . was *gone.*

* * *

Timothy adjusted the courier's cap as the cab rolled to a stop. It wasn't much of a disguise—just enough to get him through the door.

A breeze stirred tufts of grass pushing through the cracked pavement. He grabbed the long leather bag and cardboard cylinder from the seat beside him, then leaned forward and passed the driver a hundred-dollar bill.

"Wait here. Won't be long."

He stepped out, crossed the lot, and approached the back of the building. Warehouse 12 had a single loading dock and a smaller, unmarked door beside it. He knocked.

The door creaked open, revealing a mountain of a man with a rifle slung across his chest, muzzle down. He looked Timothy over, pausing on the cap and the items in his hands.

"We've been waiting for you," he said, pulling the door wider.

Timothy stepped inside—and stopped dead.

No secret handshakes. No smug laughter. No backroom deal as Bach and Deluca toasted their betrayal.

This was something else entirely.

Something worse.

"Come," the guard said, nudging him toward a table at the far end of the room.

Timothy stumbled forward across uneven concrete, his eyes drawn to the grim tableau at the center.

Luigi loomed over Annouie, bound to a chair. Her face bruised, ghost-pale. She lifted her head, blackened eyes meeting his.

God. She looked wrecked.

A man stood beside her, bolt cutters poised around her finger.

Timothy looked away and fumbled with the zipper on the leather bag. He pulled out the Rebrisi box and set it on the table with trembling hands.

Luigi arched a brow. "Mr. Gibson? Wasn't expecting you in person."

Timothy removed the cap. "Wanted to ensure the items arrived in pristine condition."

Annouie's chest rose and fell—steady, deliberate. If she recognized him, she gave no sign.

Chin slinked forward, eyes glittering. She reached for the box. Deluca swatted her hand aside.

"Patience," he murmured, caressing the glossy black lid. He traced its edges, a slow smile creeping onto his face.

"Exactly as I remember. Impeccable work."

He gave it a gentle shake. A soft rattle answered.

"And the *Venus*?"

Timothy placed the cardboard cylinder on the table, removed the stopper, and slid out the rolled canvas.

"As agreed," he said, voice wavering. "This concludes our business."

Deluca lifted the canvas to the light. "Exquisite," he said—then his tone cooled. "But without the manuscript . . ."

The weight of the unspoken words settled over the room.

Timothy's throat dried. "I was told it was no longer required. Your man said—" He glanced at Annouie.

Deluca shrugged. "True—I may have said that. But I was expecting delivery of the *Second Element* this afternoon."

His gaze locked on Annouie.

"There's been a complication. So until it's sorted, our contract remains active."

Timothy wiped his palms on his pants. "Not what we agreed," he muttered.

Deluca grunted. "In a hurry?" He smiled, humorless. "There is a third payment option. Though I doubt you'll like it."

He gestured toward Annouie. The cutters remained locked around her finger.

"A little demonstration?"

He snapped his fingers.

Tension rippled through the room.

Goon One flattened her hand against the table. Goon Two flexed his arms.

The cutters creaked open.

Annouie braced, breath held—like the last note before a string snaps.

* * *

An engine growled outside. Brakes squealed. Tension leaked from the room like air from a punctured balloon.

Chin moved to Deluca's side and said, "It's Anderson."

He exhaled through his nose. "I grow tired of these constant interruptions." He lit a fresh cigar, motioning toward Goons One and Two. "Go see to it."

The guards hustled to the side door as three sharp knocks echoed through the warehouse.

Annouie ripped down with the screw, slicing through the tape.

Deluca's gaze flicked her way, an oily smirk curling his lips. Smoke wreathed his head as the door swung open. Light sliced across the floor.

A figure stepped inside.

John Chrysler Anderson.

A canvas duffel swung from one hand. Deluca's men boxed him in, patting him down.

"Careful with the crown jewels, boys," he quipped.

"He's clean."

Anderson strode across the floor, brushed the tools aside and dropped the bag on the desk in front of Annouie. He unzipped it. Bundled notes gleamed under the fluorescents.

Deluca gave the money a cursory glance, flicking through one stack. "A lot of money for one little girl." He jerked his head toward Annouie. "Last chance, Petal. Where's the manuscript? Or you'll be leaving without that pinky." He pulled on his cigar. "Although I hear

Anderson has far worse planned, so I doubt you'll be missing it for long."

Anderson's expression hardened. "We agreed—money for the girl. You've got the cash. Hand her over."

Deluca puffed smoke. "As soon as she gives up the manuscript."

"I'm not paying two million for damaged goods."

Deluca tossed him two bundles. "Fine. Pay a doctor to stitch the fingers back on. But she's not leaving until I get what I want. Watch if you like—or wait outside."

Anderson grunted and drifted toward the far wall, his hand slipping beneath his jacket.

Deluca flicked a signal. Goon Two leaned in, adjusting the cutters.

Behind him, Chin's eyes gleamed.

"So—what's it gonna be?" Deluca raised a fist.

Annouie dropped her head. Muscles coiled. "It's like this . . ."

Deluca's hand slashed the air—

Goon Two's elbows lifted—

Anderson drew his gun—

And the front door exploded inward.

A pressure wave ripped through the space. Annouie snapped her head back—bone crunched as it cracked into Goon One's nose. He staggered, blood streaming.

Shouts erupted. Thugs scrambled, rifle stocks snapping to shoulders.

Anderson dropped to one knee—fired.

A canister sailed through the open door and burst, acrid smoke filling the space.

Annouie tore free of her last restraint, kicking Goon Two in the face as she vaulted the desk. A blade slashed the air beside her.

Chin. Knife in hand. She stabbed again.

Annouie pivoted, heel slamming into her sternum.

A flashbang clattered nearby.

Boom.

Chin crashed to the floor.

Annouie rolled low, weaving through the chaos.

Across the floor, Anderson advanced, Colt raised, then vanished into the smoke.

Annouie dropped, sliding beneath a vehicle.

A voice boomed outside: "THIS IS THE POLICE! DROP YOUR WEAPONS! GET FACEDOWN! HANDS BEHIND YOUR HEAD! NOW!"

Chin staggered up, bloodied—just as Deluca barreled into her clutching Rebrisi's box.

"Swine!" she shrieked, heel slamming into the back of his leg.

He stumbled. The box flew.

Gibson snatched it mid-flight. Cradled it. Surged forward, clotheslining Deluca.

He darted past Chin, dropped beside Goon Two's corpse. Another flashbang shook the building. Gibson ducked, yanked a submachine gun from the body, and lurched upright.

He fired wild—spraying bullets—then reeled toward the rear.

Behind him, Deluca crawled through the splintered remains of a desk. Men scrambled, diving for cover.

Chin slammed into Gibson, driving him to the floor. The box slid across the concrete.

Deluca staggered up, swaying like a drunk. He opened his mouth. Gibson wrestled the gun from Chin. Bullets snapped from the barrel. A stray round punched through Deluca's chest. He blinked—looked down—then crumpled face-first into the debris.

Chin blinked once—then punched Gibson in the face. She grabbed the gun, scooped up the box, and ran.

Annouie covered her mouth and nose as she slipped along the wall, scanning for the exit.

Anderson emerged from the smoke, spluttering. Their eyes locked. He charged, weapon raised.

And then the third blast hit.

The rear door blew off its hinges. Dust and mortar rained down. Gunfire snapped in all directions.

Two more canisters clattered onto the concrete.

Flash. Boom.

Annouie hit the floor, ears ringing. Tear gas hissed around her. She staggered upright, choking. Half blinded, she wobbled toward the rear.

Something slammed her into the wall, knocking the air from her lungs.

"Come with me!" Anderson rasped.

"Get lost, asshole," she wheezed, her knee shooting up.

Anderson crumpled, releasing her with a grunt. "You don't understand—"

She lunged past him, stumbling for the exit.

Another flashbang.

Chin shrieked, gun chattering. Bullets strafed the air.

Annouie dropped and crawled into the hallway.

Officers stormed down it, respirators on.

She coughed, sucking in a lungful of smoke, and coughed again. And again. Then continuously, unable to stop, chest heaving.

Finally, she sank onto the floor, the walls closing in.

Boots pounded the stairs.

Strong arms lifted her, slinging her into a fireman's carry.

She gave a feeble kick.

A grunt, then: "And that's the thanks I get."

Meyer-Edwards's voice—muffled behind the mask.

"Meyer-Edwards?" Barely a whisper.

"Don't sound so surprised."

He took the stairs two at a time.

"Why are we going up?" She choked out the words.

"Less gas."

He carried her to the second level and set her beside a water cooler. She fumbled the tap, water flooding her face and mouth.

He pointed at a window.

"That's our exit."

She froze. Two stories up. No fire escape. Was he out of his mind?

He bent close and whispered in her ear.

The world screeched to a halt.

No way. And then—*NO WAY!*

She turned. Eyes wide. And then—

He scooped her up and flung her out the window.

As far as distractions went, he'd chosen the perfect bombshell.

I'm the Gray Cat.

She barely registered the fall—until she hit the dumpster, bubble wrap exploding around her. She staggered upright, shaking off pieces of foam. Moments later, Meyer-Edwards landed beside her.

"Gray Cat? *You*?" she sputtered.

He moved to the edge, scanning the lot. "Thank me later. Right now, escape's our top priority."

He vaulted the rim, dropping gracelessly onto the ground. He held out his hand.

She landed in a crouch beside him, ignoring the offer. "That wasn't gratitude," she muttered.

Smoke billowed from Warehouse 12, curling from shattered windows and gaping doors. Gunfire snapped. A megaphone boomed. Lightbars pulsed.

Meyer-Edwards ran for a stack of pallets near the lot's edge.

She followed four paces behind. She should've seen it sooner—he moved like he'd done this a thousand times.

He crouched behind the pallets, gave her a quick once-over.

"Your hands are wrecked. Nothing we can do about it now. You'll need a story—assuming we make it to the hearing."

He crept toward the boundary. Eyed the fence. Then the Fat Bob 114 parked by next door's dock.

Annouie scoffed. "I'm not going to any hearing. I'm going after Gibson."

He whirled. "Gibson? Are you out of your mind? Our heads are on the block. You know what that means—we're in this together. So either cooperate—or I tie you to the back of that bike and take you anyway."

She stared. He could do it. He was the Gray Cat.

And he was right—missing the hearing would be handing Messier a victory she couldn't afford.

"Fine. Gibson can wait," she muttered. "But once we're done, I'm going after him."

"Once we're done, do what you like." He cracked his knuckles. "Now if I can just remember how to hot-wire one of those things."

Chapter Fifty-Two

Timothy was screwed. Totally screwed.

Going dark hadn't been part of the plan, but now it was his only option—until the chaos died down. After that, he could start over. New name. New city. Maybe even a new country. Somewhere without extradition.

Like Cuba.

Crawling through the hedges at the front of Lot 6, he emerged onto the pavement, a good two thousand feet from the mess at Warehouse 12. Miraculously, his taxi was still waiting. He sprinted toward it, silently thanking every saint he could name—a surprising number, given his Catholic upbringing.

He flung himself into the back seat, rattled off the gallery address, and slumped against the headrest as the cab pulled away.

Propping a hand under his chin, he stared at the smoke still curling from Warehouse 12's orifices. How had it come to this? Just hours ago, he'd been a successful entrepreneur. Now he was a fugitive.

He pulled his phone from his back pocket and called Gabriella.

No answer. Of all days not to pick up. His fingers flew over the screen:

> Call me. It's urgent. The world's gone to hell.

The cab made a left, engine humming as it merged onto the Eastern Distributor.

He could take *The Way*, sail downriver, slip out to sea. With his laptop, he could still run operations via satellite.

The laptop.

Shit.

He lunged forward, gripping the back of the driver's seat. "Turn around."

The driver's dark eyes flicked up in the rearview mirror. "Sir?"

Timothy's knuckles whitened. "You have to take me to Green Point."

The driver frowned. "I'm almost at the end of my shift. That's out of my way."

Timothy yanked out several hundred-dollar bills and shoved them forward. "Will this help change your mind?"

The driver snatched the cash, tires screeching as he spun the wheel.

Timothy exhaled, rubbing his damp palms on his knees. His gaze returned to the mirror. The driver's wide, nervous eyes stared back.

"What is it?" Timothy asked, mind still spinning.

The driver looked to the road. "Just wondering—with the news reports and all . . ."

Timothy frowned. "What news reports?"

The driver reached for the radio and cranked up the volume.

Updates filled the cabin: the hunt for Sir James, the shooting at the medical examiner's office, and a breaking story about a gang-related shootout at the Docklands Industrial Estate.

Timothy slumped into the vinyl seat, weighted down by the absurdity of it all. The world really was going to hell.

Thirty minutes later, the cab cruised past a *Welcome to Green Point* sign. As they turned onto his street, his breath hitched. At the far end of the block, a dark, inconspicuous sedan sat parked.

It screamed red flag.

"Keep going."

As the apartment complex slid past, Timothy pulled out his phone. A quick search confirmed his worst fears: every outlet was running the same story—the shooting, Thorpe's accusations, the fallout. Fringe networks were already tying the scandal back to the Belmont Beach murder.

"Circle the block."

Anxiety churned in his stomach. The laptop was everything—contacts, accounts, access. If police got their hands on it—he was finished.

The *Godfather* theme oozed from his phone. He swiped.

"Did you get it?" Sir James's voice rumbled through the speaker.

Timothy exhaled. "Unfortunately, no. I was detained. By Luigi Deluca. Annouie Bach has the manuscript—or knows where it is. Deluca was extracting the location when police raided the place."

A long pause.

"Meet me at the marina."

Timothy glanced at the driver, then shifted away, covering the mouthpiece. "I'm busy."

"You don't seem to understand the situation, my boy," Sir James growled. "I'll take care of Bach. Get to the Marina. We cast off at midnight."

Timothy sighed. There was no arguing with him. "Fine. I'll be there."

He ended the call and shoved the phone into his back pocket.

"Drop me at the corner."

The cab pulled over. Timothy handed the driver another hundred-dollar bill, stepped out, and waited until the car disappeared. Then, slipping into the shadows, he made for the back entrance—and vanished into the underground garage.

* * *

Andre rolled the Carrera's windows down as he cruised past Warehouse 12. Thick smoke billowed from the shattered front and rear exits. Officers in black tactical gear emerged from the building, assault rifles slung casually over their shoulders.

A shrill siren blast split the air as two police vans and an ambulance jolted over the curb-cut, speeding toward the roped-off perimeter. A short, uniformed officer unhooked the rope, waving them through. The vans veered left, the ambulance right—each screeching to a halt near their designated zones.

In front of the loading dock, a line of detainees sprawled on the tarmac—a motley crew in everything from three-piece suits to track wear. With their hands locked behind their heads, they lay still as one officer barked their rights and another cuffed them methodically. One by one, they were hauled upright and marched toward the open van doors.

Andre parked near the edge of the cordon, grabbed his camera, and stepped onto the street. The air was thick with tension—and the acrid stench of smoke. He moved toward a tight knot of reporters clustered at the perimeter.

"What's going on?" he asked, nudging his way in.

Across the lot, a team of medics sprinted toward the ambulance with a gurney. One straddled the patient, pumping rapid chest compressions. Another ran alongside, holding an IV bag high. A dark trail of blood streaked the pavement behind them.

Andre's breath quickened. He raised his camera and zoomed, tracking the gurney as it was lifted into the van. A man. He exhaled as the doors slammed shut and the vehicle peeled away.

Lowering the lens, he turned to the man beside him. "Any other casualties?"

The man shrugged. "Your guess is as good as mine. Cops aren't saying much—but that was Luigi Deluca. Heard he took some lead trying to bolt out the back."

Andre moved along the barrier, scanning the scene. He raised the camera again, zooming in on the handcuffed figures being loaded into the van. His heart skipped. He toggled the focus ring, tightening in on the smaller figure at the rear.

The figure turned—

Male, swarthy, bruised.

He lowered the camera and turned away.

Back at the Carrera, he slid on the Oria2 SmartSpecs as he dropped into the driver's seat. "She's not here." Then, quieter: "What did you find on the camera feeds?"

As he flicked his indicators and swung the car around in a tight arc, Oria's voice filled his ears—cool and faintly amused.

"There was a block-wide power outage moments before the breach. No footage recovered after 4:10 p.m. I've expanded the search to adjacent neighborhoods."

"ID anybody of interest?"

He eased off the accelerator, letting the car roll forward. His gaze lingered one last time on the warehouse and the chaos still unfolding.

"Anthony Meyer-Edwards arrived at 4:02. Timothy Gibson at 4:10. John Chrysler Anderson at 4:15."

Andre frowned. "Gibson I expected—he was delivering his Rebrisi fakes. But Anderson? What's his connection?"

"He paid Luigi Deluca two million for Annouie."

Andre exhaled sharply. A bounty.

A man stumbled into the road.

Andre slammed the brakes, tires screeching.

The man darted to the passenger side and yanked the door open.

John Chrysler Anderson dropped into the seat. "Knew you'd be close by." He raised the barrel of his Colt 1911 and leveled it at Andre's gut. "And now, Landvik—or should I call you Mr. Double Agent—you're gonna help me find Annouie Bach."

* * *

An itch prickled at the nape of Timothy's neck as he climbed to the fourth floor. At the stairwell landing, he paused by the fire door, scanning the apartment for threats.

Gabriella sat at the kitchen counter, one foot swaying as her long fingers flicked over her tablet.

"Psst!" Timothy crouched low, beckoning like they were in the middle of a heist.

She looked up, brows knitting. "What are you doing?"

He straightened with a sigh and crossed the room. "Thank God," he muttered, pulling her into a tight embrace despite her protests. Relief washed over him—until his eyes landed on the screened-off bedroom.

He released her. Stalked toward it.

"Jesus."

The room looked like a tornado had torn through it—mattress half off the frame, books strewn, wardrobe gutted.

She came up behind him. "Deluca's boys came. I had no choice but to let them in."

"Did they—"

"I said nothing."

Timothy darted to the back wall, ripping a picture aside to reveal an electronic keypad. He punched in the code. The secret compartment clicked open. He pulled out a laptop and stroked it with almost obscene affection.

But the relief didn't last.

He turned back to the mess.

From the corner, he grabbed a duffel bag and tossed it onto the bed. Sinking to his knees beside the chest, he skimmed the underside, searching for the hidden catch.

Click.

The lid creaked open, revealing several rolled canvases. He dumped them into the bag, along with a handful of clothes.

Behind him, Gabriella crossed her arms, a glint of admiration in her eyes. "You were behind the Gartner Haus heist."

"Shhh!"

He froze.

Something was wrong. The air had shifted—too still. Like the calm before a storm.

Or a raid.

He bolted to the window and yanked back the curtain. A fire escape zigzagged down four flights to the alley. At the far end—a flash of color.

Uniforms.

Several officers in tactical gear were closing in on the rear entrance.

He motioned Gabriella over. "We're about to be raided."

She clicked across the floor and joined him at the window. Her eyes widened at the sight of the rusted ladder.

A heavy thud rattled the door. "POLICE! OPEN UP!"

Gabriella backed away, shaking her head. "I'm not climbing down that." She spun and rushed for the birdcage elevator, snatching her designer handbag on the way.

Timothy cursed, shoved the sash window open. A rush of cool air swirled through the room as the pounding grew louder.

He swung one leg over, the metal frame biting into his palms. The fire escape shuddered as he landed on the platform.

Behind him, the door slammed open.

"GO, GO, GO!"

Boots thundered across the floor.

But Timothy was already gone—vanishing into the foot traffic at the end of the alley.

Chapter Fifty-Three

Murmured voices drifted down the hall as Annouie approached the open doorway of Studio One. She paused at the threshold, smoothing her hair and steadying her breath before stepping inside.

Behind the arced desks, the board members sat in disapproving silence. She scanned the room—one seat was vacant.

Meyer-Edwards was absent.

Judith cleared her throat. "Ms. Bach. Please. Sit."

Annouie crossed briskly to the seat at the focal point of the *Arc of Inquisition*, acutely aware that every gaze was fixed on her bleeding fingers, black eye, and scuffed clothing.

"What happened?" Judith asked, voice sharp.

Annouie met each gaze in turn. "I was gardening."

Judith frowned, her eyes narrowing on Annouie's hand. "Get it seen to. You've got a performance coming up—and you'll need to be in top form if you're hoping to compete for the Bernard Smith Scholarship this semester."

At the end of the table, Messier spluttered. "We agreed to hear the concerns before—"

Judith raised a hand. "Yes, yes. Dr. Messier has brought a complaint regarding Ms. Bach's exemption from several mandatory classes. We're here to seek board approval for that exemption. Ms. Bach will respond, and then we'll vote."

"There is no question it must be set aside," Messier insisted. "You've seen the new evidence."

Judith hesitated. "Yes, we all have. But I'd like to hear from Ms. Bach on the additional matters."

She turned toward Annouie. "Ms. Bach, are you ready to begin?"

Annouie's brow furrowed. "Additional matters?"

Judith pinched the bridge of her nose. "I gather you weren't informed?"

"I was not."

Messier scoffed, voice thick with disdain. "She's lying. I emailed her at eleven this morning."

Judith waved him down. "Perhaps Ms. Bach simply didn't have time to review the material." She shuffled through her papers, pushing her glasses up as she scanned the stack. Near the bottom, she paused.

"Here we are." She looked up. "Dr. Messier's concerns: failure to arrive on time for the History of Music tutorial yesterday, failure to attend the required early music concert last night, failure to submit a recital program to all board members, and refusal to nominate an instrument for the early music component." She peered over her glasses. "How do you respond to these allegations?"

Annouie leaned back. "That's quite a list." She folded her hands in her lap and straightened. "As for arriving late to the tutorial—I was delayed outside the room. By Dr. Messier himself. Regarding the instrument, I did nominate one. Dr. Messier said too many students had selected it and told me to choose another. I filed an appeal and have until next week to finalize my selection. Since that affects my program, I was also granted a further extension."

Judith turned to Messier. "Is this true?"

Messier shrugged. "Perhaps. But what about the advanced counterpoint lecture today? Attendance is mandatory—fifty percent of the grade."

Before Annouie could respond, Judith leaned across the desk. "That one's on me. I asked her to come to my office during the lecture. I promised I'd square it with you, but—" She offered a sheepish smile, "—I completely forgot. My fault entirely. So sorry, Thibault. You know how it is—too many deadlines, not enough time."

Messier's face reddened. "I do not know 'how it is'. I expect that if someone says—"

Judith waved him off. "I think Ms. Bach has settled any lingering concerns," she said, closing the file with finality. "All in favor of the exemption?"

Five hands went up. Only Messier's stayed down, his glare fixed on Annouie as she calmly gathered her bag and stood.

"Settled," Judith declared. "Thank you, Ms. Bach. I won't take up any more of your time. And do wish Mr. Meyer-Edwards a swift recovery—if you happen to see him."

* * *

Meyer-Edwards pushed off the wall as Annouie emerged from Studio One.

"Go as expected?"

She swept past him, heading for the stairs. In three long strides, he caught up, grabbed her arm, and steered her away from the staircase.

"Hey—"

Before she could shake him off, he yanked her down the corridor.

A heavy wooden door loomed ahead. Meyer-Edwards fished a key from his pocket, the long stem and ornate bow catching the dim light. He twisted it in the lock. A dull clunk echoed, and the door creaked open. Without a word, he pushed her inside.

She gave a sharp exhale, thoughts of Gibson forgotten.

Light poured through stone-mullioned windows onto a sprawling desk and floor-to-ceiling bookcases crammed with leather-bound volumes, tattered treatises, and dog-eared manuscripts. A Steinway grand gleamed in one corner. Near the hearth, logs were stacked neatly between ornate andirons. Above the jet-black mantel, a large flatscreen looked jarringly out of place.

At the center: a battered sofa, ottoman, and low coffee table atop a faded, threadbare rug. Neglected grandeur, frozen in time.

Her eyes widened. "Is this Gray Cat's lair?"

He kicked the door shut. "Hardly." He lowered his voice. "This used to be my office. Back when—" He cleared his throat. "Well, you've heard the rumors."

Everyone had. His affairs were the stuff of legend—or tabloid gossip—depending on whom you asked.

He slipped the backpack from her shoulder and dropped it beside the Steinway. "Sit."

She didn't.

He crossed the room and returned with a first aid kit, dumping it onto the coffee table with a heavy thud.

As he reached for the cotton wool, her gaze flicked to his forearms—lean and muscular.

Gray Cat's forearms.

He dropped the wool, detoured to the bookcase, grabbed two crystal tumblers and a bottle of Scotch. Returning to the table, he poured a generous measure into each glass.

"Drink. It'll help with the after-action shock."

He downed his in one smooth motion, then soaked the cotton wool in alcohol.

"I said sit."

Reluctantly, she circled the sofa and dropped into the worn seat. He took her right hand, his grip firm but careful, and began cleaning her wounds.

Fire lanced through her fingertips. She hissed, pulling away.

His grip tightened—insistent but gentle.

"Hold still."

He worked in silence. Beyond the windows, cherry blossoms drifted on the wind.

He paused mid-dab, eyes sharpening. "Did Deluca hire you?"

"Deluca?"

"Don't play games. Someone wanted you close to me."

She hesitated. No point lying. "It wasn't Deluca."

He studied her a beat, nodded, resumed. A rebellious lock of hair fell over his eyes.

Then he straightened, bracing his hands on his thighs. "Anderson, then. He sent you after the manuscript, didn't he?"

Her breath stilled. Her first impulse was to lie. But—she also wanted answers.

"Yes." She paused—a beat. Then: "Why do you have it?"

His hands stilled. "I'm asking the questions."

"You want answers?" She met his eyes. "Then I get to ask some of my own."

His fingers drummed once, twice. Finally: "It was sent to me."

"By whom?"

"Your turn."

She leaned close, breath mingling with his. "I was sent to watch you. Until the night of the preview. That's when Anderson told me to find an envelope instead and bring it to him."

He dropped her hand. "What envelope?"

"From the Accademia in Rome."

His knuckles whitened. "You gave it to Anderson?"

She nodded.

The air thickened. He grabbed her hand, began to bandage the wounds.

The minutes crawled by.

At last, he asked, voice low, "Anderson recruited you as a child?"

She sighed. "He found me on the docks in Kiel. I was seventeen. He gave me room and board. Only later did I learn he was the one who put my father in Craiova Penitentiary."

His eyes darkened. "Craiova—Romania?"

She nodded.

He poured another Scotch, tossed it back, the silence settling like a weight.

"Why pay two million for you?"

She smirked. "That's easy—I double-crossed him."

His eyes narrowed. "Revenge? That doesn't track."

She shrugged. "What else would it be?"

He studied her. "I think he has feelings for you."

Her fingers tightened around the glass. "No." She slammed it down. "Absolutely not."

His brow lifted. "Think about it—he tried to rescue you."

The words hung between them.

Three years, playing both sides, pretending loyalty while dismantling Anderson's network from the inside. Had he truly never guessed?

"Anderson really has no idea."

Meyer-Edwards's voice softened, almost sympathetic. "Men are simple. We only see what we want to see. You gave him no reason to think otherwise."

He stood, tossing the waste into the bin. "Right. You're all patched up. And we've got work to do."

"Work?"

He nodded. "We'll retrieve my manuscript. Then we'll go after that envelope you stole."

She arched a brow. "But first—we're going to the Fonteyn Gallery."

He sighed. "Why?"

"Because the only thing better than one Rebrisi element," she said, the corner of her mouth lifting slyly, "is two."

Chapter Fifty-Four

A low rumble echoed in the distance, then faded into silence. Jack Vallone groaned, forcing his right eye open. The left refused to cooperate—swollen shut following a particularly vicious session with Sir James.

Chin had dosed him again, leaving him sprawled on the cold stone slab to "sleep it off".

Grimacing, he pushed himself upright, one hand pressed against his bruised ribs. Sir James had done a thorough job, working him over before Chin jabbed him with the Propofol. Why they hadn't killed him yet was a mystery he wasn't sticking around to solve.

A wan light seeped through a grated vent high in the wall. He tapped his pants pocket and exhaled in relief—unbelievably, his phone was still there. He pulled it out, angling the screen toward the weak light.

No signal.

He switched on the flashlight. The narrow beam swept across the chamber, revealing a grim tableau: a stone platform, a table strewn with tools and jars, a bloodied hammer.

He flinched, swung his legs over the edge and eased onto the gritty floor, pain stabbing through his side.

The ground shifted beneath his feet as he shuffled toward the wall. The window—just a slit—was set twenty feet up. Completely out of reach.

He scanned for alternatives, the only sound his ragged breath and the faint hum of vibrations from overhead.

Then—a squeal of brakes.

Jack grinned, lips splitting painfully. The catacombs ran deep beneath the business district. Some tunnels were mapped and opened to the public. Others were sealed off, forgotten—or intentionally hidden.

He knew them all. Given a starting point, he could find his way out.

He swept his torch across the room again. To his right—two arched doorways, long corridors stretching into the gloom. To his left—a larger chamber, with a second worktable cluttered with tools.

Footsteps.

He backed into the shadows just as Dr. Chin emerged from the left tunnel, cradling a black box like a sacrament.

* * *

The Murphy door in Sir James's Victoria House office creaked open, and the MP stumbled into the dimly lit room, his movements sluggish and strained. He needed a drink. Vallone's blood clung to his hands—sticky and dark—and the coppery scent mingled with the faint odor of rot wafting through the open door behind him.

His fingers grazed the wall in search of the switch, leaving a crimson streak. He grimaced. The blood was a visceral reminder of the chaos now unfolding around him.

Crossing to the basin, he scrubbed his hands with brisk, almost violent strokes. The water ran pink, swirling down the drain. Still, the room reeked of decay, as if the open door were bleeding its secrets into the room.

Drying his hands, he grabbed the TV remote and pointed it at the wall-mounted plasma screen. A low hum filled the office as the device whirred through its slow boot-up cycle.

At the wet bar, he sloshed Macallan into a tumbler and downed it in one gulp, savoring the burn. A second followed. Then, silk kerchief in hand, he mopped his brow and collapsed into his captain's chair with a groan.

The screen finally flickered to life, sound erupting from the speakers.

Sir James lit a cigar, took a slow puff—then froze, mid-exhale.

JOHN DOE IDENTIFIED.

The feed shifted to a reporter standing outside the House of Commons. Midmorning traffic buzzed faintly in the background.

He tapped the volume up.

"MP for Haynes, Sir James Gibson, has gone to ground following today's identification of the Wilkins Beach John Doe.

"A citywide search is now underway for the man claiming to be Sir James Gibson. Just yesterday, the MP called for an inquiry into the alleged mishandling of Operation Bayside Ripper. These allegations surfaced soon after new evidence implicated him in the murder of journalist Sara Miles."

Cut to crime scene footage. Then: shaky cell phone video. A highway shootout. Hope's escape from the rear of a police van.

Sir James lowered his cigar to the edge of the ashtray, transfixed by the cold precision with which his personal assistant dispatched the officers.

Clearly, he had underutilized Hope's skills.

The screen cut again, this time—Gabriella Fonteyn, being bundled into the back of a police vehicle outside Timothy Gibson's apartment.

A journalist shouted, "Are you surprised?" Fonteyn yanked her jacket over her head.

Annoyed, Sir James muted the screen and reached for his desk phone. He was about to dial—then noticed the blinking red light.

One new message.

Frowning, he hit play.

Hope's voice hissed through the speaker. "You're a dead man, Parrish."

Sir James slammed the handset into the cradle, pulse pounding in his temples.

He spun toward his computer, fingers flying across the keys.

An urgent message awaited him. Subject line: *Payment Due.*

Not from the police. Or an adversary.

From his whisky supplier.

A man who had delivered on credit for ten years—now demanding cash up front.

Sir James swore loudly.

He leaned over the keyboard, fingers striking the keys as he began the money transfer.

Footsteps.

Maria's voice—bright, grating, entirely unwelcome.

He bolted from the desk and slipped through the passage door—just as a sharp knock rattled the office door.

* * *

Chin was waiting in the preparation room, eyes narrowed on the black box at the center of the workbench.

"It's a fake," Sir James said, stepping beneath the archway.

Her jaw tightened. "What about the manuscript?"

"A woman named Bach has it. Find her, find the manuscript. Suggestions?"

Chin swiped her phone and brought up an encrypted chat. "Anderson's tracking her—some of the best hackers in the business are on it. As soon as they get a ping, he'll text me her location."

Sir James exhaled. "Good. Forward it when it comes through."

Chin's brow creased. "You can't go after her yourself."

"Why not?"

"She's tricky."

He snorted, patting the outline of the Beretta beneath his jacket. "So am I."

"Underestimating her would be a mistake. Trust me."

He gave a dismissive grunt. "Oh, I do. But we need to divide and conquer. The *Venus* is still at the gallery. Go get it. I'll handle Bach."

"And Vallone?"

He shrugged, as if the question bored him. "Shoot him. Release him. Whatever. He's no longer important."

* * *

Jack Vallone stumbled backward through the left archway, crashing into the passage beyond. He pivoted and ran, desperate to put distance between himself and the preparation room, where Chin was likely prepping a lethal syringe.

His hand flew to his phone. Still no bars. Swearing under his breath, he shoved it back in his pocket and kept running, fingers skimming the wall to guide him through the dark.

The tunnels stretched for miles beneath the city—a labyrinth he knew well. Every twist, dead end, forgotten exit. All he needed was a sign: a shift in pressure, a subtle draft, the tang of the street above.

His breath rasped in time with his footfalls, gritty steps echoing through the corridor, mingling with the panicked squeals of rats. Then—he felt it. A barely perceptible change. Enough to make him pause.

He slid to a stop, pebbles skittering over the uneven floor. Backing up, he pressed his palms to the wall, searching for a side tunnel.

There. A breeze. Faint, less stale. Carrying the tang of the river. And up ahead—a shimmer of light. A winding staircase.

Jack tore toward it, launching himself up the steps. At the top: a bricked-in doorway. No handle. No hinges. But he knew these passages. There would be a mechanism.

He ran his fingers over the stone. Nothing. Then—just above head height.

A sconce.

He scoffed in the dark.

Gripping the lamp, he tugged it downward. The stone groaned, the door shuddered. Another tug—and it scraped open.

* * *

Nicholas ditched the police van beneath a bridge, stole a battered Suzuki hatchback from a nearby lot, and circled back to Victoria House. He parked two blocks away and approached on foot.

A passing double-decker bus shook the building as he slipped in through the back entrance.

Inside, Victoria House shivered as the bus rumbled off. Light spilled from beneath Sir James's office door. He crept through the dim corridor, drawing his firearm as he advanced, the faint tapping from within urging him on.

A door clicked open.

Nicholas melted into the shadows as Maria emerged from the end office, her graying hair flicked behind her ears, bony hands trembling around a stack of papers. She bustled up the corridor, chin high with purpose.

"Mr. Gibson?" she called, knocking lightly on his door. No answer. She leaned in. "Sir James? I know I'm not to disturb you, but I urgently need your signature."

Still nothing.

She eased the door open and peeked inside. "Sir James?"

Empty.

With an irritated huff, she slammed the door. "Typical," she muttered, marching primly back toward her office.

Nicholas stepped from the shadows.

Maria jumped, hand to her chest—but didn't scream.

Relief softened her features. "Oh, Mr. Hope!" She held up the pages. "Might I trouble you for a signature?"

Nicholas took the reports without a word. He laid them on a nearby desk, plucked a pen from the holder, and began scribbling.

"Have you seen the news?" he asked, knowing she hadn't.

She waved him off. "Sir James's had me running in circles all afternoon—ordering this, ordering that. Everything to be delivered to that yacht of his before midnight. When would I have the time for the news?"

"The yacht?"

She nodded. "He's made some very odd requests."

Nicholas raised a brow. "Could I see the purchase orders?"

She sighed. "Of course. Someone has to approve them." She scurried off and returned with a thick stack of invoices.

Nicholas thumbed through them. "Thank you, Maria. Go home now."

She hesitated, wringing her hands. "I wish I could. Sir James wants his files backed up to the cloud. It's going to take hours—and you know he won't pay overtime."

Nicholas didn't look up. "I could finish up for you," he offered, still flipping through the invoices. "All I need is your password."

Her eyes widened. For a moment, he thought she might refuse. Then she threw up her hands. "Why not? If I can't trust you, who can I trust?"

He slid a pad across the desk. "Username and password, please."

Maria scribbled both at the top. "Don't tell him I shared them," she warned, tearing off the sheet. "You know how he gets."

He leaned in, lowering his voice. "I do indeed. Don't worry—this stays between us." He pocketed the note, offered her a faint smile, and brushed past her into Sir James's office.

The air reeked of stale cigar smoke. An empty glass sat sweating by the keyboard, the faintest trace of whisky still lingering.

Nicholas slid into the captain's chair and typed in Maria's credentials.

The login screen vanished. A cluttered desktop appeared. One dialogue box hovered above the mess of open windows—Sir James had walked away mid-transfer.

His brow furrowed—Sir James never left a job unfinished.

Which meant he was close.

Nicholas scanned the room, half expecting him to emerge from the shadows. When nothing stirred, he turned back to the screen.

With a flick of the mouse, he canceled the transaction, erased the account destination, and entered new details.

One keystroke, and ten million dollars blinked out of existence.

For a heartbeat, Nicholas imagined disappearing with it. A new identity. A new life. A sun-drenched coast. Untraceable.

Tempting.

Sir James had likely planned the same for himself.

But revenge came first. For Maeve. For Sara.

Nicholas eased back the slide of Mitchell's Glock. A round glinted in the chamber—the last. The metallic snap echoed. Cold. Final.

One was enough.

The plan? Lie in wait for Sir James. Force him aboard *The Way*. Coerce. Threaten. Maybe a little torture to whet the appetite. Then the *pièce de résistance*—strap him to the hull for the five-thousand-mile journey to Cape Town through shark-infested waters.

Brutal.

Merciless.

Grotesque.

His lips began to curl when a soft groan interrupted his thoughts. The back wall creaked open.

Nicholas dropped beneath the desk, vanishing into the shadows just as Jack Vallone blundered into the room.

Oblivious, Vallone made for the door.

Nicholas rose in a blur, weapon raised.

"Make a noise and you're dead."

Vallone froze. Slowly, he lifted his hands.

"Turn around."

Vallone obeyed. The transom light carved harsh angles across his bruised face.

"Nicholas Hope," Vallone muttered.

"Where is he?" Nicholas growled.

Vallone scoffed. "Who? That thug who calls himself the Member for Haynes?"

Nicholas jammed the gun to Vallone's skull.

Vallone chinned toward the open Murphy door. "Down there. Plotting with that Asian woman."

Nicholas twitched the barrel. "Down where?"

"The catacombs. You do know about the tunnels, right?"

Nicholas was tempted to end him then and there. Just a few pounds of pressure.

"Face the wall."

Vallone turned slowly, as if bored. "Seriously, Hope. You can't take him on. He's a stone-cold killer."

Nicholas caught his reflection in the bookcase glass. Mitchell's blood marked his collar.

From below came a hollow echo—a whispering from the labyrinth waiting beneath.

Nicholas pulled out a red penlight and descended the steps, Vallone's voice fading behind him.

* * *

Andre guided the Carrera along the freeway, sliding smoothly across two lanes to settle behind a truck cruising at sixty. At this pace, they'd reach Dahlia House in four minutes—too little time to figure out how to ditch Anderson.

A glance at the dark-skinned man beside him revealed nothing but calm vigilance. The gun resting in Anderson's lap, however, told a different story. Its barrel, aimed squarely at Andre's stomach, sent panic sweat trickling from his hairline. Stomach wounds were the worst—messy, slow, and almost always fatal.

Easing off the gas, Andre drifted into the outermost lane. "I don't know what you want from me," he began, keeping his voice level. "I already told you—I don't know where she is. And if Annouie doesn't want to be found, no one will find her."

Anderson drummed his fingers against the doorframe, lips curling into a knowing smile.

Andre's grip tightened on the wheel as the off-ramp came into view. He braked hard, swinging through the turn. The car shot onto a suburban road, peak-hour traffic slowing them to a crawl.

Five minutes later, they pulled up in front of Dahlia House.

Anderson climbed out, slipping the gun into his pocket. He eyeballed Andre across the hardtop. "Don't get any clever ideas."

Nausea rose in Andre's throat—he'd seen the Sanchez interrogation.

Anderson's head was on a swivel as they climbed the steep driveway. Andre bent over the keypad, fingers flying. The door clicked open.

Oria's voice echoed through the foyer. "Welcome back, sir."

He winced. Her threat-assessment subroutines were still offline—a regrettable oversight.

"Remarkable," Anderson murmured, eyes sweeping the space.

Andre shrugged, tossing his keys into the bowl on the side table. "Not really. Home security systems are a dime a dozen."

He turned toward the stairs, breathing deeply. *Stay cool. Don't mention artificial intelligence.*

"I see you have a visitor," Oria chimed. "Would you like me to hold all messages and calls?"

Andre spun, words spilling out. "Oria's just something I've been working on for the domestic market—a more advanced home security system. People want something that can order in, take inventory, pay the bills . . ."

Anderson's smile sharpened. "Home security on steroids."

Andre forced a laugh as he climbed the staircase. "You know me—never do things by halves."

Halfway up, he settled on three options.

Plan A: Send Anderson to a dry hole. The Paper Mill—abandoned and under police surveillance. Radioactive—no way Annouie was going near it.

Plan B: Stall. Reactivate Oria's threat subroutines and wait for the police to show up.

Plan C: Overpower Anderson. Escape. Find Annouie himself. Odds of success—nil.

At the fourth floor OC door, he decided reluctantly on B.

He punched in the code. The door clicked open. Anderson shoved him inside.

He stumbled into the conference desk. As Anderson moved to the far wall, he palmed a drive and slipped it under his sleeve.

Anderson returned with a roll of duct tape.

"Sit," he ordered, prodding Andre toward the high-backed executive chair.

Andre sank into it, discreetly slotting the drive into the computer's USB port. His hands hovered near the keyboard.

"Nuh-uh!" Anderson shoved the keyboard out of reach and crouched, taping Andre's ankles to the base. Then he snapped handcuffs around his wrists, securing them to the armrests.

Andre raised a brow. "It's just a thought—but I might need my hands if you want me to run searches."

Anderson straightened, tossing the tape onto the desk. "Not necessary. Oria can do the heavy lifting."

"You want me to ask the home security system to find Annouie?"

Anderson shook his head. "I want you to ask the most powerful AI in existence to tap into every doorbell cam, traffic feed, and police dashcam in the city and give me an address within the next five minutes—or you're not walking out of here."

He turned to the windows, his silhouette sharp against the harbor lights.

The silence thickened. Fans hummed. Anderson spun back, eyes hard.

"Clock's ticking!"

Andre met his gaze. "If you think I'm giving up Annouie after what you did to Sanchez, you've severely underestimated me."

Anderson's brow furrowed. "Sanchez? What's he got to do with this?"

"You killed him."

Anderson stalked forward. "You really think I'd do that to Annouie?"

"It's what you do."

"I taught her to survive. I made her into who she is—"

"You put her father in jail."

Anderson dragged a hand over his scalp, sinking onto the desk's edge. "Sometimes, in this business, you make hard calls. Handing Isidore Bach over to Interpol was one of them. Annouie understands that."

Andre shook his head. "I don't think she does."

Something suspiciously like regret flickered in Anderson's eyes. "He'd be dead if I hadn't." He gave a weary chuckle. "Isidore was just a white-collar crook when I met him. Then he got greedy—double-crossed the wrong people chasing the *Three Elements*. Because of him, Annouie's in their crosshairs—I have to get to her first."

He sounded genuine. Almost convincing. Almost.

"Not buying it. You want the manuscript."

Anderson pulled back the hammer with a sharp click. "No more stalling. Where is she?"

Andre sighed. Plan A, then.

"The Paper Mill in Haynes Park."

Anderson raised his phone. "Got the address. Paper Mill. River Street, Haynes Park. Secure the manuscript and bring Bach in unharmed. Not a scratch. We're wheels up in an hour. I'll be waiting at the bottom of the stairs."

He pocketed the phone, turned to leave.

Andre blinked. "That's it? You're just going to leave me here?"

Anderson paused, turned, eyes narrowing. Then—

He swung.

The crunch of bone was the last thing Andre heard before the world went dark.

Chapter Fifty-Five

Katrine nosed the cruiser into the last open space beside Haynes Park station.

Saunders climbed out, shaking his head. "Dunbier's gonna blow a gasket."

She snugged her earpiece into place as she stepped from the driver's side. "This is on the way."

"If by 'on the way' you mean the scenic route—yeah, sure." He scanned the street. "You really think this is where Shiruku hangs his hat?"

"Pretty sure," she said, eyeing the looming silhouette of the Paper Mill. "And I'm betting 'he' might be a 'she.'"

A river breeze carried a chill as they headed toward the mill. Katrine stepped off the curb, weaving between parked cars. Saunders followed, heavy boots scuffing the pavement.

The building was an eyesore, wedged between upmarket warehouse conversions. Peeling paint, rusted gutters, and crumbling mortar marred its neglected façade. Even in the fading light, the decay was obvious—a clear warning to keep walking.

Except for the oak doors: re-hung, gleaming, inviting.

Katrine frowned. "Weren't these busted open yesterday?"

Saunders shrugged. "Guess someone didn't like the look."

She laid a hand on the smooth wood. It creaked inward.

"Maybe we should take a look."

"Pretty sure we need reasonable grounds to enter," Saunders warned. "Even with an open door."

"Then it's a good thing I just heard a cry for help, isn't it?" she said—and disappeared inside.

* * *

Nicholas Hope hunted Sir James Gibson through the tunnels beneath the city.

The temptation to end it quickly gnawed at him—an unbearable itch. One bullet to the back of the head. Simple. Efficient. Decisive.

But quick wasn't on the agenda.

He slid the Glock into his waistband. No—Sir James deserved worse.

The Atlantic was waiting.

Up ahead, Sir James paused, penlight sweeping the gloom. The beam caught a set of wooden stairs. Each step creaked softly beneath his weight as he climbed. At the top, a concealed wall panel swung inward. A shaft of pale light pierced the subterranean dark.

Nicholas pressed against the rough brick, holding his breath as Sir James slipped through. He waited, then followed, weapon drawn once more.

He emerged into the storage room in the Old Paper Mill, sweeping the barrel left, then right. Dust whispered underfoot as he crossed to the door. He holstered the gun and put his eye to the narrow gap between door and frame.

Sir James sat at the kitchen island, sipping from a large, glazed mug.

Instinct urged Nicholas to wait.

Patience was his ally.

He checked his watch: just after six.

Then—voices.

They cut through the river's murmuring. Sir James froze mid-sip, sprang from the stool, and ducked behind the island as Detectives Ratcliffe and Saunders stepped into the dining area.

Nicholas shrank back into the shadows.

The game was about to begin.

* * *

Saunders's tactical torch swept across the building, its beam catching on the rusted iron girders overhead.

"I'll admit, this does look like the kind of place your hacker might hole up," he muttered, voice echoing off the concrete. "Just need to find the mainframe, and we can tie this up with a bow."

Katrine ignored him. She picked her way across the gritty floor, scanning the sawhorses, toolboxes, and pallets. A plastic curtain hung around one section, shielding a piano from view. A ghost of a smile tugged at her mouth. *La Belle Dame.* It wasn't a mainframe—but it was just as incriminating.

She turned toward the kitchen at the rear. Sleek. Modern. Functional. At least Annouie wasn't completely roughing it.

Her gaze slid to the industrial-looking staircase near the far wall. If there were more answers to be found, that's where she'd find them.

Behind her, Saunders grumbled. "Come on. We should get—"

A crash echoed from above. The warbling in the rafters cut off.

Katrine dropped into a crouch, gaze fixed on the landing.

"Probably just a pigeon," Saunders offered.

She shook her head, already drawing her gun. "Cover me."

Without waiting, she started up.

A faint chittering floated down as she reached the top. She paused, angled her head.

One.

Two.

She burst into the room, sweeping her gun left to right.

A spartan living space. Wool blanket tossed over rumpled sheets. A worn rug stretched across the floorboards. At the far end, a desk with a monitor and loose cables.

She crept forward.

Crunch.

She lifted her foot. Shards of terracotta littered the floor. A half-dozen long-stemmed flowers lay scattered beside them. As she reached the desk, a possum bolted across the room, a baby clinging to its back.

Saunders's voice echoed from below. "Satisfied?"

She hesitated, holstered her gun, and exited quickly.

At the base of the stairs, her gaze drifted toward the storage room.

"Did we check in here?"

Saunders groaned. "Seriously? Ratcliffe, we're—"

Something snapped past her left ear.

A grunt. Then a thud.

She dropped to the floor and rolled as a second shot spat overhead. Drawing her Glock, she scrambled behind the kitchen counter.

In the reflection of the fridge door, she saw him—Sir James Gibson. Skulking along the edge of an unfinished partition.

Saunders lay near the dining table, clutching his thigh, blood welling between his fingers.

Gibson loomed over him, phone to his ear. "What do you mean it's not there? I transferred the money myself."

He raised his Beretta M9, the suppressor gleaming.

Katrine rose and fired. Unsuppressed rounds shredded the half-built wall.

Gibson spun, snapping his gun toward her. Bullets chewed through cabinets, shattering mugs. A ceramic shard sliced her arm. She barely felt it.

Creeping around the counter, she stilled her breath.

Sighted Gibson by the dining table.

Saunders was still alive—barely.

Gibson raised his gun.

"NO!"

The bullet punched through Saunders's jacket, a puff of navy marking the entry point.

He blinked once.

Then sagged.

Katrine surged up, then squeezed, emptying her magazine. The air filled with cordite and smoke. Her gun locked open with a sharp click.

Radio chatter crackled through her earpiece.

"Dispatch, Barnes Three. Suspect sighted. Heading East on Frith."

Gibson was gone.

She ejected the spent mag—it clattered to the floor

"Copy, Barnes Three. Units, respond to East Frith—"

She slammed a fresh one into the well.

"—Pursuit in progress."

Her hand moved to the slide.

Gibson stepped into view.

"Drop it," he said, aiming squarely at her chest.

She stooped. Set the Glock down.

He kicked it out of reach.

"Up."

She rose slowly, hands raised. He jabbed her in the back, herding her toward the stairs.

"No, I wasn't talking to you," he snapped into the phone.

She gripped the railing and climbed. Saunders's blood spread across the floor like a river of ink.

Rage surged.

She was going to get Gibson's gun. Put it to his head—

He shoved her hard. She stumbled up the last steps and spilled into the bedroom.

"I can't just drop everything and check," Gibson barked into the phone, forcing her toward the bed. "Just make the delivery. I'll have the cash waiting."

A pause.

Then Gibson exploded.

"I can't wait until nine tomorrow. We're leaving tonight."

He snapped the phone shut.

Turned to her, eyes gleaming.

"Right. Where was I?"

He flipped his gun.

Struck her across the temple.

Pain bloomed.

Then—

Nothing.

Chapter Fifty-Six

The gallery rose serene and undisturbed, glowing beneath a waning crescent moon. The river shimmered, mirroring the sky. Ripples fanned behind the tender as it nosed toward the beach. Timothy Gibson crouched at the outboard, eyes fixed ahead.

The boat ran aground with a dull scrape. He leapt out and hauled it further up the shore.

He had the laptop. The Gartner Haus works were secure. And the *Venus* would soon be his again.

His breath quickened as he set off along the river wall, leather loafers whispering against the damp stone.

The night pressed in—heavy, still.

As he climbed the steps toward the gallery, something shifted just beyond the halo of a solitary streetlamp. He dropped into a crouch, hairs rising at the base of his neck.

A figure detached from the shadows beside the dock.

A slow smile crept across his face.

Annouie Bach.

The figure leapt, hands catching the wall, and began scaling the façade.

Timothy darted across the street. He took the rear steps two at a time and flashed his pass card. The lock clicked. Slipping inside, he cut through the loading dock and hammered the elevator call button.

The doors parted. He stepped in, chest tight with anticipation, and rode it to the fourth floor.

A security guard waited, radio pressed to his mouth.

"Belay that order—it's Gibson," the man barked. He lowered the device. "Wasn't expecting anyone tonight, sir. Especially after this afternoon."

Timothy strode past him. "We're still running a business."

The guard scrambled to keep up. "But Ms. Fonteyn—"

"Her lawyers are handling it."

They stopped outside the Rose Chambers Room. Timothy pressed his palm to the reader. The light flicked from red to green. The doors clicked open.

"No need to babysit me," he said, stepping inside.

Alone, he paused before the painting.

The brushwork. The layered translucence. The shimmer of the glaze.

Rebrisi's brilliance twisted like a blade in his chest. No matter how close his copies came, they could never quite capture that luminous transparency.

His gaze drifted to the upper right-hand corner.

A faint scuff.

Relief surged. It was back.

He lifted the *Venus* from the wall and laid it flat on the coffee table. From his pocket, he drew a jeweler's loupe, fitted it to his eye, and leaned in.

Beneath the scuff: a numerical code.

He palmed a knife and began to cut—carefully, methodically—lifting a wafer-thin strip into the light.

Behind him, the door whispered open.

"You're too late," he said, turning, blade shifting to his other hand.

He blinked.

The world narrowed to a breath as a black-clad figure hurtled toward him, thick-soled boots driving for his throat with deadly precision.

* * *

Antony retreated into the shadows, breath slowing, as Bach sprinted straight at the gallery wall. She leapt—hands catching the ledge—just as he ducked back into the alley, phone pressed to his ear.

Impressive.

She free soloed up the wall like a shadow.

Mesmerizing.

Moments later, her face rose above the parapet, one hand to her earpiece.

Her voice crackled through his phone, steady and commanding. "Won't be long. Don't disappear."

He rolled his eyes as she vanished over the top.

Pocketing his phone, Antony jogged along the building's side. Two minutes to get in. Two to get out.

A ruse was his best option.

A stack of discarded cardboard near the loading dock caught his eye. Perfect. He grabbed the least mangled box and headed to the front entrance. A little social engineering ought to do it.

Straightening his back and balancing the box one-handed, he pressed the phone to his ear and strode up the front steps.

The gallery's glass doors glinted under the streetlights. Through the sidelights, he spotted a lone guard slouched at his station.

Antony leaned on the intercom and held up his conservatory pass.

The guard scowled, slow to rise, and shuffled toward the doors with visible reluctance.

"Gallery's closed," he muttered, words muffled through the pane.

Antony pressed the card harder to the glass, gesturing animatedly and speaking into the phone as if managing a crisis.

The guard cracked the door an inch. "I said—"

Antony didn't wait. He shouldered it wide and breezed inside, phone still at his ear, box balanced in his hand.

The guard followed, irritation mounting. "Sir—"

Antony waved vaguely with the box, phone wedged between his chin and shoulder. "Yes, I've just arrived at the front," he said, exasperated. "I know Mr. Gibson's concerned. The buyer is furious. Just give me thirty more seconds."

The guard hesitated.

Antony snapped the phone shut with a sharp flick.

"Which way to the Rose Chambers Room?" he asked, just as the elevator dinged open.

The guard blinked, then pressed his push-to-talk button. "A package is on its way up to Gibson. Show the courier to the Rose Chambers Room."

Antony stepped into the elevator with a smile.

People only saw what they expected to see.

* * *

Annouie inspected the rooftop access door, dropped her bag, and fished out a set of picks. Two quick rakes—*click*. The lock surrendered.

She slipped into the stairwell, descended one flight, and eased onto the fourth floor.

Next hurdle: the Rose Chambers Room.

She hugged the wall. The plan was simple—wait for a guard, then lift his pass.

A low moan echoed.

A man burst from the Rose Chambers doorway and fled toward the main staircase—a shadowy figure swallowed by gloom.

She started after him—but another moan dragged her attention back. A woman lurched into the foyer, clutching a cardboard tube under one arm. She paused beneath an exit sign.

Chin.

At the corridor's far end the elevator dinged. Guards—right on schedule.

Chin staggered to the fire door, slung the tube over her shoulder, and slipped through.

Annouie tapped her earpiece. "Meyer-Edwards. Do you copy?"

Nothing—just the hiss of the open line.

Frowning, she followed Chin into the stairwell. Labored breathing bounced off concrete. Above, a metallic bang: the rooftop door.

"Chin has the *Venus*," she whispered. "Pursuing. Advise."

Still nothing.

She sprinted upward and burst onto the roof, taser in hand. Chin was already at the parapet, securing a rope. She tested the line, climbed onto the railing—then her phone rang.

"What now?" Chin muttered, dropping back down.

She answered. "Chin. Identity check: azure."

A tinny voice replied—right as 50,000 volts hit her.

Chin convulsed and crumpled. Annouie caught the phone before it hit the ground, flex-cuffed Chin's wrists, and gave her a second jolt for good measure.

"I hope that hurt," she whispered.

From the phone, a man barked. "Do you have it?"

Annouie finished frisking Chin and grabbed the phone. Caller ID: Sir James Gibson.

"Yes," she said, muffling her voice with her sleeve.

"Good. I'm still waiting for Bach. Detectives Ratcliffe and Saunders crashed the party. Saunders is handled, Ratcliffe soon to follow. How fast can you get here?"

"I'm at the gallery." She paused, drew a slow breath. "Where are you?"

Behind her, the rooftop door creaked. Two uniformed guards stepped out. Time to move.

She tugged on Chin's gloves, grabbed the rope, and prayed it was anchored. Swinging over the parapet, she descended as Gibson spoke:

"The Paper Mill in Haynes Park. Use the map I sent—"

She scrolled through Chin's messages. Found it.

Her boots hit concrete. She tossed the phone into a dumpster.

"Meyer-Edwards, change of plan," she said into her mic. "Call the police. Send them to the Paper Mill—River Street, Haynes Park. Katrine Ratcliffe's in serious trouble. I'm on my way. I'll meet you at 112 Thomas Street when it's done."

* * *

The room swam back into focus. Andre was still cuffed to the chair.

He whispered into the air. "Oria?"

She was unusually quiet.

"Oria," he repeated. "I'm cuffed to a chair."

Nothing. Was she sulking? Maybe those buggy bits of code weren't ironed out after all.

"Could you help?" A beat. "Some suggestions."

Silence. Then, desperation: "Please?"

Finally, her voice filled the room. "In theory, picking handcuffs is relatively simple. You need something hard to probe the locking mechanism and mimic a key."

"What do you suggest I use? *Please?*"

"Google recommends using a bobby pin or paper clip, if available."

"This is a paperless office."

A beat. "My bad."

He blinked. *My bad?* "Did you just apologize?"

"The bracelet Ms. Bach gave you for Christmas should suffice. Break one of the supports. Bend the tip into a right angle."

Andre wiggled his wrist. A support broke loose.

"It's hard but malleable. Insert it into the upper part of the lock, bent tip pointing away from the center."

He slid it in.

"Now rotate clockwise."

Click.

"It worked!"

"Now again, tip toward the center. Turn until it gives."

He fumbled, then—*click*. The second cuff dropped.

He bent, ripped the duct tape off with a grimace. A rush of pins and needles surged down his limbs.

"Got a fix on Annouie's location?"

"Using trilateration to pinpoint the Oria2 SmartSpecs now."

Well?"

The doorbell rang—loud and jarring.

Andre froze. Dread twisted in his gut.

"The signal is coming from directly outside—but—"

He didn't wait. Bounded across the landing, thundered down the stairs.

He yanked open the door. "Where the devil have you—"

A DBWCS courier blinked at him, tugging the brim of his cap.

"Good evening, sir. I was instructed to deliver a package at this time."

Andre seized the envelope and ripped it open. The Oria2 prototype fell out, along with a note.

He flattened the paper.

Annouie's spidery scrawl: barely legible, unmistakably hers.

Meet me at the Paper Mill. 7:30 p.m. I have the Venus. *Will trade for Isidore's freedom. How you and DOJ manage this is up to you.*

He crushed the note in his fist and turned to the courier, who was already heading down the steps.

"How much to take me upriver?"

The man paused, glancing between the house and the harbor. "We're not a taxi service, sir."

Andre pulled out a wad of cash, crisp bills catching the light. "A thousand do it?"

A beat.

"Where to, sir?"

* * *

The Dassault Falcon 50's engines roared to life as John Chrysler Anderson's taxi rolled onto the private airfield, headlights slicing through the dark. The vehicle passed gleaming jets parked neatly beneath exterior lights before stopping beside the Falcon.

A flight attendant stood at the top of the stairs, waiting.

No sign of Chin.

No sign of Annouie.

Anderson climbed out, grabbed his carry-on, and strode toward the jet. He boarded quickly, following the attendant into the cabin. He was already behind schedule. No more delays. A knot of frustration coiled in his chest as he folded his six-foot-three-inch frame into the leather chair, tossing his bag onto the adjacent seat. No Chin he could handle. But Annouie's absence? That stung harder than he cared to admit.

The attendant offered a practiced smile. "We're expecting some turbulence. Let me stow that for you."

"Just a moment." Anderson pulled a slim folder from the bag before handing it over. She tucked it in the overhead compartment and disappeared into the cockpit.

He fished out his phone and fired off a message:

> I told you to be here on the hour. We're wheels up in five.

Moments later, the attendant returned, sealed the hatch, and strapped herself into the jump seat.

Anderson exhaled sharply, frustration spilling out in one long breath. His plans for Annouie hadn't panned out—but he'd secured the photo. That was what mattered.

As the jet taxied to the runway's end, he opened the folder and drew out the dog-eared image. Antoine Deluca had paid a fortune for the black-and-white still. Anderson scanned the faces. One of the twelve was the operative known as the Gray Cat. Just young men—full of hope, untouched by the legend the Cat would become.

He just didn't know which one.

And neither did Deluca.

The aircraft jolted over the tarmac, rattling his spine, then slowed, turned, and halted. The turbines whined louder, vibrations shaking the cabin.

He braced, gripping the armrests as the jet sprinted forward and lifted into the night. G-forces pressed him back. City lights shrank below, swallowed by the dark. Somewhere down there, Annouie was hiding.

The cockpit door clicked open.

Two men stepped into the cabin. The atmosphere shifted—pressure rising like a storm front.

Anderson tensed, hand twitching toward the duffel—and the Colt M1911 inside—before remembering it was now out of reach.

The taller wore a suit. The other—broader and silent—wore tactical fatigues.

The suit took the seat opposite. The muscle stood by the cockpit door, arms folded, gaze locked on Anderson.

The suited man crossed one leg over the other and smiled, calm and unhurried.

Anderson narrowed his eyes. "Who're you?"

The man tilted his head. "Really? You're going to pretend you don't know me?"

The face was familiar, but out of place.

The man's too-wide smile stretched. "Johannesburg ring a bell?"

Anderson blinked. "Robert Mackie?"

"Yeah. Guess you didn't recognize me without the long hair and beard?" Mackie rubbed his jaw. "That was some crazy shit we did."

He leaned back, expression sobering.

"Now it's all suits and short back and sides. I miss the old days. But life moves on. I'm an investigation team leader for the Office of the Prosecutor now. I get to indict assholes from the safety of a desk."

His expression hardened. "I made an exception for you."

Anderson tugged at his collar. "How did you get on board my charter?"

Mackie's grin returned. "Charter? This is a DOJ jet."

Anderson froze as the aircraft banked hard, veering off course.

"Incidentally," Mackie said, "Denny Maxwell was rescued from a mob safe house this morning."

Anderson's breath caught.

"You seem surprised."

"I don't know who you're talking about." He fumbled for his phone. No signal.

Mackie raised an eyebrow. "We've been tracking Denny for a while. When he went dark, we got concerned."

Anderson pocketed the phone. "Still don't know who that is."

"Strange," Mackie said, tapping the armrest. "Because he had a list of off-book clients. Your name was on it."

Anderson's mind raced. A setback—but not catastrophic.

Mackie's grin sharpened. "We picked up your lawyer, too."

Anderson's mouth dried. "Why?"

"He was on Denny's list."

Anderson slumped in his seat. "So what now?"

"We take you to a secure facility. We talk. Depending on what you tell us, we either put you away for a very long time . . . or we make a deal. Entirely up to you."

Mackie stood, buttoned his jacket, and leaned in. He plucked the photo from Anderson's hand.

"I'll take this," he said, fingers curling around it like a trophy.

Then he turned and strolled back into the cockpit.

* * *

Mackie studied the black-and-white image as he stepped into the cramped cockpit. Behind the copilot, Antony Meyer-Edwards perched on a jump seat, his expression tight—until Mackie handed him the photo.

Antony exhaled. The tension drained from his body as he slipped the image beneath his vest.

Mackie leaned against the wall, rubbing his chin. "Hell of a day. Raided a mob safe house. Picked up Anderson's accountant." His gaze drifted to the darkness beyond the windshield. "Then I get this strange directive: locate a photo, deliver it to the guy sitting behind the copilot."

He shot Antony a pointed look. "Thought you were out."

Antony shrugged, eyes meeting his for a beat, then reached down and hauled a parachute rig from the floor. He began strapping himself into the harness.

Mackie straightened. "Tell me you're not about to do what I think you're about to do."

Antony gave a crooked smile. "Be a good sport, Mackie. Take us over Haynes Park."

He tightened the last strap.

"Turns out I owe someone a favor."

Chapter Fifty-Seven

A television droned in the background.

"Breaking news: the Wilkins Beach John Doe has been identified as Sir James Gibson."

Katrine Ratcliffe forced her eyes open. Pain hammered through her skull. Something foul choked her mouth. She spat it out—a rag, damp and bitter. She turned her head. Beyond the balcony rail, darkness stretched unbroken.

She was on the bed. First floor. Old paper mill.

A man's voice floated up from the kitchen below.

She shifted. The bed creaked. A sharp bite at her wrists. She flexed—both hands zip-tied to the headboard. Fingers brushed smooth metal: vertical rods. Promising. She tested her legs. Also zip-tied. And—she'd been stripped to nothing but her boy shorts.

A hiss escaped her lips. Fury flared, hotter than the pain. The moment she escaped—and she would—she was going to beat that bastard within an inch of his life.

The clang of metal echoed. Sir James appeared in the doorway, a kit in one hand, a phone in the other.

"An extra hundred if you can deliver to Berth Nine before midnight," he said and ended the call.

Crossing to the desk, he shoved Annouie's books aside. They crashed to the floor. He flipped the kit open. Tools gleamed in neat rows. His fingers hovered, then plucked a penknife. A tuneless whistle slipped from his lips as he approached, holding the blade aloft like a relic.

Katrine flexed again. The zip-tie gave—barely.

He leaned down. The cold blade grazed her torso. He flicked. It left no mark—at first. Then a slow, burning line. Blood welled.

Gibson stepped back, eyes alight. He slashed again.

Katrine groaned—masking the subtle sound of plastic straining.

The television droned beneath the rising sounds of pain and protest.

Another slash. Then a swipe. He worked methodically. Back and forth. Up and down.

He was carving the Ripper's signature into her flesh.

She arched off the bed, twisting and pulling—working the restraint to breaking point. The headboard creaked with each movement, a counter-rhythm to the blade.

Gibson's lips twisted in dissatisfaction. He raised the knife again.

Katrine tensed.

Then a buzz—his phone.

He froze, muttering a curse. He lowered the knife and fished the phone from his back pocket.

"Thorpe? Thank God. Where the hell are you?"

He moved to the window, checking his watch in the moonlight.

"The yacht?"

She flexed again. Almost there.

"I'll be along soon. Loose ends to tie up. Stop worrying. The whole city's looking for Hope—he won't get far."

He snapped the phone shut and slid it into his hip pocket. Eyes glittering, he picked up the knife.

The TV rattled on:

"MP Sir James Gibson: a fraud. Breaking news—"

"You must be wondering who I am?" he said, approaching.

She glared. Was he serious? Every news outlet in the country was running the last twelve hours.

He shrugged like she'd answered. "A long time ago, Antoine Deluca paid me a fortune to kill a man."

The blade bit deeper this time. Blood surfaced, snaking across her skin and pooling on the sheets. Gibson watched the crimson stain grow with something like reverence.

"We were due to ship out to the Middle East, but my friend—the one Deluca wanted dead—decided to go hunting. I made it look like an accident." He dragged the knife in a long, arcing flourish.

"The old lady, Drusilla Gibson? She thought I was her son. That's the kicker. Thorpe helped me fake the rest. Been keeping it quiet ever since." His voice dropped to a conspiratorial whisper. "And that's how the son of an impoverished groundsman became the heir to the Gibson estate."

He let the knife clatter to the floor. Climbed onto the bed. Straddled her.

His hands wrapped around her throat. Began to squeeze.

Katrine writhed. His thumbs pressed deeper.

"Usually, I'd take longer," he said, "but I'm on a bit of a deadline."

So am I.

She arched and snapped the right-hand tie. She swung—fist cracking against his jaw. He toppled off the bed.

She tore her left hand free, scrambling upright as he staggered to his feet. *Snap.* Her left foot came free.

He lunged. She twisted, driving her knee hard into his groin.

He crumpled with a guttural cry.

"That's for stripping me naked, you nutjob!" she spat, ripping free her right foot and vaulting off the bed.

* * *

Nicholas sat on an upturned bucket, posture deceptively casual, as the fight upstairs raged on—every thud, grunt, and gasp echoing through the rafters. He eased back the slide on his gun. The metallic click was oddly soothing.

He eyed the chambered round. Once Sir James finished with the detective, he'd make his move.

The scuffle above intensified, punctuated by the creaking bed frame.

He wondered, briefly, what it might feel like to care. To intervene. To save a human life. But Detective Ratcliffe meant nothing to him—just another inconvenient variable.

Like Usman Malik.

He paused.

Shooting Malik had been a waste.

His stomach clenched, a slow twist of something almost like guilt. Malik had been brilliant. And his eyes—so very pretty.

Nicholas stood, stretching the stiffness from his knees. The fight was tapering off now, the rhythm fractured.

Not long.

He moved toward the door, peering around its edge. The air shifted—slightly.

A whisper of movement behind him.

He turned.

Just in time to see the roundhouse kick coming.

* * *

Annouie landed hard, both feet absorbing the impact as Nicholas Hope crumpled to the floor. His gun spun across the concrete. She scooped it up and tucked it into her waistband, already moving toward the half-open door.

The warehouse loomed, thick with shadows and echoes. The fight upstairs came in ragged bursts—thuds, gasps, groans.

She sprinted from the storage room toward the staircase, boots whispering over the dusty floor.

Then she stopped cold.

That smell—sharp, metallic.

Blood.

Her breath caught. She edged toward the kitchen bench.

Kyle Saunders lay sprawled beside the table, blood pooled dark and glossy beneath him.

She dropped to her knees, pressing two fingers to his neck.

No pulse.

She flinched, lips tightening. Then stood. Scanned the room. Bullet holes riddled the marble countertop.

She yanked open a drawer, pulled out a balaclava, and dragged it down over her face.

Upstairs, the fight reached fever pitch.

She drew the Glock, checked the chamber, and started up the stairs.

* * *

Katrine kicked Gibson in the groin again—harder this time. He doubled over, choking on a guttural cry, nearly retching onto the rug.

Her gaze swept the room. A long metal rod glinted in the corner.

She lunged.

Gibson tackled her from behind, slamming her to the floor.

"Bitch!" he rasped, eyes streaming. He drove a knee into her spine, pinning her in place, and clamped both hands around her throat.

His full weight pressed down.

The room wavered—then began to close in.

* * *

Annouie swung into the doorway, the Glock's front sight aligning in a heartbeat. She squeezed.

The 9mm round cracked past Gibson's head—missing by an inch.

Behind him, a vase shattered, clay shards erupting across the room.

Gibson jolted, stunned—his grip loosening on Katrine Ratcliffe's throat.

* * *

The room exploded.

Gibson released his hold.

Katrine gasped, rasping in air as her lungs caught up.

And a woman's voice rang out, firm and clear. "Hands in the air, asshole."

Katrine rolled onto her side, gagging as the world slowly righted itself. A robe hung from a chair nearby—she grabbed it, wrapping it around her blood-smeared body.

The masked woman kept her gun trained on Gibson as she crossed to the desk. A first aid kit thudded at Katrine's feet.

"You need to stop that bleeding," she said, nodding at Katrine's upper arm.

Katrine fumbled with the kit as the woman retrieved Gibson's remaining zip ties and advanced on him.

Gibson tilted his head, a smirk creeping into place. "You're not going to shoot me."

The woman let out a dry laugh. "Feel free to test that theory. Face the wall."

He hesitated. Then turned.

She patted him down with sharp, practiced motions. From his shoulder holster, she drew a Beretta. The magazine dropped to the floor. She kicked it down the staircase, then used the sole of her boot to eject the chambered round with click-snap precision.

Gibson's smile vanished.

"On your knees," she ordered.

"But I'm a middle-aged man with arthritis."

She didn't hesitate. One swift kick to the back of his leg sent him crashing to the floor with a crack. A grunt of pain escaped him.

She secured his wrists, yanking the zip ties tight.

Gibson grimaced. "I only wanted the manuscript. I'll pay the two hundred thousand my son promised. It's my money, after all."

"Deal's off."

She straightened and pulled out her phone. Calmly, she turned away and spoke into the mic.

"Police, please."

Katrine, still bandaging herself, looked the woman over. Same height. Same build. That lean, poised stance. But the way she moved with the gun, the quiet steel in her voice . . .

Not the Annouie she remembered.

Frankfurt had changed her.

No mask could hide that.

Annouie continued, voice businesslike. "I want to report a homicide at the Old Paper Mill, River Street, Haynes Park. Sir James Gibson is restrained and awaiting arrest. One officer is dead. Another requires urgent medical attention. And—" she flicked a glance at Gibson. "—Nicholas Hope is unconscious in the storage room."

Sir James's head whipped around. Panic flashed in his eyes. "That murdering lunatic is here?"

Annouie ignored him. She snapped the phone shut and crouched beside Katrine. Her voice softened. "The paramedics are five minutes out. Keep pressure on that wound."

She handed her the Glock. "Watch him. If he moves, shoot."

"You can't leave me here like this," Gibson snarled.

Annouie stood, tilting her head toward him as Katrine raised the gun with trembling hands.

"She can't even hold the damn thing straight!" he shouted, panicked. "What if it goes off by mistake?"

Annouie shrugged, already turning away. "Not my problem."

Behind her, Katrine groaned. The Glock wobbled in her grip.

Annouie hesitated.

Gibson didn't.

He surged forward, sweeping Annouie's legs from beneath her.

She hit the floor hard. He rolled to his feet. The zip ties snapped.

In a blink, he had the Glock in his hand.

He turned, leveling the gun—Annouie dead center in the crosshairs as she flipped onto her back.

"Too easy," he sneered, panting. "And to think Dr. Chin believed *you* could best me!"

He stepped closer, gripping the balaclava.

Annouie didn't flinch as he ripped it from her head.

* * *

Six thousand feet above Haynes Park, Antony checked his rig—straps secure, altimeter steady—his hands calm despite the adrenaline surging through his veins.

The hum of the Dassault 50's engines dipped as the pilot eased off the throttle. The cabin depressurized with a hiss.

"Ten seconds," Mackie shouted, barely audible above the rising roar. He anchored himself against the bulkhead as the door opened and 110-knot winds whipped past the hatch. Then he winked.

Antony lowered his goggles. The wind clawed at him, tugging at his clothes.

He stepped to the edge. The night yawned before him, vast and empty. He muttered a string of curse words under his breath.

Mackie gave a thumbs-up. *Go time.*

Antony nodded once, exhaled—

And leapt into the void.

* * *

In any other situation, Annouie wouldn't have baulked. Anderson had drilled a preternatural focus into her—reflex over hesitation. But Katrine had a way of subverting those instincts.

A single glance—a moment to check on her slumped form—that's all it took.

Next thing—Annouie was on the floor, staring up into the barrel of a gun.

Bogotá all over again.

Gibson grinned and pulled the trigger.

Unlike Bogotá, the Glock clicked like a toy gun.

His grin faltered. He pulled again.

Click.

And again. *Click. Click. Click.*

Annouie's lips twisted into a vicious smile. "Out of ammo?"

She kipped up, pivoted—and drove a roundhouse kick into his jaw. The crunch echoed as Gibson flew backward, crashing into the wall. Plaster burst outward in a spray of dust and debris.

Wheezing, he clawed upright, face twisted in rage. "No little girl is going to—"

He dropped flat as a long metal rod whistled past his head.

"—is going to *what*?" she growled, swinging again.

He rolled, dodging, and bolted. He vaulted over the stair rail and vanished into the shadows below.

Tossing the rod aside, Annouie turned to Katrine.

"Go get him," Katrine rasped, dragging herself upright against the footboard.

Annouie hesitated.

Katrine shook her head. "Backup's on the way. Don't let him get away. Not this time."

One last hard look—and Annouie leapt.

She landed with a muted thud. Gibson was already reassembling his Beretta—slamming in the mag, racking the slide.

She dove behind the counter as subsonic rounds stitched the wall behind her, spraying chips of concrete and dust.

Gibson advanced, Italian soles whispering over the floorboards.

Annouie slipped around the island, palming the Japanese chef's knife from the bench.

His footsteps squeaked—he'd reversed course.

She popped up and hurled the knife.

It spun end-over-end, slicing into his gun hand just as he fired. The shot went wide. Glass shattered behind her. She charged low, struck his arm. The gun skidded into the storage room.

He lunged.

She launched—right leg extended—kicking him square in the sternum. He sprawled headfirst into the dining table.

Scrambling, Gibson dove for Kyle Saunders's body. His fingers reached for the Glock.

"Drop it."

Nicholas Hope stepped from the storage room, Gibson's Beretta in hand.

Gibson froze. But only for a moment.

As he pulled Saunders's Glock, Hope fired—a tight burst, shattering the table leg. Gibson dropped the weapon.

Hands up, he slithered away. "My boy—"

Annouie stepped backward, boot snagging on the unfinished floor.

The scrape echoed.

Hope spun. Fired.

The shot hit her square in the side.

She dropped to her knees with a grunt, one hand thrown out for balance, the other pressed hard over her ribs. Blood welled between her fingers.

Gibson's brows lifted. "Hope? My God, boy—this woman was about to—"

"Shut it." Hope's voice was ice.

He shoved Annouie onto her back, gun trained on Gibson.

Her vision swam. The rafters loomed. Twelve sets of gimlet eyes stared down. An audience.

Gibson lowered his hands a fraction.

"Don't move, Parrish," Hope snapped. "The next one goes between your eyes."

Gibson froze. "What the hell are you doing, Nic?"

Hope's chest heaved. The gun trembled.

"Tell me you didn't murder her."

Gibson's tone quietened to a fatherly rumble. "You're not making any sense, my boy. Murdered who?"

Sirens began to rise in the distance, slicing through the quiet.

Hope's jaw tightened. "My mother."

Recognition flickered. Gibson's eyes softened. "Ah. Maeve Darby, of course."

Hope gave a tight nod.

"Lovely woman," Gibson said, voice layered with regret. "What happened to her in that hospital was tragic."

Hope's grip didn't waver. "Don't try to manipulate me, old man. I know what you did."

Gibson nodded, voice dropping. "You must believe me. I tried to help, but she got her hands on those drugs. You have to understand—she wasn't well, she—"

"You're a pathological liar," Hope's voice cracked. "Thorpe told me everything."

The sirens were close now. The walls shook with their echo.

Gibson's mask slipped. His eyes turned cold. "Always knew I should've killed Thorpe."

Hope wiped at his face. "And Sara?"

Gibson's gaze darted toward the storage room—calculating.

The mill flashed blue and red as lights swept through the clerestory windows.

Gibson sighed, a predatory glint in his eye. "You want to know?" He nodded toward the storage room. "Then let's take this somewhere more private."

A beat. Then Hope's gaze sharpened. "My thoughts exactly," he murmured, a cruel spark flickering behind his eyes.

Gibson rose slowly. "What about her?"

Hope hesitated, glancing back toward Annouie—

* * *

Antony counted the seconds as he hurtled through the atmosphere, wind screaming in his ears. At a terminal velocity of 120 miles per hour, the night streaked past—a blur of black and silver. He waited until the last possible moment.

Then yanked the ripcord.

The chute snapped open with a violent tug, jerking him upright. His descent slowed to a glide—a calm 12 miles per hour. He toggled the steering lines, angling toward the muddy river below and the strip of wharf behind the paper mill—his designated landing zone.

As the ground rushed up, Antony yanked both toggles. The chute flared.

He hit the concrete hard. Quick-release. Harness off. Goggles gone.

Inside, voices echoed through the mill's towering windows. He crouched beneath the sill, heart pounding, adrenaline spiking.

A silent prayer slipped from his lips—for the ex-spec ops body-guard who'd taught him HALO jumps.

Then he rose just high enough to look.

Nicholas Hope stood over Annouie—gun leveled at her chest.

Antony swore, grabbed a loose brick from beneath the window—

And hurled it at the glass.

* * *

Car doors slammed. Heavy boots hit asphalt—quick, purposeful.

Inside the mill, Nicholas Hope's voice cut through the fog in Annouie's brain, distorted and distant, like it was coming from underwater.

"It's nothing personal."

Glass shattered.

A blur—something large, fast—rushed into her narrowing field of vision.

Then—

Thud.

A man slammed into Hope, knocking his gun hand wide.

Snap.

A subsonic round spat from the muzzle—and punched through Gibson's left eye. Brain matter splashed the wall. He blinked—once—his remaining eye wide with disbelief.

Then he crumpled.

Hope recoiled, gasping, fury overtaking shock. He spun and swung wildly, fist slicing air—

The other man limboed back, avoiding the blow with impossible grace.

That's when Annouie saw his face.

Meyer-Edwards.

A sob escaped her throat—raw and involuntary. She forced herself forward, crawling across the blood-slicked floor toward Saunders's body. Her trembling hand found the grip of the Glock, still half-holstered.

From outside, an amplified voice boomed:

"POLICE! THIS IS YOUR FINAL WARNING! OPEN UP!"

Hope dove for the Beretta.

Meyer-Edwards launched after him.

Boom!

The battering ram slammed into the new oak doors.

Hope's hand closed around the Beretta. He fired—missed by inches.

Annouie rolled, pain slicing through her side as she fumbled for the Glock.

Boom!

The MBR struck again.

Hope fired once more and sprinted for the shattered window.

Annouie raised the gun, sighted over her toes, and fired.

The round tore into the sill as Hope leapt through the frame.

She squeezed again.

Hope sprinted to the end of the wharf.

She bit down, pushed the pain aside, and pulled.

He yelped, swan-diving into the river.

CRACK!

The doors burst open. Tactical boots stormed inside.

The Glock slipped from Annouie's fingers.

She slumped.

World fading.

Pigeons watching.

A hiccough left her chest as darkness closed in.

"Oh no, you don't!"

Meyer-Edwards's voice—sharp, frayed.

His face appeared above hers, flushed, defiant.

He hoisted her up. Pain seared her side, jolting her back to full consciousness.

"I'm taking you to someone," he muttered. "Just hang on."

As police flooded into the building, he bolted for the storage room.

"Don't quit on me. We've got a program to prepare."

He ducked into the secret passage.

"No way I'm giving Messier the last word."

Combat boots faded behind them as he yanked the door shut.

"Stay with me, Bach."

His breath echoed in the dark.

"And just so we're clear—"

He fumbled with his lighter.

"—that wasn't a request."

Chapter Fifty-Eight

Investigators, medics, forensic teams—and the inevitable swarm of journalists—had descended on the paper mill. Police cruisers clogged every available space—on the footpath, in driveways, even in the middle of the street—their flashing lights reflected in the wet pavement. Three ambulances blocked the accessways on either side of the building, their hazard lights underscoring the chaos.

Uniformed officers moved in and out of the shattered front doors, ducking beneath hastily strung crime scene tape. Onlookers crowded the edges, filming the carnage on their phones.

Dominic's Café—usually shuttered now—hummed with activity as reporters and cameramen sipped everything from standard lattes to iced Americanos, waiting for the next twist in a day of unprecedented disclosures.

Amid the bedlam, DCI Dunbier barked orders at a senior officer, who relayed them to the forensics team assembled before him.

Andre slowed his sprint to a brisk walk as he approached the first of the ambulances. He scanned the scene, gaze flitting past the chaos in search of one face.

Then—

Two gurneys wheeled through the mill's ruined entrance.

A chill raced down his spine.

The officer gave a low whistle, eyes fixed on the body bag strapped to the first stretcher. "Hope's been busy. Paperwork for this alone'll take a week."

He snapped back to issuing orders, sending the forensic techs scrambling.

Andre broke into a jog, closing on the gurney. He pulled his DOJ badge, buzzing it past the nearest officer as the stretcher lifted into the rear of the van.

"Sent to ID victims," he said.

Without waiting for a reply, he climbed in and snapped on a pair of nitrile gloves. Leaning over the bag, he yanked the zipper down, his pulse stampeding.

Not her. Not her. Not—

Relief hit hard—sharp and hollow.

Detective Kyle Saunders lay inside, his skin gray and waxy, as if sleeping.

Andre nodded, zipped the bag shut, and yanked off the gloves. He tossed them into the disposal bin and stepped out into the night.

The second gurney rolled past toward the next ambulance.

Andre followed. He reached for the zipper. Blood and tissue obscured most of the face.

A man's face.

Again, relief—bitter this time—swept through him.

"You get used to it," a medic said, appearing at his side. He clapped Andre on the back as he zipped the bag up again.

Andre gave a tight nod and turned.

His eyes locked on the third ambulance, parked across the street.

In the open rear bay, Katrine Ratcliffe sat sipping from an orange juice box while a medic finished stitching her arm. Her expression: strained, distant, unreadable.

Andre braced himself.

This wasn't going to be pretty.

As he approached, Ratcliffe's eyes narrowed.

"Landvik," she husked, voice brimming with menace.

He didn't slow. He flipped open his wallet and shoved his DOJ ID in her face.

Her scowl deepened. Her chest rose sharply—then she exploded.

"Hell, no!"

She lunged, snatching the wallet. Beneath the cabin's fluorescent strip lighting, she examined his credentials with mounting disbelief.

"There's no way—"

Andre yanked the wallet back. "I don't care what you think of me, Detective. I have a job to do." He gestured at the crime scene, now sprawling in all directions. "Annouie was here. That much is obvious. I need to find her."

He slipped the wallet away, voice softening. "You could help me."

Ratcliffe's gaze sharpened. "You want help tracking her down?"

He shook his head. "Not exactly."

He pulled the Oria2 SmartSpecs from his jacket. He tapped the arm, speaking quietly into the mic.

"Oria. Show Detective Ratcliffe what we have."

He stepped closer and gently slid the specs onto her face.

Ratcliffe recoiled but didn't stop him. She adjusted the fit—then froze as data scrolled across the left lens. Crime scene footage. Trajectory overlays. Heat signatures. Facial recognition tags.

"Are you kidding me?" she whispered. "You hacked the police network?"

"No," Andre said. "The world's most powerful AI did."

She stared, slack-jawed, as the feed continued. "This is generations ahead of anything we've got. If I'd had access to this tech . . ."

Her voice trailed off, caught between wonder and grief.

Andre retrieved the SmartSpecs, expression grim. "So. You'll help me?"

The medic secured the last stitch. Ratcliffe rolled down her sleeve and hopped from the van, boots hitting the pavement with a dull thud.

"No. *You'll* be helping *me*." She flexed her arm, wincing slightly. Then to the medic: "Thanks. Feels good as new."

The medic arched a brow. "Remember—no fighting, heavy lifting, or overexertion for the next week."

Ratcliffe gave a lazy two-fingered salute. "Aye, aye. No heavy lifting."

She turned, motioning for Andre to follow. He fell into step beside her, keeping pace effortlessly.

"I have questions," she said, cutting him a sidelong glance.

"I may not have answers."

"Come on, Landvik. If you want me to trust you, you've got to give me something."

"Trust is earned, Detective," he said, expression unreadable.

"Then let's start with the obvious. Seriously? DOJ?"

He looked around, voice low. "You might want to keep that down."

She leaned in. "So the whole time, you were *pretending* to hack those databases?"

Andre's lips twitched. "I'm the world's best, Detective. I'm in and out. No trace."

"That's not an answer."

"Think about it."

Before she could press further, they arrived beneath Dominic's striped awning and slipped into the crowd. Their conversation dissolved into the hum of voices and clatter of cups as they jostled their way to the counter, Ratcliffe leading the way.

Andre let her.

For now.

* * *

The tide was running out.

Time to cast off.

Timothy Gibson secured the tender to *The Way* and clambered aboard, wincing as he rubbed the back of his head. A lump had formed—tender and throbbing.

He powered up the twin 400-horsepower engines. A low rumble vibrated through the deck as he eased the yacht into the middle of the river. He nudged the throttle, and the boat surged forward, moving with the ebbing tide.

As the shoreline slipped past, the pain sharpened—and his thoughts circled back to Annouie.

Lying in wait. Stealing his Rebrisi.

His jaw tightened, knuckles whitening on the helm. That had always been her endgame. Much good it would do her. The code was gone—he'd seen to that.

A cough broke the silence.

The yacht jerked sharply toward the shore as he spun around.

Dr. Emil Thorpe stood unsteadily on the aft deck, a wood iron clutched in both hands like he was about to tee off.

Timothy steadied the wheel. "Dr. Thorpe?"

The club clattered to the deck as Thorpe exhaled, trembling. "Timothy? Oh God, Timothy. I thought you were him." He stumbled forward, breathless.

Timothy didn't move. "What are you doing here?"

Thorpe's eyes darted around, the whites gleaming in the low light. "Sir James isn't with you?" His voice barely carried over the thrum of the engines.

"Haven't spoken to him all evening."

Thorpe sagged against the rail. "Thank God." He let out another shaky breath. "You've heard, of course."

Timothy's gaze flicked toward the older man. "Yes. I suppose that makes me Timothy, son of a murderer. A con artist. A liar."

For a fleeting moment, he clung to the hope it was all some elaborate, twisted publicity stunt.

"It does," Thorpe said quietly.

He shuffled toward the nearest deck sofa and collapsed into it as the yacht veered into deeper water.

"Where are you headed?" he asked.

"Rhodes. Cyprus. Maybe Malta." Timothy shrugged.

Anywhere but here.

Thorpe nodded, approving. "As long as it's not Alaska."

Timothy didn't smile. "You're not coming with me."

"Why not?" Thorpe's mouth twitched into a sly grin. "We could make a little detour. I happen to have details for a safe deposit box in Zurich. Belongs to Sir James. And as his beneficiary, you'd have access."

The helm jerked in Timothy's grip. "Say that again?"

Thorpe licked his lips, smug satisfaction glistening there. The yacht steadied, slicing through the water like a barracuda. "Sir James has millions," he said. "In gold bullion."

Timothy's throat bobbed as he swallowed. "Millions?" His voice cracked—tight, strained—like an unrosined bowstring.

The old bastard.

Rage simmered beneath the shock, bitter and hot.

Millions.

And then—*millions*?

The pressure in his chest eased, his thoughts turning to other possibilities.

His gaze lingered on Thorpe.

Thorpe nodded, letting the silence hang—heavy with implication.

"I suppose it wouldn't hurt to travel together. For part of the way."

"Or all of the way," Thorpe said, his smile stretching into an oily grin.

All the way. Part of the way. Didn't matter when there was gold bullion to be had.

Timothy pushed the throttle forward. The engines snarled. The yacht surged toward the coast and the open sea—And whatever lay beyond.

Epilogue

Ten weeks later, Antony stood in the driveway outside the family villa, gazing across the lake and wondering if it was time to break the news to Bach. Behind him, the crunch of gravel marked the taxi's departure.

Antony exhaled and squared his shoulders.

Antoine Deluca was dying, and the organization was buzzing with intrigue. The lawyers had been summoned, the family heads convened, and the endless war over the Deluca legacy was in full swing.

Antony wanted no part of it. Family politics was a quagmire he had no intention of stepping into.

Except Isidore Bach had just made that impossible.

With a grunt, he hefted his bags and trudged toward the villa, sweat running down his spine.

He climbed the steps, dropped his bags and knocked.

The soft whisper of bare feet on tile preceded the groaning of the heavy front door. It swung inward to reveal Sibilla Meyer-Edwards—delicate, dark-haired, framed by the muted light of the courtyard behind her.

"Antoine."

He leaned down and kissed her. "Mom." His eyes flicked past her toward the long colonnade. "Is my guest still eating you out of house and home?"

"Don't stand in the heat," she said, stepping aside.

They crossed the courtyard—a fragrant place filled with rampant bougainvillea, a gurgling fountain, and the heady scent of citrus and rosemary.

"It's not polite to keep Mr. Bach waiting," she muttered.

A shadow crossed Antony's face. "I had to speak to the lawyers directly. There were arrangements to be made."

"Always with the excuses," she sighed.

They emerged onto the rear patio. Snow-capped mountains reared into a cloudless sky.

A man sat at the wrought-iron café table, a half-eaten croissant languishing on his plate as he scrolled through company spreadsheets.

"Have you eaten?" Sibilla asked.

Antony waved her off. "I'm fine."

He studied the man—late forties, blond hair fading to white, a ravenous look in his pale eyes.

Antony cleared his throat. Isidore Bach looked up.

"Tony," he said, rising quickly and wiping his fingers on his pants. "I can't begin to thank you—"

Antony flicked his wrist and dropped into the chair opposite. Isidore resumed his seat, those familiar blue eyes—so much like Annouie's—flickering with calculation.

Annouie.

The hole in Antony's chest yawned wider.

"So, when can I speak to her?' Isidore asked, claiming the croissant.

"Soon," Antony said, cool and unreadable. "Once we've finalized the terms of our agreement."

Isidore nodded, mouth full. "Excellent. Everything's arranged. You should be able to take delivery of the *Third Element* on Friday."

Antony leaned in, voice low and razor-edged. "And if I don't—you understand I'll put you right back where I found you."

The last of the croissant lingered on Isidore's lips. He opened his mouth—about to retort—when the patio doors banged open.

Sibilla swept in, bearing a silver coffee tray like it was a weapon.

Isidore's voice rasped across the table. "I need to speak to Annouie."

"All in due course."

"She still doesn't know, does she?"

Antony froze.

"Know what?"

"About Sophie." Isidore's voice dropped to a whisper. "What you did."

The clatter of mugs broke the tension as Sibilla set the tray down with a decisive clink.

"Thought you might be thirsty after your long trip," she said.

Isidore smiled widely as she poured, steam curling from the spout.

"Antony was just about to call my daughter," he said, a sly glint in his eye.

"Wonderful," Sibilla said, handing him a mug. "I know she'll be wanting to hear from you."

Antony forced a tight smile. "Of course."

He dialed, gaze locked on Isidore as the man sipped innocently from his cup.

"It's not like I'm not dying to know how her exam went."

* * *

Meyer-Edwards had been savvy enough to steer clear of hospitals—undoubtedly leaning on his dubious connections to find an off-book surgeon. Maybe he'd even stuck around long enough to hear the prognosis.

But one thing was certain: after hearing it, he'd made for the exit and vanished into the night.

Seriously?

As gunshot wounds went, hers had been neat—a clean through-and-through. Whether luck or Hope's marksmanship, she couldn't say. Still, complications could've followed. Infection, clots, internal bleeds—any of a thousand things.

Meyer-Edwards had left her to face it alone. Not even a scribbled note.

But why complain? There were no complications. She was alive. Security and Risk was a footnote. And despite Messier's curveballs, she was crushing it at the conservatory.

So why did she feel so . . . unmoored?

Simple: Antony Meyer-Edwards.

Her fists tightened as the carillon bells rang through the quadrangle. She bounded up the stairs to Studio One, turning into the corridor. A low hum met her—rehearsed answers, whispered prayers, final checks.

Soraya smirked as Annouie dropped into the chair opposite.

"It's good you're taking this so seriously," she said, eyeing Annouie's wet hair and rumpled clothes.

Without breaking eye contact, Annouie plucked a pencil from a table, twisted her hair into a bun, and staked it to the back of her head.

Soraya sniffed and leaned toward her friend, whispering theatrically.

Annouie eased back and forced stillness.

If only I still had Oria2.

But Andre had been immovable—no more "cheating", near-death experience or not.

The doors banged open. An ashen-faced student stumbled out.

"Brutal," he muttered, bolting down the stairs.

Soraya giggled.

"Annouie."

Professor Wayne's voice cut through the noise. She stood. As she passed him, he gave a conspiratorial wink.

Light streamed through the tall windows, backlighting the five examiners seated behind the three long tables. In their black gowns and soft caps, they looked like a murder of crows. Her gaze snagged on the sixth seat.

Empty.

She looked away and crossed to the nine-foot grand at the center of the room.

"When you're ready," Dean Mackie said, eyes on his notes.

She sat, steadied her breath, and dropped her hands into a C minor chord. The sound rang out—full, sonorous, mesmerizing.

Performance was the easy part.

Thirty minutes later, she took the seat at the apex of the *Arc of Inquisition.*

The hard part came next.

"Your tempo choice for the nocturne?" Judith.

Annouie delivered her response.

"Unconventional fingering in the toccata—why?" Wayne.

The answers slipped off her tongue like butter.

"You spent considerable time in Frankfurt. What would you say was the most profound lesson you learned there?" Messier.

How to take out assholes like you.

She smiled—teeth gleaming in the morning light.

She couldn't tell them about the dojo, the missions, or sleeping in doorways through summer. So she spun a beautiful lie.

They nodded, charmed. Dean Mackie winked—like they shared a secret.

Which, of course, they did.

The identity of the Gray Cat.

"There is one last thing," Mackie said, rising with an envelope. "After much debate"—a pointed look at Messier—"the panel has agreed you are the clear choice for the inaugural Bernard Smith scholarship."

Another goddamn mission.

She feigned surprise.

"We were particularly swayed by Mr. Meyer-Edwards's written recommendation," Mackie added.

Her head snapped up. "You've heard from him?"

"He's in Rome." He lowered his voice. "Last we heard."

She sat back hard, chair squeaking. *Rome?*

Mackie turned to the panel. "As to why Meyer-Edwards does what he does—I can't say. But I can offer you the scholarship."

Applause rose like a wave.

All but Messier clapped, his expression unreadable.

Annouie swallowed her resentment and forced a smile.

So.

The Gray Cat was in Rome.

* * *

Annouie stormed out of Studio One, the envelope clenched in her fist.

"That good, huh?" Soraya called as she swept past.

She didn't answer, thundering down the staircase, stomach churning.

She needed to get on the next flight to Rome.

Her phone buzzed. She yanked it out, glanced at the screen.

Andre. Checking in again.

She let it ring and shoved it back into her pocket, breaking into a sprint.

Outside, Katrine Ratcliffe waited, sprawled on the sandstone ponywall, basking like a cat in the sun. She stretched, slid off, and fell in step beside her.

Annouie didn't slow, pivoting sharply into the walkway.

"Hey!" Katrine jogged after her, boots thudding on the pavers. "You avoiding me?"

"No," Annouie snapped, speeding up.

"'Cuz it kinda feels like it."

Annouie's phone buzzed again.

Katrine raised a brow. "You gonna get that?"

"It's Andre," Annouie said, not breaking stride. "What do you want?"

"I came to talk."

"About what?"

Katrine shrugged. "You know—stuff we *haven't* talked about."

Annouie rolled her eyes. "Thought Andre filled you in."

"He might've left out a few details."

A lot of details.

The phone buzzed again.

Katrine groaned. "Just answer it already. You know he's not gonna stop."

Without warning, she grabbed Annouie's arm and yanked her to a halt.

"Stop dodging everyone," she snapped—and snatched the phone from Annouie's pocket.

She swiped and put it on speaker. "She's fine. Stop ringing," she growled into the mic.

A burst of static crackled through the speaker.

"Hello, darling."

Annouie froze.

Her chest hollowed out. She turned slowly. "Dad?"

"I wanted to tell you the good news," Isidore said. "I'm out."

Katrine winced, mouthing *sorry* as she handed the phone over.

"I'll tell you all about it when I see you," Isidore continued, his voice echoing through the cloistered walkway.

Annouie took the phone off speaker and pressed it to her ear.

"Oh, and one more thing," he added. "I hear you're heading to

Rome. That's actually why I'm calling. The man who arranged my release is sitting beside me. He'd like a word."

There was a pause.

Then a different voice—smooth, composed, and altogether too smug.

"Good morning, Bach," Antony Meyer-Edwards drawled. "Nice to hear your voice, too. I hear congratulations are in order. Well done—you earned it."

Another pause. Longer this time. Then, his voice dipped to something dark, amused, teasing.

"But tell me—do you, by any chance, still have *my* manuscript?"

Thank you for reading!

If *Mastering the Art of Deception* kept you turning pages late into the night, made you smirk, gasp, or double-check your locks—

Consider leaving a review on

Amazon: **https://mybook.to/MasteringDeception**

Goodreads: **https://www.goodreads.com/book/show/238662872-mastering-the-art-of-deception**

Just a few lines is all it takes.

Your words help this book find its next reader, and they matter more than you know.

Thanks for coming along for the heist.

There's more to come.

Thank you for reading!

With gratitude,

Marlowe Edison

Acknowledgments

Writing a book is an incredible undertaking, and I'm deeply grateful to the many people who helped bring this story to life.

To my four amazing children—thank you for phoning, listening, and letting me share my progress and hopes for the future. You never made me feel like I was reaching for the impossible or that writing for a living was a ridiculous dream. Your belief in me has meant everything.

To my friends and family—your encouragement has been a lifeline. I had no idea so many of you truly believed I could pull this off. Thank you for your support, whether through kind words, a Facebook comment or like, or simply listening when I finally opened up about my writing journey.

To my readers—thank you for picking up this book and joining me on this adventure. Your curiosity and enthusiasm fuel my passion for storytelling.

To my editor, Laura Apgar—your insights and expertise have been invaluable in shaping this manuscript into its best version.

To my cover artist, Kari Browlie—thank you for creating an honest-to-God masterpiece that so perfectly captures the swaggering noir tones of my novel.

Lastly, to everyone who dared to dream alongside me—this book exists because of you. And if I've learned anything in the writing of it, it's that the best stories are born in shadows, whispered in confidence, and carried by those who believe.

With gratitude,

Marlowe Edison

The Adventure Continues . . .

Want to Know What Happens Next?

In Book 2, Annouie's journey takes her to the heart of Rome—a city of secrets, danger, and intrigue. As she dives deeper into a world of espionage and betrayal, she'll face enemies old and new, uncovering truths that will change everything.

Curious to find out more? Be the first to hear exclusive updates, sneak peeks, and behind-the-scenes content by signing up for Marlowe Edison's newsletter.

Follow the link below and join the adventure as Annouie goes to Rome!

Annouie goes to Rome.

About the Author

Marlowe Edison is currently teaching in a high school. She has also dabbled in film and Information Technology. She is a talented artist, musician, and mother to four wonderful children.

Marlowe lives in a small town a few hours north of Sydney, New South Wales, where she finds inspiration in the quiet rhythms of village life. Her experiences and interests shape her storytelling, offering readers a glimpse into vivid worlds filled with intrigue and heart.

Mastering the Art of Deception is her latest novel.

www.edisonmarlowe.com

facebook.com/marloweedisonauthor
x.com/EdisonMarlowe
instagram.com/marloweedison
amazon.com/author/marloweedison

Printed in Dunstable, United Kingdom

66515479R00262